ALMOST A FAMILY

by STEPHANIE BOND

Life gave them a second
chance at love...

Cover by Andrew Brown at clicktwicedesign.com

ISBN: 0989912795
ISBN 13: 9780989912792

DEDICATION

In memory of my beloved, aunt,
Fonda Sue Bond,
a warm and funny lady who fostered
my love for books.

CHAPTER ONE

"SEVEN BALL IN THE SIDE POCKET," Bailey Kallihan said quietly. He squinted down the length of his cue, sliding the smooth stick back and forth through spread fingers. The stares of several dozen patrons of the Sage Saloon bored into his skin. George Jones wailed mournfully in the background. A trickle of sweat slid between his shoulder blades. Rather than think about the three hundred dollars he stood to lose on this game, Bailey focused on the three hundred he intended to win.

He drew back a final time and drove the stick toward the ball.

"Bailey!"

Startled, he jerked forward and struck the ball with a dull *thwack*, sending it spiraling toward the hole. Several inches from the target, the seven ball veered and struck the eight ball in its newfound path. Bailey winced and swore as the black ball disappeared unceremoniously into the pocket. The crowd groaned in dismay.

"Scratch!" his opponent yelled above the erupting mayhem, then scooped Bailey's money off the rail with a grin.

Straightening, Bailey scowled, turned to the crowd, and demanded, "Who the hell did that?"

The spectators shrugged and parted, heads pivoting. Bailey tossed his cue stick onto the table and scanned the gathering of cowboy wannabes and their groupies. The voice had sounded female. He would never hit a woman, but if Lisa had yelled for him, she might warrant a good shaking.

A small commotion near the back seemed to be moving forward. When a couple of catcalls caught Bailey's ear, he angled himself for a better look at the emerging woman. He heard murmured apologies before she pushed her way clear and stopped to stand ten feet from him.

Recognition slammed into Bailey. He blinked hard while his heart plummeted below sea level. His skin tingled and his throat closed. The suit and hairstyle were foreign to him, but those eyes... he'd seen those caramel-colored eyes swimming with tears so many times, there was no mistaking them now, shimmering once again.

"Virginia?" he whispered.

She clutched her purse in a white-knuckled grip. "Bailey," she said simply, her beautiful face passive, her voice an uneven croak.

Years dissolved... she could have been the same girl of eight years ago who'd told him through worried tears about the baby they'd made... or the girl who'd later repeated through happy tears her wedding vows... or the girl who'd announced through inconsolable tears their two-month-old son had been kidnapped... or the girl who'd declared through angry tears she wanted a divorce.

Well, Virginia Catron wasn't a girl anymore, but from the look in her eyes, life was still batting her around. He took no pride in the fact that he'd caused most of her early heartache. But what now? A death? One of her parents perhaps?

He walked toward her on somewhat shaky legs. She inhaled sharply, her chest rising, as if gathering her strength. As he approached her, the crowd receded but remained rapt, as if sensing some climax. Two feet away he stopped, reached his hand toward her awkwardly, then shoved it in his jeans pocket at the last second. "Virginia, what's wro—"

"They found our son."

The words echoed in his beer-fuzzed mind. *They found our son.* Four words he'd prayed to hear in the beginning. *They found our son.* Then, after months passed, words he'd dreaded to hear. *They found our son.* Finally, words he'd resigned himself to never hearing. *They found our son.*

"Did you hear me, Bailey?" Her voice trembled. She stood rigid and made tight little fists with her hands. A crumpled white tissue trailed out of one. Her face had been cried free of makeup, and her lips were pinched.

It was too much, seeing Virginia again and picturing the remains of their infant son, Bailey, Jr. He'd lost years of sleep wondering what kind of tortures his child had been subjected to. Flashes of himself walking alongside volunteers canvassing the area where their baby's blanket had been found came back to him. Had he walked right by the tiny body? Now had hunters found the miniature skeleton? Pain burned in his belly and incinerated his chest.

He stared at Virginia, his tongue thick and unwieldy. She was expecting him to say something profound, but he could manage only to nod. "I heard you." To himself he sounded like a wounded animal, and he saw her flinch in response.

For the first time, he remembered their audience. Old friends, mere acquaintances, and complete strangers gawked at them, unable to hear their conversation, but looking intensely curious nonetheless. The dank smell of beer and the thick cigarette smoke suddenly suffocated him. He reached forward and clasped her elbow, turning her around gently. "Let's go someplace to talk," he said near her ear. She nodded curtly, pulling away from him a few inches.

Bailey frowned, but his brief disappointment at her reflex passed as he anticipated the somber conversation that awaited them. As he weaved them through the crowd and toward the front doors, the music and laughter grew even louder. A wet-T-shirt contest was in high progress, with men lining up to throw buckets of icy water onto the willing contestants. Virginia averted her gaze, and he conceded a pang of embarrassment that she'd had to hunt him down in one of his tacky old haunts to tell him her sobering news.

She couldn't have looked more out of place in her tailored slate-gray jacket and fitted skirt, sheer hose and leather pumps. She'd wound her honey-colored hair into a tight crown knot, with only a fringe of bangs to soften the look. His outrageous, fun-loving coed had matured into an elegant, classy executive. They garnered more than a few looks as they wound their way toward the door.

Bailey bit back a bitter laugh. The lady and the tramp. Their divorce had ended on a sour note, but it appeared she'd fared better without him.

Virginia stared straight ahead with her mouth set in a firm line. Her back remained rigid, and Bailey felt the sudden urge to fold her into his arms, to feel her soften into him and cry against his chest. She'd done just that many times before their baby had been born, and he'd been glad to offer her his strength, trying desperately to hide his own fears of becoming a sudden husband and father. But in his grief after the kidnapping, he'd lashed out, saying unforgivable things. She hadn't been in his arms since that horrific day. Unconsciously, he tightened his grip on her arm through the soft fabric, and she tensed even more.

He didn't blame her for hating him. How could he when he hated himself?

"Bailey?" came a drawling female voice behind him.

Bailey winced. He'd forgotten about Lisa. At first he wasn't going to stop, but Virginia slowed and said, "I think someone needs to talk to you."

Bailey released Virginia's arm and wheeled toward Lisa's voice. The blonde's eyes were wide and questioning as she scanned Virginia head to toe. Hands on hips, her position accentuated her ample chest, covered by a transparent, wet tank top that left nothing to the imagination. She smirked. "Going somewhere, Bailey Boy?"

Bailey's face suffused with heat. He avoided Virginia's eyes. Withdrawing his wallet, he removed a twenty and thrust it into the young woman's hand. "Change of plans, here's money for a cab." Then he reclaimed Virginia's elbow and steered her out onto the sidewalk into the balmy midsummer air.

Nightlife in Columbus, Ohio, normally didn't get rolling until midnight, so the worst crowds and traffic were still a couple of hours away. But the street vendors and sidewalk entertainers were still busy from late shoppers who had not yet departed for home.

"My car's just around the corner," Bailey explained. "There's a coffee shop on the next block."

"Let's walk," Virginia suggested, still staring ahead.

He nodded and fell in step beside her, adjusting his stride to hers. After a few seconds of silence, he asked, "Do you want to wait to talk about it?"

She shook her head and sniffed. "No." Her voice sounded stronger, but forced. "I worked late today and had a message waiting from Detective Lance when I got home. Do you remember him?"

Bailey nodded—the man had been the lead local investigator on their son's kidnapping, had persisted even after the FBI had given up.

"Anyway, the message said he had news and needed to talk to us as soon as possible. He left you a message, too, but since he hadn't heard from you by the time I called him back, I assumed you hadn't been home yet."

A nice way of saying he'd gone straight to the saloon from work, Bailey noted.

She sought his eyes this time, and he saw her tears brimming again. Swiping at them with her tattered tissue, she said, "I'm sorry, Bailey. I should have waited for you, but I just couldn't—" Her voice faltered. "I just couldn't bear to wait another minute to hear the truth."

He wished he had been there, but he understood her anxiety. His throat ached as he tensed to keep his emotion at bay.

She wiped her mouth with the side of her hand and cleared her throat. "Then he came over, and when he told me they'd found Bailey, Jr."—her voice escalated—"I didn't know what to say." She offered him a watery smile, and his heart tripped. "Eight long years I've been waiting to hear those words, and I didn't know what to say."

Bailey ground his teeth. He ought to have been there, if only to comfort Virginia as he should have eight years before. "I'm sorry, Ginny," he said, his pet name for her slipping out. "I'm so sorry." He slowed his step and reached for her hand to squeeze it.

She stopped abruptly and stared at their hands. "Sorry?" Her forehead crumpled. "You're sorry they found our child?"

Bailey searched for the right words. "No, I'm not sorry this nightmare is finally over. I'm just so sorry you had to hear the bad news alone."

"Bad news?" Ginny looked confused for a few seconds, then her eyes rounded in astonishment. "Oh, Bailey, I... I mean, you... I thought you realized..."

Now it was his turn to be confused. "Realized what?"

"Bailey." She searched his eyes, her voice filled with wonder. "Our son is *alive.*"

CHAPTER TWO

BAILEY STOOD STOCK-STILL. His voice seemed paralyzed. He felt his mouth open and close, but no sound came out. Ginny's face faded in and out of focus, and for a few seconds he thought he might pass out. Her words were too incredible to be true. "What... how..." A passerby jostled his arm, startling him. The man apologized and kept moving.

"I need to sit down," she said, her chin quavering. Bailey looked up and saw they were only a few steps from the coffee shop. He grabbed her hand and led her to the door. For a full minute she clasped his hand tightly, and Bailey felt a strange stirring in his midsection. *Just like old times.*

They claimed a booth, sitting across from each other. He relinquished her hand reluctantly. Ginny sighed as she sank into the plush upholstery. She looked exhausted. Pink rings glowed around her eyes, nose, and lips. Bailey felt a rush of sympathy for her, but couldn't wait any longer for answers. "Ginny, what's going on?"

She inhaled deeply, still clenching the shredded tissue in her hand. "Detective Lance received a call from Fort Lauderdale this morning. A woman there passed away a few weeks ago, and before she died, she told a nurse she'd taken her son from a grocery store in Columbus, Ohio, as an infant." Her voice choked, and she bit her bottom lip to steady herself.

Bailey reached for her hand again, wanting to comfort her, but she pulled back and straightened her shoulders. "I'm all right," she said bluntly.

I'm not. Let me touch you, let me share. He lowered his hands to grip the sides of the small table, but his equilibrium still seemed off. Ginny's lips moved slowly, and he concentrated fiercely on the words coming out.

"After the woman died, the nurse reported the conversation to the authorities. When the Fort Lauderdale police could find no proof the woman had given birth, they ran a computer search on unsolved kidnappings. When they contacted the Columbus police, Detective Lance took over." She swallowed audibly. "He said he wanted to be sure before he got our hopes up, but apparently the boy's fingerprints match our son's, and the DNA sample they took at the time of the kidnapping is a match, too." Her voice turned squeaky on the last words, and she smiled tremulously at Bailey.

Panic twisted in his gut, the one question he'd worn threadbare in his mind leaping out. "Was he... abused?"

She shook her head vigorously. "No, thank God."

He released a pent-up breath and dragged a hand over his face. After being emotionally detached from everything and everyone in his life for nearly a decade, the events of the past few minutes made him feel as if he'd been gutted, with his heart on display. "I can't believe it... I just can't believe it." He spread his hands, desperate for firm ground. "What happens next?"

Her lips parted slightly. "What happens next?" Her voice was incredulous. She straightened, her back pressed against the bench seat. "I'm going to Florida to get my child. Mom and Dad are flying down with me tomorrow morning. I came to see if you wanted to go with us."

His anger flared at her insinuation. Could she possibly think he wouldn't want to claim his son? "Of course I'm going," he blustered. "I'm his father. I didn't mean to sound as if... oh, hell, I don't know what I meant." He leaned back into the cushion and glanced around the half-empty cafe. "This has thrown me for a loop, Ginny. I'm sorry if I'm not saying all the things you want me to."

She pursed her lips. "I'm familiar with your coping strategies, Bailey."

Her remark pierced his chest like a sleek blade.

"What can I get you folks?" a bespectacled young man asked.

"Two black coffees," Bailey said, his tone more abrupt than he'd intended.

"Excuse me," Ginny said as the man turned to leave. "Make mine decaf with cream." The waiter nodded, then disappeared. She turned to Bailey and lifted her chin slightly. "Things change, Bailey."

He passed a hand through his hair and sighed, his shoulders sagging. "Another good point. I suppose we need to get caught up on each other's lives before we can decide how we're going to handle this, uh"—he floundered for a few seconds—"parenting arrangement." A thought struck him and his pulse jumped as his gaze flew to her left hand. "Are you married?"

"No. Are you?"

He told himself the news cheered him because it meant fewer complications. "No." Indicating her attire with a sweep of his hand, he said, "You appear to be doing well for yourself."

"I'm a systems analyst for a brokerage firm."

"What exactly is a systems analyst?"

"I design computer systems—my specialty is stock analysis."

She'd always been smart and creative, but he was a little surprised. He angled his head toward her. "You? Computers?"

She bristled. "I went back to college and earned a degree in computer science."

Years earlier he'd resented the untimely interruption of their impromptu marriage—he hadn't considered at the time that Virginia also sacrificed dreams. "It's great that you finished your degree. I just figured you'd still be sculpting."

She smoothed a stray lock of hair behind her ear. "I wanted to be self-reliant, so I chose something with more stability."

Ginny looked a picture of independence, he had to admit. He could see her at work, all prim and aloof, with none of her coworkers suspecting that beneath the stuffy business suit lay a warm, sumptuous body—

"Here you go," the waiter said, setting down two steaming mugs. "Can I get you folks something to eat?"

Bailey looked at Ginny. "Did you have dinner?"

"There wasn't time."

"Me either. How about some soup?"

She shook her head, a movement that highlighted her sharp collarbones. He felt a twinge of concern. "Ginny, you look exhausted. Eat."

Her shoulders rounded slightly, and she nodded. "Okay." The young man bustled off to get them the house special. She swung her long legs around to slide from the booth seat. "I'm going to find the ladies' room."

Bailey tried to not watch the way her body moved as she walked away from him, but he couldn't help it. He wouldn't have believed it possible to still miss her so much after so many years.

* * *

Virginia shut the ladies' room door behind her and exhaled all of the air out of her lungs. After a few shaky steps toward the tiny vanity, she gratefully sank into a lone chair, then leaned forward to bury her head in her arms.

This morning she would have sworn she could handle anything life handed her, but she had been completely unprepared for the day's news. At thirty, she was about to become an instant mother to an eight-year-old she didn't even know. Topped with the knowledge she would have to forge a new relationship with Bailey Kallihan, she felt as if she had been plunged into a dark lake and left flailing for the surface.

Virginia raised her head and peered at herself in the mirror. In the wee hours of sleepless nights, she'd harbored fantasies of being in a stunning gown and on the arm of a gorgeous man when and if she ever laid eyes on Bailey again—not looking like a resurrected corpse in a business suit. With shaking hands she withdrew a silver lipstick case and determinedly drew color back onto her mouth.

It had taken her years to get over him. And when his rambling letter of apology had arrived at her parents' house two years before, old wounds had ruptured. Obviously written during a roaring drunk, he'd expressed regret over blaming her for their son's disappearance, and for calling her a careless mother. But instead of feeling absolved, Virginia had been overwhelmed with sadness that they were both still wrestling with lingering guilt and anger from their son's abduction and their aborted marriage.

He hadn't changed a bit. Still shaggy-haired and outlandishly handsome, still hanging out in the same bars, still driving the same old hot rod. She'd seen his black Camaro in the parking lot of the saloon. Virginia laughed a bitter laugh. And from the looks of the young woman he'd given cab fare to, commitment still ranked low on his list.

For the space of a few weeks after the birth, hope had bloomed in her chest that Bailey would be content to settle down and raise a family. Indeed, he had blazed a new trail of devoted husband and father. But when some madwoman had stolen their baby from his carrier, she'd also stolen Bailey's innocence, his optimism, and his future. Virginia had found herself married to a shell of the man she'd fallen in love with.

She'd gone looking for him tonight, desperately hoping for... what? A strong, accomplished man on whom she could rely to help raise this child. Someone who would be a good role model, someone who shared her values. But Bailey Kallihan was not father-of-the-year material. He was a willful boy in a man's body.

A body that still had the infuriating power to affect hers.

She dragged herself up and splashed cold water on her face. Slowly she dried her hands and fussed with her bangs, delaying her return as long as possible. Finally, she left to retrace her steps to the booth.

The soup had arrived in her absence and Bailey sat deep in thought, apparently waiting for her before taking a bite. Her pulse leapt absurdly at the sight of his dark profile. He'd pulled the largest portion of his black hair into a thick ponytail. He hadn't shaved in a couple of days, and the dark stubble crept all the way down to his Adam's apple. A black long-sleeved shirt tucked into faded jeans gave him the look of a displaced cowboy, seemingly capable of playing good guy or bad.

Virginia would give a week's salary to know what he'd been thinking. Years ago, her unplanned pregnancy had interrupted Bailey's plans to launch his own landscape architectural firm. What plans had her unexpected news interrupted this time?

Her appearance startled him out of his reverie. "Where do you live?" he asked as she sat down.

"In German Village." She saw a flicker of surprise in his eyes at the mention of the pricey locale. "How about you? What do you do for a living?" she inquired, lowering her gaze as she lifted her cup for a sip. The deep blue centers of his eyes were so intense against the startling whites, she couldn't look into them for more than a few seconds. Bailey, Jr.'s eyes had been deep blue, but all babies had blue eyes at that age....

"Still landscaping," he said. "I work for a commercial developer."

"Designing?"

"No," he said, picking up his spoon. "Just running a few crews."

Virginia's heart sank. He'd given up his dream. "That's nice," she said, breaking open a packet of crackers. "Do you still live at Shenoway?" The mere mention of his family's small farm sent stabs of longing through her chest.

He busied himself stirring the soup. "No. Sis and her husband renovated Mom and Pop's farmhouse, and we sold some of the surrounding land. I live above the saloon."

She took a bite of the dry cracker and swallowed her disappointment. They'd brought Bailey, Jr., home to the decrepit farmhouse, and Bailey had promised her they'd someday build a new home in the north meadow overlooking the pond. *With a big yard for Bailey, Jr., to run and play in as he grows up.* Now it seemed probable some other family lived in their meadow. "How is Rita?" she managed to ask.

At last he cracked a smile. "Sis is great, as always. She's married to a terrific guy, and they have a six-year-old, Jean Ann."

Virginia smiled her genuine pleasure. "I'd love to see them."

His hands stilled and she watched his eyes move over her hair and face. "She really misses you."

"I should have stayed in touch. With Rita, I mean."

"Well, I guess you'll be seeing more of her now," he said. "I guess you'll be seeing more of me too."

Virginia kept her face passive to hide the current of emotion coursing through her at the simple truth of his words.

"You're still wearing the locket I gave you," he said with surprise in his voice, pointing to the necklace she unconsciously fingered.

She glanced down at the shiny gold pendant, hoping he didn't read anything into the fact that she still wore his wedding gift. Looking up again, she shrugged slightly and smiled. "It always made me feel closer to him somehow."

He nodded. "Can I see his picture?"

Leaning forward, she stretched the long chain and extended the case toward him. He gently opened the locket and ran a finger over their son's birth picture—a shock of black hair over a little red face. When he closed the case, he turned over the locket, angling it in the light. "And baby makes three," he read aloud.

A shiver ran up her spine. Bailey was treading on memories that were too dear. She pulled back and dropped the pendant into hiding beneath her jacket. The locket still radiated with warmth from his fingers as it settled between her breasts.

He pushed his bowl aside and brought his hand up to scratch the stubble of his beard. Then a grin split his face, and he leaned forward to cover her hand with his. "They found our son, Ginny. *Our son.* It's pretty incredible, isn't it?"

As always, his smile was infectious. She smiled too, and nodded. "Unbelievable."

His eyes shone like two dark sapphires. "What do you think he's like? Which one of us do you think he takes after?"

She shook her head, her laughter bubbling up at his enthusiasm. "I can't imagine."

"Do you think he plays baseball or rides horses?"

She could see his mind clicking with all the father-son activities he had planned—plans he'd laid within seconds of their son drawing his first breath. Virginia fought the panic rolling in her stomach. How was she going to forge a bond with her eight-year-old son? She'd never been very good with children; since the kidnapping the mere sound of a child crying made her hyperventilate.

What if she wasn't a good mother? What if her own child didn't want her?

"Are you okay?" he asked, concern crinkling his eyes and mouth.

She felt the tears coming on and closed her eyes. "It's just the shock—it's been a very long day, and I doubt if I'll get much sleep tonight."

"I'll follow you home," he offered, waving for the check.

"It's all the way across town," she protested.

"But it's on the way to Rita's, so I'll drive over to her place and spend the night there, and meet you at the airport in the morning."

"But—"

"It'll give us more time to talk."

She wanted to inject that talking had never been a strong aspect of their marriage, but she stopped short, afraid the conversation would lead to what *had* been. Relenting with a nod, she followed him out onto the sidewalk, noting his familiar old-fashioned manners as he stepped to place himself between her and the curb as they walked.

Bright streetlamps broke the intermittent darkness into slices of near daylight. The heels of Bailey's black leather boots scraped against the cement, punctuating the quick light tap of her high heels. Bailey was one of few men who made her feel small in her five-foot-seven-inch body. Although only five inches taller, his dark looks and broad shoulders were so imposing, she'd seen him dwarf larger men when he entered a room.

"What time is your flight tomorrow?" he asked. "I'll try to book the same one, or an earlier one if I have to."

"Ten-thirty. I reserved a seat for you in case you wanted to go, just to be sure we all arrived together."

"Great. I'll write you a check—"

"That's not necessary—"

"Yes, it is."

His voice brooked no argument, and Virginia retreated gracefully. Bailey had never suffered from a shortage of pride. She gave him the airline and flight number.

"How are your folks?" he asked, his tone cautious.

Virginia smiled. "Ecstatic."

He nodded. "I'm sure they are. Do they know I'm going too?"

She hesitated. There hadn't been a great deal of love lost between her parents and Bailey when she'd divorced him. "They know I planned to ask you, but even I wasn't sure what your reaction would be."

He pursed his lips and anger flickered in his expression. "They decided to go in case I bailed so you wouldn't be alone."

She slowed her step, then stopped, tilting her head back to look at him. "They've always been there for me."

He chewed on the inside of his jaw, then said, "And I haven't, right, Ginny?"

Typical defensive Bailey behavior, she thought, checking her own anger. "Bailey, I wasn't even sure I would find you in time. Mom and Dad would have gone regardless. Don't you think it's best for our son to meet his grandparents and know how eager we all are to be with him?"

He sighed, bobbing his head in concession. "You're right, of course. I would want my parents to be there if they were still living."

"I didn't mean to exclude Rita and her family."

He resumed walking. "That's all right, it would be hard for her to get away on short notice anyway. But I'm sure she'll want to meet us at the airport when we get back." He turned to her, frowning slightly. "When are we returning?"

"The following day. Detective Lance is going too. He said we should expect to spend some of tomorrow talking with social workers and other authorities."

"Has Bailey, Jr., been told?"

"He was told this evening."

"Can we call him?"

"I wanted to, but Detective Lance said it was best to wait and let the news sink in for all of us. He said Bailey, Jr., would be told we're coming tomorrow."

Bailey grunted. "Poor kid. In a matter of weeks his mother dies, then he finds out he really belongs to someone else."

Her defenses reared and she stopped again. "*I'm* his mother. That woman who took him—"

"Hey," he said quietly, placing a hand on each shoulder. "That's not what I meant, and you know it."

She felt penned in by his arms, and pinned down by his troubled gaze. Her breathing became shallow and she was thankful the darkness cloaked her warring emotions. "I know. And you're right—even if he can't remember it all, he's been through a lot."

He murmured agreement and they fell into a companionable silence. Virginia wanted to bottle the moment and keep it, because visions of the bumpy road ahead of them terrified her. He'd turned his back on her years before in the most devastating of circumstances.

What about this time? When the going got tough, would Bailey get gone?

Her mind still swirled with uncertainties when she inserted a key into the door of her sporty sedan. Bailey whistled low in appreciation. He was standing so close, she felt his breath on the back of her neck.

"Nice wheels."

Bailey used to say he could size up people just by the car they drove. In fact, he'd admitted it had been the faded blue Mustang Virginia had been driving in college that he'd noticed first. She glanced at him as she swung into the gray leather bucket seat. "Thanks."

He stood with his arm on the open door, looking as if he were about to say something. Most of his face was cast in shadow, and Virginia felt vulnerable beneath the bright interior light. She met his gaze and waited. Had he changed his mind?

"Virginia, I..."

If he didn't have the stomach for what lay ahead, she needed to know now. "What is it, Bailey?"

The muscles in his forearm bunched as he shifted his weight and leaned forward. He opened his mouth to speak, his white teeth glistening. "I... I'll be right behind you." Stepping away from the car, he closed the door with a solid *thunk*.

She exhaled in relief, then waited until he drove up behind her before pulling out. On the forty-minute drive to her town home, she glanced often in the rearview mirror, expecting him to bail any second. He stuck with her, though, and the presence of his headlights was ridiculously comforting. Her small driveway provided a snug fit for two cars, but Bailey maneuvered in behind her expertly.

Soft landscaping lights outlined her short walkway and led them to a cobblestone stoop. As Bailey climbed the steps, she watched him peer at the bushes and flowers on either side with a trained eye and silently dared him to pass judgment on her tiny home.

Neither of them spoke as she unlocked her front door with a shaky hand and dismantled the security system from a keypad in the entry hall. The flashing "okay" light did little to settle her nerves regarding the near stranger who'd followed her inside. Virginia flipped on lights and turned to find Bailey surveying his surroundings with an impassive face. She knew him well enough to realize he would be more impressed by the hand-rubbed wood floors than by the luxurious rugs that lay upon them, and more taken by the ornate molding along the ceiling than by the chandelier glimmering above their heads.

"Coffee?" she asked, laying her keys on a slim marble-topped table, then moving through the hall toward the kitchen.

"Sure," he murmured, following her at a slower pace.

She felt self-conscious as she flooded her small, frilly kitchen with light. The wallpaper was blatantly feminine in its soft flower-and-fruit pattern, every detail of the room reflecting her bent for country English decor. She pulled a coffeemaker from a cubbyhole and scooped up fresh grounds, then added water. At last she turned to face Bailey, her heart pounding.

He balanced on a highback wicker barstool like a predator against the backdrop of a flowered meadow. Nevertheless, he looked casual and comfortable, able to charm a room full of furniture into accommodating him.

"How long have you lived here?" he asked.

"Going on four years."

He pointed to the porcelain sink and antique faucet. "This place has character."

She smiled. "All the old houses do."

"Can I get a tour?"

She hesitated, but he was already unfolding himself to explore. She went from room to room, her pride growing as she illuminated a dining room, living room, and small library accented sparingly with lustrous antiques and plush fabrics. She couldn't help but compare her hand-picked treasures to the blue-light specials they'd lived on in the aged farmhouse. But they'd been happy... for a while....

Slowly they circled the first floor, making their way back to the entry hall. He paused before the staircase and asked, "Are the bedrooms upstairs?"

Virginia nodded, but made no move toward the second floor.

Bailey shifted his weight to his other foot. "Do you have a room for Bailey, Jr.?"

"Well, my guest room isn't exactly a boy's dream, but I guess it'll do for now."

"Oh?" Bailey's eyebrows shot up. "Are you planning to move?"

"No. I meant the room will do until I can redecorate it for him." She experienced a niggling of awareness, a dawning of the implications of discussing bedrooms with her handsome ex-husband. In the next instant she discarded the thought. He simply wanted to know where his son would be sleeping, that's all.

"Maybe I can do something to help," he offered. "Build some bookshelves or something?"

She nodded, the silent seconds stretching into a cavernous minute. Clearing her throat, she asked, "Want to take a look?"

"Sure."

She gripped the banister tightly, her feet automatically landing on the spots where the floorboards did not creak or complain as she climbed. At the top of the stairs she turned left and led him to a small bedroom draped with pink and cream curtains, and a comforter, complete with lacy pillows. Bailey winced.

"I know," she said in an apologetic voice. "But it'll suffice."

"He could stay with me—"

"No!" At his startled glance, Virginia amended hurriedly, "I mean, no, there couldn't be room at your place."

His frown confirmed her statement, then he offered a halfhearted grin. "But I do have a nice, plain brown couch that sleeps pretty good. Do you work at home?" he asked, effectively tabling the issue of his living accommodations. He pointed into the room across the hall. A desk and computer workstation dominated the shadowed room.

"Sometimes." She walked over and switched on the office light.

Following, he peered in. "Nice setup." Something caught his eye, and Virginia's heart vaulted when he entered the room and picked up a framed photograph from a credenza. He smoothed a finger across the glass. "I remember taking this picture," he said, his voice scratchy.

Virginia blinked rapidly. She didn't have to see it—she'd memorized every detail in the photo of her holding Bailey, Jr., in her arms outside the hospital, just before they'd driven him home. She'd worn a loose yellow jump suit, and he'd been bundled in pale blue. Her heart had been full to bursting. But even more vivid than her emotions on that day had been the splitting grin of happiness on Bailey's face as he adjusted the camera lens. *Smile. Wave to Daddy. Smile, Mommy.*

"Did you keep other pictures?" he asked, his voice stronger.

She hesitated, then walked to a closet in the converted bedroom and withdrew a large photo album. Carefully, she wiped and blew the dust from the cover, its faded golden letters proclaiming "Our Son." With trembling hands she opened the album, vaguely aware that Bailey stood just behind her, looking over her shoulder.

Memories slammed into her, leaving her shaken, but with fewer tears than the last few hundred times she'd thumbed through the pages. A younger, smiling Bailey feeding the baby a bottle, giving him a bath, changing his diaper—breaking all the macho-daddy rules. How long had it been since she'd tortured herself with the faded pictures of her infant son, so beautiful and trusting?

From the pages, a sheet of folded paper escaped, floating to the floor. As Bailey bent to retrieve it, Virginia realized with a nervous jolt it was the letter he'd sent her two years before. She remembered now... that night had been the last time she'd looked through the baby album.

Her heart thumped against her chest at the implication of her keeping the letter. Bailey retrieved the sheet, straightening as he unfolded it, his face transforming from confusion to... something... when he recognized what he held in his hand. His gaze met hers, and long-slumbering emotions stirred in her heart with the fierceness of a drowsy giant awakening.

"I wondered if you'd gotten my letter."

She swallowed hard. "I got it."

He opened his mouth to speak, but the shrill beep of the coffee-maker downstairs interrupted. Suddenly exhaustion weakened her limbs. She lifted her gaze to Bailey, and attempted a weak smile. "I'm sorry, Bailey, but I have to get some rest."

"Sure," he said agreeably. "I'll take a rain check on the coffee."

They walked wordlessly down the stairway together, her heart tripping double time as she stopped to let him move ahead to a safe distance.

He turned to stare at her, filling up her entryway with denim and attitude. "Well, I guess I'll say good night."

"I'll see you tomorrow at the airport," she said.

He nodded. "Tomorrow."

She stood awkwardly, not knowing the proper ex-spouse etiquette for late night departures after earth-shattering news. "Good night, then."

He turned and opened the door, giving entry to a warm, fragrant breeze that teased the ends of his ponytail.

Virginia stepped to the door and held the knob as he walked out. At the last second he turned back and lifted his hand to rub a rough thumb over her cheekbone. The intimate contact startled her, and she instinctively drew back. He dropped his hand and smiled.

"Tomorrow we see our son, Ginny." Then he was gone before she could reply.

She closed the door, but waited until the sound of his rumbling engine faded before she moved.

No, no, *no*... she couldn't have feelings for him still. She'd been down this road before and heartache lay at the end. Tomorrow she would be thinking more clearly. Tomorrow she would be strong and resistant to his charms. Tomorrow she would have enough to worry about just being a mother. Virginia climbed the stairs, weak-kneed and light-headed.

She didn't dare think past tomorrow.

* * *

"Bailey, are you drunk?"

He whooped and lifted Rita off the floor, whirling her around. "Stone sober since Ginny told me the news."

His sister's look of disbelief transformed into pure delight. "Oh, Bailey!" She clasped him in a tight hug. When she released him, tears shone in her eyes. "After all these years... this is incredible!"

He laughed with her, his happiness mushrooming. "It's a miracle all right."

"Virginia—oh, she must be beside herself! Will she... will the two of you... how is she?"

"She's fine." He grappled for some detail that wouldn't betray the revived emotion he felt stirring in his swollen, stupid heart. "She works in computers and is doing well for herself. Has a town home in the Village."

"Does she have other children now?"

"No, she never remarried."

One graceful black eyebrow shot up. "Really."

"Don't start, sis."

"What?" she asked, bringing a hand to her chest, her eyes wide in innocence.

"You know what," he admonished with a stern look. "Don't get any romantic ideas about me and Ginny picking up where we left off. We're completely different people now." He hoped some of his logic would sink into his own hard head.

"Which is precisely why your relationship might work this time."

"Rita—"

"Bailey, you share an eight-year-old son, what better reason could you have for getting back together with Ginny?"

"I know it would be better for him if we were still married," he admitted, "but our marriage wasn't that great, and after all these years she's not going to just welcome me back into her life with open arms, not the way we left things." Guilt stabbed him, and he averted his eyes.

His sister smiled, and touched his hand. "Ginny's a good woman, I'm sure she'd want what's best for—"

"Trust me on this one," he said abruptly. "She wouldn't want me."

Rita blinked, then narrowed her dark eyes at him. "Is there something I don't know? Was there another woman?"

He frowned. "Of course not. I partied a lot, but I was never unfaithful."

"What, then?"

Bailey turned away from her piercing gaze, shame burning in his stomach. "I said some hurtful things to her after the baby disappeared."

"What kinds of things?"

He swallowed hard and closed his eyes. "That... that she was careless—"

"Oh, Bailey—"

"—and not a good mother."

"Oh, God, no, Bailey."

The sorrow in her voice increased the pain swirling in his gut. "I know." He sighed. "It was... unforgivable."

Her arms wrapped around him from behind, and she pressed her cheek against his back. In a soft voice she murmured, "You were hurt and angry and young—"

"And stupid and thoughtless." He ground the words out.

"Have you tried saying you're sorry?"

"Yeah. I wrote her a letter a couple of years ago and told her what a jerk I was."

"And?"

"And nothing. She didn't respond—not that I expected her to. She has every right to hate me." *Although she did keep the letter...*

Rita unwound her arms and moved to face him. "You're right," she said, angling her head. "She should hate you. So you've got some serious making up to do."

He pursed his lips, nodding slowly. "I know... but how?"

She smiled and reached forward to squeeze his shoulders with her little hands. "Bailey, there are things more important than being the life of every party. You might even have to give up your reputation of being the biggest lady-killer in town. It's time to grow up, little brother."

Bailey bit the inside of his cheek to allow the flash of anger to subside. Slowly, the warmth of acceptance seeped into his heart. "You're right, sis," he said finally, inhaling deeply. "I've been given a second chance, and I'll try to make the most of it."

A few minutes later Bailey left to drive back to his apartment, still vibrating with nervous energy. On impulse, he turned the car onto the dirt road that led to the north meadow overlooking the pond. He stopped the car and retrieved a flashlight from the glove compartment before climbing out, but when he walked to the top of the hill, the moon shone so bright across the meadow, he switched off the beam. For a long time he simply stood and stared across the lush field, listening to the tall grass whisper in the wind. Silver light gilded the huge old white oak tree that loomed enormous in the exaggeration of shadows, drawing him, as always.

Insects fell silent, then resumed their chirping in rounds as he waded through the dew-laden grass to stand in the silhouette of the Kallihan heirloom tree—his tree. His father had planted it the day Bailey was born, and thirty-three years later, its branches spread wide and inviting, begging to be climbed. At first it had been hard to reconcile the sentimental act with his hard-nosed father, whom he missed dearly, but Bailey had come to realize his father had possessed a soft center. Out of respect and love, Bailey had taken a single acorn from the immense tree and planted it the day his own son came into the world.

He turned slowly and walked toward the smaller tree growing several yards away. Bailey, Jr., had already been snatched from their lives by the time the tiny sprout had emerged from the ground. His heart had nearly broken each time he visited the tree, but he'd nursed it determinedly. Despite a fragile beginning, it now stood tall and straight as a sword, casting a fifteen-foot shadow, its leaves rustling in the night breeze. Decades from now its branches would spread to meet those of the older tree. Long after he left this earth, his and his son's trees would live and touch and breathe. The thought filled his veins with deep satisfaction.

He crouched and lowered himself to the ground to sit beneath the canopy of the smaller tree, then leaned back against the rough bark. He and Ginny had planned to build a home in the meadow and raise their son here. Instead, they'd all been scattered in separate directions.

From what he could gather of Ginny's current tastes, he doubted if she would've been happy for long with the simple home design they'd chosen years earlier. He probably still had the dog-eared blueprints somewhere. Lot of good they would do, except remind him of what he'd had, of what he'd thrown away. Even if he did manage to get his life back on track, Ginny was probably lost to him forever.

Or was she?

Sitting amid the sweet-smelling grass under his son's tree, he suddenly realized he'd been given a miracle today and right now anything seemed possible, even a notion as remote as having Virginia Catron's love again.

Bailey felt a boulder of grief and guilt slide from his chest. His shoulders drooped in relief, and his cheeks felt wet. He tilted his head and gazed up through the branches into the star-winking heavens.

"Thanks," he whispered.

CHAPTER THREE

"I KNEW HE'D BE LATE," Virginia's father said, a deep frown creasing his weathered face.

"Edward," Virginia's mother chided, laying a hand on his arm.

Virginia ground her teeth and silently agreed with her father—Bailey was nothing if not unreliable. When the gate attendant announced the final boarding, she gripped the handle of her tapestry carry-on bag and reluctantly rose to her feet. "We'd better go," she said in her strongest voice.

"Let me get that, honey," her dad said, reaching for her bag. He squeezed her shoulders and gave her a smile. "Everything's going to be just fine, you'll see."

She nodded and straightened her shoulders, turning to signal Detective Lance. The salt-and-pepper-haired man was already on his feet, looking grave and protective in his navy suit. He settled a hat on his head with both hands, then stopped to stare at something down the concourse.

Virginia heard Bailey before she saw him. "Ginny!" he yelled. "Wait—I'm coming!"

She shook her head in grudging relief. Bailey rounded the corner in a flurry of flying arms and legs, the bag slung over his shoulder bouncing against his hip. Virginia blinked in astonishment at his appearance. Was this the same man she'd seen the previous night?

His hair had been neatly shorn into short, thick layers, his jaw cleanly shaven. He wore dark jeans and boots with a white dress shirt and—wonder of wonders—a tie of muted colors that complemented the charcoal-gray sport coat covering his wide shoulders. Her throat went dry at his transformation from plain good-looking to downright gorgeous.

Then he grinned and vaulted from gorgeous to drop dead devastating.

"I made it," he announced. "Hello, Peg... Edward." He inclined his head, then extended his hand to Virginia's father.

Edward Catron considered the hand offered to him for several seconds before he clasped it in what appeared to be an iron grip, considering the flash of pain on Bailey's face.

"Bailey," her father acknowledged.

Her mother gave Bailey a tentative smile when he squeezed her hand in greeting. Detective Lance had just finished reintroducing himself when the harried gate attendant rushed over to hustle them onto the plane.

At the doorway the head flight attendant met Virginia with a warm smile. "Your parents mentioned the purpose of your trip to one of the gate crew. We've arranged for you and your husband to sit in first class."

Before Virginia could react, the captain appeared and extended his own congratulations, again addressing them as a married couple. Avoiding Bailey's gaze, Virginia smiled and nodded her way through the uncomfortable misunderstanding, immensely relieved when they were shown to their seats.

"How about that?" Bailey said cheerfully while the plane taxied to take off. "We're celebrities."

Rather than putting her at ease, though, Bailey's carefree smile left her unsettled. Despite the new clothes and tame hair, the gravity of the situation still had not sunk into his irresponsible head. Suddenly the shock, the worry, and the fear of the last fifteen hours rose in Virginia's chest like a suffocating bile. She gagged, jamming her hand to her mouth as she dropped her chin and closed her eyes.

"Ginny?"

She lurched forward as the plane became airborne. Her stomach dipped precariously, then she felt his hand at the small of her back.

"Here's an airsick bag. Are you okay?"

She started to nod agreeably, as she had a hundred times since she'd heard the news, then changed her mind. "No," she gasped, grabbing the bag. She heaved her meager breakfast into it, then sat back, purged and weak, only to find Bailey and the attendant hovering over her.

"Are you all right, ma'am?"

Bailey requested a wet cloth, concern evident in his voice, but he didn't push Virginia to talk. She squeezed her eyes shut and concentrated on taking deep, even breaths. Suddenly a cool, soothing cloth was applied to her forehead by gentle and disturbingly familiar hands. "Can't blame you, Ginny," he murmured. "I felt a little queasy myself this morning. After all, this is a pretty big day for us."

Us. The word reverberated through her fuzzy brain, and a lump of hurt and anger formed in her throat. They should have been able to present a strong, united, happily married front for their son today, but Bailey hadn't loved her enough to stick it out. Deep down, she knew she shouldn't blame him for feelings he hadn't been able to manufacture, but his rejection of her had hurt badly, and if truth be known, it still did.

She opened her eyes, reached up to take the cloth from his hand, and slowly wiped her mouth. "There is no *us*, Bailey," she whispered hoarsely.

He searched her face for a moment, and she hoped her newfound resolve was evident. Her life seemed to be in a state of free fall, and she had to regain some measure of control. Her breathing became shallow as the silence between them ballooned.

After a full minute he reached forward to cover her hand with his, then wet his lips. "There could be an us." He angled his head, his eyes disarmingly hopeful.

Tiny hairs sprang up on the back of her neck as his words sank in, then a slow burn started in her chest. Bailey Kallihan had more nerve than ten men to think he could erase years of hurt with a charming smile and a soft touch. She must look like a fool if she seemed that desperate.

Humiliation bloomed and spread to the ends of her tingling fingers as she carefully extracted her hand from his. She struggled to keep her voice even as she gripped the cloth so hard, water dripped onto her shirt. "Let me make one thing perfectly clear, Bailey—if our son had not been found, I would have had no reason, and no desire, to see you again." He shrank back from her a few inches, and she felt a bite of satisfaction, a dimension of control returning. "I love my child enough to make the best of this situation, but don't try to turn this into something it's not."

Bailey shrugged. "Okay, I didn't mean to—"

"Yes, you did mean to," she cut in, then held up her hand to bring the subject to a halt. She closed her eyes and sighed. "I called an attorney this morning, Bailey, and we've got a lot to discuss before we land, so let's just get through this, okay?"

A muscle ticked in his jaw. "Sure."

Another flight attendant stopped to take their drink order and Virginia gratefully accepted a glass of ginger ale. She longed for the mild sedative her mother had offered her earlier. Her stomach pitched and rolled with a myriad of emotions she tried to pin down. In only a few hours she'd be face-to-face with her son... her *son*. She worried her bottom lip and dug her fingernails into her palm.

"What things?" he asked, jarring her out of her racing thoughts.

"What?"

He pushed his hair back from his forehead, looking frustrated. "What things do we have to discuss?"

"Oh." She straightened in her seat. "Well... the custody arrangement."

His brow furrowed. "What's to discuss? We'll both have custody—he can stay with me on the weekends."

"Stay with you? You mean on your couch in an apartment above a bar?"

He flushed angrily. "We'll stay at Rita's so he can get to know his cousin."

Virginia had two panicky visions—her son alone with her in a stifling town home, and her son with Bailey's rowdy family on a farm; it didn't take a child psychologist to guess where the boy would prefer to spend time. "I work during the week, I'd like to spend weekends with him too."

"Can't you cut back on your hours?"

Anger flamed through her, but she fought to keep her voice calm. "I arranged for a month of leave, which should take me up to the start of school, but after that I'll be back to working at least forty-five hours a week. Raising a child is expensive, Bailey."

"I'll help," he declared hotly.

She averted her eyes so he couldn't read her doubts. Ever the good-intentioned, Bailey's fault lay in his follow-through. His idea of savings used to be buying old cars, hoping they'd appreciate in value. He'd let her down before in a big way—she wasn't about to sacrifice a portion of her income on the basis of a verbal promise. "I'm not cutting my hours. He can stay with you at Rita's every other weekend."

"Wait a minute!" Passengers around them turned to stare. He leaned toward her and lowered his voice, his eyes still flashing. "Four or five days a month isn't enough. He's my son too, and I want to get to know him just as much as you do."

"Well," she said coolly, "we seem to be at an impasse."

His eyes narrowed, then his face relaxed as if a solution had occurred to him. "Not necessarily."

She angled her head toward him suspiciously. "What do you mean?"

"In the beginning we can both spend time with him... we can all do things together."

Virginia frowned, wary.

"It's only fair to Bailey, Jr.," he asserted, "that he get to know both of us. We both want to spend time with him, and we can't split him down the middle." He flashed her a charming smile. "You can't convince me you've grown *that* tough, Ginny."

Her stomach contracted at his reminder that he used to know her well, that he used to know her intimately. "What about holidays and school vacations?"

He shrugged. "We'll work it out when the time comes."

"I think we need to get this down on paper," she insisted.

"Ginny, for God's sake, you make this sound like some kind of business deal. You used to be easygoing and spontaneous—now you want every detail planned out. What's happened to you?"

His words stung, but she wasn't about to let him know. "What happened to me? I grew up, Bailey, which is something you might think about doing someday. Living life shooting from the hip is amusing for a man in his twenties, but not very flattering for a man in his thirties."

As she watched raw emotion play across his handsome face, Virginia almost felt sorry for her ex-husband. But she knew him, and knew that he had to be forced to face the truth. It was too late for them, but he needed to extend himself beyond his hedonistic lifestyle for their son.

Bailey dropped his eyes and swished a stirrer in the whiskey sour he cradled in one hand. "I guess I deserve that," he said, his voice resigned. Then he set his drink down and twisted in his seat to face her. "But, Ginny, you have to believe me when I say I'm going to settle down and be a good father to Bailey, Jr. I want to be there for him." He gave her a sad smile. "I want to be there for you too, but I understand how you feel about me."

Her stomach pivoted again, but this time it had nothing to do with the altitude or her anxiety over meeting her son.

"Could you put up with me being around long enough to allow our son to adjust?"

Warning bells screamed in Virginia's head. Spending time with Bailey sounded too much like playing house. He might charm her into letting her guard down long enough for him to get his hooks into her heart again.

"Only," she said in a threatening tone, "if you give me your word we can be adult about this and keep things on a strictly platonic level."

He laid a hand over his heart. "I give you my word."

But Virginia's chest tightened in dreaded premonition. When had Bailey Kallihan *ever* lived up to his word?

* * *

As soon as he stepped into the gate area, Bailey spotted a small but conspicuous group of police officers and other official-looking people. Detective Lance took the lead, first introducing himself to a fellow officer, then presenting Virginia, Bailey, and her parents.

A kindly gentleman in a maroon jacket clasped Ginny's hand warmly, his eyes shining. "I'm Kendall Maybry, from the children's services bureau. It's a real pleasure, Mrs. Kallihan," he said. The title sent a tiny shock wave through Bailey, and he was remotely pleased that Ginny didn't correct the error.

After a few minutes of awkward pleasantries, Bailey asked, "Mr. Maybry, where is our son?" He knew he was probably breaking protocol, but he wasn't sure if protocol existed for such a situation.

"He's been living at a children's shelter since the death of his mo—" The man broke off, embarrassed, and offered Ginny an apologetic smile. "I mean, since the death of the woman who... took care of him. This is Ms. Andrews—she's been counseling Chad through this ordeal."

"Chad?" he and Ginny asked in unison.

"The boy goes by the name Chad Green," Ms. Andrews said, shaking their hands in turn.

The news hit Bailey like a knee to his stomach. Of course the woman who'd kidnapped him hadn't known the child's real name, and wouldn't have used it if she had. The one link he had with his son had been stripped away.

"Are you the one who told him about us, Ms. Andrews?" Ginny asked, gripping her purse tighter and tighter. Bailey's heart constricted at her pinched, expectant expression.

"Yes."

"What was his reaction?"

Ms. Andrews hesitated only a few seconds, but long enough for dread to wash over Bailey. "Well... as you can imagine, it was quite a shock for him, but we can talk about it on the way to the shelter. Shall we?" She swept her arm toward an exit, and the group moved forward as a unit.

Minutes later Bailey helped Ginny climb into a minivan with Mr. Maybry, Ms. Andrews, and Ginny's parents. He settled into the space beside Ginny, experiencing a twinge of pleasure at the sensation of her leg pressed against the length of his. Seeking diversion from the sudden rush, he blurted out, "Tell us what's going on with our son. Is he okay?"

The counselor turned in her seat to face them. "Physically, he's fine, just an ordinary, healthy eight-year-old."

Bailey felt a small amount of relief.

"But," the woman continued, "he's understandably upset about leaving the area he grew up in to live with parents who are strangers to him."

"The woman who"—Ginny swallowed audibly—"who took our son—Detective Lance told me she didn't mistreat him. Is that true?"

The woman smiled encouragingly. "As far as we know, yes. Neighbors say that Lois Green was a person who sometimes acted a little strange, but was very protective where Chad was concerned."

Bailey bit the end of his tongue. It wasn't fair to Ginny that another woman had been allowed to be protective of their child. But considering all the alternatives their son could have been exposed to, it wasn't the worst scenario by far.

"There was no father figure in the home, and I gather from my sessions with Chad that he grew up quickly, and assumed the role of caretaker when Lois became ill."

"How did she die?" Bailey asked.

"Cancer," Ms. Andrews replied.

"Was she—" Ginny hesitated, and he saw her clench her hand into a fist. "Was she a decent sort of person?"

The counselor nodded. "Lois Green held a secretarial position and rented a small apartment. It wasn't in the best part of town, but she made certain Chad went to school, and you'll be glad to know he's a good student."

"What grade?" It sounded like a stupid question, but Bailey had no time for pretenses.

"Fourth. I understand you have no other children, Mr. and Mrs. Kallihan?"

Bailey squirmed, and Ginny's cheeks flushed dark pink before she said, "Actually, Ms. Andrews, we're no longer married. I go by the name of Catron."

Mild surprise registered on the woman's face. "Oh? Which family will Chad be living with?"

Bailey coughed. "Neither one of us have a family."

"We're both single," Ginny clarified, "and Ch-Chad will be living with me."

"I see," Ms. Andrews said slowly. "Well, for Chad's sake, I'm sorry you're not living together, but I guess this is the next most desirable situation, if you're both agreeable to the living arrangements." She glanced at Bailey.

"We've reached a compromise." He met Ginny's gaze, and felt a stab of determination to breach the wall she'd erected.

The counselor nodded, then explained they were forty minutes away from the home where they would meet Chad after they signed the necessary papers.

He felt Ginny stir beside him before she asked, "What does he look like?" He glanced at her, but had to look away when he saw the tears gathered in her eyes.

Ms. Andrews smiled. "He's a fine-looking boy. I'm sure you will be very pleased."

The forty minutes crept by. No one spoke, as if conceding that words could not prepare them for what lay ahead. Bailey alternately concentrated on the traffic outside and the tightening and loosening of Ginny's iron grip on her purse. Unable to help himself, he reached over to close his hand over her white-knuckled one, but he didn't look at her for fear she'd pull away. She didn't, and he welcomed her warm skin against his to calm his own jumping nerves.

At last they pulled into the shelter's crowded parking lot. Bailey squinted at the gathering of people and equipment just outside the entrance. "What's going on?"

Mr. Maybry banged his fist on the steering wheel and Ms. Andrews shook her head angrily. "Reporters," she said. "Someone must have leaked the story to the press."

He heard and felt Ginny's sharp inhale, and felt a surge of protectiveness. "Damn. Is there a back entrance?"

"Too late," Mr. Maybry said as the crowd turned and ran toward their van, microphones held high and cameras rolling.

Detective Lance and another police officer were on their feet before the van rolled to a stop. "Follow us," he instructed.

Bailey clasped Ginny's hand and held on, even when she started to pull away. "Stay close to me," he murmured. The din of the crowd exploded around them when the van door opened. A dozen microphones were thrust into their faces and camera flashes blinded them.

"Mr. and Mrs. Kallihan, what are your feelings as you prepare to meet your son for the first time in eight years?"

"Do you know anything about him?"

"What if he doesn't want to live with you?"

"Will you give us a statement before you leave?"

The police officers cleared a path, with Mr. Maybry and Ms. Andrews offering protection from behind. Bailey focused on the home's entrance, his strength growing each time Ginny leaned into him. Finally they reached the steps, the sounds and voices receding behind them as they ascended to safety.

The door closed behind them. Bailey looked around, forcing his eyes to adjust to the dimness, expecting to see his son in any corner of the room. His heart pounded in anticipation.

"I'm terribly sorry about that," Ms. Andrews said. "I guess it was bound to capture the media's attention. It's quite a fantastic story—we've never heard of a reunion like this one."

Bailey had already dismissed the commotion. "Where's my son?"

Mr. Maybry stepped forward. "If you could give us just a few more minutes to sign the necessary paperwork to release Chad into your custody—"

"Show me the papers," he demanded.

At a signal from Mr. Maybry, a secretary scurried out of the room, then returned with a handful of documents.

"Now, Mr. and Mrs.—I mean, Mr. Kallihan and Ms. Catron, if you will—"

Bailey snatched the pen. "Where do I sign?"

The man abandoned whatever rules he'd been prepared to defend, and simply pointed to a blank line on each paper, where Bailey hastily scrawled his name, then handed the pen to Ginny. She hesitated only a second or two before following suit. Bailey suspected it was the first time she'd signed anything with such abandon since their divorce papers.

When she set down the pen, he said, "Now, Mr. Maybry, take us to our son."

"Right this way."

They were led down a carpeted hallway with numbered doors on either side. Ginny gripped his hand tightly. He caught her worried glance and gave her a wink and a comforting smile.

The end of the hall opened into a recreation room, complete with game tables, bookshelves, and bean-bag chairs scattered in front of a TV. Bright fluorescent lights reached into the corners of the room, dimmed by blinds that had been pulled, Bailey realized, to keep out prying cameras. His eyes scanned the quiet room, alighting on a small figure sitting at a table against a far wall. At their entrance the woman sitting with the boy stood and moved away.

Bailey's eyes were riveted on the child as he turned to look their way. His heart threatened to explode as he took in the boy's familiar features. Same dark, unruly hair, same deep widow's peak and slight cowlick, same dense brows, same cobalt-blue eyes. It could have been himself at eight years old.

He heard Ginny's sharp intake of breath, felt her death grip on his hand. "Oh, my God," she whispered.

The boy stood up, his eyes guarded, his expression wary. He wore a baggy blue-and-white-striped T-shirt over denim shorts and high-top athletic shoes. As they walked closer, he dropped his gaze and flicked a paint chip from the surface of the table. When at last he looked at them, Bailey saw pain and fear in the boy's wide, dark eyes. Blood pounded in his ears. *My son... my son... my son.*

"Hello," Bailey ventured, pleased that his voice worked at all.

"Hey," came the cautious reply.

Ginny seemed speechless, unable to tear her eyes away from the boy. Bailey wasn't sure what to say next, but his son had apparently been giving this moment a great deal of thought.

"So you're my real parents, huh?" He spoke with the low tone and casual grace of a street-smart kid.

"Yes," Ginny said, her voice wavering only slightly. "Bailey is your father, and I'm Virginia, your m-mother."

The dark eyes scanned them both head to toe, and Bailey held his breath.

"I can see you're my old man," Chad said to Bailey. "We got the same face."

Bailey nodded, confirming the obvious. He was going to have a heart attack if his pulse didn't slow soon.

Then Chad turned to Ginny, and tilted his head. "But you don't look like any mother I've seen."

Bailey had to agree. She looked too young and too slim in a blue wrap dress and high heels. He watched as she smiled, her face lighting with wonder. "But I am," she said gently. "I'm your mother."

His son considered Ginny's words for a few seconds, then turned belligerent eyes her way. "What kind of mother lets her kid get stolen in a grocery store?"

CHAPTER FOUR

BAILEY BLINKED. Ginny dropped his hand, her shoulders falling, her hand covering her open mouth. Anger bolted through his stomach as he looked back to his unruffled son. The boy even had a slight smile on his face. "What did you say?" Bailey demanded.

Chad rolled his eyes. "I said what kind of mo—"

"Never mind," Bailey interrupted. "I heard you." He turned to the small knot of people in the back of the room. "We'd like some privacy, please."

Ginny's father puffed up and opened his mouth to respond, but her mother quieted him and pulled him from the room along with the others. The door closed noiselessly. The only sound in the room was Ginny's soft sniffling as she struggled to regain her composure.

Bailey wanted to comfort her, but his immediate concern was the cocky cause of her tears.

Chad stood with his arms loosely crossed, challenging Bailey with his eyes and his stance. He was apparently unmoved by tears, and unafraid of a reprisal.

Even as Bailey's mind raced for the appropriate reprimand, he cursed himself. What right did he have to chastise? The boy's words to Ginny were almost identical to the words he'd said to her after the kidnapping. And Bailey had been old enough to know better, not a confused eight-year-old kid.

Whether by design, Bailey wasn't sure, but Chad had lashed out at the very person who would be the most devoted to him. *Like father, like son.* He rubbed at the ache forming in his temple, then leveled his gaze on Chad. "This is strange for all of us, but you had no cause to say that."

Chad shrugged, his eyes remaining passive. "It's a free country, I can say whatever I want."

Bailey straightened, placing his hands on his hips. "Then I hope you want to say you're sorry."

His son's chin raised a notch. "And I suppose you're going to make me, *Daddy?*"

The taunt stung Bailey, and it took him a few seconds to recover. The boy was as belligerent as he'd been at that age. He took a deep, steadying breath to rein in his anger. "You can be a jerk to me if you need to blow some steam, son, but"—he took a few steps closer to Chad and assumed an authoritative stance of his own—"don't take it out on your mother."

Chad's eyes narrowed. "My mother was Lois Green."

Bailey remained completely still. "Then consider yourself lucky. Some kids don't have a mother at all, and you've had two."

The boy jerked his thumb toward Ginny. "I'm not calling her Mom, and I'm not calling you Dad."

His heart squeezed over yet another intangible loss.

"That's fine," Ginny injected, her voice much stronger. "Virginia and Bailey will do for now." She looked at Bailey, nodding encouragement.

"Sure," Bailey said stiffly.

"And I *don't* want to be called Junior. A counselor told me I could have my name legally changed to Chad Green."

Another pause, and he and Ginny shared another glance. The kid sounded like an eight-year-old going on sixteen. Bailey conceded. "Okay, we'll talk about the name change later."

"So what's this place like, this Columbus, Ohio?" Chad's tone sounded as if he were already decidedly unimpressed with his destination.

Bailey shrugged, immensely relieved to be on more neutral ground. "It's flat, and big, and busy, not unlike here."

"A friend of mine used to live there and said he froze his ass off."

Bailey frowned. "Do you always talk like that?"

"It's a free country—"

"I know," Bailey cut in. "But watch your language."

Chad gave a dismissive wave and turned back to the table. "I changed my mind—I don't want to live with you."

Bailey tamped down his anger. "You're not going to live with me, you're going to live with Ginny."

At last he was rewarded with Chad's undivided attention as the boy sorted the words in his head. He snorted. "You mean you guys are divorced?"

Regret washed over Bailey—he didn't dare look at Ginny because he knew he'd find no remorse there. "That's right."

The boy threw up his arms in resignation. "Great. How many half and step brothers and sisters do I have?"

"None," Ginny said.

"But I have stepparents, right?"

"No," Bailey said.

Their son frowned, the wind taken from his sails. "When did you get divorced?"

Bailey exhaled a long, noisy breath. "A few months after you were kidnapped."

"No more kid, no more marriage?" Chad hooted. "What was I, an accident or something?" One look at Ginny's face, and his smirk disappeared. "You're kidding—I was an accident?"

"Unplanned," Ginny said quickly, "but we wanted you very much."

"Oh, right," Chad declared haughtily. "You were probably glad I was kidnapped! You probably left me alone on purpose!"

"No," Ginny whispered, shaking her head. "We looked everywhere—"

"That's enough," Bailey said, his voice low and just short of threatening. He buried his hand in his hair and bit back a curse. "You're my kid all right. I'd have known it if you didn't look like me because you don't know when to keep your mouth shut."

"Bailey," Ginny began, but he held his hand up to silence her.

"From the minute we arrived, you've been nothing but rude, disrespectful, and downright mean."

"Don't like me, huh?" Chad's voice had lost some of its bravado. "Well, maybe I don't like you either, mister."

When he noticed moisture gathering around the corners of the boy's dark eyes, Bailey experienced his first glimmer of hope that things might work out someday, somehow. He reached over to squeeze Chad's shoulder, and the boy turned his head, but didn't pull away. Another good sign.

"My daddy always told me it was a shame you couldn't pick your relatives like you pick your friends." Chad's hooded gaze darted back to him and Bailey shrugged. "But you can't, so I guess we're stuck with each other."

His son pondered the words a few seconds, then asked, "Are you the only family I got?"

Bailey reluctantly withdrew his hand, shaking his head. "An aunt, uncle, and six-year-old cousin in Ohio—"

"A boy cousin?"

"Jean Ann's a girl, but she's no sissy. Throws a baseball so hard it'll burn your hand through a glove."

Chad seemed mildly impressed. "Who are those old people who came with you?"

"They're my parents," Ginny said softly, stepping forward. "Your only grandparents, and they're dying to meet you." She smiled and wiped at her lingering tears with the heel of her hand.

Bailey left and returned a few minutes later with Edward and Peg. Chad shuffled over to them with little enthusiasm, but surprised Bailey by shaking hands with Edward and allowing Peg to give him a hug. As he watched his son nod and answer questions, pride filled him and he struggled a few seconds with his own emotions. He wondered if his expression matched Ginny's.

She positively glowed. Her eyes never left Chad, soaking him up like a thirsty sponge. The top of his dark head nearly reached her shoulder. At times her fingers hovered just above his skin, as if she wanted to touch him, but didn't dare. She looked as tentative around Chad as Bailey felt around her.

Taking advantage of her distraction, he allowed his gaze to roam over her figure. He'd always loved her slender neck, and the topknot she wore gave him a tantalizing view. The fabric of the dress she wore clung softly to her shoulders and slight curves. He remembered the skin on her stomach being satiny smooth—flat muscle before the baby, stretched during the pregnancy, then softness afterward on the way back to muscle tone—his fingers had been explicably drawn to her abdomen at every stage. Her legs were long, her calves well defined, narrowing to slender ankles.

Desire welled within him. The sexual aspect of their relationship had never been lacking—Ginny had been a warm, enthusiastic lover, at times leaving him too tired for his physically demanding job. He remembered the ribbing he'd taken at work on days he'd moved with less energy than usual.

His prevailing memory of their lovemaking was her whispering his name in urgency. Every time he'd lain with a woman since his divorce, he'd imagined Ginny's satisfied gasp... *Bailey... oh, Bailey...*

"Bailey," Ginny said, snapping him out of his reverie. She volunteered her first genuine smile since their reunion and motioned him to the table where the four of them were pulling up chairs. "Join us."

As he walked toward them, Bailey locked his gaze on Chad and Ginny. The last eight years seemed to disintegrate. Here was his family, his son and wife, the two people he loved most in the world. Guilt slammed into him with the force of an anvil.

He'd failed miserably at his husbandly duties. How well would he handle parenthood?

* * *

Virginia had never experienced such a deluge of emotions in such a short time span. As an hour slipped by, then two, her pulse finally slowed to just below the dangerous mark, only to leap again when Chad revealed some interesting tidbit about his life. In fidgety, staccato sentences, he admitted that he skateboarded, hung out at the video arcade, and could hit a three-point shot on the basketball court in his school gym. And that he liked animals, hated girls, and tolerated homework. While not exactly warming to his new family gathered around the table, Chad seemed to become less confrontational as the sparse conversation progressed.

But he avoided all eye contact with her.

The ceiling, the floor, and every other person at the table seemed worthy of his attention, but not Virginia. His earlier outburst still rang in her ears, but she tried to push it from her mind. And she really didn't mind his averted eyes, because then she didn't have to worry that he would discover her secret.

She was terrified at the thought of taking him home.

Virginia could scarcely reconcile this belligerent, gangly boy with the baby she'd carried home in her arms so many years earlier. As she watched him move and speak, she felt twinges of happiness and longing, but the fear... the fear dwarfed every other sensation. She kept smiling while her skin prickled, and her blood raced.

Before this moment, only one other person had ever made her feel so completely overwhelmed—Bailey.

She lifted her eyes to find her ex-husband engrossed in Chad's explanation of why the South Eastern Conference was *definitely* the best college basketball conference in the country. Bailey nodded thoughtfully, his eyes warm and rapt on his son. Then he offered his own argument for Ohio State's conference, the Big Ten. Bailey sat back in his chair and splayed his hands, then cracked his knuckles with a bend of his wrists. She'd once hated his noisy habit, but now found it oddly familiar and comforting.

He had removed the gray sport coat and rolled up the sleeves of his starched dress shirt to reveal impressive, darkly tanned forearms. The calluses on his large hands further attested that he often abandoned his position of crew chief and pitched in to help his men, a revelation that didn't surprise Virginia at all. She smiled sadly to herself. Bailey had never been afraid of hard work—it had been the more abstract demands of life he'd found too challenging. Like loving her...

A rap sounded at the door, then Ms. Andrews's head and shoulders appeared. "Would you like to break for a light meal?" Though not the least bit hungry, Virginia felt immensely grateful for a return to the mundane details of living. The group rose and filed from the room, following the counselor.

With a pang Virginia noted the identical father-son saunter, originating from the carriage of the same wide shoulders, and the gait of the same long legs. The child was created from the joining of her and Bailey's bodies, but as she watched them move in near perfect synchronization, she realized that little to none of herself had made it past the dominance of Bailey Kallihan's genes.

Bailey and Chad were formed from the same mold—it was she who didn't belong. Her ex-husband and her son had both voiced their doubts about her ability to be a good mother, and they didn't even know the extent of her own apprehension. From the recesses of her mind, the thought materialized that perhaps they'd be happier together—without her. Premonition shivered through her, but she shook it off.

A cold meal in the dining room was a quiet affair, with conversation contributed mostly by Ms. Andrews and Mr. Maybry. As dusk approached, Detective Lance reappeared to announce reporters were still camped outside the building.

"Chad," Virginia said across the table. "This is Detective Lance. He was assigned to our case when... from the very beginning."

The officer smiled. "Good to finally meet you, young man."

Chad acknowledged him with a nod, swallowing the last of his sandwich. "So Lois outsmarted you, huh?"

She thought she detected a hint of pride in Chad's voice, and her anger at the woman who'd taken him flared once again.

Detective Lance glanced from her to Bailey, who was taking his time wiping his tightened mouth with a paper napkin. She nodded for the officer to speak freely.

"I guess she did, son."

"Those other cops wouldn't tell me what really happened."

After another encouraging nod from Virginia, Detective Lance pulled up a chair beside Chad, then opened a brown accordion folder and removed yellowed newspaper articles. "The suspect," he began to explain in an official-sounding voice, then stopped and removed his hat. When he resumed, he encompassed all of them in his sweeping gaze, and spoke in a softer tone. "Lois Green was born and raised in Detroit, Michigan. She was an only child, kind of quiet, with no criminal record. She married young and, around eight years ago, became pregnant. Her husband abandoned her when she miscarried.

"She left Michigan and made her way south, moving from diner to diner as a waitress. She quit a job at a truck stop in Westerville, Ohio, a few days before the kidnapping. We'll probably never know if she planned the kidnapping ahead of time or made a split-second decision in the grocery store." He pushed a newspaper account of the story toward Chad, who picked it up and began reading in earnest.

She remembered the article. The *Columbus Dispatch* headline read "Infant Boy Stolen from Grocery," and had created a stir up and down the East Coast. For weeks, volunteers had poured in to search for their missing baby. The article's accompanying picture showed the face of a young, angst-ridden Bailey tramping through the woods. Virginia had stayed home, feeling helpless as she waited by the phone for a possible ransom demand. But the call never came, and the only tormenting clue had been the discovery of their son's blanket in a ditch along a busy highway. Lois Green must have discarded it as she drove out of town with her tiny victim, Virginia surmised.

Chad's eyes moved rapidly over the story, then sifted through other accounts, recaps, and updates. Long-forgotten memories crashed over Virginia. The inevitable waning public interest, bitter fights with Bailey, separate beds, her leaving, then filing divorce papers. Ironically, on the day their divorce had been final, nearly a year after the abduction, a reporter called for her comment on the rumor that the investigation had been unofficially closed. The next day Virginia began picking up the remnants of her life.

Chad suddenly pushed the pile of paper back toward the detective. "She was a good mom," he asserted in a challenging voice, his chin jutted high. "Maybe she made a mistake, but she was a good mom." At last he looked directly at Virginia. "She must have wanted me really bad to risk getting into trouble." She saw his unspoken words in narrowed, accusatory eyes. *She wanted me, and you didn't.*

"Chad," Ms. Andrews cut in, standing up, "why don't we have one last chat this evening? I've got some free time right now, then you'll need to finish packing."

He frowned, but shrugged reluctantly. "Whatever." He pushed himself away from the table with a heavy sigh, threw the remains of his meal into an

43

industrial-sized waste can, and followed Ms. Andrews out of the room without a backward glance.

Virginia took a deep breath and made her best effort to appear cheerful. "I suppose we should check into the hotel soon, but I don't look forward to facing that crowd."

"Ms. Catron," Mr. Maybry said, his face flushing a deep pink. "Ms. Andrews and I assumed you both would want to be as close as possible to Chad tonight, but we weren't aware of your, um, status, and we have only one guest room available." He coughed. "However, it is equipped with twin beds, and we can—"

"That was very thoughtful." She caught Bailey's wide-eyed reaction. "We'll work out something," she assured the embarrassed man, her insides churning at the mere suggestion of intimacy with her ex-husband.

"Meanwhile," Bailey said, "we probably should decide what to do about the press."

"Just run 'em off!" Edward sputtered.

"But it's not often we hear of such a happy ending," Mr. Maybry reminded them, his expression gentle. "The attention might help some other child be reunited with his parents."

"You could prepare a statement and your father and I can read it when we leave for the hotel, dear," her mother offered.

"Thanks, Mom, but I think this is something Bailey and I need to do."

"Together," he added, meeting her wary look with a conciliatory smile.

Red flags went up in her mind. *Darn him*, she fumed. He was so, so... accommodating.

"How about getting it over with?" he asked, standing and lifting his palms.

She hesitated a few seconds before rising to her feet. "Okay."

He held out his hand for hers. With an audience, she couldn't refuse such a friendly gesture, which was all it meant anyway. She placed her hand in his, a rush skittering over her as their fingers entwined and their palms met. Her heart raced with the realization this wasn't the first time they'd held hands that day, but it was the first time she'd participated deliberately and for a reason other than pure fear.

They walked to the front of the building, preceded by Mr. Maybry and flanked by Detective Lance and her parents. As soon as the doors opened, a murmur rose and the crowd of about fifty onlookers pressed toward the tiny sheltered stoop where they stepped into the humid evening air. Cameras flashed and microphones bobbed high.

Mr. Maybry unceremoniously yanked a microphone out of a young man's hand and waved his arms to silence everyone. He quickly introduced himself, then announced, "The child's parents, Ms. Virginia Catron and Mr. Bailey Kallihan, will make a short statement." He then thrust the borrowed microphone into Virginia's hand.

She held it for a few seconds, registering the cold heaviness, wondering what on earth she was going to say. Every eye was riveted on her, and she could read the anticipation in their eyes, hands poised to record her every word. They wanted tears of happiness, an embracing Norman Rockwell-type family touting plans for their future. How could she confess they were the epitome of the modern dysfunctional family—a divorced couple juggling a troubled child?

Bailey slipped his arm loosely around her waist, his hand resting casually on her side after giving her a slight squeeze. Her heart rattled in her chest, quickened by his touch. She somehow found her voice. "E-eight years ago the media came to our aid when our son was taken from us. I can't tell you how much it means to me"—Virginia stopped and swallowed hard before continuing—"to see my son again after all these years. *Please* pay attention to posters, fliers in the mail, milk cartons—any pictures of missing children. Someday you may be the one to reunite a family." *A family of strangers*, she added silently.

The crowd applauded loudly, but began to fire questions before the noise even died down.

"Ms. Catron," an older, pleasant-faced woman asked, "how does your son look to you?"

Virginia smiled. "He looks very much like his father."

"Handsome?" the woman pressed, her eyes twinkling.

"Well, um... of course." Her face burned and she heard Bailey's low chuckle beside her.

"How is your son taking the news?" another woman asked.

She hesitated. "He's confused, naturally, and as surprised as we are, but I'm sure things will work out fine." *Liar,* her mind nagged.

"Ms. Catron," a man near her asked, "I assume from your name that the two of you are no longer married?"

"That's correct," she said calmly. A disappointed murmur resounded.

"Have you both remarried?"

"No, neither of us," Bailey piped in helpfully.

"Are you planning to get back together?"

The crowd tittered, and every reporter waited, straining forward for a juicy tidbit of gossip. She felt Bailey's arm tighten and she tingled with humiliation. *There could be an us,* he'd said, as if now that their son had been found, things were right with the world again. He'd never turned his back on her, never broken her heart.

One woman grew bolder following Virginia's hesitation. "How about it, any chance of you two getting back together?"

"No," Virginia said with confidence.

"Anything is possible," Bailey said at the same time.

CHAPTER FIVE

BAILEY SCANNED THE SMALL, sparsely furnished room, eyeing the disappointing distance between the neatly made twin beds in opposite corners. A floor lamp situated behind mismatched armchairs in the center of the room cast harsh light to the perimeter. The air hung stale and prickly hot. A vase of wilting cut flowers sat on a round coffee table between the chairs. Plain navy curtains hung at the single half-window above an ancient television with a rabbit ear antenna.

"Looks cozy," he said cheerfully, crossing the faded green carpet and dropping his garment bag on one of the chairs. "Reminds me of when we lived in the old homeplace, Ginny." He spun and caught the flash of panic on her face, then told himself to slow down. She'd barely uttered ten words since his spontaneous public announcement that he wouldn't mind them getting back together. He laughed to ease the tension, then said, "Of course, Rita has done such a great job with the place, you wouldn't recognize it."

She walked over and claimed a bed with her lone piece of luggage. "It wasn't all that bad before," she said, her gaze darting around the room.

"Hey." He spoke softly. When she looked at him, he continued. "Are you okay with this? I can go to the hotel."

"No," she said hastily. "I mean, yes, I'm okay with it." She laughed nervously, tugging on the zipper of her bag. "We're adults, Bailey, not teenagers hopped up on hormones."

"You're right." Bailey carefully kept his voice light. "After all, what's one night? We've spent hundreds of nights together."

With a final jerk the zipper on her bag gave way. "And thousands more apart," she reminded him.

Properly chastised, he cracked his knuckles. "Well, what do you think of our son?"

Pausing, she pursed her lips, looking thoughtful. "He was different from what I expected, but I'm not even sure what I expected."

"He seems like an okay kid, but I think he's got a bit too much spunk for his own good."

She smiled tightly. "You know what they say about the apple not falling far from the tree." She pulled out a handful of toiletries and headed for the bathroom, visible through a narrow door next to her bed. Nudging the door open with her elbow, she then arranged shampoo and toothpaste on the tiny vanity in the vintage room.

Anticipation stabbed him as she bent to fuss with the water faucet of the avocado-green bathtub. Her dress rode up to reveal her thighs. As she swished her fingers under the spray of water to find the right temperature, Bailey felt himself begin to harden at the tantalizing outline of her legs. It suddenly became apparent that the next eight or so hours might be excruciatingly long and painful.

"No shower," she announced when she emerged, drying her hands on the towel. "Would you mind if I went first in the tub?"

"No." He jammed his hands in his pockets. "Go right ahead."

She rummaged in her bag, presumably for sleepwear, and Bailey found himself unable to look away. Ginny used to sleep in a pair of his boxers topped with any of several sexy camisoles. He swallowed hard. Whose boxers might she be wearing these days? He hadn't thought past her not being married, but now it seemed likely that a woman with her beauty and success would be involved with someone.

"Ginny."

She raised her face, eyebrows lifted. "Yes?"

"Are you, um, seeing anyone?"

Her brow furrowed. "Romantically?"

He rolled his shoulders awkwardly. "Uh, yeah."

"Not at the moment." She went back to rummaging, then gave up, lifted the bag by the handles, and headed toward the bathroom.

"Ginny?"

With one hand on the knob, she stopped and turned.

"Aren't you going to ask me if I'm seeing anyone?"

She adopted a wry expression. "I don't have to ask, Bailey. Last night at the saloon I saw almost as much of her as you've undoubtedly seen."

She turned and entered the bathroom, closing the door with a firm *clunk*.

Frustration propelled him to the bathroom door. "I'm not seeing her," he said loud enough to penetrate the wood. "Lisa's just a... an acquaintance."

The faucets were shut off, followed by the sound of light splashing, as if she were testing the water.

"Are you jealous?" he asked hopefully.

After a few seconds of silence he heard her walk back to the door. He held his breath in anticipation. Was she going to invite him in?

The distinct *click* of the lock sounded.

Bailey swore softly under his breath, but he remained at the door, riveted by the sounds of Ginny removing her clothes, then sliding into the water. Only supreme restraint kept him from kneeling to find a keyhole. He closed his eyes and pictured her naked skin, slick and glistening. A full minute passed, his desire for her swelling, literally, as he listened to her move around in the water. He opened his mouth to say something, anything.

"Go away, Bailey," she said.

Damn. He turned from the door and retreated to his bed, then removed his shirt and kicked off his boots before dropping onto the lumpy mattress. The day's events swirled in his head, culminating in a knot of pain over his left eye. Less than forty-eight hours earlier he'd been a happy-go-lucky bachelor, surrounded by laughing friends and willing women. Now he was father to a too-wise eight-year-old, and trying to patch things up with an ex-wife who barely tolerated him.

And who just happened to be bathing in the next room.

Bailey groaned, massaging his aching temple. Running his tongue over his dry teeth, he acknowledged how welcome the taste of whiskey would be to his throat. The tasks before him suddenly seemed overwhelming, and he wondered how most men dealt with the crushing weight of family responsibility. His own father had mostly ignored his wife and children unless they disobeyed. His boss had a running string of complaints about his ungrateful, spoiled children and wife. The attitudes of most of the married men who worked for him typically ranged from begrudging loyalty to downright resentment.

Then there was Jerry, his brother-in-law, the one man he knew who seemed eager to go home to his wife and child, content to watch television on the weekends rather than shoot pool and down a cold one at a bar with Bailey. What was it between Jerry and Rita, Bailey had often wondered, that was strong enough to keep Jerry coming home every night with a smile on his face?

Since his divorce, Bailey had experienced a couple of near misses at the justice of the peace, but he'd always come to his senses at the last minute. He frowned, eyes closed. Although he'd loved Ginny, he remembered feeling trapped during their brief marriage. Even now he wanted her so much his body hurt, but he couldn't be sure it would translate to long-term commitment. And despite his promise to her on the plane, he worried if he'd ever settle down long enough to become a permanent fixture in anyone's life, even his son's. Although he knew in his heart the best thing for Chad would be to rebuild a lasting relationship with Ginny, he still had doubts about his ability to live up to his end of the bargain. And Ginny had made no secret of her opinion on the matter.

When the bathroom door opened, he sat up. Ginny floated into the room on a cloud of fruity fragrance, wrapped in a satiny knee-length robe, her dark gold hair shimmering damp and loose on her shoulders. Her legs were long and lightly tanned, her feet slender and shapely. The troubling thoughts behind his headache dissolved. His heart thudded against his chest wall at the overpowering impact she had on his senses.

"It's all yours," she announced as she folded her clothes and stacked them in a neat pile on her bed.

"It used to be all mine," he said softly, meeting her gaze when she lifted her head. He rose to his feet and took a few seconds to absorb her, to memorize her all over again. Every muscle tensed, tingling with anticipation. Instinct spurred him. He took one tentative step toward her, then another. As he neared her, she inched backward, but the awareness and desire in her eyes kept him moving forward. She came up short when the bed prevented her from going any farther. He stopped, leaving mere inches between their bodies.

Moisture glistened where the deep vee in her robe revealed the base of her throat. The locket he'd given her nestled in her cleavage. Her chest rose and fell rapidly. Her caramel eyes shone, her pink lips parted slightly. Her cheeks glowed from the effects of the bath. Bailey studied her face, looking for a sign to stop, praying for a sign to continue.

He lowered his mouth to hers carefully, poised to retreat at the slightest resistance. But as his lips touched hers, her mouth came alive, and the realization fired his arousal. The kiss deepened as she opened her mouth to allow him full entry. With a groan he wrapped his arms around her waist, pulling her damp body to his. Familiarity cloaked him as her curves melded against him, as she nipped at his tongue and ran her nails lightly across his naked back.

With controlled urgency he slipped his hands down and underneath her robe, his breath catching at the feel of her muscles clenching as she strained to meet him. His fingers found the waistband of scant panties, then slid inside to knead her bare bottom, sliding her up and against his hard arousal. She lifted her mouth to gasp, rolling her neck and shoulders.

He fumbled with the tie of her robe as she pulled at his belt buckle. Within seconds the robe was discarded, revealing a peach-colored camisole and matching undies. Her nipples were straining at the sheer lace. He ached to touch them, to taste them, but stopped long enough to shed his jeans.

When he came back to her, though, a slight frown marred her smooth complexion. Her eyes were worried. "I'm not sure this is right, Bailey."

Panic gripped him. He was so close to reminding her—reminding himself—how good things could be between them. He folded her into his arms. "Ginny," he whispered, his heart hammering, "I want my family back."

At his words Virginia stiffened. A sensation akin to shame washed over her. Bailey didn't want her, he wanted a tie with the mother of his child. A guarantee he could always have access to his son. From the beginning she'd been part of a package deal. What had Chad said? No kid, no marriage? Out of the mouths of babes.

She straightened her arms and pushed against his bare chest. Bailey stepped back, confusion evident on his face. "What did I say?"

"The truth—this has more to do with you wanting to be with your son than wanting to be with me," she murmured, fighting to control her breathing. He shook his head and reached for her again, but she held up her arm to stop him. She yanked up her robe from where it had fallen on the carpet and gathered it around her, tying it securely with a double knot.

"Leave Chad out of this, Ginny. You're not that good an actress—you wanted me as much as I wanted you."

She turned her back and bit her bottom lip hard as she straightened her folded clothes again. "You're wrong, Bailey." *More... I wanted you more than you wanted me. Always have, always will.* "On the plane you promised our relationship would be strictly platonic, and I expect you to keep your word." She crossed her arms over her breasts. "I think you'd better take your bath now."

He grunted in frustration, then strode to the bathroom. When the door closed, Virginia sagged onto the bed, hugging herself hard. How could she be so stupid? Having Chad meant having to see Bailey regularly. It was going to be hard enough on her without adding casual sex to the equation.

She hurriedly cleared her bed, turned off the lamp, and climbed in, intending to be fast asleep when he emerged. But adrenaline was still pumping through her body when he opened the bathroom door. Unable to resist, she watched him move by her bed and across the room in the shadows.

The light from the window provided enough silhouette to reveal he'd wrapped a towel around his waist. He paused by his bed long enough to fling back the covers and drop the towel. Virginia squeezed her eyes shut and listened to the creak of springs as he lowered his big body onto the old mattress. She counted as he punched his pillow four times and rolled over twice before settling down. Same old routine, she thought sadly, minus the part where he'd lay his hand on her stomach before falling asleep.

As pain ballooned in her chest, she twisted the sheet in her hands and brought it to her mouth, fighting the urge to call out his name. She had to regain control of the situation, and fast. She'd once heard that in any relationship, romantic or otherwise, the person who cared the least had the most power. A wry laugh died in her throat. If the saying was true, between the two of them Bailey definitely had the most power.

Then a thought occurred to her. She could be the person who *appeared* to care the least. Bailey Kallihan was wrong—she was a great actress, and she would play the part convincingly until her heart healed completely. Eventually, she'd get over him.

But her heart squeezed sadly, reminding her that if she pulled off this part, she'd deserve an Academy Award.

* * *

Bailey started awake, disoriented at first, then remembering where he slept: in Fort Lauderdale, Florida, in the shelter where his son was staying, in a hot room exactly five strides from Ginny's bed.

Moonlight streamed through the opening of the curtains at the small window. He estimated approximately an hour had passed since the last time he'd awakened, with about four more hours to go until dawn. He knuckled his scratchy eyes, then swung his legs to the floor and sat on the side of the bed.

Ginny lay in the shadows of the wall, her figure barely discernible. After a few seconds passed and she hadn't stirred, he stood up gingerly and padded over to her bedside, standing close enough to make out her features. She lay on her back, one arm folded across her stomach, the other flung wide. She was so lovely. High cheekbones and finely arched brows, a sculpted nose and full mouth. Her hair fanned over the pillow, tangled and wild.

His gaze roved lower. She'd kicked off the covers, as was her habit. A spaghetti strap from her camisole had slipped off her shoulder, offering a tempting glimpse of the curve of her breast. The silky fabric had crept up, displaying her flat, sexy stomach. The skimpy panties were nearly hidden in the valley created by her slightly raised knee. And underneath all that luscious, smooth skin lay a heart of pure gold and a passion of pure intensity.

His naked body responded to his musings, and it took every ounce of discipline he had not to crawl in beside her and stroke her to full consciousness. She had wanted him earlier, he was sure of it. Ginny had always been forthright about her feelings—he'd been the accomplished cover-up artist. So why had she pulled back?

A disturbing thought struck him. Perhaps she did want him, in the physical sense, but felt no affection, no love for him. To a woman like Ginny, sex without emotion would be a mistake. Maybe that's why she'd changed her mind—because she had absolutely no feelings for him.

Although many obstacles blocked the road toward a long-term relationship between them, Bailey had never doubted their true affection for each other. If that one flickering flame had been doused in Ginny's heart, his chances of winning her back were bleak indeed. He took an enormous breath and exhaled slowly, then limped back to his bed. The worst of the night was yet to come.

* * *

"Did you sleep well?" Ms. Andrews asked.

Virginia nodded, lying. Her normal ten-minute makeup application had stretched to thirty that morning in an attempt to camouflage her tired, puffy eyes. Bailey and his luggage had been gone when she awoke, his bed passably made. Her momentary relief had given way to growing concern because she would have preferred their first exchange after the awkward evening be conducted in private.

Chad's counselor pushed a newspaper across the table. "I thought you might want to see this."

Frowning, Virginia picked up the paper. It was startling to see herself standing next to Bailey in a picture after all these years. She looked scared and shy, he looked confident and comforting, his arm draped around her protectively. *Return of Kidnapped Boy After Eight Years Could Reunite Divorced Parents.* The story gave scant details of the kidnapping and of the reunion, giving the most space to Bailey's quip implying they might get back together.

Virginia rolled her eyes. Love conquers all, love is the answer, all you need is love—the media portrayed romantic love as some kind of panacea, but she'd learned long before that it took more than love to keep a relationship together. Her love for Bailey had been unshakable, yet her marriage had crumbled anyway. Pushing the paper aside, she laughed dryly. "Don't believe everything you read, Ms. Andrews."

The woman gave her a bolstering smile. "Ms. Catron, the media would like to wrap up this miracle like a pretty package and put a big bow on top— everyone loves a happy ending. But make no mistake—all of you will have some trying times ahead. If I can be of help, don't hesitate to call me."

"Do you suggest family counseling?"

Ms. Andrews hesitated. "I never discourage anyone from seeking family counseling if they feel the need. But I've spent a lot of time with Chad these past few weeks, and he seems like a well-adjusted boy, if a little mature for his age. And you seem to have a supportive network in your parents and your ex-husband."

Virginia nodded. "My parents will help anyway they can." Bailey seemed eager to get to know his son, but she wasn't sure yet how much she could rely on him.

"Then I think the most healing therapy is love and time."

Virginia thanked the woman, while wondering if her fear was so transparent. When Ms. Andrews said she was going to make sure Chad was awake and packed, Virginia washed down her butterflies with a swallow of coffee and offered to go instead. Through a maze of hallways, she found the room Chad shared with another boy and quietly knocked on the door.

When the door opened, Bailey stood on the other side, looking well rested in a pale blue polo shirt tucked into neat jeans. His smile was blinding. "Morning, Ginny."

"Good morning," she said cautiously, stepping inside.

Chad stood on his side of the room, stuffing clothes into a green duffel bag. He glanced up and acknowledged her presence with a sour frown. Virginia squashed down the hurt. "Good morning, Chad."

"Hey," he said, his voice low and sullen.

She glanced around the shared room, noting his roommate was absent, probably at breakfast. The furniture and comforters were generic but colorful, the wall and floor coverings basic and functional. "Nice room," she offered with a smile.

"It's not mine," Chad pointed out.

Remembering the feminine guest room awaiting his arrival, Virginia cringed inwardly and asked, "What was your room like?"

Chad shrugged, barely glancing up. "Lots of posters. I had a sign on the door that said 'Keep Out.'" He looked up as if to gauge her response. "I'm bringing the sign with me."

She nodded. "Everyone needs privacy." She tried a different tactic and nodded to the handheld Nintendo gaming device lying on top of his duffel. "Do you like to play video games?"

He nodded warily.

"I'm pretty good at them myself," she said, holding out her hand. "Can I try?"

He grabbed the Nintendo and held it down to his side protectively. "My mom gave this to me for Christmas last year. It was expensive."

Ginny swallowed hard. Again she'd overstepped her bounds.

"I spoke with Mr. Maybry this morning," Bailey interjected. "I arranged to have all your things shipped to Ginny's house later this week."

"Do you have a yard?" Chad asked her.

She nodded. "A small one in the back."

"Is there room for a basketball goal?"

She hated to disappoint him, but shook her head. "No, but there's a park just a few blocks away." When he didn't respond, she asked, "Did you play on your school team?"

The frown returned. "No. You got to have lots of money for uniforms and shoes and stuff."

Her heart squeezed for him. "Maybe you can play at your new school this fall."

He looked up. "Are you rich?"

She laughed. "No, but you can participate in any sport you want to, as long as you keep up your grades."

He waved off her concern with a cool flip of his hand. "School's a breeze. You just got to listen and ask lots of questions so the teacher will think you're interested."

"Ms. Andrews told us you're a good student."

Another shrug. "Whatever."

"Well," Bailey said with a wink, "looks like you inherited something from Ginny after all—plenty of smarts."

Chad scanned Virginia head to toe, doubt evident on his face.

She cast for a new topic and settled on the trip home. "Have you ever been on a plane before?"

"No," he said defensively. "But me and my mom went to see the space shuttle launch two years ago. It was real cool."

"I'll bet it was," she agreed, the repeated references to his "mother" not lost on her.

"Are you all packed?" Bailey asked.

Chad looked around the room. "Yeah."

Bailey reached for the duffel bag. "Is there anyone you want to say good-bye to before we go to the airport?"

After pondering the question, Chad angled his head at them, a challenge in his eyes. "Yeah—I want to stop by my mom's grave."

Virginia inhaled sharply but kept her face immobile. She traded glances with Bailey, who raised one eyebrow slightly in question. She nodded, then looked back to her son. "I think that would be a very nice thing to do."

Chad stared at her for a few seconds, chewing on the inside of his cheek, then grabbed his Nintendo and walked out the door.

Once again they were offered the taxi services of the shelter's van. They used the back entrance of the building to avoid lingering reporters, but if anything, the throng had grown in size. They were mostly interested in Chad, angling and shoving one another for the best shot. To shake the reporters tailing them, Mr. Maybry took a zigzag route across town to the cemetery where Lois Green had been buried less than eight weeks before.

Her heart pounding, Virginia accompanied Bailey and Chad to the unmarked grave on a steep incline, mounded with crumbly dirt. A single rusty white metal basket and bits of dead, dried flower stems were the only signs that anyone had acknowledged the woman's passing.

Virginia had prepared herself to be overcome with feelings of hatred and resentment for the woman who had cheated her out of her family, but as she stood in the scorching sun watching Chad stare forlornly at the baked earth, pity for the dead woman was the only emotion that seemed appropriate at the moment. Chad knelt down on one knee, pulled a weed from the loose dirt, and tossed it aside. He held his precious game player tightly in one hand.

"Hey, Mom." His voice sounded steady and grownup, and Virginia felt precariously close to tears. "These people have come to take me to Ohio to live with them. I don't know when I'll be back to see you, but I'll think about you all the time. Just remember I love you, and that no one can take your place." His voice cracked on the last words, and his head dropped for a few seconds.

Virginia bit down hard on her tongue. In Chad's eyes, no one would ever be able to replace Lois Green. His resentment toward Ginny was palpable. Did she have a prayer of ever growing close to her son?

Bailey shifted, coughing lightly. Chad stood up quickly, dragging his hand across his face, then walked back to the van.

The ride to the hotel to pick up her folks and Detective Lance was a quiet one. Only Ms. Andrews and Mr. Maybry broke the silence with light conversation. Virginia sat immersed in guilt, confusion, and the ever-present fear. And the emotions Bailey had stirred up the night before only cluttered the situation further. At least their exchanges had been cordial, if strained, with no mention of their mutual lapse.

Prearranged airport security met them curbside to keep the persistent cameras at a safe distance until they were processed through the general security lines. At the gate, Bailey kept a protective hand on Chad's shoulder while they waited to board. She was glad to see Chad had abandoned his surliness for the time being in his excitement over getting on the plane. Standing with his face and hands pressed against the window, watching the planes depart and land, he appeared to be a typical eight-year-old, mesmerized by the giant machines, anticipating a new adventure.

Chad's engaging grin evoked mixed emotions in Virginia—extreme joy at seeing her son happy, and extreme anxiety at the challenge to keep him that way. After watching father and son interact for several minutes, she realized with a start that Chad had begun to seek Bailey's attention. When momentary envy subsided, the touching moment triggered an additional sobering thought.

She and Chad did have one common trait—they were both captivated by Bailey Kallihan.

CHAPTER SIX

"THE RESEMBLANCE IS AMAZING!" Rita cried, pulling a flustered Chad into a bear hug. "Would you look at this, Jerry?" she asked her husband. "Jean Ann, this is exactly what your uncle Bailey looked like when he was a boy—so handsome!"

Still recovering from her own exuberant airport greeting from her former sister-in-law, Virginia watched the exchange, envious of Rita's easy way with children. It was early afternoon, and Rita insisted they all caravan back to Shenoway and stay for dinner. Virginia's parents begged off and, after promising Chad a camping trip in the near future, left for home. Detective Lance also took his leave after Virginia and Bailey both gave him a grateful handshake.

They left the terminal, dodged yet more reporters, and finally made it to Virginia's car. To her chagrin and relief, Bailey had asked to ride with them since Rita had given him a ride to the airport. She wasn't eager to spend more time with him, but she wasn't ready to be alone with Chad either.

Before they could put on their seat belts, Chad said, "Is this your car?"

Virginia laughed at his wide-eyed expression. "Sure is."

"You *must* be rich."

Bailey turned around. "What do you know about cars?"

Chad lifted his shoulders in what was fast becoming his signature gesture. "Lots. I put models together—I hope none of them get broken on the way here."

"I like cars too," Bailey confided. "I'll show you my collection when we get to the farm."

"You have a model collection?" Chad asked.

Bailey smiled. "Not models—the real things."

"Wow!"

A finger of apprehension nudged Virginia. How financially reliable could Bailey be if he was still investing in jalopies? Just one more reason why, when push came to shove, she could count only on herself. She knew Bailey would never intentionally neglect his son financially, but he was the kind of man who didn't see the use of planning ahead. She grimaced. Which was just as well, since he couldn't seem to stick with long-term commitments.

About a thirty-minute drive from the airport, Shenoway had once been a remote location. But no more, Virginia quickly discovered. The area had changed so much, Bailey had to give her directions to the house in which she'd once lived. Subdivisions had popped up everywhere, along with strip malls, schools, and manicured parks.

But soon the development gave way to familiar surroundings, sending her pulse jumping. She pulled onto the gravel driveway and began the steep ascent to the house at the top of the hill, now hidden by the growth of surrounding trees. At the top, the land leveled to a spacious plateau of nearly fifty lush acres. She frowned when she saw rooftops in the distance—Shenoway lots Bailey and Rita had sold. "How many acres do you have now?" she asked.

"About thirty-five," Bailey told her, his voice shaded with regret. "We used the money to build a new barn and re-fence the base acreage. We had some great offers, but we refused to sell to developers. The three families who bought from us purchased five-acre plots to build large homes. And we kept an acre between each plot to guarantee a developer couldn't gobble them up."

Chad jumped out of the car to explore before it came to a complete stop.

She laughed, and Bailey grinned. Then an awkward silence followed, during which Virginia realized it was the first time they'd been alone since the previous night.

She put the car in park and switched off the ignition.

"Look, Ginny," Bailey began, "about last night—"

"No need to apologize," she interrupted, keeping her voice light and carefree. She even managed to laugh. "I've forgotten it already."

He scowled. "I wasn't going to apologize, and I haven't forgotten it."

The low rumble of his voice sent a thrill along Virginia's spine, unraveling threads of desire. *The person least interested controls the situation.* Self-preservation kicked in. "It was no big deal, Bailey, you're making too much of a harmless kiss. Let's just get past it."

"A harmless kiss?" he repeated. "Is that all it was to you?" He exhaled in exasperation, then clasped her hand. "Look at me, Ginny, and tell me last night meant nothing to you."

Tell him, her heart pleaded. Tell him he's the only man you've ever loved.

Go ahead, her head teased. Trade a few months of pleasure for another decade of pain when he tires of you, except now with Chad, you'll have to see him every week and keep the wound fresh.

She pulled her hand from his, looked deep into his cobalt-blue eyes, and said in her calmest voice, "Last night meant nothing to me, Bailey."

Hurt narrowed his eyes, but she didn't flinch. His ego was a little bruised, that was all. He obviously wasn't used to his sexual advances being rejected.

Bailey expelled a long, noisy breath. "Rita says I'm pretty dense sometimes, that I have to be hit over the head with the truth." He laughed harshly. "I guess she's right." The smile he offered her seemed resigned. "So... where do we go from here?"

"Nowhere," she replied casually, her heart splintering. "We'll need to keep up appearances for Chad's sake, but that shouldn't be too difficult."

He worked his mouth, pursing his lips. "Appearances... you mean *pretend* to like each other?"

"Not pretend—I'd like to think we can be friends."

He turned in his seat to look out the window, across the farm, in the direction of their meadow. Her nerve endings tingled, her muscles tensed for his response. She drew a deep breath for strength—she wasn't sure how much more resistance she had in her.

Finally he turned back to her and gave her a watery smile, then surprised her by extending his hand. "Friends it is," he said softly.

Virginia stared at his broad, tanned fingers, trying to push aside the memories of the fire his hands had unleashed the previous night. She slipped her hand inside his and squeezed slightly in a firm handshake. *Bravo, Virginia.*

"Hey, you two!" Rita's voice startled her. She jerked around to see the petite brunette shaking her finger at them through the car window. "Aren't you coming in? You can hold hands out here!"

A flush burned Virginia's cheeks as she withdrew her hand from Bailey's clasp. He said nothing as they climbed out of the car, but a frown creased his dark brow.

Chad came running up with his sandy-haired cousin at his heels, his face consumed with a grin. "Jean Ann says there are fifteen cows and four horses!"

Bailey's expression lifted instantly. "Do you ride?"

Chad's face fell. "No."

"Well, I guess we'll have to fix that, won't we?"

Virginia couldn't help smiling when her son's face lit up.

"Can you teach me?" he asked Bailey.

Bailey pulled at his chin. "I could, but Ginny used to be the real horseman in the family." Her expression must have mirrored Chad's one of surprise, because he added, " 'Fess up, Ginny, you ran our little stable single-handedly."

"But I haven't ridden in years."

Chad frowned. "I want *you* to show me, Bailey," he said earnestly, "not some *girl*."

Virginia bit her lip, telling herself she was going to have to stop letting these two men hurt her.

"Son," Bailey said, "I learned some of life's best lessons from this girl right here. You could do worse."

"Where's your car collection?" Chad asked, obviously clever enough to know when to change the subject.

"Go ask your aunt Rita for the key to the barn, and I'll catch up with you."

Chad ran off at top speed. She watched him bound across the yard, then up the porch steps, worry rooted deep in her heart.

He reached out, then stopped before touching her arm, plowing his hand through his hair instead. "He's pushing your buttons, Ginny, that's all. He's a scared, confused kid and he's taking it out on you—don't let him. After our conversation today"—he paused, making it clear he wasn't satisfied with the outcome—"it looks like I won't be with you all the time, so you have to stand up for yourself."

Frustration and anger bubbled inside her. They'd been parents for less than a day and it seemed to be coming naturally to Bailey—why was she grappling with it? She was the one who had her life together, who was he to give her advice? She lifted her chin with false bravado. "Thanks for the pointer, Bailey, but I figure if I can handle you, I can handle my son."

His nostrils flared slightly, then he inclined his head. "Touché."

"Bailey!" Chad yelled from the front of the house, holding high a ring of keys.

"I'll be right there, buddy." When he looked back to Virginia, his face was still anger-flushed. "Want to come?" He held up a hand in mock defense. "Just for appearance's sake, of course."

She didn't acknowledge his sarcasm. "I think I'll visit with Rita."

* * *

Bailey strode across the driveway, gravel crunching beneath his boots. As he neared Chad, he tried to force the angry thoughts from his mind. Virginia Catron was without a doubt the most infuriating woman, he'd ever known. Now that he had her back in his life, how was he supposed to adjust to being mere friends? His desire and love for her had lain dormant for years. How could he now look at her week in and week out and not reveal them?

"Where's the barn?" Chad asked eagerly.

At the expression on his son's face, the corners of Bailey's mouth lifted automatically. He pointed west. "Through that grove of trees. See the tin roof?"

Chad was gone before he finished the sentence. Bailey laughed to himself and walked quickly to catch up with his energetic son. A few minutes later he was unlocking a series of padlocks on a black wooden door that spanned sixteen feet. When he swung out the heavy door, he stepped aside to let Chad enter first, then felt along the wall for the light switches.

"Wow!" Chad exclaimed as light flooded the mini showroom. "Look at all the cars! Are all these yours?"

"Yep."

"How many?"

"Twelve."

"This is so cool! Is that a Corvette?"

"Nineteen fifty-four. Needs a lot of work."

"There's a Skyliner!"

"Nineteen fifty-seven. Original retractable hardtop. Mint condition."

"Man, oh, man—there's a Cadillac!"

"Nineteen fifty-nine, Series 62 convertible. Everything's original but the windshield, the tires, and the paint job."

Chad's mouth hung open in awe. "Which one's your favorite?"

Bailey wound his way through the maze of classics to stop beside one fully-covered vehicle in the far corner. He pulled back the canvas, and Chad's eyes bugged.

Patting the immaculate baby-blue paint job with a loving hand, Bailey said, "Nineteen fifty-three—"

"Packard Caribbean convertible," Chad finished. "I have a model just like it—same color and everything! This is awesome! Did you do all the work yourself?"

"Most of it. See all my tools in the back? Rita's husband, Jerry, helps me some—"

"I can help!"

Bailey's chest expanded. How fortunate that his son also shared a love of cars. "Great, I could use a helper. I was going to work on the 'Vette next. A mechanic friend of mine trades me use of his repair bay for free trees."

His son frowned. "Free trees?"

"I'm a landscaper for big office buildings and stuff. You know, bushes, trees—"

"Flowers?" Chad made a face.

Bailey laughed. "Yeah, even flowers."

Chad jerked his thumb toward the cars. "Can I lift some of the other tarps?"

"Sure, I'll help."

As he pulled back the heavy canvasses, Bailey suddenly felt a pang of sympathy for Ginny. Chad was ignoring her, and all the reprimanding in the world from him wasn't going to make things better. In fact, it would probably make things worse. Ginny had no experience to draw from when relating to Chad. She'd been an only child, a goody-two-shoes kid raised in a loving family. Dysfunctional was largely a TV term to her. And while he didn't consider himself an expert on parenting difficult kids, he did have a qualifying background.

When he was growing up at Shenoway, his parents were married, but had never really gotten along. He and Rita had grown used to them fighting at all hours of the day. Occasionally, his mother would kiss or hug her two kids, but not often, and he couldn't remember his dad ever touching them, except on the backside. So not only did he know what it was like to be an eight-year-old boy, but he knew what it was like to be an eight-year-old boy who'd largely relied on his wits to get by.

As he watched his son touch and study details of the old cars in various stages of restoration, an idea began to germinate. Ginny had made it painfully clear there was no future for them, so he needed to make provisions to be able to see Chad as much as possible. And he couldn't do it living in a one-bedroom apartment above a saloon. He knew Rita wouldn't mind him bringing the boy to her house when he had visitation, but she had her own family, and it wasn't fair to impose. He needed a home of his own.

The meadow was the only location he'd consider, but he felt a twinge of sadness. He'd hoped he and Ginny would have a home there someday, but it wasn't to be—he'd clinched that decision long ago when he'd let their marriage sour. So a home for him and his son would be the next best thing.

Except he needed money to start building. He could talk to his boss tomorrow about his salary. And the only savings he had was sitting there under protective canvas covers. One dealer had been pestering him for years about a couple of the cars. He'd call the man, then try to find the original house plans.

He watched as his son's dark head disappeared inside a battered 1954 Hornet. "Double wow!" came the muffled appraisal.

Gratitude filled his heart, but then he thought of Ginny, and a tiny selfish part of him cried out for more.

* * *

"It's so great to see you, Ginny," Rita said, elbow deep in flour.

Virginia sat at the kitchen table slicing tart green Shenoway apples for the pie Rita was making. "You too—you haven't aged a day."

Rita laughed. "Not true, but nice to hear. You haven't fared badly yourself. And Bailey tells me you're a successful executive—computers, isn't it?"

A blush warmed her cheeks. "Yes, computers. It's not as glamorous as it sounds, but I enjoy my work."

"So, how do you feel about all this?"

She took a deep breath, grateful to have a woman close to her age to confide in. "Shocked. It was so sudden—I feel like I've been turned inside out, emotionally and physically."

Rita clucked sympathetically. "I can't even imagine. When Bailey told me, I was floored—delighted but floored. Are you going to be okay?"

She nodded. "I guess so. It's hard becoming an instant mom to an eight-year-old."

"Remember you can call me if you need anything at all." Rita stopped kneading and angled her head toward Virginia. "I mean it."

She smiled fondly at her former sister-in-law. Though younger than Virginia, Rita had always been mature and thoughtful. "Well, the truth is," Ginny ventured, "I'm a little scared."

Rita smiled, tossing her black bangs out of her eyes. "You'll be a great mom, Ginny, just give it some time. He seems like a good kid."

"He's the spitting image of your brother, complete with attitude."

"Well, since you're the only woman Bailey ever listened to, I'd say you're the woman for this job too."

"Thanks for your vote of confidence, and your offer."

"By the way." Rita's voice took on an innocent tone. "Bailey also told me you never remarried."

Virginia's hand slipped and she gasped as the sharp knife sliced into her skin. Luckily, the cut wasn't deep. "That's right." She sucked her finger, eyeing Rita warily. "I guess I never met the right guy."

"Well," Rita said lightly, "maybe that's because you'd already met the right guy and married him."

Shaking her head and laughing at Rita's transparent tactics, Virginia said, "Right, Rita, and that little thing called a divorce never happened."

The petite brunette smiled wryly. "Well, I tried." She reached for a rolling pin, then her mouth pulled down in a deep frown. "Seriously, Ginny, I know Bailey isn't the easiest person to love. He told me the things he said to you, the jerk—he doesn't deserve you."

Virginia's cheeks flamed. She'd never told anyone the terrible things Bailey had said to her after the kidnapping.

Rita's voice softened with affection. "But I think it's great to see you coming together for Chad's sake."

She had to fight the urge to be carried along with Rita's fantasies. "It's the right thing to do."

"Bailey will be a good father, Ginny."

Resuming her peeling, Virginia murmured, "I know, Chad's already completely taken with him."

"My brother's never loved anyone else, you know."

Virginia's heart skipped a beat, but she didn't lift her head. "Other than himself, you mean."

Rita chuckled. "So he's not the most humble man, but maybe after you and Bailey spend more time together..." Her voice petered out on a high, hopeful note.

Virginia threw her an impatient look.

Up went Rita's hands, flour buffeting around her head. "Okay, okay, I'll stop—for now." Her black eyes twinkled merrily. "I'd love to have you back in the family, but for now, I'll take what I can get."

They heard male voices approaching the kitchen door. Bailey and Jerry walked in, heads high and noses sniffing. "Need a taster?" Jerry asked, his smile wide and teasing for his wife. He swooped down on her neck with a noisy kiss that brought a blush to Rita's cheeks. She elbowed him playfully, shooing him out of her way.

Watching the affectionate exchange, Virginia felt a tug of longing. To avoid Bailey's gaze, she looked around the room, admiring the Americana colors of navy, brick, and cream. This was the kitchen she and Bailey had once nuzzled in, had shared late night cookie raids, had warmed formula for their baby....

"Brings back memories, huh?" he asked softly, too close to her ear. She jumped, tipping the bowl of apples. He caught the bowl without sacrificing any fruit, and settled it back in her lap.

Embarrassed that he'd practically read her mind, she said evenly, "Good and bad."

Undaunted, he turned to Rita. "Sis, have you shown Ginny the rest of the house?"

"Just the living room when we walked through," she said. "Why don't you show her around? Jerry can finish those apples for me."

Virginia hesitated, but Bailey's expression looked harmless enough. Reluctantly, she relinquished her knife to Jerry. Her back became moist with perspiration as she followed Bailey out of the kitchen and into the living area.

"In here we stripped and sanded the floors, plus replaced some rock in the hearth," he said as they walked through the family room.

"It's beautiful. Rita said you did most of the work."

He waved off the credit. "My schedule is more flexible than Jerry's. I just pitched in is all." Giving her a devilish grin, he said, "I'm still good with my hands."

She rolled her eyes, unable to suppress a laugh.

"I knew there was a good mood in there somewhere," he teased, walking close to her down a narrow hallway.

The Shenoway farmhouse was a rambling two-story structure, made larger still by the addition of sun room and garage. Memories rushed over Virginia at every corner turned—in the den, the dining room, the cubbyhole hideaways. When they climbed to the second floor, her heart began to pound. Five bedrooms in all, and two full baths. The first was Jean Ann's room, scattered with sports equipment and books. The master bedroom had new windows and updated lighting and ceiling fans—Virginia and Bailey had used the leaky, drafty room for storage when they'd lived there.

The next two rooms were guest rooms, small but neat and quaint. When they approached the last room, she tried to concentrate on the new carpet instead of the fact it had once held their marriage bed.

And still did, she noticed immediately, her pulse leaping. She'd wondered what Bailey had done with their one passable piece of furniture, but hadn't dreamt he'd kept it. Fashioned from pale gray wrought iron, the bed gleamed, the headboard a series of thin bars about six inches apart, a web of metal ivy climbing across the top. Simple posts and an overhead frame formed a canopy. Now it hung bare, but when they'd purchased it years before, she'd draped it with yards of gauze. They'd drawn the cloth together when they lay down, shutting out the world, shutting in the sounds and scents of their lovemaking.

A multicolored handmade quilt adorned the bed, its simple design belying the heated passion that had taken place on the mattress. Her heart pounded against her ribs as she felt Bailey's eyes on her. He wanted a reaction, some signal that their past held relevance with her. That knowledge gave her the strength to adopt a bland smile of disinterest.

"I kept our bed," he said unnecessarily, an obvious attempt to unnerve her.

"I see." She turned her attention to other details of the room.

"This is where I sleep when I visit," he pressed.

Heat suffused her midsection, but she said lightly, "I don't blame you—the view is nice from this window."

The palladium window had been the primary reason she'd chosen the room as theirs. The view of the farm was still spectacular. The ornate window dwarfed the modestly sized room, by far the most architecturally interesting in the house. The roof lines were angled, with plant shelves hugging the ceiling. Near the head of the bed, the sliding door to the working dumbwaiter remained camouflaged. To her immediate right, a door—another reason she'd chosen this room, for the adjoining nursery.

"It's a bathroom now," he said quickly, opening the door.

Virginia peeked inside, relieved to see no vestige of the pale-blue and white wallpaper she'd labored to paste on the uneven, deteriorating walls. "Nice," she said smoothly, then turned a smile his way. "We'd better go back down and check on Chad."

He looked at her as if he wanted to say something, but simply swept his arm ahead. "After you."

She descended to the first floor, her knees wobbly, and grateful to be out of close quarters with Bailey, relieved to have pulled off another act.

The rest of the afternoon passed uneventfully. Chad had fallen in love with the farm, as she knew he would. He surprised her by making friends with Jean Ann, although she suspected it had something to do with the slingshot his cousin had given him. Dinner was sprawling and noisy, punctuated with tantalizing smells and satisfied sighs. Chad ate like he'd never tasted fried chicken, consuming only one piece less than Bailey's four.

As Virginia watched her son, she felt love flourishing in her heart. When he dropped the sullen, tough persona, he was a charming child. He was open and talkative with everyone at the table except her. With a start, she realized that since his arrival, he'd not once addressed her by her name, or even addressed her at all. Easy enough to overlook in a rowdy roomful of people, but ominous with the impending night alone with him.

Glancing down the table at the identical dark heads thrown back in laughter, she lifted her iced tea glass with a shaky hand. These Kallihan men were going to be the death of her yet.

CHAPTER SEVEN

"THIS IS IT?" Chad asked, climbing out of Bailey's car to stand in front of Virginia's town home. Disappointment weighted his voice.

On the solo drive home, Virginia had steeled herself for his reaction, knowing her home would fall woefully short next to the allure of Shenoway. Still, she had to struggle to keep her voice cheerful. "This is it."

Bailey obviously heard the disparaging remark because he frowned at Chad when he walked up. "You haven't even seen it."

"Can't I stay at the farm with you?"

Bailey glanced at Ginny, then back to Chad. "I don't live at the farm, I have an apartment downtown."

Chad wheeled and headed back to Bailey's car. "Great, I'll stay there!"

Catching him by the shoulder with one arm, Bailey said, "No, you're staying here with Ginny."

"You don't want me to live with you?" The same hurt she felt colored her son's voice as he stared at Bailey.

"Sure I do..." Bailey began, then sighed. "Look, my apartment is no place for a kid to be, okay? Your mother and I agreed you'd be better off here."

"But when will I see you?" Chad whined.

Bailey looked to her for help.

"All the time," she said brightly, fighting her rising panic.

"When?" her son demanded.

"Tomorrow?" Bailey asked, his eyebrows raised for her confirmation.

She nodded, relieved.

"Tomorrow afternoon," Bailey continued, "we'll go shopping for things you need."

A spark of interest flashed in Chad's eyes. "A new bike?"

Again Bailey looked to Virginia.

"Sure," Virginia said, glad to be able to give the boy *something* he wanted.

"And a motorcycle?"

"Whoa," Bailey said, laughing, "we'll talk about that when you're older, okay?" He steered their son toward the front door.

The early evening air blew warm against her moist neck as she led the way into the house. Bailey brought up the rear, carrying Chad's duffel bag.

Chad circled the entryway and scanned the contents of the rooms with a telling frown. "Do you have a TV?"

She pointed into the living room. "In that cabinet. Why don't you turn it on and I'll get us all something to drink."

"I want a Coke," Chad said.

From behind, Bailey placed a hand on his shoulder. "But we'll take whatever you have, right, Chad?"

Chad worked his mouth and shrugged. "Whatever." He shuffled into the living room.

Bailey rolled his eyes heavenward, then set the duffel on the bottom step. Somehow she knew he would follow her into the kitchen, and he did. He walked to the refrigerator, opened the door, and bent over to rummage around, whistling under his breath. With hands on hips, she watched him with no small amount of amusement. Apart for eight years, back together for two days, and he'd hardly missed a beat. For a few seconds her perception of time dissolved. She half expected him to emerge wearing boxers and lifting a milk carton to his mouth.

He turned his head. "Hey, Ginny, do we have any—" He stopped and straightened.

She said nothing, eyebrows raised.

He laughed awkwardly. "That is, do *you* have any salsa?"

"Second shelf."

"Uh, right." He withdrew the jar, and glanced around the kitchen, looking sheepish.

"The bowls are over the sink, right cabinet."

"I assume you have chips."

"I'll get them," she offered with a wry smile.

Emptying the red sauce into a bowl, he said, "I didn't mean to come in and take over—"

"Yes, you did," she said, but then laughed and added, "I'll let it slide." With having to maneuver around Bailey, her neat kitchen suddenly seemed cluttered and close. She put the iced drinks and a platter of chips on a tray, then headed toward the living room, feeling Bailey uncomfortably close at her heels.

At the doorway of the living room she came up short, and Bailey jostled her from behind.

"What—" Bailey's sentence ended when he saw the scene of the movie Chad was watching. A half-clothed man and woman were making love against a wall, their moans reverberating from the stereo speakers. Bailey strode over and snatched the channel changer, finding a nature documentary in two clicks.

"Hey!" Chad yelled. "I was watching that!"

"Well, you're not watching it anymore," Bailey said firmly, his eyebrows drawn together.

"I know what sex is," Chad grumbled from his prone position on the rug.

"Knowing is good, seeing and doing is *not* good." Bailey ran a hand through his hair. "We'll talk about this later."

She watched Bailey once again handle the situation like a pro while she felt like a helpless bystander. A revelation washed over her: She was utterly ill equipped to raise this child. Her eight-year-old son knew about sex—or said he did—what else had he been exposed to? And what things had he missed?

It was becoming abundantly clear just what *she* had missed.

She set down the tray with unsteady hands, then fled to the guest bath across the hall in search of aspirin. After a full minute of shuffling bottles and jars, she found the painkiller and swallowed two with a paper cup of water. When she closed the medicine cabinet, she jumped. Bailey stood behind her, staring at her in the mirror. He stepped closer in the small room, triggering a shiver that raised the hair on her arms.

"Headache?" he asked with a small smile.

"Yeah, imagine that," she replied without turning around.

"This whole situation feels pretty strange, doesn't it?"

"You always had a gift for understatement, Bailey."

"I know he's a handful," he offered. "I'd be glad to stay tonight."

Desire curled low in her stomach. She searched his eyes for ulterior motives, but his dark irises revealed nothing. So soon after last night, she didn't trust him or herself with that kind of proximity.

He read her mind. "I'll take the couch." Still no hint of teasing.

The thought suddenly occurred to her that Bailey wasn't as interested in getting next to her as much as he was concerned about her handling Chad by herself. Remembered words echoed in her head. *My God, Virginia, what were you thinking? Even I know not to let a baby out of my sight....*

"We'll be fine by ourselves," she said firmly. "After all, you won't always be around to pick up the pieces." She held his gaze level in the mirror.

He inched closer, placing his hands on either side of the sink, penning her in from behind without touching her. His angry eyes bore into hers. "If you won't give me a chance to prove I've changed," he said, his voice low, his words deliberate, "I may have to resort to drastic measures."

Her mind spun. What did he mean? Acquire sole custody of Chad?

"Whoa," came Chad's voice from behind. "Why watch it on TV when I can just watch you two?"

They both whirled around at the same time to face their son. Embarrassment flooded Virginia as Chad stared at them with knowing eyes.

"I thought you wanted to watch TV," Bailey said, frustration plain in his voice.

"If you're only going to let me watch whales and stuff, what's the point? Where's my room?"

"I'll show you." Virginia brushed past Bailey with as much dignity as she could muster. "Keep in mind," she said to Chad as they climbed the stairs, "up to now it's been only a guest room—we can change it any way you like."

75

Her heart pounded, anticipating the likely explosion when Chad saw the frilly room. She pushed the door open and switched on the light.

"No way!" he shouted without even stepping inside.

"It'll do for now," Bailey said.

"It's a girl's room!"

Virginia hated herself for scrambling to make amends. "I didn't have time to take down the curtains. And we'll buy new linens tomorrow."

"I'm sleeping on the couch," Chad declared.

"Fine," Virginia said quickly. "We'll have your room fixed up in no time. We'll make a shopping list for tomorrow. Then, when your stuff gets here, it'll seem more like home."

Immediately, she wished she could take back the last word. It hung in the air between them, and she waited for Chad to lash out.

He stared at her, blinking furiously to rid himself of the tears she saw forming. "Wrong again," he said in a dull voice, then spun and pounded down the stairs. She started to follow him, but Bailey put out his arm.

"Let him be," he said. "Almost anything we say right now will upset him."

The TV blared from the first floor.

His voice softened. "Ginny, don't expect too much too soon. He'll come around."

Virginia nodded, hoping her ex-husband was right. He seemed to be able to read the boy better than she could.

She walked to the hall linen closet and withdrew extra bedclothes to take downstairs. Bailey offered a hand and she tossed him a pillow, trying to ignore the reminders of the previous night. She wondered if he, too, was remembering, because he was unusually quiet, as if he were watching her.

And the more he watched her, the more she thought about their kiss, the heat of his skin under her fingers, his raging arousal. She felt a light sheen of perspiration emerge at her hairline and desperately tried to push the thoughts from her mind. But the uneasy feelings persisted as they descended the stairs.

"Bailey," she said carefully, "I appreciate everything you've done today." She conjured up a smile, then continued. "But it's getting late and I think we could all use a good night's sleep."

He stopped in front of the door and winced at the volume coming from the living room. "Good luck," he said, grinning. Then he relented. "Okay, I know when I'm being thrown out."

She laughed, grateful he wasn't pressing the issue. "Why do I get the feeling it hasn't happened to you that often?"

He lowered his armload of bedclothes onto a stool by the stairs. With one arm on the banister, he bent toward her, his eyebrows wagging. "I take that as a compliment."

Sexual energy leapt through her as she felt the intensity of his gaze. She wet her lips, casting for something to throw him equally off balance. *The one who appears to care the least.* She drew herself up and said in her coolest voice, "Being a skirt-chaser isn't a very becoming characteristic for a father, Bailey."

His eyes narrowed as her words hit the mark. He straightened and worked his mouth thoughtfully, then said, "And bitterness isn't a very becoming characteristic for anyone, Ginny."

As he strode away from her into the living room, she allowed his blunt observation to sink in. After the emotional beating she'd taken these past two days, she'd expected her body to have triggered some kind of defense mechanism by now, to lessen the impact of her internal response.

But apparently, she'd not yet reached her threshold for pain—she'd only surpassed the previous day's capacity.

* * *

Bailey cranked the ignition on his aged Camaro, then sat in the confines of his darkened car, staring at the windows of Ginny's town home.

Both of their shadowed figures moved around in the living room, illuminated by the glow of the television. After nudging down the volume, they'd finally settled on a G-rated comedy before he'd left. Walking out the door had been difficult for him. Chad made no bones about the fact that he wanted to go with Bailey, and from the flashes of panic he observed on Ginny's face, he had the feeling he could have worn her down about letting him stay the night.

He sighed, pounding his fist lightly on the steering wheel. He felt distinctly divided—he wanted to be with her, but he was scared to succumb to the temptation to throw caution to the wind and play out his fantasy—woo Ginny into falling in love with him because she found him to be desirable and noble, not because she felt obligated, like she had years before. Then they'd get married.

Except he choked on the happily-ever-after part. What if after a couple of years he couldn't hack it? What if he grew to resent her late working hours and Sunday dinners with the in-laws? What if he became distant and drove her away again? The next time he'd not only be uprooting their lives again, but Chad's as well.

When he was alone, he could tell himself it wasn't fair to pursue Ginny's love, to insinuate he was ready for permanence, especially when she'd indicated her disinterest. But Ginny's presence was like a mind eraser, removing previously well-laid plans, reducing him to a childlike state where instincts and impulses reigned.

He looked back to the window. Chad and Ginny. The two people he held more precious than anything in the world. It was as if an incredible prize were dangling above him, just out of reach no matter how far he stretched, no matter how high he leapt. As he reluctantly backed out of the driveway, he felt angry with himself for the unshakable feeling that he was cheating Chad, cheating Ginny, and cheating himself out of something wonderful.

It was only ten o'clock when he nosed the Camaro into a cramped parking spot outside the saloon. The walls fairly jumped with the volume of the live music inside. Sunday night and the place was packed. After only a few seconds' hesitation, he slipped out of his car and headed toward the front door. He hadn't yet gotten to slake the previous night's craving for whiskey, and he didn't feel like going upstairs to an empty apartment.

"Hiya, Bailey," Big John said at the door. As usual, Bailey pulled out his wallet to pay the cover, and as usual, the burly bouncer waved it aside.

A smile crossed his lips when he entered his familiar haunt. He felt comfortable here, among people he knew, people who enjoyed life minute by minute. Making his way toward the bar, he nodded and exchanged greetings with several people he knew. A southern rock band played on the stage where the wet T-shirt contest had taken place Friday night. They sounded pretty good, he acknowledged, then a split second later found himself hoping the noise wouldn't travel up to his bedroom. Oh, well, it was just a minor bother for the convenience of living so close.

He claimed his regular seat at the bar, then signaled the bartender. A whiskey sour appeared before him in a flash. He held the drink up to his lips with a slight frown, observing in a moment of self-discipline that it wasn't necessarily a good sign that the aproned man was so well acquainted with his drink order.

Studying the ice cubes, he surmised that few respectable fathers were in a bar on Sunday night, drinking whiskey. He lowered his drink and glanced around the room. Mostly single people, with a few straying marrieds thrown in. He wrinkled his nose. Everyone seemed so damn young. Bailey winced. And come to think of it, the lead singer was butchering that Lynyrd Skynyrd classic.

A comely brunette sidled up next to him. "Bailey," she shouted, touching his arm. "Long time no see. Mind if I sit?" She didn't wait for an answer, falling onto the stool beside him.

"Hey, Mia."

Long and lush-bodied, Mia had been his bed partner several months earlier, before he'd been distracted by Lisa.

"What're you up to these days?" she yelled over the music.

Chad's face flashed through his mind, and Bailey had the sudden urge to tell someone about his newfound son. "Funny you ask. I just found out I'm a father."

Her thin eyebrows shot up. "Really? Lisa's pregnant?"

He scowled. "No. I had a son when I was married years ago, but he was kidnapped. They found him Friday, and now he's living with my ex-wife."

Mia's eyes bulged. "No fooling? That's some story."

"It's true."

She smiled. "Kids—you learn to love 'em."

He squinted at her. "You have kids?"

"Three. Two girls and a boy."

Bailey looked back to his drink and bent the stirrer. "I never knew you had kids."

"Yep," she said, nodding. "My mom keeps them for me."

His first thought was what was she doing here, but his next thought was what was *he* doing here? He looked around him, shifting uncomfortably. The thought of his son walking in and seeing him spurred him to his feet. "I just remembered something," he yelled, scooting away from the bar. "See you around."

"Sure," she said, taking out a cigarette.

He tossed money for the untouched drink on the counter and exited the door he'd just entered a few minutes earlier.

"That was quick," Big John said. "Been to church today, Bailey?" He guffawed at his own joke, clapping Bailey on the back.

Bailey walked quickly toward the stairs that led to his apartment, his ears ringing from his short exposure to the blaring music. He felt disoriented and panicky, like a kid who'd done something wrong and was scrambling to cover it up before anyone realized what a mess he'd made.

The clock read nearly ten-thirty when he tossed his keys on the cheap nightstand by his water bed. He clicked on the lamp, then remembered the bulb had burnt out weeks earlier, and felt for the flashlight he kept nearby. By the dim illumination he opened a drawer full of rumpled papers and rummaged around until he came up with the business card he sought, then pulled out his phone.

He dialed the number on the card, and a man answered on the third ring. "Jackson? Bailey Kallihan here... fine, fine. Listen, I've had a change of heart on the Caddy and the Caribbean—when can you come by? Tomorrow morning is good, say around eight? Fine, see you then."

He looked for a place to set down his phone, but the nightstand was cluttered with beer cans and Lisa's overflowing ashtray. He frowned, then put the phone on the bed next to him, in case Ginny called during the night. He pulled his shirt over his head and tossed it on the floor, then expelled a long breath as he settled back against a lumpy pillow and waited for the waves around him to subside.

Pounding on the door of the living room brought him to his feet again. He took his time getting there, looked through the peephole, and groaned at the distorted image of Lisa waving.

He swung the door open, his mouth already forming words to send her away. She fell upon him, a mass of giggles and exposed flesh, her breath stinking of bourbon.

"Where ya been, Bailey Boy?" she slurred, running her hands through the hair on his bare chest. "Someone said they just saw you downstairs."

Patiently, he removed her hands and held her by the wrists, cursing himself. He'd been sleeping with this woman? "Lisa," he said firmly, "you can't come up here anymore."

Her lipstick-smeared mouth formed a slow pout. "Why not?"

"Because I found out this weekend I have an eight-year-old son."

She angled her head at him and smiled dreamily. "Don't you think I'd make a good mommy?"

He didn't voice his thoughts. How could he criticize the girl, when he'd been content with her company only a few days before? "Like I said, you can't come up here anymore. It's over between us."

She straightened her shoulders and jerked her wrists away, stumbling back out into the hall. "Are you sleeping with that dressed-up little miss who came in and dragged you away the other night?" she yelled, her eyes glassy with drunken tears.

"No," he said through gritted teeth.

"Bet you she's an uptight little thing between the sheets."

He closed his eyes and counted to five. "I'm going to call you a cab."

"No! Just leave me alone!"

He took a step toward her, then sighed. "Go home, Lisa, and don't come back. Do you understand?"

"Yeah," she spat out. "Loud and clear." She lurched away, and he watched her half walk, half fall down the stairs. "Screw you, Bailey!" she yelled just as she opened the hallway door to admit the sounds of a thumping bass guitar.

Distaste for his bad habits and bad judgment erupted in his stomach, roiling as he made his way back to the unmade water bed. He cursed—he could definitely hear the band. His nostrils flared at the lingering scent of stale sex on the tangled sheets. God, when had he last changed them? He searched for the remote control among the musky bedclothes, but frowned when he came up with the device, sticky with food and lint.

Disgusted, he pulled himself up and went to the kitchen in search of a lightbulb, then realized the chance for success among the chaos there was slim to none. He turned on every working light in the apartment and cringed at the sight that lay before him. Newspapers, magazines, pizza boxes, beer bottles, and clothing were strewn among and over the dilapidated, dusty furniture. An unidentifiable but foul odor permeated the rooms, probably some spoiled carton of takeout food.

He wrinkled his nose, then scavenged in the utility room for a bucket and a handful of rags. Further searching uncovered an unopened bottle of household cleaner left by the former resident. He ran water in the rusty utility sink until it steamed, then filled the bucket with suds and set to work.

At two in the morning he fell into bed, exhausted, but between clean sheets, and with the feeling that literally and figuratively, he was finally getting his house in order.

The early appointment with Jackson caused him to be a little late reporting to work, but he knew his boss, Lenny Banks, wouldn't mind. Besides, Bailey was so pleased with the deal he'd struck for the two restored cars, he didn't care if Lenny did yell a little.

" 'Bout time you showed up, Bailey," Lenny barked when he walked in the office. "I was ready to send a couple of guys over to your place to see if some jealous boyfriend had strung you up."

"Sorry, Lenny, I need to talk to you for a few minutes, then I'll get right out to the McClain job."

Once they'd entered Lenny's office, his boss spoke up anxiously, "You can't quit, Bailey, we got to finish—"

"Relax, Lenny, I'm not quitting." He told his friend of six years the events that had occurred since Friday evening, trying to weed out the melodrama.

"Man." Lenny shook his head in disbelief. "And I thought I had a big weekend."

"So," Bailey continued, "you can see that my financial obligations have taken an upswing. I know I turned you down when you asked me about taking over Dean's job when he leaves, but now I'd like to take a stab at it."

Lenny pulled on his chin, clearly pleased. "Why, sure, Bailey, I've been after you to join the design team for years. Be nice to see you exercise that brain of yours instead of those overdeveloped pecs." He laughed and extended his hand. "I'll talk to Dean this morning about turning his current projects over to you starting next week. Be thinking about your replacement, and have a name to me by Friday." He reached to pick up the phone, ending the conversation. When Bailey opened the door to leave, his boss called, "Oh, and Bailey—congratulations on your new family."

Bailey thanked him, his boss's words leaving his chest tight. He was a long way from having a family, but making progress. He left the office and climbed into his company truck. When Lenny had offered him the design job a couple of weeks earlier, Bailey turned him down flat, saying he didn't want to play politics with the city planners. But in fact he'd turned down the job because he didn't want to be reminded of the ambitions he'd abandoned years before. Mindless hours of cleaning the previous night had given him time to think, and he'd begun to realize that not only had he ditched his responsibility to Ginny when they were married, but he'd also ditched his responsibility to himself over the years. Accepting the design job was one small step toward reversing the cycle.

On the way to the job site, he called to line up an appointment with an architect and a builder later in the week. When he ended the calls, he smacked the steering wheel in satisfaction.

He spent the rest of the morning overseeing two skeleton crews on a job that was near completion, and the early afternoon with three large crews newly formed to landscape an entire industrial park. The blistering hot day seemed to creep by. He looked at his watch every few minutes, already anticipating the moment he would see his son again. His eagerness was further fueled by the knowledge he would also see Ginny, a thought that sent a stab of desire to his groin. Toward late afternoon his fantasies began to run so rampant, he abandoned his clipboard and joined two men hoisting sledgehammers just for the physical release.

At three o'clock he left the job site and went home to shower. The clean scent of the scrubbed bathroom was a welcome change, but not enough to make him dally. In and out in a flash, he was ringing Ginny's doorbell just before four o'clock, their agreed meeting time.

He'd barely taken his finger from the button when Chad threw open the door, then covered the steps in one leap. "Let's get outta here," he grumbled loudly.

"Hey to you too," Bailey said, not bothering to hide his sarcasm.

Chad looked up. "Oh, hey."

"Where's Ginny?"

"Right here," she answered, stepping into the door frame, purse and keys in hand. Striking as always in snug white jeans and navy shirt, she looked a little worse for wear around the eyes. She'd pulled her thick gold hair into a low ponytail and through the back of a red ball cap, and except for the dark sleep circles, looked all of twenty-one.

"I see you're both ready to go," he said dryly.

"Yep," Chad responded.

"Got the list right here." She waved a long sheet of paper and walked quickly toward her car parked by the curb.

"Bad day?" he asked under his breath.

"Don't ask," she said.

"We can take my car."

She stopped and frowned slightly, considering his offer to drive.

"More trunk space." He pointed to her list, then leaned close to her ear. "And remember how big the backseat is?"

She jerked back as if she'd been shocked. "We'll take my car," she said firmly.

"Want me to drive?" he offered. "You can navigate." She relented and handed him the keys. He ordered Chad from the front passenger seat to the back, then paused until everyone was buckled in. Heading down the highway, he noticed they looked every bit the upper-middle-class family: one kid in the backseat of a luxury sedan, headed for the mall. The thought rather pleased him that at least outwardly they looked like they belonged together.

He followed them from store to store to buy furniture, a comforter, curtains, paint, wallpaper, clothes, tennis shoes, and last but not least, a bicycle. Chad seemed to be on his best behavior. Bailey argued with Ginny over paying for the items, then finally agreed to split things down the middle. Four hours, one hamburger, one cookie, one ice cream, and three sodas later they dropped into chairs in the waiting area at the center of the mall, laden with bags, boxes, and delivery slips.

When his bottom met cushioned comfort, Bailey exhaled in relief, wriggling his cramped toes inside his low-heeled boots. He rolled his shoulders and groaned. He'd fared better with the sledgehammer today than with the cumbersome shopping bags.

Ginny laughed, and he realized she, too, was exhausted and hurting. "So much for aerobics," she said, her eyes closed, her head leaned back.

Chad sighed with impatience. "Can I go over there?" He pointed to the neon sign of a multimedia store blasting music.

Bailey opened his mouth to say yes, but Ginny cut in. "Not by yourself. Let us rest for five minutes and we'll walk over with you."

"But it's just right there!" Chad complained, waving his arm. Wheeling to face Bailey, Chad crossed his arms. "She wouldn't let me go to the park alone today and ride my skateboard—she followed me there and sat and watched the whole time. It was embarrassing—I was the only kid there who had a baby-sitter."

Bailey tried to hide his smile, then looked at her. "I can see the front of the store from here, Ginny."

She looked back and forth at them, then sighed. "Be back in twenty minutes to wake us up." Chad's new sneakers squeaked as he took off.

Silence stretched between them, punctuated by the sounds of shoppers leaving for home.

"I'm beat," Ginny said unnecessarily.

"Me too."

She laughed and leaned her head back. "And broke."

"Me too." He rubbed his eyes in big circles. "How do people do this on a regular basis?"

She yawned loudly. "It's become entertainment for families who have money—or credit cards."

"We never did this."

"That's because we never had money or credit."

He sat up, eyes open. "I shopped for you... sometimes. I remember bringing home one fun little turquoise number that you enjoyed—"

She lifted her head and narrowed her eyes. "Until I found out you'd spent a week's grocery money on it."

He grinned. "It was worth every bologna sandwich."

She reddened adorably, and he felt his body tense with longing.

"You wouldn't happen to still have that little number, would you, Ginny?"

She opened her mouth to respond, then glanced away and straightened when something across the mall caught her eye.

He looked too, and immediately jumped to his feet. Chad was at the door of the store he'd begged to visit, being yanked by two men.

"Help!" he yelled, struggling. "Let me go!"

"They're taking him!" Ginny shouted.

Bailey dropped the parcels he held and bounded over, with Ginny only a few steps behind. As he neared, he heard an alarm beeping shrilly, drawing the attention of passersby. The two men wearing nametags weren't taking Chad, they were restraining him.

"What's going on here?" he demanded of one of the men who held Chad by the wrist.

"Do you know this kid?"

"He's my son," he retorted, widening his stance. "What's the problem?"

"The problem, sir," the other man said in a monotone, "is your son is a thief."

"What?" Bailey bellowed. "There must be some mistake," he said as he looked at Chad's panicked face.

"No mistake, sir." The first man reached into the front of Chad's jeans and withdrew two compact discs. "The police are on their way."

CHAPTER EIGHT

VIRGINIA FELT FAINT, but anger kept her on her feet. Chad had been caught shoplifting—what a fitting end to the roller-coaster day she'd spent with him.

She'd awakened to the sound of a blasting TV. Then he demanded pepperoni pizza for breakfast, which he ate in sullen silence while playing his Nintendo. Then he refused to budge from channel-surfing all morning. After lunch he'd asked to go to the park by himself, but she'd insisted on going, so he hadn't stayed very long. When they returned and she asked what he wanted to do about his bedroom, he made a gagging sound and said he could fix it all with a match and a can of gasoline.

The one bright spot had been when her parents called to talk to him. He'd changed colors like a chameleon, politely answering their questions and enthusiastically agreeing to go camping with them in their RV one day the following week. When he hung up, he flopped onto the couch.

If he'd asked once where Bailey was and when was he going to get there, he'd asked thirty-five times. Cozy little fantasies she'd harbored about getting to know her son that day were banished when he announced he needed to make a few phone calls to friends back home. She'd agreed, retreating to the kitchen. She was going a little stir crazy herself because of her abrupt hiatus from work, so she resorted to cleaning windows. She hadn't meant to eavesdrop—in fact, she'd been pretty certain he'd purposely talked loud enough for her to overhear his comments.

"Yeah, he's real cool, but I have to live with *her*...Expects me to sleep in some sissy pink room, *yuck*...Drives a fancy car, but lives in a cracker box with no yard...I feel like I'm in prison."

Ironic word choice, she thought, considering he was now courting detention time.

Frightening visions popped into her head: Chad shoplifting, then stealing cars, then armed robbery... an exaggeration perhaps, but she knew criminal behavior could usually be linked back to petty crimes at a young age. She had the feeling Chad's behavior, at least in the immediate future, would depend on the way they handled this infraction.

One thing was certain—she did not intend to raise a thief.

"Bailey," Chad whined, crocodile tears spilling down his cheeks, "help me! I was going to pay for the stuff—honest! I was coming to get some money from you."

She watched her son carefully. He was lying. She'd bet he'd shoplifted before, and if given the chance, he'd do it again.

She saw Bailey waver.

Obviously attempting to wear him down, Chad said, "I was trying to get your attention, but you weren't watching like you said."

Virginia pursed her mouth. The little hustler.

Bailey looked at the two men still holding Chad. "Can't we settle this before the police get here?" He removed his wallet. "I'd be happy to pay for the merchandise."

"No," she said.

Everyone turned to look at her. Bailey frowned. "What did you say, Ginny?"

She set her chin. "I said no, let the police handle it."

Bailey took a step in her direction. "But, Ginny, he said—"

"Can't you see he's working you? I won't have a hoodlum living in my home."

Chad's eyes narrowed in contempt. "I don't want to live with you anyway."

She arched an eyebrow. "So you're trying to get yourself thrown in jail?"

"Jail would be better than living with you," he yelled. "I hate you!"

She ignored the sharp pain that shot through her chest. "I'm sorry to hear that, because I happen to love you."

Chad's mouth tightened and he turned his head.

Bailey touched her arm and spoke for her ears only. "Ginny, getting the police involved might be too much for him."

She shook her head. "He's testing us. He needs to know now what he can't get away with."

He studied her face for a moment, then gave a short nod of concession. "You're his mother," he said quietly, then turned back to the men. "We'll wait for the police," he affirmed.

"But I didn't mean it!" Chad yelled.

She watched to see if he was getting to his father, but Bailey simply looked at him. "Like I said before, you need to learn when to be quiet."

The police arrived within fifteen minutes, and Ginny gave thanks the two officers were both brawny and intimidating-looking. By the terrified look in Chad's eyes, she concluded he'd never been caught before. She and Bailey listened patiently while the store personnel explained the situation and presented the merchandise they'd removed from Chad's clothing. A closer search also revealed a keychain and a pack of temporary tattoos.

The older officer filled out a report while he shook his head. He looked up. "You the parents?"

"Yes, officer," Ginny volunteered, stepping up. Bailey did the same.

"Ma'am, I'm afraid we're going to have to file a juvenile complaint."

"What does that mean?" Bailey asked.

"It binds the case over to juvenile court. It'll take a few minutes, then we'll release him into your custody until the court date."

Virginia nodded gravely.

Chad had mustered a little bravado. "Are you taking me to jail?" His voice held only a tiny tremor.

"Nope." The cop ripped off a copy of the form. "Not this time anyway. We're releasing you to your folks."

Chad looked relieved.

"But you're not off the hook," the officer warned him. "You'll have to deal with Judge Brice in a few weeks, and that's a scary prospect even for an adult. You'd better clean up your act, kid." He handed a copy of the report to Bailey and said good night.

Bailey and Virginia apologized to the two men at the store for their trouble, and at Bailey's urging, Chad finally mumbled he was sorry. They shuffled back to their mound of abandoned packages in the center of the mall, where a security officer waited for them. The mall had been closed for thirty minutes, and they were the only customers left.

They loaded Chad down with packages and silently made their way back to Virginia's car.

"When will my bike be delivered?" Chad asked, breaking the quiet on the drive home.

"It won't be," Virginia said.

"What?" Chad screeched.

She looked at Bailey in the dimly lit interior, challenging him to defy her, but he simply nodded. She turned her head slightly toward the backseat. "After the stunt you pulled tonight, you're not getting a new bike."

Chad slammed back against the seat and grunted in frustration. He turned on his game and the car was soon filled with the sounds of jarring music, beeps and sirens. Ginny prayed he was playing an age-appropriate game, but that was a battle for another day. She could almost feel the hatred aimed at the back of her head. She swallowed, remorse filling her, but she bit her tongue hard. No one said parenting was easy.

After they arrived at her place and carried in all the packages, Chad huffed off to the television room.

Ginny followed him, with Bailey close behind. "Wait just a minute." She held out her hand for the remote control. He frowned and gave it to her. "Sit down."

Chad dropped onto the couch, his eyebrows knitted together.

"I'm appalled at your behavior," she said. "Shoplifting is a crime. You might get off with a hand-slap the first time, but if you keep it up, you'll wind up in jail."

He worked his mouth, saying nothing.

"Is that what you want?" Bailey asked. "To go to jail? To have an arrest record that will haunt you the rest of your life?"

"No," he mumbled, as if they were stupid.

"Then the next time you want a CD," Ginny said, "ask for it."

He frowned. "You wouldn't have liked the music, I knew you wouldn't buy it for me."

"Try me next time," she urged.

"Meanwhile," Bailey said, "Ginny and I will talk about an allowance, so you'll have your own spending money."

"Now go to your room," Ginny said.

"I'm not sleeping in that pink room."

"I took down the curtains and removed the comforter."

"The walls are still pink!"

She pointed to the stairs. "Go."

He grabbed up his Nintendo, flounced out of the room and bounded up the stairs. His bedroom door slammed.

Ginny sagged onto the couch, removed her ball cap, and leaned her head back.

Bailey sat down, his leg brushing against hers. "Are you sure we did the right thing?" he asked, his brow furrowed.

"No," she replied honestly, trying to ignore her bodily response to his nearness.

"Aren't you afraid it'll only make him more hostile toward you?"

She smiled and shrugged. "I have experience taking grief from Kallihan men."

He had the grace to blush. "Can't argue there. Did he give you a rough time today?"

She glanced at him sideways. "He's just feeling me out, I think, seeing how I react to certain things."

"Smart boy," Bailey said, his voice suddenly husky.

Her stomach jumped when she realized how close he'd gotten. He studied her face, his eyes hooded with desire. She lifted her head and held up a hand. "Remember our handshake, Bailey."

He wet his lips. "I think the memory of our kiss has blocked it out," he said, his face grave.

Uh-oh. She could handle the teasing, the flirting. But when he turned serious, her resolve always weakened. Why did he have to be so damned desirable?

The touch of his fingers against her hand roused her to move. She sat up, prepared to stand, but he gathered her hand in his and gently pressed her to stay. "Ginny, I need to talk to you about something that should have been said long ago."

Her heart thudded as he begged her with his eyes to listen. She inhaled and nodded for him to continue, not sure what to expect.

He dragged in a ragged breath and expelled it noisily. "I was a terrible husband to you. I guess I've known for a long time, but it took me a while to admit it."

Tears gathered in her eyes and she looked away from him. His grip on her hand tightened.

"Our marriage didn't fail because I didn't love you, Ginny—I was never unfaithful."

She raised her eyes to him and blinked them free of tears. A small frown marred his brow.

"I just wasn't mature enough to handle the responsibility of being married."

Ginny chewed on the inside of her cheek, then said, "And you're telling me this now because you've changed, is that it?" Her voice sounded amazingly strong—and dubious.

He sighed. "I'm working on it."

A choking laugh escaped from her throat, and she shook her head slightly. "And what's all this supposed to mean to me, Bailey?"

"I don't know," he said. "I just wanted to tell you I'm trying to turn my life around. If there's any love for me left in your heart, please be patient. I can't do anything about the past except say I'm sorry, but I want the three of us to be together, Ginny, as a family."

She turned his words over in her mind, separating emotion from fact. "Forgive me, Bailey, for not jumping into your arms." She heard the pain clearly in her own voice. "But it's hard to erase the past with a few nice words, even if they are sincere." Withdrawing her hands, she pushed herself up from the couch and walked over to the window.

For a few seconds the only sound was muffled noise coming from the TV. Her miniature grandfather clock chimed the half hour, then she heard Bailey shift on the couch and rise to his feet. His footsteps made a whooshing sound as he walked across the rug to stand behind her.

"Just tell me there's hope, Ginny," he said, his voice cracking.

She bit her bottom lip and clasped her hands together, then turned to face him. "I can't do that to myself, Bailey," she whispered. She raised her chin, realizing she'd just admitted she still had feelings for him. "I *won't* do that to myself."

Pressing his lips together, he nodded sadly, glancing at the floor. Then he placed his hands on his hips, inhaled deeply, and said, "Well, I guess I'd better be going."

She followed him to the front door, her chest tight, her nerves frazzled. Bailey turned and gave her a small smile. "I'm going to make my standard offer to stay."

Her pulse vaulted with the knowledge that she was getting much too used to Bailey's company, especially in light of the words they'd just exchanged. "Then I guess I'll make my standard reply of 'thanks anyway.' "

He nodded and smiled tightly, then caught her gaze. His eyes darkened and he stepped toward her. When she realized he meant to kiss her, Ginny pulled back. Bailey stopped, his face inches from hers. She watched his eyes move over her face, regret imprinted in their blue depths. He lowered his mouth to sweep a kiss across her cheek, then walked out the door.

* * *

The next couple of days found Ginny and Chad at a stalemate. He didn't talk, and she didn't cave. She offered to take him to the pool, but he refused to move, just played video games for hours on end. She mentioned the zoo and going out to eat, but he wouldn't budge. In fact, he'd hardly made eye contact with her since the night of the shoplifting incident. Bailey came by in the late afternoons to help wallpaper and paint, plus arrange the new bedroom furniture. Around him, Chad acted excited about his room, only to slip back into a funk when Bailey left.

It seemed that Bailey, too, was not his usual flirty self. Unfailingly cordial, he kept his distance during his evening visits, staying busy but seeming to go out of his way to avoid all physical contact with Ginny. In the beginning she was grateful not to have to keep up her guard, but near the end of the evenings, she found she missed his playful banter. And even though he was noticeably exhausted after lifting and bending for hours, he didn't ask to spend the night, an action that bothered her more than it should have.

By Thursday morning she'd had enough of Chad's cold shoulder. She put on her running shoes, retrieved his new basketball from his room, and trotted down the stairs to find him in his standard position, prostrate in front of the television. She reached over and clicked it off, only to be assaulted with loud protests.

"Come on," she said. "We're going to the park."

He scowled. "I don't want to go."

"I didn't ask you if you wanted to go, I said we're going."

"You can't make me," he challenged.

"I'd planned on bribing you with money," she said bluntly.

"What?"

"A game of horse. If you win, I'll give you twenty dollars."

He looked suspicious, but at least she had his interest. "What if you win?"

She shrugged. "If I win, you have to wash my car. That's the best deal you'll get all day."

He frowned and reached for the remote. "What do you know about basketball?"

"I know that when it comes to shooting, women players top the men."

Chad lifted one eyebrow. "Can you really shoot?"

She smiled. "Bailey practically lived in the gym when we were in college. I rebounded for him, so I picked up a few pointers."

He still looked skeptical, but pulled himself up to a seated position.

She took it as a good sign and nodded toward the door. "Put on your new shoes."

After much huffing and sighing, he dragged himself up the stairs, but when he came back down wearing baggy shorts and the spanking new shoes, he had a decided bounce in his step. He leapt up to smack the door frame, grabbed the ball from her hands, launched over the steps, and zigzagged as he dribbled down the driveway.

She smiled to herself, feeling her heavy heart lift a fraction. It was just a walk to the park, but it was something.

The sun shone high and gloriously white in a cloudless sky. They passed other people on the sidewalk, mothers with strollers, groups of kids.

"You know," she said carefully between his pronounced dribbling, "school starts in a few weeks."

"So?" The sullen tone had returned.

"So, I was wondering if you'd like me to arrange a visit before the first day, you know—so you can check things out."

He shrugged, bouncing the ball between his legs. "Whatever."

She took that as a yes. "You'll have to tell me what kind of supplies you'll need. This will be a first for me."

He stopped dribbling and angled his head at her, then tried to spin the ball on his finger. "Are you going to be one of those mothers who hang around a lot and do the PTA stuff?"

Momentarily shocked at his acknowledgment, she stammered. "I—I honestly don't know." She swallowed and took a gamble. "What kind of mother was Lois?"

He jerked his head up and stared at her with wide blue eyes. She kept her expression passive, her gait casual. The ball hit the pavement one, two, three times before he said, "She was a great mom."

She nodded. "I'm sure she was. Did the two of you do things together?"

Bounce, bounce. "Sometimes, before she got sick."

She felt a pang of sympathy for her son. "That must have been really hard on you."

Bounce, twirl, bounce. "Not as hard as it was on her." He looked up at her. "She cried a lot."

"From the pain?"

Chad stopped, bent over, and retied his shoe. "Yeah, and she worried about me." Bounce, bounce.

"I know how she felt," Virginia said softly. "I worried a lot about you too."

He tossed the ball in the air and caught it, then tossed it up again. Looking ahead, his face split in a grin. "Wow! Four goals, with nets and everything!" He was off like a shot toward the nearly vacant courts. Virginia sighed and jogged after him.

His driving layup was impressive as he pivoted, dodging imaginary defenders. By the time she caught up with him, he'd taken several shots, making more than he missed.

"You're pretty good," she said breathlessly. "You'll have to go easy on me—I haven't played in years."

"Here." He bounced her the dark orange ball. She took a minute to adjust to the weight and feel of the nubby surface, dribbling tentatively.

"You dribble like a girl," he scoffed.

She stepped behind the free throw line, aimed, and let the ball fly. It passed through the goal so cleanly, the net barely moved. Chad's mouth dropped open, and she laughed out loud. "I shoot like a girl too."

They decided to play a hybrid version of horse, earning letters to spell the word by making baskets at different spots on the court. After marking the shot areas on the court with a piece of scavenged chalk, they agreed on two practice games. Chad won the first game convincingly, and Virginia won the second game by a nose. By the time the third game rolled around, they were laughing and sweating.

"Ready?" Chad asked, poised for his first shot.

Virginia nodded. "Ready."

He made the H shot handily, then stalled out. "How'd you meet Bailey?" he asked after she'd missed her first shot.

"In college," she said. "He liked my car."

He shot and missed. "Yeah, he showed me all of his cars at the farm."

She made two baskets and moved up to R before missing again.

He made his O shot, then missed. "You two going to get back together?" he asked.

Virginia missed badly. "What makes you think that?"

Chad chased the loose ball, then made the shot and moved on to S, where he missed again. "He likes you."

She made the basket and moved to S. "How can you tell?"

His shot swished in and he moved to E. "He makes googly eyes at you when you're not looking." He missed, then bounced the ball to her.

Her stomach churned, and it had nothing to do with the pressure of the game. "Well, unfortunately, there's more to marriage than googly eyes." She made the basket and moved to E, then missed.

"You don't like him?" He missed.

"It's not that simple." She missed.

"I know people who *hate* each other and still stay married." He missed.

"Well, I don't hate your father, but we couldn't live together." She missed.

"Don't you want more kids?" Mercifully, his shot fell in and saved her from answering the very question she'd been asking herself for years. Chad whooped around the court holding his two fingers high in the victory symbol. "You owe me twenty bucks," he crowed.

She held up her hand for a high-five. "I'll pay you when we get back. I guess I'm stuck washing my own car."

He worked his mouth, spinning the ball on his palm. "I'll help you," he said simply, then pivoted off and drove away from her for a layup.

She had a feeling they'd just turned a corner in their relationship, but she knew better than to make a big deal of his offer. "Great," she said. "Let's get something to drink."

They walked home sipping lemonade from a concession stand, then sat on the small shaded stoop until they'd both cooled off. She could tell Chad had something on his mind by the faraway look in his eye. He was so handsome, her heart squeezed with pride. Her hand itched to smooth his hair or erase the smudge on his cheek. Instead she watched the pedestrian traffic and waited for him to talk.

"Do you have any pictures of me when I was little?" he finally asked.

Stunned, she nodded. "A few. Would you like to see that?"

He shrugged. "Whatever."

She stood and entered the house, her heart pounding. He followed her as she climbed the stairs to her office and withdrew the album from the closet. When she turned around, Chad was studying the framed shot of her holding him.

"Is this you and me?"

"Yes. Bailey took it before we left the hospital on the day we drove you home to Shenoway."

"You mean you lived on the farm?"

She nodded. "For a while." Laying the album on the desk, she opened the book and angled it so he could see the photos. She pointed out significant events and items. "This is your first bath... your favorite teddy bear." Tears rose to clog her throat, but she swallowed them.

"You and Bailey look funny," he said, laughing at their hairstyles.

She smiled too. "We were very young."

He turned a couple of pages, then frowned when the pictures ended. "Is that all?"

"You were only two months old when"—she scrambled for the right words—"when you disappeared." Then a thought struck her. "I do have one more picture." She reached up to touch the flat locket hanging beneath her shirt. She pulled it over her head and, with trembling fingers, opened the case.

Chad studied the picture and the locket with a grave expression. "It's pretty," he said, sounding enchanted. "Did Bailey give it to you?"

She nodded. "On the day we were married."

"Do you wear it all the time?"

"Most of the time, yes."

He studied the picture carefully, then handed the locket back to her. Suddenly his expression changed, as if he'd had enough heavy stuff. "I thought you wanted to wash your car."

Virginia nodded. "I'll get the bucket and meet you out front." She carried the locket to her room and laid it on her dresser.

Minutes later they were sudsing her car in small sections, and rinsing before the soap dried in the hot sun. Virginia had the water hose, and when Chad turned his back, she couldn't resist giving him a squirt.

"Ughh!" He lifted his arms and arched his back, then spun around and dove for the hose. She squealed and ran the other way, trying to keep the hose from him, but dousing them both in the process.

After several minutes of water war, Virginia surrendered and they called a truce, both of them soaked and laughing. She tingled all over, trying to remember when she'd had so much fun. They made quick work of the rest of the car, and were towel-drying it when a package truck pulled up.

Virginia realized the boxes being removed were packing cartons. "It's all your stuff that was shipped," she told Chad. "Now you can finish setting up your room."

He jumped up and down enthusiastically, pitching in to help carry the eight boxes into the house and up to his bedroom, then ripped open the lids. "My model collection! I don't think any of them broke," he said, the excitement clear in his voice. He pulled them out carefully, one by one, then set them on a reserved shelf on his new bookcase. Stereo cube, speakers, comic books, sports equipment, games, clothes, and miscellaneous items came out of the boxes. Little by little, the bare spaces in his room were filled with toys, his newly papered walls cluttered with posters.

Only one box remained, smaller than the others, and Chad seemed reluctant to open it.

"What's in this one?" Virginia asked.

He frowned and bit his lip. "Some things my mom gave me, pictures and stuff."

She inhaled and exhaled quietly, not sure she was ready to see the face of the woman who had stolen her child, who had cheated her out of seeing her son grow up. Today especially had shown her how much she'd missed. "Go ahead and open it," she said finally.

Gingerly he tore the strapping tape and folded back the top flaps, reaching in to pull out a handful of pictures. "I don't remember all of these," he said. "I was too little, but she wrote on the backs so I'd know when I grew up."

Virginia withdrew one photo with a shaky hand. Lois Green smiled back at her, her pale features unremarkable but pleasant, her eyes shiny. Chad was an adorable, laughing toddler standing on a table bent over a cake, and she held him by the waist... as if she had given birth to him, as if she had every right to pose for a picture with him, as if she were his mother. She turned over the photo. *Chad's second birthday with Mom.*

Tears of frustration welled in Virginia's eyes, and she tried mightily to blink them away. Hurt ballooned anew in her chest, smothering her. This woman had taken everything. Because of her, Virginia's life had been devoid of her child's love. Eight years of her life, of her son's life, she could never recapture.

She stood up and clutched her burning chest, watching the picture spiral to the floor.

"Are you okay?" Chad asked, concern in his voice.

"I'm sorry," she said weakly, swiping at her tears. "I just can't... I can't look at these."

She turned and stumbled from the room and down the hall into her own bedroom, where she dropped onto the padded bench seat of her vanity and tried to harness her emotions. But one look in the mirror at her own hurt, and the dam burst. All she could see was the glassy-eyed expression of the woman who'd ruthlessly uprooted her life. "I... hate... her... I... hate... her," she said over and over, punctuating her anger by pounding her fist harder and harder onto the cold marble vanity top.

In the mirror she saw a movement behind her and drew a shuddering breath when she saw Chad standing in the open doorway, tears streaming down his face. His eyes met hers, then he shot off. His feet pounded down the hall, then came the teeth-jarring slam of his bedroom door.

CHAPTER NINE

VIRGINIA KNOCKED SOFTLY on Chad's closed bedroom door. "Chad, I need to talk to you. Can I come in?"

She pressed her ear against the door and thought she heard him sniffling. Closing her eyes, she sagged her shoulder against the door. *I've done it now.* She quietly turned the knob, but met the lock's resistance. Knocking again, she said, "Chad, please let me in."

"Go away." His voice sounded muffled.

"I need to explain some things to you." When she heard him rise from the bed and cross to the door, relief flooded her limbs. She stepped back from the door and wiped her cheeks. Then she heard a swishing sound and felt something hit the toes of her shoes. Defeat washed over her as she stared down at his Keep Out sign.

The doorbell rang, startling her. She expelled a frustrated sigh, then headed for the stairs. At the top step her foot hit something solid, sending it airborne. Her heart froze as she watched Chad's handheld Nintendo bounce from step to step before landing on the wood floor with a terrible crash that left it in at least three pieces. His most cherished item... Lois's last Christmas gift to him.

She stood paralyzed, staring down at the mess, her hands covering her mouth. How could she *ever* make it up to him?

He must have heard the noise, because suddenly he was standing beside her.

"Chad—" she began, reaching for his arm.

"My Nintendo!" he cried, then ran down the stairs. He turned a tear-stained face up to her. "Why'd you do it?" he yelled.

Somewhere in the distance Virginia heard the doorbell ring again. She started down the steps slowly. "I'm so sorry—it was an accident."

"No, it wasn't!" he yelled, crying harder. "I heard you! I heard you say you hated my mother—you threw it down the stairs because she gave it to me!"

She shook her head and raised her hands, beseeching him. "No, it was on the floor. I accidentally kicked it—"

"You did it on purpose!" he shouted, his face red. "I'll get you back!"

The insistent ringing of the doorbell gave way to loud knocking. "Ginny?" Bailey yelled. "Are you all right? Chad?"

Chad yanked up the pieces of the broken device and fled through the hall. The patio door slid open, then vibrated with his slam. The only sound remaining was Bailey's pounding.

"Ginny! Ginny, open up!"

She descended the stairs, then walked around tiny broken pieces that remained of the game and opened the door. Bailey nearly fell inside.

"What's going on?" he asked, scowling. "I heard shouting—where's Chad?"

"In the backyard, I think," she said wearily.

He closed the door and reached up to touch her cheek. "You've been crying. What's he done now?"

She shook her head, mostly to dislodge the disturbing touch of his hand. "Nothing. In fact, he's been great all day." She smiled. "We shot a few hoops at the park and he helped me wash the car. Then his stuff came from Florida and—" She couldn't stop the tears from coming again. "Oh, Bailey, I've made a mess of things."

He looked alarmed at her fresh tears, and reached to draw her into his arms. Virginia went, crying against the soft denim of his shirt, pressing herself into the familiar hardness of his chest. With each sob she filled her lungs with his scent, snuggling deeper into his cocoon of comfort.

"Shh," he murmured, kissing her hair. "Tell me what happened."

In a muffled voice she told him about the pictures and what Chad had overheard her say. She kept her eyes down because she didn't want to face his recrimination. He hadn't approved of the way she'd handled the shoplifting incident, and from his silence she surmised he didn't approve of her behavior this time either.

She could admit when she'd made a mistake, and standing in Bailey's arms looking for sympathy wasn't going to help matters. Responding physically to his embrace, she reasoned, was just her body's way of delaying a resolution with Chad.

Forcing herself to pull away, she turned her back to him. "Chad and I were finally making progress, and I blew it." She pressed her lips together. "To top it off, I knocked his Nintendo down the stairs and broke it, and he thinks I did it on purpose."

He was silent behind her for a few seconds, then asked, "Did you?"

She turned back to him. "How could you ask that?"

He put his hands on his hips and averted his gaze. "All I'm saying is I wouldn't blame you if you did throw it down the stairs. You've been under a lot of pressure—"

"And it's obvious I can't handle it, is that what you're saying?"

"I didn't mean it like that," he said, his voice taking on a soothing tone.

"What kind of mother do you think I am?" she snapped. Then, holding up one hand, she added, "No, don't answer that." She turned and headed toward the bathroom.

He followed her, grunting in frustration. "Ginny, I think under the circumstances you're doing a great job."

She reached for a tissue. "You didn't want the police involved the other night."

He shrugged. "He's a confused kid in new surroundings—I was going to cut him some slack."

"So I was the bad guy."

Sighing, he shook his head. "No one saw it that way."

"Chad did."

"I'll talk to him." He swung his arm wide, encompassing the broken pieces of the game in the foyer floor. "I'll talk to him about all of this."

Bailey to the rescue. After blowing her nose, she took a deep breath and said, "No, I need to handle this."

"It sounds as if he's too upset right now to listen to you. He might say things he doesn't mean."

She wavered. Bailey was right on one count. She didn't want to keep building on Chad's hurt and anger. "Maybe I should let him cool off."

"I came over early to invite myself to dinner." His smile was tentative. "Let's all try to relax for a few hours. I thought we could grill out—I still make a mean garbage burger." He wagged his dark eyebrows.

Virginia couldn't help laughing. Back when money was tight and their meals had consisted mostly of hamburger, they'd resorted to adding leftovers to ground meat patties for variety. On any given night they might have eaten mashed potato burgers or pork and bean burgers. Bailey had dubbed them "garbage burgers," and had eaten them with relish.

"I think I have a container of broccoli in the fridge," she teased, wiping the last of her tears.

He made a face. "I was afraid of that, so I stopped on the way and picked up steaks."

Her stomach growled. The idea of a backyard barbecue suddenly seemed appealing, and she tried not to analyze her relief that Bailey seemed to be more himself than he had been the last few days. "I need to run down to the corner for a few groceries." She nodded in the direction of the back door and smiled. "He's eating me out of house and home."

"Why don't you go and I'll get the grill started?" His voice softened. "I'll feel him out, then you can talk to him when you get back. By that time he'll probably be more settled."

Unable to argue with his logic, Virginia nodded and picked up her purse. "I'll be back in a few minutes." To be honest, she was looking forward to a few minutes alone and away from the house to help clear her head.

* * *

Bailey stepped onto the patio, then slid the glass door closed behind him. He passed an admiring, professional glance over the tidy fenced backyard, keeping an eye out for his son. The redbrick patio measured about ten feet by fifteen feet, large enough for a green wrought-iron table and four chairs, plus a gas grill. The masonry yielded to tall plant boxes, and finally, a strip of lush fescue. Ginny had compensated for her legendary lack of a green thumb by planting perennials and evergreens, and connecting the beds with impressive walkways. A three-foot fountain gurgled in a far corner, flanked by crape myrtles, the dwarf trees blooming brilliant fuchsia in the heat.

The toe of a white tennis shoe protruded past the edge of the fountain base. Bailey noisily uncovered and lit the grill, then sauntered over to his son's hiding place. Chad stared straight ahead, clutching the broken game, his lashes wet. Bailey sighed. "Want to talk about it?"

Chad remained completely still. "No."

Bailey squatted and lowered himself to the ground, his back against the fountain. "She's hurting too, you know."

His son scoffed. "Yeah, right."

"She's been crying on my shoulder."

Chad rolled his eyes. "Bet you liked that."

Bailey blinked in surprise. "That obvious, huh?"

"That you're still hung up on her? Yeah, it's pretty obvious."

Exasperated, Bailey asked, "So how did you get so wise?"

Chad glanced over with a lopsided grin. "I keep my eyes open."

Grunting in response, Bailey said, "So tell me what happened today."

His son shrugged. "She was the one who told me to get out the pictures of my mom, then she freaked out and went running to her bedroom. At first I felt kind of bad, but when I heard what she was saying about Mom"—his voice choked—"I got really mad."

"Hm. Then what?"

"I went to my room and locked the door. When I wouldn't let her in, she threw my game down the stairs."

"Did you see her do that?"

Chad bit his lip. "No, but I know she did it. She wants me to forget about my other mom, but I can't, and I don't want to."

Bailey took a deep breath and folded his hands together. "Well, Ginny thought she could handle seeing the pictures of you and Lois, but she couldn't. And she wouldn't have said what she said if she'd known you were listening. Besides"—he reached over and carefully withdrew the broken game to inspect it—"can't you understand the way Ginny might feel toward Lois, even a little bit?"

"No," Chad insisted.

"After you were kidnapped, your mother was inconsolable. She used to sit in your nursery for hours, rocking in her rocking chair. She wouldn't eat or sleep. She was worried sick about you. We both were."

"But Lois took good care of me."

Bailey frowned. This was a touchy subject. "And we're grateful that Lois took good care of you, but that still doesn't make up for the fact that you were *our* baby, *our* son, and she took you away from us."

"Do you hate Lois too?" Chad asked.

Angling his head, Bailey answered as honestly as he could. "I used to hate some nameless, faceless person who stole you from us, but since the minute I heard you'd been found, I haven't really thought about it. I'm just happy to have you back. And so is Ginny."

Chad looked at the game, then raised his eyebrows hopefully. "Can it be fixed?"

Clicking his jaw in doubt, Bailey said, "It doesn't look good. Sorry, buddy. But we'll get you a new one."

"Maybe not—she wouldn't let me have the bike," Chad pointed out.

"She had a good reason for that," Bailey said in a stern voice. "This is different."

"I want to come live with *you*."

Bailey's heart contracted. *Few things would make me happier.* He set down the radio and looked back to his son. "We already talked about that."

"But I hate it here, and I can't get along with her."

"*Her* name is Ginny."

"Whatever. Why don't you move out to the farm and let me come live there?"

I'll pour footers tomorrow and have it finished in ninety days, the builder had promised him, standing in the meadow less than an hour earlier. A home for himself, Chad, and hopefully, Ginny. He chose his words carefully. "Son, I'd like nothing better than for us to live together at Shenoway, and if things go the way I plan, maybe we can be there by mid-fall."

Chad's face lit up. "That would be great!"

"Now, wait a minute," Bailey warned, holding up a finger. He leaned close and lowered his voice. "This has to stay between me and you—Ginny doesn't know yet, and I want to wait to tell her, okay?"

"Sure." Chad nodded happily.

"Meanwhile," Bailey said gravely, "if Ginny says that breaking your game was an accident, then it was. And as far as what you overheard, well, promise me you'll try to see her side when she's ready to talk about it, okay?"

"Okay," he grumbled.

"That's my boy." Bailey smacked Chad on the knee.

Chad smiled back, then leaned over and picked up a leaf. He twirled it idly by the stem, and a tentative expression crossed his face. "Bailey." His voice had a strange timbre, and he didn't look up.

Worry flooded him. "What, son?"

"I, uh..." Chad kept his gaze riveted on the leaf. "I was thinking maybe Chad Kallihan wouldn't be too bad of a name to be stuck with." He flicked the leaf away, then looked up.

Bailey's chest expanded to bursting. "I think it has a nice ring to it."

* * *

The little jaunt might not have been so beneficial, Ginny decided as she pulled back into her driveway. Her anxiety about talking to her son was now compounded by frustration when she realized how thankful she felt that Bailey had arrived to act as buffer between them.

Sighing, she allowed the painful realization to sink in. Although she was grateful he'd come just when Chad needed him, she'd been just as glad he'd arrived when she needed someone... needed him. After her earlier breakdown, she'd have to try even harder to convince him and to convince herself she could handle Chad without him.

Virginia carried the bag of groceries into the house, surprised to see the debris from the game had been cleared. She heard Chad's animated voice from his room, and caught occasional words about his model collection.

She threw, "I'm home," up the stairs on the way to the kitchen, then froze. Such a simple phrase, yet years had passed since she'd had anyone to inform she was home.

"Be right down," Bailey yelled. A strange sense of déjà vu washed over her.

Virginia slowly unpacked the groceries, eyeing the plate of seasoned raw steaks. She lined up salad ingredients by the cutting board. Her heart pounded in anticipation as they descended the stairs. How would Chad react to her? What was she going to say?

"Salad?" Bailey asked as they swept into the kitchen. "My body won't know how to react." His smile was casual and encouraging as he nodded to her.

Her eyes quickly darted to Chad, who stood with his eyes down, holding a Monopoly game.

"Well," Bailey said cheerfully, "why don't I get the steaks on the grill and let you two get things going in here." He grabbed the plate and disappeared.

Virginia watched her son fidget, then said, "Would you help me cut up tomatoes for the salad?"

He frowned. "I don't like tomatoes."

She laughed softly. "I'm not surprised—Bailey doesn't either. How about carrots?"

"Nope."

"Mushrooms?"

"Uh-uh."

"Well," she tried to keep her voice light, "at least wash your hands and help me tear up the lettuce."

He sighed and set his board game on the table, then walked to the sink. After washing his hands, he climbed up on a barstool, facing her, but not making eye contact.

She handed him half a lettuce head, then began tearing her half into bite-sized chunks.

He followed suit with little enthusiasm.

"Chad, I'm sorry."

He worked his mouth but didn't reply.

"I'm sorry you overheard me say something bad about Lois." She expected him to bolt any second, but continued. "It was wrong and I have no excuse other than to tell you that my reaction sprang from my love for you." She choked on the last couple of words, but recovered. "I would never hurt you intentionally." She ached to hug him tightly, but she knew her foothold was precarious at best.

He remained silent, but glanced up quickly and tightened his mouth. He began to tear the pieces with more vigor, obviously angry.

She rushed on. "I'm sorry, too, about your game—I know it meant a lot to you."

His scowl deepened and he chewed on the inside of his cheek.

"You don't have to say anything," Virginia added. "I don't expect you to forgive me, but I hope you'll give me another chance. I had fun with you today, and I'd like us to be that way again." With a start she realized how similar her words were to Bailey's a few nights before.

After a few seconds of silence, Chad shrugged. "Whatever."

Her nerves eased somewhat. At least he hadn't lashed out. And while he wasn't exactly accepting her olive branch with open arms, she had hope they could start rebuilding their relationship. As far as she and Bailey were concerned, however, she'd have to give it more thought.

The glass door slid open and Bailey stuck his head in. "How're we doing in here?"

She smiled, throwing in the last of the lettuce. "One plain lettuce salad coming up."

The next few hours were the most enjoyable she'd spent in recent memory. The steaks were delicious, and she'd fried a skillet of potatoes to go with their plain but healthy salads. Doused with honey butter, the angel flake rolls she'd bought at the bakery were mouth-watering. For dessert they had bowls of strawberry ice cream.

Chad became more lively as the evening progressed, beating them soundly in Monopoly. Her parents called and asked to take their grandson to a laser show the following evening. To Virginia's delight, he agreed and seemed to be looking forward to going. Later, when he challenged Bailey to arm wrestling, she found herself mesmerized at the two of them interacting—grunting, concentrating, and laughing. What a complex little person, this son of hers.

With a guilty pang she found herself again wondering if it was wrong to keep Chad with her when he so plainly preferred to be with Bailey. Worry crept into the crevices of her brain. Was she resisting the inevitable? Would she withstand emotional contortions over the next several months, only to end up losing him to Bailey anyway?

Bailey... the man already owned everything of hers that mattered—her heart and soul. Why not take her son too?

A fantasy began to take shape, and for a few uninhibited seconds Virginia allowed herself to picture the three of them together as a family. Not an I'll-take-him-for-weekends-and-you-get-him-for-the-summer kind of family, but an honest-to-goodness have-dinner-together and go-to-the-Grand-Canyon kind of family. She sighed. Did such an animal exist anymore?

She looked at Bailey's laughing profile, her temperature rising with the knowledge that if she had made love with him in Fort Lauderdale, they would now most likely be engaging in an affair—enjoying every moment with their son while anticipating the time they would lie down together. Bailey had been a wonderful lover, the first man to introduce her to the finer textures of sex. Even while she was pregnant, they'd spent hours—

"Ginny, I'm getting eaten alive."

"Hmmm?" she murmured at his words, momentarily suspended between her fading fantasies and the present moment.

"Mosquitos," Bailey asserted, smacking the back of his neck. "They're eating me alive under these lights."

"Me too," Chad grumbled, leaning over to scratch his ankle.

Virginia rose and swatted at her own skin and headed for the door, the guys right behind her. Inside the kitchen, she stopped and surveyed the dirty dishes.

"We'll help," Bailey said immediately.

Chad wrinkled his nose and Virginia laughed. "Don't worry, I don't think there's room in here for all three of us."

"Then I'll help," Bailey clarified, reaching for the frilly half-apron she'd left draped over a barstool. Meant to be worn around the waist, he tied it underneath his arms, the ruffled hem barely brushing the waistband of his jeans. She and Chad both burst out laughing.

"I'm getting outta here," Chad said, backing out of the room.

"Find us something to watch on TV," Bailey said, then added with raised eyebrows, "and make sure it's G-rated."

Chad saluted, then bounded away.

Still smiling, Virginia slipped on a second apron and began loading the dishwasher as Bailey handed rinsed dishes to her. In the end there were only a few items that needed to be hand washed, so she ran a sink half full of suds and scrubbed while he waited patiently, holding a dish towel to dry with. He looked so comical, she started giggling again.

"What?" he asked, his eyes wide.

She shook her head. "You."

"I used to help you with the dishes all the time."

"You're right," she admitted, scrubbing harder, trying desperately to erase the chain of good memories that had surfaced.

He snapped his fingers. "Except we always had music." He turned on the radio on the counter and tuned in a classic country music station. Don Williams crooned from the speakers and Bailey nodded in satisfaction. "Perfect. Remember this one?"

Virginia swallowed, the hair on the back of her neck tingling. "No," she lied. "I haven't listened to country music in years." *That* at least was the truth.

He leaned on the sink, too close for comfort. "The old stuff is still the best," he said huskily. "The fads come and go, but the classics—the originals—those are the ones you remember late at night." His eyes glinted with desire.

Hoping the hot water would explain away the heat she felt climbing her neck, Virginia's mind whirled for a suitable wet blanket to douse the flame between them. When she found her voice, she forced a light tone. "Who are you calling old?"

Too late, she realized her banter only fueled him.

He grinned wide. "Did I find a weak spot?"

"No," she said too quickly.

"Ginny." His voice was silken. He placed a finger under her chin and turned her face toward him. "If it's possible, you're even more beautiful now than the day I first laid eyes on you."

She felt helpless with her hands in the water. "Bailey, don't," she said softly. Pulling away from his hand, she dunked the clean pan in the rinse water.

"I can't help it, Ginny." He moved behind her to rest his chin on her shoulder. His sigh feathered the hair around her face, adhering it to her moist cheek. "You always drove me crazy—isn't Chad living proof of that? I couldn't keep my hands off you... I still can't." His arms encircled her waist, his hands pressing her back against him.

"Bailey," she whispered urgently, trying to move away from him, "that's enough." Her knees threatened to buckle if he didn't stop touching her. "Chad's in the next room."

"I can hang around until he goes to bed," he murmured into her ear, sending shivers dancing across her shoulders. He closed in to kiss her earlobe. "Please let me stay tonight, Ginny."

When he descended on the taut, sensitive cords of her neck with his tongue, she felt herself waver.

CHAPTER TEN

BAILEY KNEW SHE WAS WAVERING, could feel her teetering on the brink. He continued to probe and nibble on her neck, remembering well what it did to her, and feeling the full effect on his own straining body.

"Hey, Bailey," came Chad's muffled voice from the living room. "You gotta see this!"

Ginny's neck stiffened beneath his mouth.

He stepped back with a frustrated groan and leaned against the kitchen bar. "Be right there, buddy!"

She turned around, wiping her hands on a towel, the color high in her cheeks. "We have to try to be a good example, you know," she said, her chest rising and falling rapidly.

He dragged his gaze from her breasts and glanced down at his telltale arousal. Reaching around and jerking free the knot between his shoulder blades, he then lowered the apron and retied it around his waist, the dainty flowered fabric effectively covering him.

As he left the kitchen, he heard Ginny laughing. He smiled wryly to himself. At least she wasn't angry—he was still in the running.

Chad was sitting cross-legged on the floor in semi-darkness, watching a sports documentary on legendary stadiums. "This is cool!" he said, grinning up at Bailey.

Bailey nodded his enthusiastic agreement, then sat on the edge of the couch to watch with his son. Ginny joined them in a few minutes, giving him a warning glance, then sitting a few inches away from him on the deep, comfy sofa.

"When can we go back to Shenoway?" Chad asked a few minutes later.

Bailey's heart lurched, hoping his son would keep his pact about not telling Ginny of his plans. Looking at Ginny, he asked, "Got any plans for Saturday?"

She shook her head.

"Then Saturday it is—I have a few chores to do around the farm, then we'll take a picnic down by the swimming hole."

"Can we go horseback riding?" Chad asked.

Bailey nodded. "In fact, Rita, Jerry, and Jean Ann will be out of town for a wedding, and I promised to stay overnight to keep an eye on things. I sure would like some company."

"Yaaaaay!" Chad cheered.

"I don't know..." Ginny hesitated, and he guessed at what she might be thinking.

He lowered his voice. "There are plenty of bedrooms, Ginny. Come on—don't you want to teach him to ride?"

"Well... all right."

Relieved, Bailey settled into the sofa cushions. Wincing, he massaged a knot of tension between his neck and shoulder. He was a bundle of tense, hormone-laced muscles, a walking wad of pent-up frustration and longing. He glanced over at her profile. A man shackled within view of the finish line.

His gaze traveled down to where her buttoned blouse gapped open. Wetting his lips, he angled for a better look. The lacy top of a pink bra beckoned to him, and he itched to touch it, his fingers curling against his palm. Bailey put his head back and closed his eyes, cursing silently. He wouldn't be getting rid of the apron anytime soon.

His next conscious moment was Chad shaking him awake. "Bailey," he whispered, "I'm going to bed."

"Huh?" Bailey sat up, rubbing his eyes.

"It's late and I'm going to bed. You both fell asleep."

He looked over and saw Ginny was sleeping on the other two-thirds of the couch, her head on the armrest, her arms crossed and her feet tucked up to her rear end, compactly nestled into the space. "What time is it?"

"Around midnight."

Bailey yawned. "Okay, you're going out with Ginny's folks tomorrow night, aren't you?"

"Yeah."

"Then I'll see you Saturday morning."

"Won't you be here in the morning?" Chad asked.

Bailey took in Ginny's sleeping form, all closed up and inaccessible, and the firm set of her chin, even in her sleep. He frowned. "Don't count on it."

"Okay, see you Saturday."

Chad loped out of the room and Bailey listened as he climbed the stairs, then closed his bedroom door. Yawning widely, he rubbed his knuckles over his face, then stood up for an all-body stretch. Reluctantly, he leaned over to shake Ginny awake, then changed his mind in a split second.

The couch felt too good, and Ginny looked too good. He removed his boots and belt, then stripped off his shirt. He had no intention of making love to Ginny while she slept, but he wasn't going to pass up the opportunity to snuggle with her all night. He lowered himself behind her onto the couch, easing in little by little, nudging her body forward. She moaned and murmured incoherently, but eventually lay spooned in his embrace.

He punched down the pillow lightly, but skipped his customary habit of turning over to find the sweet spot. He reached up and carefully unclasped her hair, then buried his nose in its silkiness and inhaled her scent. Pulling her as close to him as he dared, he lay his hand on her stomach and sighed into her ear. She wriggled against him, and he felt his love for her swell in his heart.

Ginny was the sweet spot.

* * *

Virginia blinked and winced. Her neck hurt, her back hurt, her—

She jolted wide awake, realizing where she slept and who was snoring softly in her ear. She remembered lying down, thinking she'd doze until Chad's television show ended. And she distinctly remembered *not* entwining her body with Bailey's before lying down. His legs were wrapped around hers, and his bare, muscled arm lay across her waist. She swallowed. Oh, God, was he naked?

She glanced down, glad to see in the breaking morning light that she was still fully clothed, and that he at least was wearing jeans. She moved gingerly, but at the first sign of withdrawing from him, he responded by tightening his grip on her.

Struggling harder, she hissed, "Bailey, wake up. It's morning."

"Mmmmph," he murmured in her ear, sending goose bumps down her arms.

"Wake up—you have to go to work."

"No," he whispered sleepily. "I have to stay right here."

"Let me up!"

"Stay with me," he urged, pulling her closer and rubbing his arousal against her behind.

Longing knifed through her, and she yielded to her impulse, rolling her neck and arching her back, pressing into him. He groaned into her hair, then reached around to cup her breast through her thin shirt. Desire bolted through her, and she reached behind her to massage the smooth skin of his back.

"Ginny," he whispered huskily, "you make me crazy with wanting you." He devoured her neck, sending miniature convulsions through her body. Her nipple hardened beneath his hand, and he ground his hips against her.

Reality seeped into the fog of her rapture, and she stiffened slightly. "Bailey," she whispered hoarsely, "Chad could walk down those stairs any minute."

Bailey sighed, clearly frustrated. "And what would he see? His mother and father lying together on the couch." He resumed his ministrations on her neck.

She laid her head back, easing into him a little more. "It's gone a little beyond lying together, don't you think?"

"Let's go to your bedroom," he whispered urgently, nipping the top of her shoulder.

"He'll know," she insisted, still moving against him.

He planted a kiss just below her ear, his breath coming in short gasps. "Relax, Ginny. Nothing would make him happier than for us all to be together."

At his words, Virginia pulled away from his embrace and swung her feet to the floor.

He groaned his disapproval and shifted to his back, throwing an arm over his brow. "What did I say?"

She pushed to her feet and looked down at her ex-husband, her mind spinning with indecision.

Impressive—that was the word that came to mind as she scanned his half-naked body. His dark hair, almost blue in its intensity, fell against the light-colored cushion. His arm covered his eyes, but his mouth was soft with drowsiness, his chin darkened with morning beard. Spanning the width of the couch, his shoulders were gloriously muscled and tanned, his chest matted with dark, springy hair that extended from throat to flat navel. *And beyond,* she remembered, unable to miss the hard ridge of his arousal through his jeans.

"Ginny." He sat up and raked his fingers through his hair. "Talk to me."

She sighed and rubbed her throbbing temple. "If Chad wants us to be together, it's only because it would mean he could be with you all the time."

"You'll grow closer in time, Ginny, I know you will."

"Maybe we will," she admitted, "but what happens if you and I play house for a while and things don't work out between us? We'd be harming him even more if we split up again. You said yourself, Bailey, that commitment isn't your strong suit."

He sighed. "I know, but I'm working on it."

She scoffed, anger flaring through her. "What the hell does that mean"—she raised her arms—"you're *working* on it?"

"Ginny." He stood and reached for her. "We can make it work this time, I know we can."

She stepped back out of reach. "Not unless I mean more to you than just a vehicle to get to your son."

He frowned, exasperated, jamming his hands on his hips. "How can you say that? Are you blind, Ginny? We're good together."

Her laugh was short and humorless. "Our sexual compatibility was never in question, Bailey, but I need more from you."

She captured his gaze and leveled her chin at him. "What can you offer me?"

His chest rose and fell as he pondered her question. Finally, he said, "Marriage, if that's what it takes."

Disappointment washed over her. The words were right, but the circumstances were wrong, and she knew it. She'd backed him into a corner, and he'd given her the answer she wanted to hear. She turned away from him. "You should leave."

"Not like this." He walked up behind her. "I love you, Ginny."

A sound of disbelief emerged from her throat. She pressed her lips together and shook her head.

"I do, Ginny. I always have. But I don't want to make you long-term promises this time until I know I can keep them. That's why I asked you to be patient."

She spun. "And while I'm being patient, you also expect me to warm your bed."

He dropped his gaze. "You're right, it's not fair. I'm sorry."

She took deep, even breaths to control the emotions racing through her. She didn't want to provoke any more discussion—she just wanted him to leave. "You're going to be late for work," she said calmly.

Bailey stared at her for several seconds, frustration clouding his eyes. Slowly he nodded, then reached for his shirt draped over the couch arm. He shrugged into it, buttoned two buttons, then pulled on his boots one at a time, leaving his jeans tucked haphazardly inside.

"I'll call you later," he said.

She watched him walk out of the room, then heard the front door open and close. Tears welled in her eyes, and she angrily wiped them away. He was the one who had overstepped his bounds. So why did she feel so miserable?

* * *

"Rough night, Bailey?" Lenny asked when he walked into the office.

"I'll be in the shower," Bailey barked, ignoring his boss's chuckle.

At the first burst of hot spray from the shower head, Bailey sank forward, supporting himself with both arms on the tiled wall. He rolled his head, loosening his stiff neck, and allowed the therapeutic water to work its magic. The rising steam helped to lighten his head, but his heart still felt heavy in his chest.

Although his first priority was Chad's well-being, Bailey felt sure his son's future would most benefit from living with both him and Ginny, from seeing their love for each other. Except Ginny wanted a commitment. Why couldn't she just enjoy the time they spent together? He scrubbed his face with a rough cloth, then lathered up his beard.

Marriage. He loved Ginny, but the thought of marriage still spooked him. He'd hoped they could live together for a while, give it a dry run before putting it in ink again. Holding a razor angled on his chin, Bailey frowned at his own image, then lowered his hand. And what kind of message would they be sending to Chad? He could hear him now. *My folks are shacking up.*

While he shaved with the dull razor, he tried to sort things logically. He wanted to be with Chad, and he wanted to be with Ginny. Chad wanted to be with him, but he suspected deep down he wanted to be with Ginny too. Ginny wanted to be with Chad, and had hinted she wanted to be with him too, but only if he offered her a long-term commitment. Bailey sighed, wincing when he nicked himself on the chin. He had two choices—commit and have them both, or don't commit and lose Ginny, plus see Chad on a sometimes-only basis.

He rinsed the razor, then wiped the fog from the small hanging mirror to look at himself. He studied his own eyes, searching them for a shred of doubt, a trace of hesitancy. None. Having a wife and a son was a huge responsibility... but he could handle it.

He'd asked himself before what was it between Rita and Jerry that kept Jerry coming home at night... but it wasn't anything Rita did or didn't do—she just loved Jerry. Jerry came home every night because he knew loving his wife and child made him a better man. It was worth the tradeoff of being a carefree bachelor.

And suddenly Bailey knew the same thing about himself. Being a husband to Ginny and a father to Chad were worth any sacrifice he had to make.

He dragged a washcloth over his skin, enjoying the invigorating friction. He sighed in contentment, thinking through the day ahead of him.

Fridays were normally a light workday, but he had three jobs to visit, two of which he suspected would be problematic, plus he had to get Lenny a name for his replacement. And he was hoping to get out to Shenoway to take a look at the footers the builder had promised would be set.

His pulse quickened at the thought of breaking ground on his new home. A sprawling four-bedroom, three-bath ranch with a full basement—a slightly upscale version of the plan he and Ginny had originally chosen. Lots of room for a big family, he thought with satisfaction, his imagination galloping ahead. Then he shook his head, laughing to himself.

First he'd have to convince Ginny to marry him again. *Then* they could think about growing their family.

He turned off the water and emerged from the shower with a kernel of a plan. Chad would be with Edward and Peg for the evening, so Ginny would be free. Maybe she'd agree to go out with him. A bona fide date, complete with flowers and everything. But he'd have to come up with a charming invitation over the phone. He smiled... he'd think of something.

With the phone call to look forward to, the morning's schedule seemed more tolerable. As expected, he encountered trouble at one of the jobs with a city inspector who didn't like the sprinkler system his crew had installed. Bailey kept his cool and handled the man deftly, reaching a compromise on the modifications.

Before he left, every member of his crew stepped up to shake his hand and wish him luck with his new job. Bailey felt a few pangs of regret, knowing he'd miss some aspects of his old job, but his anticipation of joining the design team overrode any sentimentality.

He laughingly assured his men he'd be back to check on their progress on his own time, just to make sure they didn't try to pull anything with the new crew chief. A group of them wanted to take him out for a drink after work, but he politely refused, saying, "If my plans work out, I'll be drinking with someone a lot prettier than you guys."

When he broke for lunch, he called Ginny, as nervous as a sixteen-year-old.

"Hello?" she asked softly.

"Ginny, hi, it's Bailey."

"I was hoping you'd call."

His pulse spiked. "You were? Is everything okay?"

"Yes," she said quickly, then sighed. "No. Bailey, I'm sorry for the way I acted this morning. You're right, it would be foolish to make promises that couldn't be kept—I'd never want you to do that."

Surprised, he swallowed. "Okay," he said simply, his mind spinning. "So, where does that put us now?" he managed to ask.

"Let's just play it by ear, okay?" she asked. "And move slowly."

"Sure," he said, still searching for firm ground.

"So why did you call?"

He cleared his voice. "I wanted to check in to see how things are going today, you know, with Chad."

"Not great." She sounded tired. "He hasn't really talked much, and I know he's still upset with me, but I got him to agree we'd go somewhere this afternoon to look for a new game console."

"That's a start."

"I suppose."

"What time are Edward and Peg picking him up?"

"Around six, I think. They're going to take him to eat before the laser show starts."

"When will they bring him home?"

"Around eleven."

"Great, that gives you plenty of time."

"To do what?" Her voice was cautious.

"To go to dinner with me."

She was silent.

"A real date, Ginny. Put on something nice and let me buy you dinner for me being such a pain lately."

She laughed. "Lately?"

"Okay, for being such a pain *always*."

"I don't think Columbus has a restaurant *that* nice."

"That's why I'm throwing in flowers and candy."

"It sounds like you're sucking up," she said carefully.

"Guilty," he admitted. "So, what do you say?"

She laughed again. "You certainly are persistent."

"What time can I pick you up?"

"Six-thirty?"

He blinked in surprise. "I'll be there."

"I expect you to be on your best behavior, Bailey Kallihan. No funny stuff."

His heart sang. "No funny stuff," he agreed.

* * *

Virginia slowly hung up the phone. A date with Bailey. She felt schoolgirl foolish with anticipation, but reasoned that a nice dinner in public would be both relaxing and safe. After their emotional exchange that morning, she looked forward to them being on friendly terms again.

She noticed a spring in her step as she moved through the rest of the day. Chad had adopted his sullen act again, dodging her hugs, refusing to look at her or utter anything but grunts. They drove to an electronics superstore after lunch. Remembering the incident of their last shopping trip all too well, Virginia nervously kept an eye on her son's hands. The salesclerk announced the game console model they were looking for as already being outdated, which put a defensive frown on Chad's face. They were presented with the latest model, and Ginny glanced at Chad.

"What do you think?"

"I want the same one," he insisted. "It's the one I like."

"Maybe we can find one somewhere else," she suggested, but the salesclerk shook his head no.

Chad's mouth and shoulders drooped. "I guess it'll do, even if it's not as good."

The salesclerk opened his mouth to argue, but she silenced him with a look. "We'll take it."

But Chad was morose while their purchase was being rung up. And when they returned to the car, he slammed the door and maintained his silence for the drive home. The bag with the new Nintendo remained untouched.

He retreated to his room when they arrived home with another door slam. Ginny cleaned the house, burning pent-up frustration over dealing with her son and nervous energy over her impending date with Bailey.

Fifteen minutes before her parents arrived, Chad descended, looking clean-cut and all-American in his jean shorts and red and white striped T-shirt. He wore a pleasant expression, and even whistled under his breath as he kept watch out the window.

"It makes me happy that you want to do things with my parents," she ventured.

He shrugged. "They're cool. Besides, I've never had grandparents before."

His words hit her like an open-handed slap. He'd never had a father before, and he adored Bailey. He'd never had an aunt, uncle, or cousin before, so he liked Rita and her family. He'd never had grandparents before, so he looked forward to spending time with her folks.

But he'd had a mother before, and he wasn't about to let Virginia take Lois's place.

"They're here!" he yelled, throwing open the door.

Virginia hugged her parents and chatted for a few minutes before seeing them off with a wave.

She tried to put aside her earlier revelation about Chad's attitude toward her as she readied herself for Bailey's arrival.

After a leisurely shower, she opened her closet door and frowned. At last she decided on a white knit miniskirt topped with a V-necked yellow summer cardigan. The thin fabric had a sexy sheen and draped nicely around her shoulders and waist. She stepped into a pair of white leather sandals, then dried her hair. For once, she left it loose and swinging around her shoulders, then applied her makeup carefully.

When she appraised her image in the full-length mirror, she was relatively pleased with the result. Then she frowned—she needed jewelry. Virginia pulled her favorite gold hoops from her jewelry case, then decided the locket would be the perfect foil for the low-necked sweater. And fitting for the occasion, she thought happily. She rummaged through the case, frowning when she didn't find the necklace in its usual compartment. Fifteen minutes later she had removed and separated every piece of jewelry, but still hadn't found her precious locket.

Desperately trying to stem her rising panic, she forced herself to remember the last time she'd worn it. She'd shown it to Chad before they washed the car yesterday—had she then worn it outside? She thought she remembered putting it on the dresser, but she couldn't be sure. She ran down the stairs and outside to look all around her car and in the driveway. She even moved her car, but still couldn't find it.

Her worry escalated as she climbed the stairs to her bedroom. She performed another search of her dresser and jewelry case, then fell to her hands and knees to search the carpet in her room. Nothing. Spent, she sat on the floor with her back against the bed, no longer able to ignore her rising suspicion. In her mind she saw Chad's tear-streaked face and heard him yell, "I'll get you back!"

She leaned her head against the mattress and sighed.

Chad had stolen her locket.

CHAPTER ELEVEN

WHEN THE DOORBELL RANG a few moments later, she dragged herself to her feet and walked down the stairs, wrestling with whether to divulge her suspicions to Bailey. At the last second she decided against it, thinking if she confronted Chad and he owned up to it, no one would be the wiser. Resolved, she conjured up a smile reflective of her earlier anticipation, and opened the door.

She was greeted by the largest bouquet of wildflowers she'd ever seen. Laughing in delight, she asked, "Is my date in there somewhere?"

He peeked around the side, then whistled low. "Wow, you look great."

Her cheeks warmed. "Thanks. I'd ask you to come in, but I don't think you'll fit through the door."

Somehow they managed to get the flowers inside. Ginny was stunned to see that Bailey had traded in his jeans and boots for tailored slacks and dress shoes. A white collarless dress shirt fit his broad shoulders to perfection. "You look great, too," she said, swallowing hard.

"Then I guess we make a great-looking couple," he said, his teeth flashing.

Her throat went completely dry at the thought of them once again being a couple. She busied herself finding enough vases, pitchers, and water glasses to hold all the flowers. When they finished, she looked around at the bouquets and laughed aloud. "It looks like you raided one of your wholesalers."

His sheepish grin confirmed her guess. "DiNaldo's has the best plants in town."

"They're lovely… and I'm certainly impressed with the quantity."

"Size matters," he said with a mischievous grin.

She rolled her eyes, smothering a laugh, and glanced at the clock. "Should we get going?"

"Sure. We'll have time to have a drink at the bar before dinner."

"Where are we going?"

"We have reservations at Crosby's."

She raised her eyebrows. "Well, well."

He opened the front door. "After you."

At the bottom of the steps she froze in her tracks. "Oh, Bailey." At the end of the driveway, a small knot of pedestrians had gathered to get a look at a perfectly restored baby-blue 1953 Packard Caribbean convertible. "It can't be the same car you dragged out of that old woman's shed in Havensport."

"Yep—I gave her five hundred dollars for it and you thought I was getting ripped off."

She walked toward it, her mouth agape. "It's unbelievable! This car must be worth a small fortune."

"I wouldn't go that far," Bailey said, opening her door.

Sliding across the smooth white upholstery, she admired the sparkling chrome, the precise attention to restored detail. Suddenly Bailey's saving plan seemed more sensible than before. "You did this yourself?"

"With some help," he said, swinging into the driver's seat. "I'm glad you like it, because this is a farewell excursion." He started the engine and carefully turned the vehicle around.

"You're selling it? Why?"

He shrugged. "I found a motivated buyer, and money talks. Now I'll be able to do some things around Shenoway I've been wanting to do for a long time."

Warning bells chimed in her head. Unless she was hearing things, Bailey Kallihan was starting to sound... responsible.

She settled back into the comfy seat, enjoying the warm summer air blowing through her hair. Bailey drove at the minimum allowable speed on the expressways, garnering lots of attention and thumbs-ups from other drivers. It was a clear summer night, and Virginia felt special—in a special car, with a special man. Tonight she would put aside the past and see him through different eyes—maybe he *had* changed. She would try to be more open-minded where Bailey was concerned, but not let her guard down completely.

When they arrived at the restaurant, the valets scrambled for the honor of driving the Packard. She saw Bailey slip the guy a twenty tip in advance. "Don't let anyone touch my car," he said simply.

Once they'd given their names to the host, they claimed seats at the bar. Suddenly Virginia felt ridiculously nervous at having to converse with Bailey alone for an entire evening.

"What'll you have?" the bartender asked them.

From the wine list, she selected a glass of pinot noir.

"Same," Bailey told the man.

She glanced at him in puzzlement. "What happened to whiskey sours?"

He cleared his throat and gave her a small smile. "Turning over a new leaf."

Virginia fidgeted with her napkin, growing more nervous with each passing second at this new side of Bailey.

When the barman brought their glasses, Bailey raised his toward her. "To our reunion," he said, a smile crinkling his eyes.

She nodded and offered him a watery smile when she clinked her glass to his. The drink she took from her glass was deeper than she'd intended, the alcohol instantly warming the back of her throat.

"So how was the shopping today?" he asked.

"Not so good. Apparently, they don't make that gaming model anymore. I bought a newer one, but he barely talked the rest of the day."

He made a rueful noise. "He'll come around."

"I hope so. At least he was nice to my parents when they arrived. "

"Have you been notified yet about a date for juvenile court?"

She shook her head. "A woman at the police station told me over the phone it should be in the mail any day now."

"Well, let's hope the whole thing will scare him enough to keep him from doing it again."

Don't bet on it, she thought, her mind on the locket. Involuntarily she reached for the spot the pendant normally hung, her fingers touching bare skin instead.

He noticed the movement. "Where's your locket?"

Unable to look him in the eye, Virginia took another deep drink from her glass. "I must have left it at home."

Their name was called, and a hostess led them to a secluded table on the second floor of the restaurant, with a nice view of the city lights. A pianist played classic romantic tunes in the background, and a few couples turned slowly on a tiny dance floor.

Virginia perused the menu, feeling languid and sentimental. Her menu didn't even have prices—they could never have afforded to eat there when they were first married. Suddenly she longed for a platter of barbecue from a little dive where they used to go when they found extra money or wanted to treat themselves.

"Bailey."

He looked up from the menu, one eyebrow raised in response.

"Is Blackey's still in business?"

He looked surprised, then pursed his lips in concentration. "I think so... yeah, I heard some guy at work mention it the other day."

"Let's go."

He frowned and leaned forward. "Excuse me?"

"Let's go eat barbecue at Blackey's."

He looked all around them, then whispered, "Ginny, are you drunk?"

She laughed. "Not on one glass of wine."

"Are you saying you want to leave?"

"It's a nice place, but suddenly I had a longing for something more... familiar."

This time both eyebrows shot up.

The waiter suddenly reappeared at the table. "Are you ready to order, madam?"

"No." She fanned herself furiously with the menu. "In fact, I'm suddenly feeling very ill." She took several deep breaths, inhaling and exhaling in an exaggerated fashion.

"Can I get you something?" the man asked, his face crumpled with concern.

128

"I'm sorry," she said, "but I think we'd better leave."

Bailey barely concealed his amusement. "I think she's right." He moved behind Ginny's chair and made a big show of trying to help her from the chair.

The waiter looked completely perplexed. "I hope your wife feels better, sir."

Ginny stiffened slightly at the title, but tried to maintain her "sick" demeanor.

"She'll be fine," Bailey said to the man, then lowered his voice. "She's pregnant."

Virginia choked, and Bailey massaged her back. "Are you okay, sweetheart? Do you need a drink of water?"

"No," she gasped, "just some fresh air."

They hurried downstairs and out the door. The valet recognized them, and sprinted off to collect their car.

Once in the car, they looked at each other and started laughing.

He captured her gaze and shook his head slowly. "What on earth made you think of Blackey's?"

She shrugged, raising her hands. "I don't know, it just came to me that we were there getting ready to buy an overpriced meal when we could be having a good time at Blackey's."

He frowned slightly. "I wanted to take you to a nice place, Ginny. I can afford more than Blackey's now."

It hadn't occurred to her that she might have accidentally bruised his ego. She touched his arm. "I know you can afford more than Blackey's now, Bailey, but that's the point—we can go wherever we want, and tonight I want to go to Blackey's."

He smiled, and reached up to twine her fingers with his. "Then Blackey's it is."

* * *

Memories assailed Bailey as soon as the door opened to admit them in a rush of air. The fact that the word "authentic" was misspelled on the sign in the window of Blackey's Authentic Pit Barbecue was a customer's first signal to lower their expectations about the interior. But what Blackey's lacked in decor, it made up for in atmosphere.

Blues music blared from cheap stereo speakers hung haphazardly on the walls. Ceiling fans whirred frantically overhead in a failing attempt to circulate the smoky, greasy air. Long, scarred wooden tables butted up to each other cafeteria-style in three strips across the square, squatty room. Dozens of chairs, each different, lined the edges of the tables, about half of them full.

He noted most of the diners looked college-aged, which seemed logical since Blackey's sat in a rundown part of town only a few blocks from the campus of Ohio State University. He might have balked at bringing the Packard there had it not been for a secure parking garage nearby, and had he not been so eager to please Ginny.

Along with a lot of other students, he and Ginny had spent many mornings there studying, which hadn't bothered the owner since mornings were slow anyway. When he'd graduated, he'd met Ginny there regularly for lunch. After she'd withdrawn from school and they married, they occasionally splurged and came for dinner.

He turned to look at Ginny, her cheeks flushed and full, her figure still as lithe as a coed's. Their rendezvous at Blackey's seemed like a lifetime ago... and only yesterday.

"Grab you a chair," a waitress yelled as she passed, laden with two huge trays of food.

They claimed two chairs side by side in as secluded a spot as they could find. The menus were stacked in irregular little piles up and down the tables, more often than not splattered with barbecue sauce. He chose two of the cleanest-looking and handed one to Ginny.

She scanned the food items, her eyes shining. "It's the same menu," she said. "I'll have my usual—"

"Number seven," he supplied. "With dipping sauce on the side."

She grinned. "You remember."

"Sure I do. And I'll have—"

"Number twelve, extra hot sauce, extra napkins."

This time a grin tickled his lips. "Right." Then he glanced down at his snowy shirt. "I might need a bib too."

"What'll it be?" yelled the waitress, one hip cocked. They placed their food orders and requested bottles of good beer, their one deviation from the old days when they drank the cheapest draught.

The brews were delivered right away, the food, they knew, would take a bit longer. Ginny lifted her bottle in the air. "To Blackey's."

Buoyed by her good mood, he clinked his bottle against hers. "To Blackey's."

After a long drink, Bailey settled back, draping his arm around the back of Ginny's chair. Graffiti was encouraged at Blackey's, every customer could write their name and any bits of wisdom they could find room for on the cracked plaster walls. "Do you remember where we wrote our names?" he asked her.

Squinting, she looked around the room as she worked her mouth in concentration. Suddenly she brightened. "Over there, by the far window."

He nodded. "Think they're still there?"

She shrugged and grabbed her beer bottle. "Let's see."

Bailey followed her, feeling as if he were walking on eggshells. Which memories to touch on, which to avoid? For some reason, Ginny seemed more open and fun-loving tonight—but was it because she was becoming more receptive to him, or because he'd promised her a night on the town with "no funny stuff?"

They stood shoulder to shoulder, studying the hundreds of signatures and sayings which mostly merged into illegible garble.

"I see them!" she cried, pointing just above his head.

"Where?"

"Right there! See the red V? You can barely make out the rest of it, but I see your name just underneath."

He spotted their names, and smiled. "Yeah, there they are."

"We were just kids when we wrote our names up there," she said.

"And now we have one."

She tilted her head slightly, looking into his eyes. "Isn't life strange?" she asked, her voice soft.

He studied her caramel eyes, his heart skipping a beat. "Seems to have come full circle for us."

She bit her bottom lip. "Which reminds me, I'm going to call Mom to see how things are going." She gestured to the alcove where the bathrooms were located. "I'll be right back."

Before his eyes she'd transformed into a worried mother. As he watched her make the phone call, Bailey felt a pang of guilt—he hadn't even thought her parents might be having problems with Chad, or vice versa. She caught his glance and gave him a thumbs up, then ended the call. Lover, mother, friend—Ginny was a total package. He craved her so badly, her body *and* her companionship, he felt real physical pain.

"Order's up," their waitress yelled, slamming the trays down in front of their seats.

"I'm starved." Ginny patted her stomach, her eyes wide.

"Me too," he said, watching her walk back to the table, and feeling his groin tighten. "Me too."

* * *

Ginny chewed the saucy meat slowly, savoring the textures and spices. Worth waiting for, the platter of chopped pork barbecue and sweet corn bread satisfied her hunger and her senses.

"What have you been doing for the past eight years?" she asked between mouthfuls.

His eyebrows climbed as he pondered her question, then grinned. "Not a whole hell of a lot, I guess." He raised his beer for a drink.

"Oh, come on," she urged. "Restoring cars?"

He nodded. "Landscaping during the week, working on the cars on the weekends. And there's always plenty to do around the farm. I took up cross-country biking a couple of years ago."

"Really?" she asked. "Where have you been?"

"This spring a couple of guys from the cycling club I belong to invited me to ride to North Carolina. Next year we want to go out west, where the bicycle trails are more rugged."

"Do you still play basketball?"

"On a winter league." He shrugged. "It's good exercise. How about you? What have you been doing besides going back to school?"

She tilted her head. "A coworker of mine has a sailboat on Lake Erie, so I spend weekends there sometimes."

He wiped his mouth with a napkin. "Is this a male friend?"

Glancing up from her plate, she realized what he was asking and smiled impishly. "Yes, Robert is definitely a man, but his wife and grandchildren make it awfully hard for us to carry on our torrid affair."

He smiled wryly and picked up his fork "Did you ever come close to remarrying?"

She nodded slowly. "Once."

Virginia noticed Bailey had tightened his grip on his fork. "What happened?"

"He was divorced and had shared custody of his two children. The kids saw me as the obstacle for their parents getting back together. I decided it wasn't worth all the trouble it caused his family." And she couldn't be around his children without thinking of her own lost child...

He stabbed his fork into a chunk of meat. "So you really loved this guy?"

Lifting the beer to her mouth, she said, "I thought I did, but I got over it pretty quickly, so I guess I didn't." She took a swallow, then said, "How about you?"

"I came close a couple of times, but it didn't pan out."

Why did that hurt? "Your decision?"

"Yes." He wrapped his hand around his beer. "Are you still sculpting?"

Shaking her head, she sighed. "Not in years. I have good intentions, but never seem to get a piece started. I'm on my computer a lot in the evenings, catching up on work."

"Which reminds me, I'm starting a new job Monday and—"

"What new job?" Another surprise.

He seemed sheepish. "I'm joining my company's design team."

Smiling, she straightened. "That's wonderful, Bailey. When did this happen?"

"Last week."

"Why haven't you mentioned it?"

Shrugging, he said, "It seemed as if we always had more important things to discuss."

"Another toast," she declared softly, holding up her half-empty bottle.

He held his bottle up to hers.

"To new beginnings."

Beaming, he said, "I'll drink to that." They clinked their bottles, then pushed their empty plates to the center of the table. Bailey revealed he needed to learn spreadsheet basics, and Ginny offered her assistance.

When the bill was settled, she glanced at her watch and reluctantly said, "I guess we'd better call it a night if we're going to make it home before our son."

He agreed and pushed away from the table. Immediately she missed his arm around her shoulders, but attributed it to the old memories they'd stirred up all evening. Bailey had certainly kept his word—he'd been a gentleman throughout.

On the drive home she laid her head back and smiled up at the stars. "You know, Bailey, we had a lot of good times."

He smiled and nodded. "It's human nature, I guess, to dwell on the bad, but you're right—we had fun before…. before."

She turned her head and studied her ex-husband's face, still incredibly handsome, but older and perhaps wiser since their ordeal eight years earlier. "We were young," she murmured. "Perhaps we gave up too quickly."

Nodding again, he held out his hand in invitation to hers. "I was too young to realize how much I was giving up."

She smiled and offered her hand in a slow, intimate clasp. He raised her fingers to his lips for a soft kiss, then lowered their hands to rest between them on the seat.

For the remainder of the drive, her midsection pulsed with desire, her need for him almost tangible. Their evening had been deceptively casual and friendly. She desperately hoped he wouldn't ask to spend the night, because tonight she would say yes. And as much as she knew they wanted each other, she wasn't sure if they were ready for the emotional plunge. Her heart pounded faster when he pulled into her driveway.

He turned off the engine and said, "I'll walk you to your door."

She stopped rummaging in her purse. "You aren't coming in to wait for Chad?"

Bailey shook his head. "I told him I'd see him in the morning."

"Okay," she said, hiding her disappointment.

She led the way to her door, her heart pounding. Would he at least kiss her good night?

Unlocking the door, she quickly stepped inside and dismantled the alarm. Bailey remained on the stoop, his hands in his pockets.

"I had a great time," she said, laughing nervously.

"Good, because I did too." His eyes shone in the semidarkness, the angular planes of his face alternately shadowed and highlighted. "You surprise me sometimes, Ginny."

She swallowed. "I sometimes surprise myself."

"Can I have a kiss?"

Her throat went completely dry. "Since when have you become such a gentleman?"

His grin was slow and warm as he leaned forward. "It's my new strategy."

She raised her mouth to his and he kissed her, soft and teasing at first, then with mounting urgency. His arms circled her waist to pull her closer, and she looped her arms around his neck, tangling her fingers in his hair. Their moans mingled and echoed into each other's mouth, fueling the fire between them. Virginia felt her resistance dissolve as he lowered his hands to press her against him. If he asked right now, she'd give him anything she had to offer.

Suddenly his embrace loosened, and his kiss relaxed.

He raised his head and stepped back from her, his breathing ragged, his lips pressed together. "I think it's time for me to go." He inhaled deeply, then gave her a slow, heart-stopping grin. "I'll swing by around ten in the morning, okay?"

She nodded.

"Good night."

"Good night," she murmured, her nerves still quaking, her muscles still tense, her mouth still burning.

After closing the door she walked into the darkness of the living room and peeked out the curtain. Bailey started his car, then slowly pulled out of her driveway, only to stop at the curb. He looked toward her house, and Virginia debated whether to turn on a light or give him some other signal, but then he shifted into gear and drove away.

She didn't have long to ponder the events of the evening, because her parents arrived soon afterward with a well-fed, well-entertained Chad. It warmed her heart to see him accept their good-bye hugs and kisses. They asked Ginny if he could go camping Monday night, and she agreed.

After her parents left, Ginny decided to confront Chad about the locket right away, because it didn't seem right to pretend that everything was okay.

"Chad," she said after he'd told her about his evening, "I've lost something and I hope you'll be able to help me find it."

His eyes narrowed slightly, then he shrugged, a little too casually, she thought. "What is it?"

"It's my locket with your baby picture in it."

"I haven't seen it," he said too quickly, reaching for the television remote.

She stopped him with her hand, covering his fingers with hers. "It's very special to me and I hope if you find it, you'll bring it to me. I might have lost it outside when we were washing the car."

"Okay," he said in an annoyed voice. "What's the big deal anyway? It's just a necklace with a dumb old picture in it."

"It means everything to me," she whispered.

"Kind of like my game?" he asked, convincing her he'd taken it.

"Please give it back to me," she said.

"I don't have your stupid necklace." He pulled his hand from underneath hers. "Leave me alone."

Later when she stepped into his shadowed bedroom to soak in his sleeping form, her eyes swam with tears. Would she ever make peace with Chad and Bailey at the same time?

One step forward, then two steps back. And now she was going to spend the entire weekend with both of them.

CHAPTER TWELVE

THE SHENOWAY FARMHOUSE was quiet as they unlocked the front door. "Would you mind getting the picnic together while I feed the cattle?" Bailey asked. "It shouldn't take more than forty-five minutes."

"Not at all," Virginia said, only a little apprehensive about rattling around in the house by herself.

"Can I help?" Chad asked Bailey.

"Absolutely," Bailey said. "I expect you to pitch in when you're here."

"Sure!" Chad agreed.

"I'll take the luggage upstairs," Bailey said. "You help Ginny take the groceries to the kitchen."

Chad didn't argue, but she could tell his heart wasn't in it when he thunked the bags down on the counter.

"Thanks," she said.

"Whatever."

He turned and walked out, then she heard Bailey come back downstairs. "We'll be back soon—be sure to put on your bathing suit," he called from the living room, the screen door slapping closed.

"Whatever," she mumbled, hands on hips, eyeing the mounds of groceries. Her son had made it perfectly clear all morning that as far as he was concerned, she didn't exist. She'd woken to ear-splitting music coming from his room, which he reduced to just plain loud when she pounded on his door. He'd refused to come out of his room or answer her until he heard the doorbell signaling Bailey's arrival, then he'd ridden over with Bailey leaving her to follow behind in her car, solo.

And her locket hadn't shown up, but she still held out hope it would turn up soon.

At least Bailey was cheerful and friendly this morning, which meant he hadn't lost as much sleep as she had over their good-bye kiss. Sighing, she began to pull out food and assemble sandwiches.

Once she'd packed the basket with as much food and drink as possible and straightened the kitchen, she felt restless, and decided to unpack the clothes she'd brought. She peeked into the guest rooms alternately to see where Bailey had placed their bags. Chad's duffel sat just inside the first room. She frowned when she saw Bailey's gym bag in the room next to Chad's room. She chewed the inside of her cheek as realization began to dawn. Sure enough, she found her bag sitting in the room she and Bailey had once shared. A large vase of cut flowers sat on the dresser, and an envelope propped against it read *Ginny*.

With one eye on the card, she changed into her bathing suit, then pulled on black knit shorts and a pink T-shirt. She picked up the envelope, her heart pounding in anticipation, and sat on the edge of the bed. With trembling fingers she loosened the flap and withdrew a card covered with muted watercolor designs. The inside had no preprinted message, only a few lines in Bailey's handwriting.

Thanks for such an enjoyable evening. I look forward to the day when I don't have to leave you after kissing you good night. Bailey

Her smile extended all the way to her toes. Her skin tingled and she felt as giddy as a teenager. Hugging herself, she lay back onto the soft bed, suddenly wishing Bailey was stretched out beside her. She looked around the room and sighed. It might not be so bad sleeping in here after all.

The screen door slammed downstairs, and Virginia shot up. She smoothed the covers and tucked the card back into the envelope, then walked to the staircase landing.

Bailey stood alone at the bottom. The sight of him sent jolts of sexual awareness through her limbs. He'd traded his polo shirt for a snug white T-shirt. His face and arms glistened with sweat, and bits of hay stuck to his skin. His jeans were tucked into a pair of old workboots. He dabbed at his forehead with a bandanna. She stopped on the next to last step, a couple of feet above him, her body tingling.

"Hey," he said, smiling up at her.

"Hey, yourself. Thanks for the card."

He wet his lips. "You're welcome."

"And the flowers."

He nodded.

She gazed into his eyes, and descended one more step. "You look... hot."

He studied her carefully. "I am... hot."

"Where's Chad?"

"He found Jean Ann's tire swing. I thought I'd take a shower before we go on the picnic."

Her fantasies whirled free. "A shower?"

"Uh-huh," he said just as slowly. "A hot shower."

She stepped down again, coming to stand within inches of him. "A hot, soapy shower?"

He reached for her and crushed her into a deep kiss. She tasted the salt from his skin and felt the heat from his mouth. She inhaled the musky scent of him, and her legs weakened. Her tongue swirled over the smooth surface of his teeth, then probed deeper. Their kiss became more urgent as their hunger for each other escalated. She clenched at the muscles on his back, feeling the soaked, flimsy shirt beneath her fingers. She tore it from his waistband and raked her nails against the moist, warm skin of his back.

Behind them, the screen door slammed. "Oh, brother," Chad said loudly.

They parted quickly, both breathing hard, and stared at their son.

Bailey shoved his hand through his hair. "I thought you were on the tire swing," he said raggedly, a hint of annoyance in his tone.

"I thought you were going to take a shower," Chad said, just as annoyed.

"I was," Bailey sighed in exasperation. "I am." He climbed the stairs in long strides.

Her chest rose and fell as she fought to regain control of her breathing. Chad stared at her with narrowed eyes until she started to squirm. "You got hay all over you," he said, then turned and walked back outside.

She looked down and saw bits of straw on her arms and clothing, then stepped out on the front porch to brush herself off. Chad sat in an old metal glider a few feet away. She walked over and leaned on the rail near him.

"It's a great day for a picnic."

"Yeah, if we ever get there."

After a few seconds of silence Virginia tilted her head and asked, "Chad, does it bother you when Bailey kisses me?"

He looked at her and rolled his eyes. "No."

"Then why did you act so mad just now?"

He looked away and said nothing.

"Chad?"

He jerked his head toward her. "Because," he yelled, "you're always in the way, that's why! I want to spend time with my dad, and every time I turn around he's kissing you instead!"

She flinched. "Chad, I—"

"I don't want to hear anything you have to say!" He jumped up and leapt off the porch, then disappeared around the house.

Virginia sat down on the porch steps and contemplated her next move. Sighing, she rolled her head back and closed her eyes. Even a fool could see where this flirtation with Bailey was leading. The question she had to answer was whether she believed he'd become a man with staying power; otherwise, she couldn't afford to invest any more of her life and love in Bailey Kallihan.

The one thing she was sure of was that Chad needed to be with Bailey. Maybe it was his age or maybe it was his genetic tendency, but he flourished around his father and Bailey benefited from Chad's company as well.

She opened her eyes. So where did that leave her?

The door opened and she sat up. His hair still wet from the shower, Bailey walked out wearing navy swim trunks, a pale gray T-shirt, and low-top athletic shoes. He smelled like soap and carried the picnic basket in one arm, an old quilt and three faded life jackets in the other. "What are you thinking about?"

"You," she said.

He sat down beside her. "What about me?"

She looked him in the eye. "Where do you see yourself in five years?"

His eyebrows knitted and he toyed with the frayed thread of a life jacket. "I plan to be right here at Shenoway, but I don't think that's what you're asking."

"No, it isn't."

He lifted his gaze to hers. "Ginny, I can't imagine any other woman in my life except you."

Tears gathered in her eyes.

"Uh-oh, the tears I can't handle." He leaned over to kiss her nose and she smiled. "That's better—are you ready?" He stood up and offered her a semi-free hand.

"Yeah." She pulled herself to her feet and took the life jackets. "I don't know where Chad's run off to, though."

Bailey put two fingers in his mouth and whistled shrilly. Chad burst out of a grove of trees, carrying his slingshot.

"Can we go now?" he yelled, running toward them, making it perfectly clear the adults had been the holdup all along.

"If you carry your weight." Bailey tossed him the quilt.

The walk to Milton Creek, the Kallihans' west property line, took about thirty minutes, but it was well worth it. They were lucky enough to have a family of persistent beavers on their land who'd dammed up a portion of the creek, just enough to form a deep swimming hole.

Virginia's cheeks warmed when she saw the shady blue-green pool. She and Bailey had skinny-dipped there on more than one occasion when they'd dated. She caught his eye, and from his smile knew he, too, was remembering. In fact, she suspected that Chad might have been conceived on this very bank.

Chad's expression was dubious. "It looks deep."

"It is in some places," Bailey said. "Can you swim?"

Chin jutting, Chad said, "Sure… a little."

Immediately, Virginia said, "Then you should wear your life jacket."

"No," Chad whined. "That's for sissies!"

"Hey," Bailey said, raising an eyebrow. "You heard Ginny."

"All right," he grumbled, frowning.

They spread the large quilt on a mossy stretch of bank, the weeping willow above them providing dappled sun and shade as its spindly branches swung to and fro. Within minutes Bailey had stripped off his shirt and shoes and waded into the water. Virginia watched the muscles in his back ripple as he made a series of shallow dives to stake out the depth of the water.

He surfaced to their far right and threw his head back. "It's deepest here—more than fifteen feet—everywhere else it seems to be running from five to eight feet." He swam back to the bank using powerful strokes, then stood up and waded out.

Virginia was unable to tear her eyes from his dripping body. The water found every rippling valley as it rushed down. The hem of his nylon trunks dragged, pulling the waistband a half inch beneath his tan line, and outlining his manhood in jarring clarity. He walked over to them and shook like a shaggy dog, laughing when she squealed and Chad jumped up to run out of range.

Bailey lowered himself to the quilt with a sigh, stretching out his long legs in front of him. "Feels good, doesn't it?" he asked her. "Coming back here, I mean."

"Yes," she agreed, glad it felt special to him too. She pulled her T-shirt over her head a bit self-consciously. His gaze roved over her body as eagerly as hers had taken in his. To her embarrassment, her nipples hardened, plain to see in the pale pink swimsuit.

"What's for lunch?" he asked with one eyebrow cocked.

She reached over and gave his shoulder a playful shove, then he grabbed her hand and kissed the fleshy area between her index finger and thumb. The contact from his tongue triggered head-to-toe responses. Remembering Chad's accusation, she glanced around nervously, then said, "I'll get out the food."

"I'll take him in before he eats." Bailey grabbed two life jackets as he stood up.

While she unpacked sandwiches and opened bowls of coleslaw and baked beans, Virginia kept an eye on her men. Chad looked pale and thin in his baggy trunks, but his shoulders were wide and his legs were long, both guarantees that his father's good build would be his destiny. They spent several minutes collecting smooth stones for Chad's slingshot ammunition, tying them up in Bailey's bandanna, then they both waded out into the deeper water. Chad seemed tentative at first, his eyes widening in fright when his feet couldn't touch bottom. But he soon learned to trust the life jacket, and Bailey showed him some basic strokes and kicks he could do while wearing the flotation device.

"Hey, Ginny!" Bailey called after a few minutes. "Aren't you coming in?"

"I don't know..."

He began to make chicken noises and flap his arms, Chad readily joining in.

Laughing, she stood up. "Okay, okay." She slid her shorts down her legs, a move that earned her a catcall from Bailey. She waded in, strapping on her jacket.

The water felt wonderfully cool and invigorating to her warm skin, the rocks smooth to her bare feet. She swam out to them in a few strokes, then rolled over on her back to wet her hair. Bailey's fingers grazed her toes, which triggered a tickling match, which triggered an all-out water fight, reminiscent of many.

Finally they were all exhausted and traipsed back to the bank to refuel.

Chad and Bailey both ate so much, she began to wonder if she'd packed enough food—she'd forgotten how much food a hungry male could put away. But at last the two were sated, stretched out in the sun, and patting their stomachs as if they'd spent every Saturday of their lives together, dozing away the afternoon.

* * *

Bailey opened his right eye and glanced at Ginny. Her eyes were closed, but she wasn't asleep. He opened the left eye and glanced at Chad. Definitely snoresville. Quietly rolling up on his right side, he stared down into her face for several seconds. If ever he'd seen a classic beauty, it was Ginny. But more than beautiful, she was striking—a head-turner—with those huge eyes and full lips... a look all her own... memorable.

To that he could surely attest. Had a single day passed since their divorce when he hadn't thought of her at least once?

"Hey, beautiful."

She started and her eyes snapped open. "Oh." She put a hand to her chest. "Bailey, you scared me to death."

"Ginny," he said gravely, *"you* scared *me* to death."

When she realized he was serious, she frowned. "What?"

"When we were married," he said slowly, "you turned so serious and so responsible overnight, I was scared."

"Bailey, we were having a baby—"

He put a finger to her lips to stop her. "I know. You *should* have been serious and responsible, but I should have been too, and I wasn't. I was scared because I didn't want to change."

Her eyes misted and she breathed heavily for a few seconds, holding his gaze. "And now?"

"And now," he said hoarsely, leaning over her, "I'm strong enough to change." He lowered his mouth to hers, a feathery, airy kiss. He sampled the tastes and textures of her mouth slowly, with no driving need, no immediacy, no straining. Just an unhurried, thorough exploration of her plump, memorable mouth. She moaned and offered up the velvety tip of her tongue for his to dance with.

A loud splash broke the silence, startling both of them. He jerked his head around. Chad was gone!

"Help!" he heard him call from the water, followed by the sounds of thrashing arms and legs.

Ginny was instantly on her feet. "He went under!"

Bailey stood and ran to the water's edge and made a shallow dive. He got a handful of the boy's trunks and yanked him to the surface. Chad lunged for his neck, wrapping his strong little arms and legs around Bailey's body, nearly dragging him beneath the water as well. Bailey swallowed a mouthful of water, coughed, then shifted Chad's back to his own chest and slowly swam back to the bank.

Ginny half dragged Chad from the water. He appeared shaken, coughing violently. "Are you okay?" she gasped, bent over him, clutching his hand to her heart.

"Yeah," he murmured, struggling to sit up. "I'm okay."

Still gasping for his own breath, Bailey watched as Ginny's expression changed in a split second. "How dare you sneak off—I told you to wear your life jacket! I'm not strong enough to pull you from the water. If Bailey hadn't been here—" She burst into tears.

Bailey pulled her away from Chad, up and into his arms. "Shh," he said, rubbing her back. "It's okay."

But Chad had recovered enough to stand, and his defenses were up. "I didn't sneak off! If you two hadn't been rolling around—"

"That's enough." Bailey held up a finger in warning. He turned his attention back to Ginny, who cried silently in his arms. "Let's go home," he whispered, stroking her hair.

After a few seconds she nodded, sniffing mightily and swiping at her cheeks.

He looked at Chad. "Start packing things up."

The late afternoon sun was unforgivingly hot, bearing down on Bailey's sudden headache. They walked back to Shenoway in near silence. Conscious of the warring emotions between Chad and Ginny, Bailey knew it was up to him to make reparations. "How about going to see a movie?"

Chad looked suspicious. "Which one?"

Bailey shrugged. "I'm sure we can find one we all agree on."

Chad looked sideways at Ginny, then back to him. "I doubt it."

"Oh, come on," Bailey urged. "Popcorn, nachos—"

"Hot dogs, chocolate-covered peanuts," Chad finished, his eyes lighting up.

Ginny laughed softly, and they both looked at her. "I've never seen two people so preoccupied with food."

Bailey grinned, glad to see her sense of humor returning. "How about it?"

"Sounds good to me," she said.

"Me too," Chad chorused.

Two hours later they were walking into the theater to see the summer's biggest action thriller. They juggled seats for a couple of minutes until Chad finally settled happily between them. Bailey strongly suspected the seating arrangement was his son's attempt to keep them apart. It was becoming clearer to him that Chad was trying to squeeze Ginny out of the picture. No wonder she was having such a hard time with him at home.

Bailey looked over at Chad and pursed his lips. He was planning to take Ginny to the meadow the following day and tell her about the house. He hoped she would see how much he wanted them all to be together. Then he would have to have a talk with his son.

* * *

Chad's little separation scheme hadn't gone unnoticed by Virginia. She looked over at her son and shook her head. He wanted Bailey all to himself, and she was his only competition. Chad had made it clear he didn't like to see them kissing, which surprised her a little. If he were so eager to live with Bailey, one would think he'd be matchmaking instead of trying to keep them apart.

She shuddered when she thought of the swimming incident. She felt sure he'd jumped in on purpose to break up their kiss, not realizing how dangerous the stunt could be. Then he'd been quick to induce guilt by implying they were too wrapped up in each other to keep an eye on him. Virginia bit her bottom lip. The worst part was the knowledge that he might have drowned if not for Bailey—a sobering fact that once again stirred her own doubts about being able to take care of her son.

Perhaps rekindling her relationship with Bailey would be the answer to their problems. If they remarried, Chad could live with Bailey, which would make the two of them happy, and she could share her son's development as well. She was optimistic enough to think that someday she would be able to have a good relationship with Chad, but she knew the chances of that were slim if she remained the single obstacle between him living with his father.

And, she had to admit, a future with Bailey was not entirely unappealing. His confession to her today had gone a long way in repairing the holes in her confidence about his level of commitment. Perhaps he was driven in part by his desire to be with Chad, but if he truly loved her—

She looked over at her ex-husband and he winked at her.

The lights lowered and the movie started rolling, beginning with a spectacular explosion, then jumping from scene to dramatic scene. Every brief kissing scene was accompanied by Chad's loud "Yuck!" followed by a pointed glance in Virginia's direction. Chad's hostility toward her seemed to be growing every day.

The drive home was a little more relaxed, the afternoon's incident fading with distance. Virginia's thoughts turned to her decision to allow, even foster, the relationship growing between her and Bailey. She wasn't sure where it was going, but she felt good about its prospects. If she was going to give it her best shot, she'd have to do more than just abandon her previous plan to be the one who appears to care the least—she'd have to make herself vulnerable to him again, a notion that shook her to the core.

"We're still going horseback riding tomorrow, aren't we?" Chad asked Bailey.

"Uh-huh. I want to show you more of the farm."

"Great!"

"It's straight to bed when you get to the house, so you won't be tired tomorrow," Bailey added.

Chad sighed. "Okay."

Panic bolted through Virginia as a thought occurred to her. She knew Bailey well enough to realize that coming to her bed would be a likely move—perhaps the reason he'd put her things in "their" room to begin with. Had he planned all along to seduce her that night? The idea partly annoyed, partly thrilled her. Her nipples pebbled with anticipation. If he came, she knew she would let him stay.

At the house she felt virginally tense while she made sure Chad had everything he needed before she closed his bedroom door. Bailey stood in the hall when she turned around.

"Will he be all right?" he asked unnecessarily.

"I think so," she said softly.

"Will you?" he asked, his eyes smoldering, "You had quite a scare today."

Virginia swallowed. "I'll be fine." After many seconds of gazing into his eyes, she nervously pushed a strand of hair behind her ear. "I guess I'd better turn in." She turned to go. "Good night."

"I certainly hope so," she heard him murmur, leaving her certain he would make an appearance before morning.

Her hands shook as she undressed and showered quickly in the bathroom, but she couldn't be sure how much of her nervousness was due to memories resurrected by the room and how much was due to Bailey's impending visit. She tried to calm herself afterward by massaging perfumed lotion into her skin, using long, soothing strokes. The sole nightgown she'd brought was papery white cotton, short and adorned with ribbon roses where the thin straps met the smocked bodice. Despite its near transparency, it suddenly looked very girlish to her. She slipped on sheer white panties, then pulled the gown over her head and switched off the light. After toweling her hair dry in the semidarkness, she sat on the edge of the bed, brushing fullness into her fine-textured hair, gazing out the splendid window at the moonlit view.

Thirty minutes passed, then forty-five, and she was beginning to think she'd misinterpreted their exchange, when a faint knock sounded at the door. Her heart jumped to her throat, and she stood with her back to the window. Her voice didn't work, but she didn't have to answer because the knob turned and the door opened.

Bailey paused in the doorway, wearing white boxers, his hand on the doorknob. She inhaled deeply, then realized her body was completely silhouetted to him by the light of the window.

"Ginny?" he ventured to say, his voice hoarse.

"Bailey."

"I thought you'd be in bed by now."

She slid her tongue over her lips. "I was waiting for you."

He stood motionless for a few seconds, then stepped inside the room and closed the door noiselessly behind him. She waited for him at the window, holding her breath.

Inches from her, he stopped. "You look like a dream, standing in the moonlight," he whispered.

She exhaled. "But I'm not a dream. Touch me, Bailey."

With a deep groan he pulled her to him in a hungry kiss. His arousal was already hard against her belly. He cupped her bottom and squeezed her against him, then slid his hands beneath her gown and caressed the back of her waist, her spine, her shoulder blades.

Fire spread through her limbs, and she weakened under his seeking hands. She moaned into his mouth and ran her palms over his muscled back, reveling in the smoothness of his skin. He smelled of soap and talc, his hair curled damp against his neck. She buried her fingers in its softness, pressing his mouth harder against hers.

He dragged his mouth away with a moan, then picked her up and laid her on the bed. Before he joined her, he stripped off his boxers, his erection and muscled behind outlined to her briefly. She gasped when he rolled in next to her, scooping her up to hold her in an iron embrace.

"Ginny," he whispered, "I thought I'd never get to make love to you again."

He began kissing her ear, then moved to her neck, then lower, teasing a nipple through the thin fabric of her gown. His tongue left a trail of fire, causing her muscles to dance and her body to moisten itself in preparation for him. Lifting the sheer garment out of his way, he fell upon her breasts, greedily kissing and sucking, the electric barbs paralyzing her with pleasure.

He eased down her panties, moaning as his fingers encountered her wet anticipation. Virginia's knees rose at his explosive invasion, clenching around his fingers, urging him deeper. Using his thumb, he massaged her most sensitive spot, moving his fingers inside her in unison. The waves began to build, and she rode them, moaning his name. "Bailey, oh, Bailey... "

At the crest, she bit down on his shoulder, remembering with sudden clarity how quickly he could bring her to climax. He brought her back down gently, slowly. She groaned in utter satisfaction.

He grinned and whispered, "Like riding a bicycle."

She laughed, swinging at him playfully.

His arousal branded her thigh, hot and unyielding. She reached to encircle him with her hands, rousing a sharp gasp from his open mouth. Moistening him with her own wetness, she stroked him slowly, the way she knew he liked it, then began to move under him, with him, as if he were already inside her.

His head went back, a look of rapture on his face. "Ginny," he whispered, "you know just what to do to make me crazy." He lowered his mouth to draw on her breast, and she arched into him, her thighs sliding against each other, slick with satisfaction and growing need. Bailey moved lower still, kissing her abdomen and navel, nipping at the outer edges of her private mound, licking her thighs. Suddenly his tongue probed her womanhood, and Virginia gasped, throwing her head back. For several vaulting moments he made love to her with his mouth as she writhed under him, then once again carried her past the brink of ecstasy.

He slid back up to kiss her mouth, his lips tasting of her musk. "I can't hold out much longer," he gasped, "I want you too much."

"I'm not protected," she warned him.

Then he laughed. And she laughed.

"Which is what got us in trouble in the first place," he said. "But this time," he added with a quick, tender kiss, "I planned ahead." From out of nowhere appeared a condom, which he broke open quickly and unrolled on his erection.

He went to her swiftly, kissing her deeply as he probed her entrance. She was more than ready for him. His breath was ragged. "I have to have you now," he said, taking a deep breath, then plunging inside.

Virginia's body convulsed when he entered her. He filled her completely, physically and emotionally. She wrapped her legs around his body and clenched her inner muscles, letting him ride her as slowly as he wished. She threw her arms over her head, her fingers wrapping around the metal bars of the headboard to allow her more leverage to move under him.

Bailey was a vocal lover; she knew which of her movements he found the most pleasurable by listening to his moans. Arching to meet his thrusts, she followed his pace from sensual to urgent to frantic until he shuddered on top of her, moaning low and long with each spasm. Bailey's breath was ragged and shallow, his sighs satisfied. Their rhythm slowed to a lazy grind, then stilled.

She lay beneath him, his weight comforting and warm. She had come full circle... back to Bailey's arms, where she'd always belonged.

CHAPTER THIRTEEN

"JUST RELAX," Virginia said to Chad. "Horses can sense when you're afraid."

"I'm not afraid," he scoffed, but his eyes told a different story. "Am I doing it right, Bailey?" he asked, pointedly ignoring Virginia's attempt to instruct him.

Before he stepped in, Bailey looked to Virginia with a raised eyebrow. She nodded for him to go ahead, and slowed her horse to fall in behind Bailey's and Chad's mounts.

She yawned, then winced when her horse shifted, the saddle rubbing against too-tender skin. A not-so-marvelous reminder of Bailey's marvelous night of lovemaking. Predawn, he'd slipped from her room to prevent any awkward hallway encounters with Chad.

Strange, but despite the passionate night they'd shared, she felt irritable this morning—headachy, short-tempered—nothing that could even be remotely called afterglow. As the morning wore on, the more she replayed last night's script, the more she suspected her unease was due to the fact that not once had Bailey mentioned the word *love*. Or *marriage*. Or *commitment*.

"Hey, Ginny," he called, interrupting her thoughts.

"Yeah?"

He stopped his horse until she caught up. "Let's ride over to the meadow."

She swallowed. Not really in the mood for more unsettling memories, she stalled. "The meadow? Hasn't someone built a house there?"

"Just getting ready to," he said. "The footers were poured Friday."

The knowledge saddened her beyond belief. She couldn't imagine anyone else living in their meadow, overlooking their pond. But if it didn't bother Bailey, she supposed she couldn't get too upset about it. "Sure, why not?"

She knew the way by heart, but followed a few paces behind so she could be alone with her reactions. Since they rode slowly for Chad's benefit, it took several minutes to climb the gentle rise that leveled and gave way to the north meadow.

Her heart sank. It was more beautiful than ever—more lush, more inviting, more stirring. The pond was about the size of a football field, opaque green in the center, brown around the muddy banks, edged with giant sunflowers, cattails, and thistle.

On the back of the property, a framing semicircle of trees had matured and would provide the family and their home with valuable shade. She squinted and spotted the wide strip of land that had been staked off, saw the concrete corners that were the beginnings of the foundation. She felt as if something had just slipped through her fingers and out of reach.

"What do you think, Ginny?" Bailey asked.

She stared out over the meadow, her throat tight. "The owner is lucky to have this place."

"Yeah, well, I'm just a lucky guy."

She jerked around to look at him, amazed. "You?"

"Yeah, me, a homeowner, imagine that." His eyes crinkled with pleasure.

"Wow," Chad said, his voice and eyes excited. "Will it be a big house?"

Virginia could see the wheels turning in his head, and she felt a flash of panic. Of course he'd want to live there with Bailey.

"Big enough," Bailey said.

Her stomach churned. "Th-that's great, Bailey." She forced a smile to her lips. "When will it be finished?"

"If the weather cooperates, about three months."

Her alarm increased. "That soon?"

"Wow! I can't wait!" Chad said.

"But with my new job, I may not be able to get out here during the day as much as I'd like to check on the progress."

"What kind of house are you building?" she asked, her voice weak.

He looked into her eyes, then said, "I'm sure you'd find the plans familiar."

She dropped her gaze and pretended to be engrossed with adjusting her horse's halter. "Those old plans we ordered from a magazine?"

"With a few modifications. I guess I have my sights set a little higher now than I did in my twenties."

He was building *their* house in *their* meadow—did he intend to ask her to share it with him?

"Look at that tree!" Chad yelled, pointing across the meadow. "It's huge!"

Virginia looked up and smiled in spite of her muddled thoughts. It was Bailey's tree, the one his father had planted for him.

"Want to ride over?" Bailey asked Chad, who responded with an eager nod.

The three of them rode abreast slowly, and Bailey recounted the story of Chad's grandfather planting the tree. The sprawling oak was a magnificent sight, having grown exponentially since she'd last seen it. She estimated the trunk at ten feet in diameter.

"That's awesome!" Chad exclaimed.

Bailey smiled. "I'm glad you think so," he said as he reined in next to a smaller, lone oak tree, about fifteen feet tall. "Because this tree is yours."

"Really?" Chad asked.

Virginia was as surprised as Chad.

"Yep. I took an acorn from my tree and planted it the day you were born."

Chad didn't say anything, just stared at the tree with an awestruck expression.

The news shook Virginia to the core. "You never told me, Bailey."

He shifted in his saddle. "I wasn't even sure it would germinate, and by the time it started growing..." He trailed off and smiled sadly.

By the time it started growing, Lois Green had ripped their son from their lives. She bit her tongue—God, would she ever stop hurting?

"You mean that tree is the same age as I am?" Chad asked, grinning.

"To the day," Bailey responded.

Chad looked at the older tree. "Is it okay to climb it?"

Bailey pursed his lips as if he were pondering the question. "Well, if you're going to find a good place to build a tree house, I guess you'd better scout it out with a good climb."

"Oh, boy!" Chad said, kneeing his horse forward.

"Be careful," Bailey called sternly. "Walk him over to the fence to climb down, just like you mounted, then tie him off like I showed you."

"Okay, Bailey."

Virginia watched the exchange, feeling more and more like an outsider. The house, the tree, the open space, the paternal guidance—in Chad's eyes she could never compete with any of those things. Her face must have betrayed her emotions, because Bailey asked, "Ginny, what's wrong?"

She shook her head, smiling sadly. "Chad loves it here."

"I loved it when I was his age too." Bailey dismounted, then offered her a hand.

She swung down, her body inches from his, her head still spinning.

Bailey held her gaze for a few seconds, then cleared his throat. "Listen, Ginny, I don't know if this is the right time, but I realize you're having a rough time with Chad, and I was hoping you'd consider letting him move in with me at Rita's while you and I work things through."

Stunned, she only stared at him. Let Chad move in with him while they "worked things through"? "I don't understand," she murmured.

"Well, I've been giving this some thought," he said, his words sounding rehearsed. "School will be starting in a few weeks, so it would be best to get him settled in now, rather than move him in the middle of the school year."

"Move him in the middle of the school year?" she parroted.

"Well, yeah, the house should be finished by mid-October."

Her mouth tightened in dawning realization. It had all been a ploy. Butter her up to let Chad move in with him, knowing full well it would be next to impossible to revert if she and Bailey couldn't "work things through."

"No," she said.

He frowned slightly. "What?"

"I said no," she said, her voice louder. "Chad's not coming here to live. He belongs with me—his mother."

"But I don't want to live with you!" Chad shouted.

She spun in surprise, as did Bailey. They hadn't heard him approaching on foot.

"Chad—" She took a step toward him.

"No!" He backed up. "Tell her, Bailey, tell her about our plan!"

"Chad." Bailey's voice held a warning note.

Virginia narrowed her eyes. "What plan?"

Chad turned on her, his eyes flashing. "Bailey told me last week that I could move in with him and live at Shenoway, but you weren't supposed to know because you'd probably try to ruin it like you're trying to ruin it now."

Her blood ran cold, her limbs were paralyzed. No wonder Chad had been alienating her more and more. Bailey must have promised him it would be just the two of them, without her in the way. All she could manage was a steady stare at Bailey. What had he said one night at her house? That he would have to resort to drastic measures? How foolish could she have been? A few flowers, a few kisses, and she'd jumped right back into his arms like a naïve coed.

"Ginny." He raised his hand in stop-sign fashion. "He's taking my words out of context."

"You can't keep me from living with my father!" Chad yelled.

"That's enough, Chad," Bailey said, his voice low and commanding. "I need to talk to your mother alone."

"She's not my mother!" Chad shouted as he walked away sniffling, pulling out his slingshot.

"Be careful with that thing." He turned to her. "Ginny—"

"How dare you," she said through gritted teeth, tears scalding her eyes. "How dare you pretend to care for me, take me out, even make lo"—she choked—"have *sex* with me... it was all a setup."

"Ginny," he growled, clasping her arms, "listen to me! I meant that I wanted us all to be here together—Chad misunderstood, that's all."

She pulled away. "Don't touch me." Turning her head, she yelled, "Chad, come with me. We're going home."

Virginia climbed back into her saddle, avoiding Bailey's eyes. She burned with humiliation... her heart felt raw.

"No." Chad jutted out his chin, then rocketed another stone onto the pond's rippling surface.

"Get on your horse and come with me," she said evenly.

"Do it," Bailey said to his son, his voice sounding resigned.

She watched as Chad moved to obey Bailey, biting her tongue to control her fury. Bailey had to get in one last demonstration of how well Chad minded him and how well he ignored her. Wheeling her horse away from Bailey, she waited until Chad's mount caught up with hers, then began a slow walk back.

Bailey watched them ride away through watery eyes, his hands fisted in frustration. How had things gone from promising to impossible in the span of a few minutes?

* * *

"But I don't want to go," Chad said, his tone belligerent as he slung his duffel into the trunk.

Ginny shut the trunk lid firmly. "I'm sorry. I know you don't want to go, but we have to."

"But why?" he persisted.

"Because," she said calmly, swinging into the driver's seat, "we can't stay here."

"I can."

She bit the inside of her cheek as she started the engine and shifted into gear. "You're coming home with me."

"I hate that place—it's boring."

"I've been thinking about that. I'll talk to a realtor next week about finding a house with a bigger yard."

"Big deal," he said miserably.

"I'm trying to make things better for you," she said, looking both ways before pulling into traffic and driving away from Shenoway.

He looked out the window for several seconds quietly, then asked, "Why?"

She frowned slightly. "Why am I trying to make things better for you?"

"Yeah, you couldn't care less about me."

Virginia nearly ran off the road, then slowed her speed. "How could you say such a thing?"

"Because it's true," he said. "When I got in trouble at the mall, you wanted the cops to take me away."

She gasped. "I didn't want them to take you away, I only wanted you to understand the consequence of your actions."

"You won't let me do things by myself because you don't trust me."

"That's not true," she said, shaking her head. "I guess I'm a little overprotective—I'll work on it."

"You said you hated my mom."

She closed her eyes briefly. "I said those words out of frustration and anger. I wish I could take them back. I don't hate Lois, I hate only that you and I lost all that time together."

"You broke my game," he said, his voice growing more angry.

She inhaled deeply. "You're right, I did, but it was an accident. I swear I didn't see it lying there."

"Then you accused me of stealing your locket."

She bit her lip to stem her welling tears. He was building quite a convincing case against her mothering skills. Despite her intuition about the locket, he was right, she had no proof. "I apologize, Chad," she said in a low voice. "It must have fallen off while I was wearing it and I didn't notice."

"And now you're using me to get back at Bailey."

Virginia's speed fell off and the car behind her blared its horn. "What did you say?"

"You're using me—"

"You're way out of line, young man."

"It's true," he yelled. "You didn't mind him coming over to see me as long as he kissed you all the time! Now you're mad because he wants it to be just the two of us, so you're not going to let him see me at all!"

His words reverberated in her head, triggering a low hum of panic. Chad was treading closer to the truth than she cared to admit. She had begun to anticipate Bailey's visits nearly as much as Chad did. Now, after discovering he was only trying to get next to Chad, she had retaliated by taking Chad away. In one week she'd already made the mistake she'd seen coworkers and acquaintances make, the one thing she'd promised herself she'd never do... use her child to get back at the other parent.

Tears slid down her cheeks. "I'm sorry," she whispered. "I'm so sorry."

He frowned, exasperated. "You don't have to cry." He shifted in his seat to look out the window.

But the dawning truth laid her heart wide open, and she couldn't stop the steady stream of tears.

CHAPTER FOURTEEN

"YOU LOOK A LITTLE PEAKED, DEAR," Peg said, touching Virginia's arm.

"I'm fine, Mom, just tired, that's all." She sipped her coffee, trying to avoid her mother's probing gaze until Chad and her father returned from loading his things into the RV.

"Ginny, being a mother is difficult," she said. "And you've had it much harder than most. Don't be too rough on yourself—he's a good boy."

Virginia nodded, smiling faintly.

"Is Bailey helping?"

Another nod. "He's great with Chad, and Chad adores him."

Peg laughed softly. "You know, I kind of wondered if you and Bailey might get back together."

Her heart squeezed. "No chance of that."

"Oh? He seems to have grown up a lot since you were married."

"He has," she admitted. "He's building a house, he's cut back on drinking, and he has a new job." She tilted her head and bit her bottom lip. "Mom, I know this is hypothetical, but if you and Dad had divorced, who would I have lived with?"

Her mother's eyebrows inched upward as she considered the question. "Probably me, if only because of logistics."

"What if I'd wanted to live with Dad?" Virginia pressed, hoping for some kernel of wisdom.

Peg sighed. Her mother could see where her questions were leading. "And your dad wanted it too?"

"Yes," Virginia said softly. "Very much."

"You're asking if I would break my own heart to save my child's?"

"Yes, I suppose that's what I'm asking."

After a long sip of coffee, Peg raised her gaze to her daughter's. "If I truly believed you would have been at least as healthy and more happy with your father, then I would have let you go. Especially," she added, "if you had been a boy." She smiled sadly. "Like I said, being a mother is difficult."

"How do I know if I'm making the right choice?"

Peg squeezed Virginia's hand. "You don't."

The front door creaked open, then two pairs of heavy footsteps came toward them.

"Peg?" her father called good-naturedly as he entered the kitchen. "If you're finished yakking, we men have got everything loaded up and ready to go." He winked at Virginia, and she stood to give him a hug and a kiss.

"Bye, Pop," she said, then turned to her mother and gave her an extra-hard squeeze. "Thanks," she whispered.

They filed to the door, Virginia trailing. "Chad," she said.

He'd been strangely quiet and cautious around her since her tearful trip home the day before. "Yeah?" he said, his voice sounding normal for a change.

She reached over to brush back his bangs, love washing over her at this tentative contact. He hadn't often allowed her to touch him. "Here's some spending money." She pressed a twenty-dollar bill into his hand. "Have fun." She smiled, then leaned down and kissed his forehead. He blinked in surprise, but didn't jerk away.

Virginia stood on the stoop and watched as they drove away, waving at Chad as he stared at her through the back window. At the last second he raised his hand in a small wave, then he was gone.

Ignoring the midmorning heat, she walked down the steps and knelt to weed her front mulch beds. If she kept her hands busy, she might not dwell on her impetuous behavior where Bailey was concerned. What a mess she'd made of things. For now it felt good to be able to tidy up some small part of her life. She tore at the wild plants, ripping them out by the roots. When she finished, she tossed the weeds into her garbage can, then wheeled it to the curb.

On the way back inside, she checked the black metal mailbox beside her door, then sifted through the mail as she slipped off her shoes inside the entryway. Two official-looking envelopes caught her eye, one addressed to Chad, the other addressed to "Guardian of." After tearing the flap of the second envelope with her thumbnail, she withdrew a short letter informing Chad Green, also known as Bailey Kallihan, Jr., along with a parent or legal guardian to appear in juvenile court in two weeks. She assumed the other letter was a duplicate, so she walked upstairs to leave it on his desk.

She opened his bedroom door and placed the letter where he'd find it. As she turned to go, she saw the small packing carton of Chad's pictures shoved under his desk. Virginia stared at the box for a full minute, torn. Then she slowly bent over to slide it across the carpet, and sat down cross-legged. With a deep breath she opened the lid.

The odor of old paper enveloped her. On top of the pictures lay the broken pieces of the beloved Nintendo game. She carefully set them aside to thumb through the curled photos. Some of the older pictures were Lois Green as a little girl. She had not been a happy child, nor had her parents, from their dour expressions.

Each time Virginia found a photo with Chad in it, she laid it aside to assemble some kind of chronological order. After an hour she had exhausted the pile, and Chad's childhood lay spread before her. She then lovingly scrutinized each photo, at long last experiencing his first step, his first Christmas, his first tricycle, his first day of school. The abundance of photos made it clear that Lois was a doting mother, and for a few quiet seconds Ginny looked heavenward, closed her eyes, and gave thanks to the woman for at least preserving these precious moments.

From the gap in pictures she estimated the time when Lois began to get sick. Suddenly Chad was nearly his present age, and all his poses with Lois were from her bed, where successive photos chronicled her deterioration. One photo in particular caught her eye because in it Lois was smiling especially wide, her thin arm around Chad and his arm around her. It couldn't have been long before she died—the developing paper was new and slick.

She fingered the photo, an idea blooming.

She went to a crafts store and bought a shadow box, then she spent an hour gluing the Nintendo device back together—it would never work again, but she made it look passably good. With adhesive she mounted the game console and other mementos Lois had saved—photos, amusement park tickets, school programs, and Chad's artwork—inside the shadow box in an artful composition. She set it in her bedroom to dry, suddenly more happy than she'd felt in days.

The phone rang. When she saw Bailey's name on the display, she let it roll to voice mail, then listened to the message he left.

"Ginny, hi, it's Bailey. I wanted to tell Chad goodbye before he left, but things have been crazy here at the office—God, I never thought I'd hear myself say that." His laugh was short and dry, then his voice grew softer. "I need to talk to you—I'd like to come over. I hope you'll let me explain about Sunday. I'm sorry... I should have talked to you before I said anything to Chad. As usual, I only made things worse. I'll be here until around six-thirty." He rattled off the number. "Please call me."

Virginia felt remarkably calm listening to his words. She suspected that her humiliation and anger had simply yielded to numbness. She'd always had a blind spot where Bailey Kallihan was concerned, but now she had a higher priority—her son.

For Chad's sake, she would develop and maintain a cordial relationship with Bailey, even if it killed her... or broke her heart. If she were going to give up her son to him, she would at least keep a little of herself. And just like that, the decision was made... the decision she had feared from the very beginning.

She would allow Chad to live with Bailey.

She would learn to be satisfied with occasional outings, with stolen hours here and there, with being a spectator in her son's life. Within time her own loss would be offset by seeing him happy under Bailey's care.

Virginia inhaled deeply. No more tears.

* * *

164

"Bailey." Lenny walked into his office and tossed a note on his desk. "Cassie forgot to give you this message. Lady named Virginia called about an hour ago."

Frowning, Bailey snatched up the note. *No need to stop by—will be out this evening. Everything's fine.* "Everything's fine," he muttered. "What the hell does that mean?"

Lenny looked perplexed. "Means everything's fine, Bailey."

"Not with Ginny, it doesn't."

"I take it she's your ex?"

"Yeah."

"Mine's a heap of trouble too."

Bailey pulled a hand down his face, then loosened his tie. "That's not the problem, Len. Ginny's the one that got away."

"Oh, I see. Well, she must be the only woman in the world to turn you down."

"No," Bailey said, smiling faintly. "Just the only one to turn me down who mattered."

When Lenny left, Bailey reached for the phone and dialed her number again, but hung up when it rolled to voice mail. He banged down the phone in frustration, then glanced at his watch. She was already gone.

* * *

Virginia passed the evening shopping for Chad. She gathered underwear, socks, shirts and pajamas—it made her happy to rummage through the racks alongside other mothers shopping for their children. She bought him a pair of workboots, sturdy jeans, a ball cap, and a new life jacket—all things he would need at Shenoway.

It was strange, but after making the decision to let him leave, she felt more like a mother. Perhaps to fully appreciate the privilege of motherhood, one had to first experience personal sacrifice.

She dozed fitfully that night, missing Chad in the house and wrestling with the consequences of her own bad judgment where Bailey was concerned.

But near morning she fell asleep, content with the knowledge that it wasn't as bad as nights she'd spent wondering if her baby was dead or alive, and wondering what had happened to her marriage. Considering her previous heartbreak, this was a mere crack. She'd make it.

She slept late and awakened to her phone ringing. It was Bailey again, and he left another message. "Please call me, Ginny. I need to talk to you."

Swinging her feet to the floor and pushing herself up, Virginia grabbed her robe and reached for her absent locket. She played the message twice more, listening to his deep, husky voice. Then she erased the message.

Her parents brought Chad home after lunch. When Virginia hugged her mother, Peg whispered that Chad had been subdued most of the trip. Virginia assumed he was still upset about not living with Bailey, so she decided to tell him her decision as soon as her parents left. She carried the wrapped shadow box to the kitchen, then called his name from the bottom of the stairs. For once, his music was at a normal level.

"Hungry?" she asked when he came to the top of the stairs.

He shook his head.

She waved him down. "I have something for you, and we need to talk."

Looking apprehensive, he descended the stairs. "Is it about the letter?" he asked.

She frowned, then remembered the court date. "No, we can discuss that later."

He followed her to the kitchen table and sat down, arms crossed.

Pulling the wrapped shadow box from behind the snack bar, she said, "I know this can't make up for my behavior, but I hope you like it."

Frowning slightly, he tugged at the heavy paper, then uncovered the shadow box a little at a time, saying nothing. He studied the frame, squinting. "It's my game—and all the stuff my mom gave me."

Virginia nodded nervously. "You can open the door and add more things if I left out something that's important."

"You did this yourself?"

She nodded again. "I hope you don't mind me looking through your pictures—I didn't touch anything else in your room, I promise."

He chewed on his lip, studying the contents. "I like it," he said finally. "Thanks." Then he stood and walked over to her and gave her a hug.

Not a quick, little obligatory hug, but an honest-to-goodness hug. Virginia could have held on forever, desperately fighting her tears of happiness. When he pulled back, she said, "There's more. Sit." She patted the chair.

He sat, waiting.

Taking a deep breath, Virginia began, her voice only a little shaky. "Chad, I love you very much, and I'll never be able to tell you how thankful I am to have you in my life again." She felt herself begin to choke up, but she fought it and held on. "But I know you'd rather be with your father, and because I want you to be happy, I've decided that you should move to Shenoway and live with Bailey."

For a few seconds he said nothing. Then he asked, "Tomorrow?"

Her heart sank lower. She was hoping to have a few more days with him. "If that's what you want," she said softly. "You can call your dad later and the two of you can decide on a day."

"Are you coming too?" he asked, his dark brow furrowed.

"No."

"But Bailey wants you to live with us, doesn't he?"

She shook her head and chose her words carefully. "Grownups are funny. I think Bailey talked about us all living together because he thought it was the only way he could be with you. Does that make sense?"

He shrugged. "I guess." After a few seconds he began to squirm in his seat. "Can I take this to my room?"

"It's heavy, I'll help you."

Together they carried it to his bedroom and set in on a shelf. "It looks nice," he said. "My mom—I mean Lois—would really like it."

Virginia smiled. "I'm glad." She squeezed his shoulder, then glanced at her watch. "Are you going to call Bailey?"

Chad frowned slightly. "I'll call him later. Can I go to the park and skateboard—by myself?"

She started to shake her head no, then remembered her promise to stop being so overprotective. "I think that'll be okay if you promise to be careful."

He nodded. "I promise."

She ruffled his hair. "Okay, but be home before dinner."

She walked downstairs, then heard him gallop down several minutes later. "Bye," she yelled from the kitchen, but she was drowned out by the slam of the front door. Five minutes later the phone rang. Bailey again. Sighing, Virginia picked it up. "Hello?"

"Hi, Ginny, it's Bailey."

"Chad just left to go to the park."

"That's okay, because I called to talk to you."

"Bailey," she said calmly, "I've been doing a lot of thinking, and you were right—you and Chad were both right—he belongs with you. I've decided to let him come live with you at Shenoway."

After a few seconds of silence he asked, "Why don't I have a good feeling about this?"

"Relax," she said quickly, "I've already told him and he's very excited."

"Ginny—"

"If he's agreeable, I'd like to see him at least a couple of times a week, but we can work out the details later."

"Ginny, we need to talk about us."

She couldn't think of a statement that wasn't provocative, so she simply said, "Okay."

"I get the distinct feeling that you didn't believe me when I said I wanted all of us to live together in the house. I asked Chad not to tell you because I wanted to ask you in private."

"Look, Bailey," she said carefully, "you don't have to take the package deal. I appreciate you being nice to me—"

"Being nice to you?"

"—but I'm not putting conditions on Chad living with you."

"You think I made love to you so you'd let Chad move in with me?"

"I wouldn't have used those exact words," she said.

"I'm coming over right now," he growled.

Frowning at the dial tone, she replaced the handset and took a deep breath. A confrontation was inevitable, but she'd be calm and collected. Once Bailey had custody of Chad, he'd eventually feel free to drop the boyfriend act, then perhaps they could be friends. Until then, she'd be as cordial as possible, for Chad's sake.

A few minutes later, Virginia heard the sound of Bailey's car door slamming. He rang the doorbell twice, then started knocking before she could walk the length of the hall. When she opened the door, she swallowed her surprise at his work clothes—a dress shirt with the sleeves rolled up and a loosened silk tie. His face was anger-flushed as he stepped into the entryway.

She closed the door and turned to face him, carefully keeping her face impassive. For several seconds they simply looked at each other, Bailey's breathing becoming more and more erratic. He put his hands on his hips and glared at her.

"I assume you have something to say," she prompted softly.

"I'm so angry right now," he seethed, "I don't trust myself to talk."

"Angry at me?" she asked calmly.

"Angry at you, angry at myself," he said, raising his hands. She could see his big fingers were trembling.

"Do you want to sit down?"

"No!" he barked. "I don't want to sit down. I want you to tell me you don't love me, dammit!"

She blinked. "Excuse me?"

"If you expect me to walk out this door and never come back, you have to tell me you don't love me."

She opened her mouth and shook her head. "I..."

"Say it!" he demanded. He grabbed her by the arms and pulled her to him, holding her in an iron grip. "Say it and mean it."

"You're hurting me," she whispered.

"And you're hurting me," he said in a choked voice, then released her suddenly.

She stumbled backward a half step. "What's this all about?"

He took a deep, shaky breath, his eyes clouding with tears. "I love you, Ginny, and I'm not leaving here until you're convinced of that. I want to marry you, and I want us all to live at Shenoway as a family, but if you tell me you don't love me and there's no chance of it happening, then I'll leave you alone."

Speechless, Virginia stared at her ex-husband, realizing with sudden clarity that he was a different person from the one she'd taken her vows with years before. That Bailey had been a scared boy, pure of heart, but immature and selfish. This Bailey was a strong, capable man, unafraid to show his love, and willing to fight to keep his family together.

"I love you, Ginny, and I want you back in my life." He bit his bottom lip and inhaled sharply. "I've been kicking myself for eight long years, and I'm not about to let you go this easily."

She studied his eyes, overwhelmed at the love she saw there. Smiling tremulously, she murmured, "I—I don't know what to say."

"Just give me some hope we can work things out. Just tell me if there's a chance you might be able to love me again."

"Again?" she asked. This was her moment of truth. Could she risk laying her heart out for him to see? "I can't remember *not* loving you, Bailey."

He straightened and swallowed, then narrowed his eyes. "Say that again."

"I love you, Bailey... I never stopped."

A faint smile lifted the corners of his mouth as he took a step toward her. "Say it louder."

She smiled. "I love you, Bailey."

Another step, a bigger grin. "Louder!"

"I love you, Bailey Kallihan!"

He stopped in front of her. "I love you, too," he whispered. "So much."

Seconds passed and her gaze remained locked with his.

"Are you just going to look at me?" she asked.

His blue eyes narrowed. "No," he said softly, grabbing her arms more gently this time and pulling her to him. Virginia's heart thudded against his. He lowered his mouth until his breath brushed her lips. "I'm going to kiss you until you lose consciousness."

He descended on her mouth with force, kissing her fiercely. His lips were bruising and ruthless as he foraged her mouth, tongue on tongue, teeth on teeth. Virginia felt his need for her transferred through his kiss, his moans savage and his mouth unrelenting. Desire flooded her body, setting fire to her breasts, stomach, thighs. She surrendered to his demands and angled her mouth against his, matching him moan for moan, bite for bite.

He lifted his head long enough to bend, put an arm under her knees, and sweep her up into his arms.

"Where are we going?" she murmured, her eyes half shut.

"To your bedroom," he growled, charging up the stairs. At the top he veered into her room, then laid her on the bed. Immediately he began tugging at her clothes, and she felt herself being swept away in the tide of his passion.

"Bailey," she said after her shirt was removed and her bra discarded, "I'm still conscious." She raised her mouth for a kiss, and as soon as he rolled off her panties, he obliged, this one more tender.

"Ginny," he whispered, nipping at her chin, then moving downward, "when I said I'd kiss you unconscious, I wasn't talking about your mouth."

* * *

Around five-thirty Virginia thawed three pork chops and peeled potatoes to mash for dinner, all the while humming under her breath. She couldn't keep a smile from her face because she still felt Bailey's mouth and hands on her body. He'd left about an hour before, his hair and clothing a little worse for wear, but sporting a huge grin. Their good-bye kiss on the stoop would have the neighbors talking, she was sure.

She was waiting for the water to boil for the macaroni and cheese, when she started to worry about Chad. Virginia sighed and looked at her watch. He should have been home by now.

Ten minutes later she'd grown impatient enough to go to the front stoop and look down the street. Nowhere. When he hadn't returned in another fifteen minutes, she turned off the stove, grabbed her keys, and drove the few blocks to the park, her heart thudding in her chest.

She parked and walked toward the skateboard ramp, feeling relieved when she saw a small crowd of kids taking turns. She scanned their faces when she walked up. "Does anyone here know Chad Green?"

The kids looked at one another, then one rangy boy asked, "Black hair, red and blue skateboard?"

She nodded hopefully.

He shook his head. "Haven't seen him—but Buddy found his skateboard a couple of hours ago."

Virginia's heart dropped to her stomach. "His skateboard?"

The boy nodded, then a second boy stepped forward, holding out the skateboard. "Found it over there, near the trees." He pointed.

"Sh-show me," she whispered, reaching for his skateboard with trembling hands. She frantically searched the area the boy showed her, but she didn't find anything else of Chad's. A horrible sense of deja vu washed over her. She had visions of a stranger dragging Chad into his vehicle, and her heart nearly leapt out of her chest.

Clutching the skateboard, she stumbled toward her car. Tears blurred her vision, and she gasped for every breath. She didn't have her phone, and how she drove the few blocks home without causing an accident, she didn't know. She ran for the phone, then stabbed in Bailey's number.

He answered, his voice low. "Ginny, I'm in a meeting—is everything okay?"

"No," she whispered, tears dripping into her mouth as she talked. "I can't find him."

"Chad?"

"He's not at the park, and the other boys said he hasn't been there all afternoon. One of them found his skateboard." She broke down, sobbing.

"Call 911. I'll be right there."

CHAPTER FIFTEEN

WITH HIS HEART IN HIS THROAT, Bailey doubled every posted speed limit on his way to Ginny's house. Dusk was beginning to fall—it would be dark soon, the streets too dangerous for a lost eight-year-old. He pulled to a tire-squealing halt, ran past the police car at the curb, and through a knot of milling neighbors. Then he bounded up the steps and through the front door. "Ginny?"

She was sitting on the edge of the sofa in the living room, her face gray and pasty. Two police officers stood in front of her, taking notes and asking questions.

She jerked her head up when she heard him, then her face crumpled. "Bailey, we can't find him!" The officers stepped aside for him. He pulled her to her feet and into his arms, rocking her back and forth as she sobbed against his shoulder.

"I shouldn't have let him go by himself," she cried hysterically. "Someone's taken him again, I just know it."

"Shh," he said, blinking back his own tears. "You don't know that. Maybe he went home with some kid he met and lost track of time."

One of the officers coughed. "We were just wrapping up, sir. We've already talked to the kids at the park and put out an Amber alert. We're also notifying all patrol cars on southbound I-23 and I-35. I understand he's from Florida."

Bailey rubbed Ginny's back. "That's right. Fort Lauderdale. Do you think he's run away?"

"Could be hitchhiking back to Florida. Kids run away more often than they're kidnapped, sir."

"You have to understand how we're feeling right now, officer. Our son was kidnapped when he was an infant. We just got him back into our lives a few days ago."

The man nodded sadly. "I saw it in the papers. I've been on the phone with Detective Lance—he filled us in and said he would contact the Florida State Police and the shelter where the boy stayed."

Stroking Ginny's hair, Bailey asked, "What can we do?"

"Someone needs to stay by the phone, of course. Call everyone he knows." He turned to Ginny. "Ma'am, check his room again and let us know if you can figure out what he was wearing when he left."

She pulled away and dabbed a shredded tissue at her puffy eyes as she explained to Bailey. "The clothes he was wearing when he asked to go to the park are on his bed, and"—she started crying again—"I didn't see him before he left." Looking into Bailey's eyes, she said, "I didn't even tell him good-bye." She bit her bottom lip, tears streaking her face.

"That's all we can do now, sir," the man said. "I'm Officer Handler. Be sure to call the station and ask for me if he turns up or if you think of something else. I'll keep you informed."

Bailey shook hands with the policemen, but let them find their own way out.

He made Virginia sit down again, then asked her to repeat everything that had happened since Chad had returned home from camping. She told him about the shadow box and the talk they'd had. "He seemed a little quiet," she said, sniffling, "but I figured it was everything happening so suddenly."

"Did you check to see if his duffel bag is missing?"

"It's still in the laundry room with his camping stuff in it."

"Did he have any money?"

"I gave him twenty dollars before he went camping—I don't know if he had any left over. And Mom or Dad might have given him some." She shook her head. "It doesn't make sense that he would run away. Besides, his skateboard... oh, Bailey"—her voice rose in panic—"it's happening again—"

174

"Hey." He snuggled her against his chest. "We don't know that. He's a big boy now, not a helpless infant." *And still prey for all kinds of sickos,* he thought, his gut twisting.

"What are we going to do?" she whispered desperately.

"Wait," he said firmly, squeezing her. "We'll wait together."

"But what if someone has him—"

He cut her off. "We can't think about that."

"What if we never see him again?"

"We will," he assured her. "And we still have each other."

She smiled through her tears and touched her finger to his mouth lovingly.

He kissed the tip of her finger, then wrapped his arms around her and squeezed hard. "I know this isn't the best time to propose, and I don't want you to give me an answer now"—he pulled back and brushed a strand of hair out of her wide eyes—"but if the worst has happened and we never see our son again"—he choked, his voice resuming a rusty tone—"I couldn't bear to go on if you're not with me."

She pressed her lips together tightly, her eyes spilling over again, then lay her head against his chest. She clung to him like a lifeline, and they stood pressed together for several minutes, filling up on each other's love.

Suddenly a thought occurred to him, and he could have kicked himself for not thinking of it sooner. Pulling back, he said, "Ginny, where's the one place you would go if you were Chad?"

She started to shake her head, then her eyes widened. "Shenoway! But it's so far—how would he get there?"

"He's a smart kid—too smart for his own good."

Bailey pulled out his phone and called Rita, talked for a few seconds, then disconnected the call. "She hasn't seen him, but I don't think he'd knock on the front door. I'm going over there."

"I'm going with you," she said. "I can't stand just sitting here."

As they sped toward the farm, he prayed his intuition was right. In fact, he wouldn't allow himself to think otherwise.

The moon was in its early cycle, so the meadow lay darkly shadowed when they topped the crest, each carrying a flashlight. Immediately, however, Bailey breathed a sigh of relief. A faint beam of light shone from the back of the meadow, from his tree, the mammoth oak his father had planted. They trotted to it as fast as Ginny could move through the tall, wet grass, then stopped underneath, panting.

The small flashlight beam had been extinguished. Bailey cleared his throat and said, "Chad, we've been worried sick about you."

There was a scrape on one of the lower branches, but no response.

"Why did you run away, son?" he asked gently.

Silence.

Virginia felt strength returning to her weak limbs, and laid a hand on Bailey's arm when he started to speak again. "Chad," she said, "if you won't come down here, then we're coming up there."

She shone her light overhead until she saw him, his hand thrown up to shield his eyes. Her heart shivered in relief to see he was okay. She motioned and Bailey hoisted her up first, then pulled himself up into the nearly room-sized opening the tree's lower branches provided. Using their flashlights, they carefully picked their way over to where Chad sat, crying softly.

"Hey." Virginia sat down close to him and squeezed his shoulders.

He didn't look at them, only cried harder.

"If you don't tell us what's wrong," Bailey said, sitting on the other side of him, "we can't fix it."

Chad studied the flashlight he clenched in his hands. "I did something real bad, and I didn't want you to find out, so I ran away."

"*Nothing* could be that bad." Virginia covered one of his hands with her own.

He glanced up, then down again. "It is, it's terrible, and you're going to hate me." He started crying again, but Virginia patted his hand, her heart turning over for her son.

"We could never hate you, Chad," she said quietly. "You're our boy—we love you, no matter what. Just tell us."

"I s-stole your l-locket," he said, "and th-threw it in the p-pond with my s-slingshot."

Anguish barbed through her chest at the loss, but she didn't react.

"What's this about your locket?" Bailey asked. "I didn't even know it was missing."

Chad looked up at her, his eyes miserable. "You didn't tell him?"

She shook her head.

"But you knew I took it, didn't you?"

She nodded.

Chad's face crumpled again. "I was feeling bad about it anyway, and then I got home from the camping trip, and you'd made me that neat picture box, and said nice things even after I broke you and Bailey up—"

"You didn't break us up, son," Bailey injected with a smile. "We're adults, we make our own mistakes."

"Well, I know I caused your fight. And I know it made Ginny sad." His lower lip trembled again. "And that letter was there saying you have to take me to court—I'm too much trouble."

"Hey," she said softly, planting a kiss on his temple, "you let us be the judge of that. Why did you leave your skateboard in the park?"

"I figured if you thought someone had kidnapped me, you'd be glad I was gone and wouldn't come looking."

Horror bolted through her, and she pulled his chin up to look directly in his eyes. "Chad, if I ever lost you again, I would never stop crying, do you understand?"

"I'm sorry," he said, tears sliding down to wet her fingers. "I wouldn't blame you if you still wanted me to leave, but I want to stay with you, Ginny."

Amazed, she exchanged a glance with Bailey, then wiped a few of Chad's tears with her thumb. "But I thought you wanted to live with Bailey."

Chad straightened his shoulders and sniffed, then jutted out his chin. "Sons are supposed to take care of their mothers."

Joy ballooned in her heart and filled every cell of her body. She smiled through her tears. On the other side of Chad, Bailey cleared his throat, then winked a glistening eye at her in the flashlight beam.

She clasped Chad's hands with hers. "I'm honored you feel that way, but you've got it turned around—it's my job to take care of you." Smiling wide, she said, "Besides, it'll be the two of us for only a little while."

Chad frowned, confused.

"Your father and I are getting married," Virginia said with a grin.

Chad's eyes widened, then he looked back and forth between them. "Really?"

Bailey's gaze flew to hers. "Really?"

"Really," she said, laughing. Bailey reached over to squeeze her hand, smiling at her from the shadows.

"Hm," Chad said, suddenly thoughtful. A small frown furrowed his brow.

"What?" she probed.

"Well, with all the kissing you two do, I guess you'll be having babies and stuff."

Exchanging glances with Bailey, she ventured carefully, "And how would you feel about that?"

Chad shrugged and grinned, clearly happy at the prospect. "Whatever."

EPILOGUE

VIRGINIA SMOOTHED THE SLIM SKIRT of her short wedding dress, taking a deep, calming breath. The music had started, her mother and Rita had just left the dressing room, and she had all of five minutes before once again becoming Mrs. Bailey Kallihan. She was as nervous as she'd been all those years before. Unlike her first wedding day, however, she wasn't plagued with doubts about Bailey's level of commitment, and the child growing within her then was now the joy of her life.

A small knock sounded at the door. She turned away from the mirror. "Yes?"

"Mom?" Chad asked, poking his head and shoulders in the room. "Can I come in?"

She smiled. "Absolutely. You can help me tame these butterflies."

"Wow, you look great." He walked toward her with his hands behind his back.

"Thanks," she said. "You don't look so bad yourself." She straightened his bow tie, her heart swelling with pride at the sight of him in his small black tux. "Are you excited?"

He nodded. "We're almost a family."

Tingling with happiness, she stroked his cheek. "We always were, sweetheart, we were just a bit... scattered."

"I got something for you," he said shyly, withdrawing a small package from behind his back.

She took it, swallowing the lump in her throat. The paper, silver with white wedding bells, had been mangled a bit, then repaired with yards of cellophane tape. A big white bow sat crookedly on top.

"I wrapped it myself."

"It's so pretty," she whispered.

"Open it."

Carefully, she tore away the paper to uncover a jeweler's box. She glanced at her son suspiciously, but he was wide-eyed with anticipation.

"Hurry, you don't have much time."

She lifted the hinged lid to reveal a shiny gold locket on a gold chain. She pressed her lips together to stem her welling tears. "It's lovely," she whispered, pulling the necklace from the box and fingering it lovingly. She slipped her thumbnail into the groove and opened the case to reveal a recent picture of Chad. Her heart swelled.

"Do you like it?" he asked. "I bought it all by myself."

She reached for him and gathered him in a powerful hug. "I absolutely love it, but you didn't have to do this—it must have cost a lot of money."

He shrugged. "I took my new Nintendo back to the store and got a refund."

"Oh, Chad."

He bit his lip. "I didn't deserve a new one. I left my game lying on the floor. What if you'd tripped on it and fallen down the stairs?"

Ah—now she knew why he'd never played with the new game, because he'd felt guilty. "But I didn't," she said lightly, and kissed his nose. "You never cease to amaze me, you wonderful boy. Do you know how much I love you?"

He blushed happily. "Yeah, Mom, you only tell me ten times a day."

Another knock sounded, and Rita stuck her head in. "Ginny, everyone's waiting!"

"Be right there," Virginia said. She handed the necklace to Chad. "Will you put it on for me?"

He nodded, lifting the chain over her head, lowering it carefully to avoid messing up her hair.

"How does it look?" she asked.

"Beautiful," he breathed.

"I'll never take it off," she promised.

He grinned.

"I think they're ready for us," she said.

He straightened, then cocked his arm out, elbow bent, just like he'd practiced. She tucked her hand inside, and they walked out into the hall.

Jerry and Detective Lance opened the doors to the chapel, smiling and nodding. Virginia and Chad stepped to the back of the church, the wedding march chiming louder to announce her arrival. The small congregation stood as she entered, and at the altar, Bailey turned toward them. She saw her future in his eyes, hers and Chad's. She squeezed her son's arm, smiling, and they walked toward him together.

The End

A NOTE FROM THE AUTHOR

Thank you so very much for taking the time to read my heartwarming romance ALMOST A FAMILY. This book is the only book I've written in my career that isn't a comedy and doesn't feature a mystery—it's simply a story about a family I wanted to tell way back in 1997. A publisher bought the manuscript and released it (with a dreadful cover) under a pen name I used back then, Stephanie Bancroft. I think it sold about 10 copies, and my mother bought 9 of them! The book quickly disappeared from shelves and eventually, I got the rights back to it, then put it in a drawer. In 2011, I resurrected the ancient files and updated the story (took out the boom boxes and the pagers) and tweaked the writing extensively. After all these years, I'm still happy with this story...I hope you enjoyed it, too.

If you did enjoy ALMOST A FAMILY and feel inclined to leave a review at your favorite online book retailer, I would appreciate it very much.

And are you signed up to receive notices of my future book releases? If not, please drop by www.stephaniebond.com and enter your email address. I promise not to flood you with emails and I will never share or sell your address. And you can unsubscribe at any time.

Also, although I can't count the times this book has been edited and proofed, I am human, so if you do spot a typo, please email me at stephanie@ stephaniebond.com to let me know! Thanks again for your time and interest, and for telling your friends about my books. If you'd like to know more about some of my other books, please see the next section and/or visit my website.

Happy reading!
Stephanie Bond

OTHER WORKS BY STEPHANIE BOND

Humorous romantic mysteries:

TWO GUYS DETECTIVE AGENCY—*Even Victoria can't keep a secret from us...*
OUR HUSBAND—*Hell hath no fury like three women scorned!*
KILL THE COMPETITION—*There's only one sure way to the top...*
I THINK I LOVE YOU—*Sisters share everything in their closets...including the skeletons.*
GOT YOUR NUMBER—*You can run, but your past will eventually catch up with you.*
WHOLE LOTTA TROUBLE—*They didn't plan on getting caught...*
IN DEEP VOODOO—*A woman stabs a voodoo doll of her ex, and then he's found murdered!*
VOODOO OR DIE—*Another voodoo doll, another untimely demise...*
BUMP IN THE NIGHT—*a short mystery*

***Body Movers* series:**

PARTY CRASHERS (full-length prequel)
BODY MOVERS
2 BODIES FOR THE PRICE OF 1
3 MEN AND A BODY

4 BODIES AND A FUNERAL
5 BODIES TO DIE FOR
6 KILLER BODIES
6 ½ BODY PARTS (novella)
7 BRIDES FOR SEVEN BODIES

Romances:

ALMOST A FAMILY—*Fate gave them a second chance at love...*
LICENSE TO THRILL—*She's between a rock and a hard body...*
STOP THE WEDDING!—*If anyone objects to this wedding, speak now...*
THREE WISHES—*Be careful what you wish for!*
TEMPORARY ARRANGEMENT—*Friends become lovers...what could possibly go wrong?*

Nonfiction:

GET A LIFE! 8 STEPS TO CREATE YOUR OWN LIFE LIST—*a short how-to for mapping out your personal life list!*

Made in the USA
Lexington, KY
13 June 2019

Race, Campaign Politics, and the Realignment in the South

Race, Campaign Politics, and the Realignment in the South

James M. Glaser

Yale University Press   *New Haven and London*

BFP 7392-0/2

Designed by Rebecca Gibb. Set in Bell type by Keystone
Typesetting, Inc. Printed in the United States of America by
Edwards Brothers, Inc., Ann Arbor, Michigan.

Library of Congress Cataloging-in-Publication Data

Glaser, James M., 1960–
    Race, campaign politics, and the realignment in the South /
James M. Glaser.
        p.   cm.
    Includes bibliographical references and index.
    ISBN 0-300-06398-9 (alk. paper)
    1. Southern States—Politics and government—1961–
2. United States. Congress—Elections.   3. Elections—Southern
States.   4. Party affiliation—Southern States.   5. Political
parties—Southern states.   6. Southern States—Race relations.
I. Title.
JK2683.G58   1996
324.975′043—dc20   95-32636
                                                              CIP

A catalogue record for this book is available from the British
Library.

The paper in this book meets the guidelines for permanence and
durability of the Committee on Production Guidelines for Book
Longevity of the Council on Library Resources.

10 9 8 7 6 5 4 3 2 1

To my parents, Harold and Judith Glaser,
and to my grandmother Mae Kramer,
with love and thanks

Contents

List of Illustrations ix

Preface xi

One   The Puzzles of the Southern Realignment 1

Two   The Case for Context 25

Three   Racial Issues in the Congressional Campaign 43

Four   Courting White Voters 80

Five   The Majority Black District 142

Six   Resolving the Puzzles 175

Notes 197

References 213

Index 223

Illustrations

Figures

1.1 Party Identification of Southerners, 1952–1992

1.2 Party Identification of White Southerners, 1952–1992

1.3 Presidential Electoral Vote in the South, 1952–1992

1.4 Percent of Southern Democrats in Congress, 1952–1992

1.5 Percent of Democrats in Southern State Legislatures, 1952–1992

2.1 Congressional Districts in the Study

Tables

1.1 Southern White Attitudes on Racial Questions

1.2 Congressional Votes in the 1980s

2.1 Demographic Considerations of Southern Strategists

2.2 Summary of Cases

2.3 Turnout in Special and Off-Year Elections

Preface

"EXACTLY WHAT ARE YOU DOING HERE?" asked an Alabama campaign manager back in 1989. "*Rashomon*," I responded. The man looked at me blankly. "You know," I explained, "the Kurosawa movie where he shows the same event from the perspective of everybody who participates in it." He rolled his eyes: "I don't know no *Rashomon*."

My answer, which made some sense when I first uttered it as a graduate student in a Berkeley coffeehouse, did not go over well in this Anniston, Alabama, coffeeshop. It was a rookie mistake. Still, over all these years the metaphor has guided me. The point of this classic Japanese movie, which shows an attack on a couple from the very different perspectives of the attacker, the man and woman who are attacked, and an "objective" observer, is that the truth is to be found by putting together all their accounts (the objective observer also is shown to have biases that shape his point of view). Likewise, my purpose has been to gather the perspectives of many different actors on the same events, some congressional elections in the South, to construct some narratives of these elections, adding my own observations, and to analyze and interpret them.

The result is a book that is quite different from most other work on southern political behavior. This is not to say that analyses of public opinion data or electoral data are not of value. There are any number of good, detailed quantitative studies of southern voters. Understanding southern politics, however, comes also from knowing about the context in which mass political decisions are made, and that is the purpose of what follows.

Much of the work on southern politics, going back several decades now, starts with the assumption that the changes that took place in politics and society in the 1960s would lead inexorably to Republican domination in the region. In particular, changes in race relations and the infusion of blacks into the electorate—and into the Democratic party, at that—have long been viewed as fueling Republican growth and providing for the party's very promising future. Although the Republican party has grown enormously since the 1960s, it has not achieved the full-scale electoral success many expected. Even in the 1980s, Republicans did not come to dominate in the South except at the presidential level. Only after the midterm elections of 1994, thirty years after passage of the Voting Rights Act, have they achieved even partisan balance at the congressional level. Most indications point to continued and perhaps dramatic Republican congressional success. The fact remains that it has been a surprisingly slow development.

This book on the choices offered to southern voters in congressional elections will shed light on why Republican success in presidential elections in the South has been so slow in translating to lower-level electoral success. One major argument I make is that the Democratic party's fate was not sealed by the civil rights movement and the political changes it engendered. Democrats, in fact, adjusted well to the dramatic changes in the political environment, including the racial changes in this environment, and political strategy surrounding race actually helped the Democratic party keep its tenacious hold on many lower-level positions in the South. In the decades after the passage of major civil and voting rights legislation, Democrats were better at reading and understanding the requirements of the campaign, the constraints that the racial balance in the South posed, and the opportunities it provided. Moreover, they were better able to construct biracial coalitions in race-sensitive environments. In the thirty years following the Voting Rights Act, they stayed in political contention and even dominated at the congressional level on down for a variety of reasons. But this ability to manage the challenges of race in the South certainly was vital to their success. They must continue to manage these challenges if they are to continue to hold off Republican domination at all levels of southern politics.

It has been exciting putting this story together and writing it. Much of the pleasure of doing this work came from the people I encountered along the way, and I wish to thank them here. I talked with many people, some at great length, about their experiences in the campaigns described in the upcoming pages. In many cases, these interviews came during the heat of the campaign, when time was very valuable. In some cases, the interviews came with a ride to the next campaign event and even assistance in getting into that event. For their time, their candor, and in many cases their kindness, I want to thank James Anderson, C. F. Appleberry, Linda Arey, Sam Attlesey, Edith Back, Unita Blackwell, Betty Jo Boyd, Bob Boyd, Glen Browder, Sarah Campbell, Jim Chapman, William Coleman, Joe Colson, Dave Cooley, Chris Crowley, Dwayne Crump, Hayes Dent, Wayne Dowdy, Pat Duncan, Thom Ferguson, C. J. Fogle, Johnny Ford, Sheila Gilbert, Dylan Glenn, Jerome Gray, Reed Guice, Edd Hargett, Charlie Horhn, Paul Houghton, Lee Howard, Jim Humlicek, Craig James, Ron Jensen, David Jordan, Tom King, Jim Merrill, Pat Murphy, David Murray, Trudy Nichol, L. F. Payne, Clarke Reed, Ken Reid, Chip Reynolds, John Rice, George Shipley, Brent Shriver, Christopher Smith, Mike Smith, Sharon Souther, Carolyn Stuckett, Gene Taylor, Worth Thomas, Bennie Thompson, Charles Tisdale, Cora Tucker, Bobby Vincent, Steve

Walton, Jim Warren, Jim Yardley, Lauren Ziegler, and Bill Zortman. I owe an additional thank you to Tom Anderson, Unita Blackwell, Glen Browder, Hayes Dent, John Rice, Gene Taylor, and Bennie Thompson for opening their campaigns to me and permitting me to attend their campaign events.

Many organizations helped me through the lengthy process of writing this book. My visits to Alabama, Mississippi, and Washington, D.C., were expensive, and without support from these different sources I would not have been able to do this research. I am most grateful for the financial support I received as a graduate student at the University of California at Berkeley. The Department of Political Science, the Institute of Governmental Studies, the Berkeley Chapter of Phi Beta Kappa, and the Dean of Graduate Studies at Berkeley all provided me with funding that made it possible to write a dissertation that has evolved into this book. I also received funding later in the process, which enabled me to return to Mississippi in 1993 and to complete this project. I would like to thank the Political Science Department at Tufts University and the University Faculty Research Award Committee for their generous support. I also received funding from the American Political Science Association Small Grant Program and wish to thank Michael Brintnall, director of professional affairs at the APSA, for helping me obtain permission to use some of that grant for this project when the opportunity to go to Mississippi arose.

I am especially grateful to Raymond Wolfinger, who, as my dissertation chair and mentor, originally encouraged me to do this research and helped me plan a research design that eventually would yield so much wonderful material. I have greatly valued his guidance, his wisdom, and his friendship. Paul Sniderman gave me sage advice throughout this process as well. He has contributed so much to my thinking and my development as a political scientist, more than he even knows, and I feel fortunate to have linked up with him early in my graduate career. I also thank Jack Citrin, Martin Gilens, Marissa Martino Golden, Michael Hagen, Michael Hout, and Jonathan Krasno, who read and critiqued several early chapters of this book (Professors Citrin and Hout as members of my dissertation committee). Jon Krasno deserves a special thank you for helping me enormously at a critical point in this process. More recently, David Mayhew read and critiqued the manuscript for Yale University Press. His very smart observations and advice were invaluable to me as I worked to improve it. Jeffrey Berry, Pamella Endo, and Kent Portney also read later versions of the manuscript and helped me to make it better. My colleagues, particularly Professors Berry, Portney, and Frances Hagopian, and the staff of the Political Science Department, Lidia Bonaventura, Paula Driscoll, and Jini Kelly, have been very supportive of me during my years at Tufts, and I am thankful.

In the final stages of this project, I was lucky to have connected with John Covell. He and his staff at Yale University Press have made this a most pleasant experience. Lawrence Kenney, the manuscript editor, did a superb job preparing it for publication.

Most of all, I thank my wife, Pamella Endo, for her love, her understanding, and her encouragement from beginning to end, and my daughter Alison, who came along in the middle of this process. They were my inspiration.

Race, Campaign Politics, and the Realignment in the South

1 The Puzzles of the Southern Realignment

"I never should have been a Democrat. People like me made the Democratic party strong." *Alabama State Senator John Rice (Rep.—Lee County)*

"I'm a Democrat, but I vote for the man. All the men are Republicans though." *Former Democratic county chairman, Mississippi*

THROUGHOUT THE SOUTH, a lot of old Democrats are finding themselves at various stages of conversion to the Republican party. Born Democratic, raised Democratic, they have had difficulty letting go of their old affiliation, which in many cases was burned into them. "Daddy would have whipped me if I was anything but a Democrat," said one former Democratic county chairman from East Texas. "There's no rhyme or reason for [my being a Democrat] anymore, except it's all I know" (Taylor 1985a). Still, he and many other white southerners slowly are working their way toward a new identity.

People like this have made the South competitive territory, but it has been a painfully slow process, slow not just in the conversion of old Democrats, but also in the Republican realization of the fruits of their efforts. Republicans have yet to experience full-fledged success in the South, though many have been expecting it for years, indeed decades. What has impeded Republican progress and how the Democrats have held back the future is, in fact, the subject of this book.

V. O. Key and the Politics of the Old South

The story begins in the Old South, where a political system based on segregation and the subjugation of blacks flourished. V. O. Key, in his classic work *Southern Politics in State and Nation* (1949), describes the southern political system and the relation of race to politics in the region.[1] His analysis is based upon the contention that race had been and continued to be the fundamental structuring force of southern politics. Almost every feature of southern politics—the peculiar electoral rules and regulations, the practices, rhetoric, and styles of politicians, the concentration of political power in black belt whites, the nature of public opinion, the unity among southern representatives in Congress—fit into his scheme. Writes Key in 1949, "In its grand outlines the politics of the South revolves around the position of the Negro. It is at times interpreted as a politics of cotton, as a politics of free trade, as a politics of agrarian poverty, or as a politics of planter and plutocrat. Although such interpretations have a superficial validity, in the last analysis the major peculiarities of southern politics go back to the Negro. Whatever phase of the southern political process one seeks to understand, sooner or later the trail of inquiry leads to the Negro" (5).

My interest in V. O. Key is his argument that the nature of the party system, if it can be called that, rested on the power of racial issues. Democrats reigned supreme because the "race issue," the issue or set of issues of segregation, eclipsed any other issue that could possibly generate a cleavage in the electorate and upset the prevailing partisan situation. As Key writes, "The maintenance of southern Democratic solidarity has depended fundamentally on a willingness to subordinate to the race question all great social and economic issues that tend to divide people into opposing parties" (315–16). So long as this issue remained atop the political agenda, there was little to split the Democratic party.

The leadership of the Democratic party, according to Key, thus worked hard to keep the race issue festering. It is hardly surprising that this leadership was dominated by conservative black belt whites and that their fears, concerns, and priorities on the race question permeated the politics of the entire region.[2] As Key argues, these "black belt whites succeeded in imposing their will on their states" (11) and were the most important southern voices in national politics as well. Key also documents a strong relation between black populations and white support for these types of politicians. Blacks in the most heavily black counties of the South were the most shut out of politics, and whites in these counties were most supportive of keeping it that way. The Solid South was white supremacist and solidly Democratic, two tendencies that reinforced each other.

Given this status quo, Republicans, as "the party of Lincoln," were unable to gain a foothold in the electorate except in a few remote places in the hill country of the region.[3] In a party system whose genesis lay in the Civil War and Reconstruction, they had no natural constituency to appeal to, particularly as blacks were disenfranchised. As Democrats were not about to yield the overwhelming advantage the racial issue gave them, the situation was bleak for the Republican party. Southern Republican leaders, however, accommodated themselves to this situation rather well. Many were, as Key describes them, "patronage farmers" and "palace politicians" whose "chief preoccupation [was] not with voters but with maneuvers to gain and keep control of the state party machinery" (292). Although not all Republican leaders fit this description, Key's point is that Republican leaders, having no divisive issue to call upon, were ill equipped and in many cases not even inclined to challenge Democratic dominance.

One of the important consequences of this partisan situation was that class issues were, for the most part, kept off the political agenda. Appeals to racial hatred were designed to distract lower-class whites from challenging the prevailing economic order. By keeping emotions high on racial issues, elites were able to minimize the possibility of a class-based political movement emerging. Of course, there was (and is) a populist strain in southern political culture, and southern political history is peppered with characters like Huey Long and the Georgia radical Tom Watson. But these populist figures are notable as exceptions, not as the rule.[4] Class-based politics was largely subordinated to a race-based politics in the South, and southern Democrats worked hard to keep it that way.

Key's interpretation of the politics of the Old South ties together the one-party system, the black belt domination of politics, and the subordination of class issues to racial issues. The South he describes is the baseline from which all political change is measured, and since Key wrote his famous book, much has happened to change politics, society, and the economy in the South.

Most notably, the civil rights movement abolished de jure segregation, a set of events that altered southern politics forever. The civil rights movement and the passage of civil rights and voting rights legislation represented the death knell of the old political system as the basis upon which it rested—the disenfranchisement and officially sanctioned subjugation of blacks—crumbled in the years to follow. These pieces of legislation had profound and inevitable consequences for the southern political system as blacks entered the electorate in large numbers and became an important new constituency and as the defenders of the Old South lost the most potent issue in their political arsenal.

The civil rights movement and the changes it brought to the South are not the only reasons the old southern political system began to change. Changes in the economy had some bearing on partisan change in the region. Through the 1950s, a growing, prosperous urban and suburban middle class, for instance, gave the Republicans a new and important base of support (Bartley and Graham 1975, 185). Industrialization and the desire to attract northern investment to the region led to some new political priorities (Wright 1986) and placed power in a different set of elites.

Changes within the national parties starting in 1948 were also partly responsible for the decay of the old southern political system. In that year, skirmishing in Congress over President Truman's new civil rights policy was followed by a southern walkout from the Democratic national convention. The Dixiecrats bolted over a civil rights plank in the Democratic party platform and ran their own ticket throughout the South in the presidential elections of 1948. Their rebellion (which cost the Democrats thirty-seven electoral votes in the South) made clear that the partnership of southern and northern Democrats was the source of potentially large problems.

There was little change in the racial positions of the parties through most of the 1950s. The Democrats managed to balance the programmatic wing of the party and the southern Democrats, and the Republican position on racial change was not clarified by the actions of the Eisenhower administration. Although the administration did little to advance civil and voting rights during the decade, the president did call out federal troops to resolve the Little Rock school crisis. Moreover, as Sundquist (1983) notes, "The white South could not forget that it was a Republican chief justice, appointed by Eisenhower—Earl Warren—who molded the unanimous Supreme Court decision outlawing the South's segregated schools" (357). A transformation in party positions on race really can be traced to the end of Eisenhower's term. In the congressional elections of 1958, liberal Democrats defeated several prominent liberal Republicans (including some active civil rights supporters), and the complexion of both national parties began to change considerably (Carmines and Stimson 1989). When the Kennedy and Johnson administrations started to take a more active role in advancing civil rights in the South and when Barry Goldwater partially based his presidential campaign in 1964 on his opposition to the Civil Rights Act of 1964, a polarization of the national parties over race began to set. Though this polarization was certainly not complete, particularly in the South, the parties became distinguishable on racial issues.

At about this time, many important political analysts started predicting a new party system in the South, one predicated on this different racial cleavage. Philip Converse (1966), for instance, wrote, "Of the current issues on the American scene, the Negro problem comes closest [in the South, but not elsewhere] to showing those characteristics necessary if a political issue is to form the springboard to large-scale partisan realignment" (240). In their book on the "new" southern politics, Donald R.

Matthews and James W. Prothro (1966) said, "One or two more presidential campaigns like that of 1964, in which the Republicans appealed explicitly to the racial prejudices of the white South, and an abrupt and
thoroughgoing party realignment might well be brought about" (474).
And Samuel Lubell (1966) described Republican opportunities this way:
"In nearly every Southern state racial emotions were—and still are—
sufficiently powerful to constitute the balance of voting power. When
these racial feelings lie bedded down, the political balance favors the
Democrats. But a popular recoil against efforts to enforce desegregation
could swing much of the South out of the Democratic fold" (172). Though
all these analysts were predictably careful in their predictions, they saw
the challenge to the racial status quo as a potentially great boon to the
Republican party.

The Republican political strategist Kevin Phillips was even bolder.
Noting that as blacks entered the electorate, they would become almost
completely incorporated into the Democratic fold, he enthusiastically
argued that realignment was imminent. "Negroes are slowly but surely
taking over the apparatus of the Democratic party in a growing number
of Deep South Black Belt counties," he wrote. "This cannot help but push
whites into the alternative major party structure—that of the GOP" (1969,
287). As Phillips predicted, the entry of blacks into politics did have profound implications for the Republican party. So long as blacks were denied
access to politics, the Democrats could continue to speak for southern
conservatism. Blacks' full entry into the political system and inevitably
into the Democratic party put white Democratic politicians in a new and
different situation. The play of events was certain to work in the Republican party's favor, and Phillips urged the GOP to work with, not against,
these trends.

The Republicans essentially followed the plan sketched out by Kevin
Phillips. As the party began to be associated with racial conservatism and
as the Democratic party incorporated blacks into its ranks, the Republican party in the South began to grow and become a viable political force
in the region. Perhaps it was because the Republican party was becoming
more racially conservative than the Democratic party. Perhaps the social

and political events of the late 1950s and early 1960s simply released many conservative southern whites from a race-based allegiance to the Democratic party, enabling them to connect with the party that most appealed to their other conservative political beliefs. Perhaps *liberalism* lost its New Deal connotation and became associated with social engineering and the presence of the federal government in changing the racial status quo. Whatever the case—all three explanations are plausible and not mutually exclusive—there was no returning to anything resembling the Solid South described by V. O. Key.

The Republican party has grown considerably since the civil rights era, and a new party system now defines the politics of the region. But some aspects of this growth and this new party system are perplexing. Given the strong possibility of a "thoroughgoing," "large-scale" realignment and given commonly held assumptions about the long-standing nature of southern politics, there have been some surprises. In the remainder of this chapter, I discuss two of these surprises, two puzzles that arise from a study of Republican growth in the South since the 1950s and most notably since Ronald Reagan's election in 1980. This book is structured around these puzzles.

The Puzzle of Mixed Republican Success

Whatever one attributes Republican growth to, it clearly has not been an overnight phenomenon. From 1952 to the present, the Republicans have gained steadily. But, as noted at the beginning of this chapter, the process has been slow and, in fact, it is likely not over.

The growing strength of Republicanism is apparent in the partisan affiliations of southerners over time (fig. 1.1). In 1952, fully 83 percent of all southerners were Democrats; only 14 percent were Republicans, and a fair proportion of these people were black.[5] Democratic affiliation dipped to 64 percent in 1960, but actually rose to 73 percent in 1964, as blacks were driven into the Democratic camp. In spite of a Republican presidential campaign that attracted many southern whites, only 19 percent of southerners counted themselves as Republicans in 1964. The Republicans have made almost continuous gains in the years since. From that

Figure 1.1 Party Identification of Southerners, 1952–1992

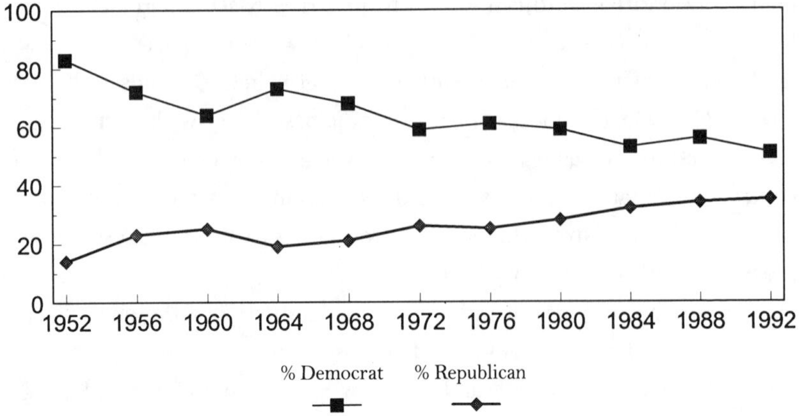

Source: American National Election Studies, 1952–1992

low, Republicans have come to comprise 35 percent of the southern popu-lation (as of 1992), and this growth of 16 percentage points has been almost monotonic.

Republican gains, of course, have come at the expense of the Demo-cratic party. The Democrats have lost 22 percentage points in the years between 1964 and 1992. Their losses have been marked by dramatic dips and mild recoveries rather than a steady, monotonic decline. As of 1992, Democrats comprised 51 percent of the southern population. There is little doubt that there has been a major change in the aggregate party balance. Yet, perhaps the most important point here is that, as of 1992, in spite of the attrition the Democrats had experienced, they still held an advantage—a 16-percentage-point advantage—in partisan identification in the South. Although things look promising for the Republican party, they are still the minority party in the region.

If one looks at blacks and whites separately, the picture is sharpened somewhat. By the election of 1964, southern blacks had almost all turned to the Democratic party. This shift had started earlier as blacks became part of the New Deal coalition put together by Franklin Roosevelt (Weiss 1983). But a good many blacks, particularly southern blacks, still felt a tie to the Republican party, the party of Lincoln and the party of their parents. Of course, prior to the election of 1964, not all that many southern blacks were registered to vote. About one-quarter of southern blacks voted in the presidential election of 1960, up from 13 percent in 1952 (Jaynes and Williams 1989, 230). As they entered the electorate in much more significant numbers, the civil rights movement, the Goldwater campaign, and the Democratic response to these two developments led many blacks to align themselves with the Democratic party. By 1964, more than 86 percent of southern blacks were Democratic, up from 60 percent in 1960. Since then, southern black support for the Democratic party has continued to be close to complete. Throughout the 1980s, southern black Democratic support fluctuated quite a bit from year to year, but still ranged between 76 and 94 percent. The percentage of blacks identifying themselves as Republican through the entire time period is quite small, at no time greater than 12 percent.

While blacks have moved almost entirely into the Democratic camp, many southern whites are now in the other camp. If one looks only at the partisanship levels of whites (fig. 1.2), the shift toward Republicanism is dramatic. In the early 1950s, about 85 percent of white southerners called themselves Democrats, 13 percent Republicans. Democratic affiliation fell significantly in the 1950s and early 1960s to 65 percent, but rebounded some in 1964 (70 percent versus 22 percent for the GOP). Since then, conversions and generational replacement have had a steady effect on party balance. Perhaps in response to Wallace's independent campaign, many white Democrats left the fold in 1968, though they were not yet prepared to call themselves Republican. Republican gains that year did not amount to even half the Democratic attrition. Republican growth and Democratic decline among southern whites continued through 1972 but then held steady through the decade, the trend likely retarded by Jimmy Carter's candidacy and presidency. Republican growth among southern whites resumed in the 1980s, and by 1992, 43 percent of white southerners were Republicans compared to 42 percent calling themselves Democrats. Among whites, the Republicans had finally caught up.

Republican gains in the electorate mean little unless they can be con-

Figure 1.2   Party Identification of White Southerners, 1952–1992

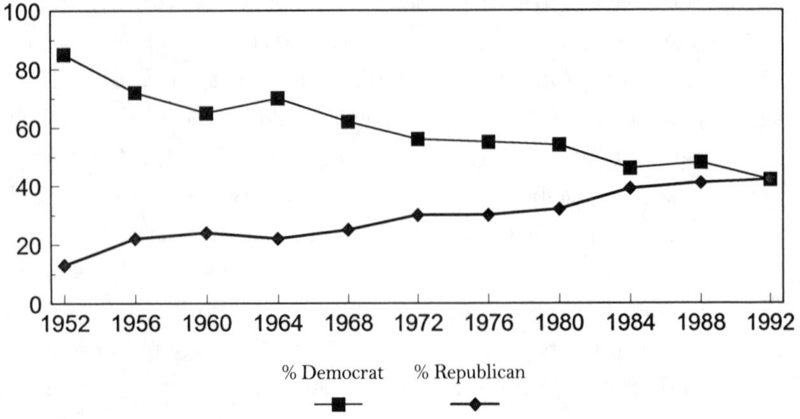

Source: American National Election Studies, 1952–1992

verted into electoral victories, into Republicans in office. The South has contributed to Republicans in one office in particular—the presidency. In recent elections, the South, with one exception, has gone overwhelmingly for the Republican ticket (see fig. 1.3), a fact that has been very important to the party's national chances. Black and Black (1992) even call the region the Vital South, the key to Republican success in the electoral college. A Solid South accounts for almost two-thirds of the electoral votes required to win the presidency. And although the Republican lock on the electoral college failed in 1992, it was not because of the South. Almost two-thirds of President Bush's electoral vote came from the region.

Even before the civil rights movement, the Republican ticket was competitive in electoral votes and in popular votes in the South. In 1952 and 1956, Dwight Eisenhower picked up about half the electoral votes in the South, even breaking through in the Deep South in 1956 with a victory in Louisiana. Richard Nixon won more than one-quarter of southern electoral votes in the election of 1960, taking the peripheral southern states of Florida, Tennessee, and Virginia. But the election in 1964 saw the biggest breakthrough. Although Lyndon Johnson and the Democrats

Figure 1.3   Presidential Electoral Vote in the South, 1952–1992

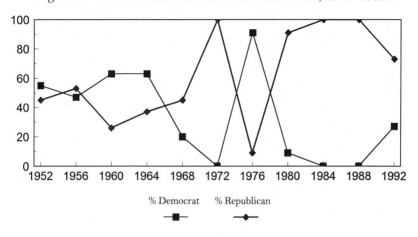

again won eighty-one electoral votes (as they had in 1960), Barry Goldwater won forty-seven electoral votes, reaping rewards for his staunchly conservative, anti–civil rights campaign and sweeping the Deep South. In 1968, George Wallace's candidacy complicated the election in the South. In spite of Wallace, Nixon won a plurality of the popular vote (35 percent compared to Wallace's 33 percent and Hubert Humphrey's 31 percent) and of the electoral vote. Nixon won five states for fifty-seven electoral votes while Wallace took five states for forty-six electoral votes. Humphrey won only Texas's twenty-five electoral votes.

Since then, with the exception of 1976, Republicans have overwhelmingly dominated the presidential contest. In 1972, 1984, and 1988, the patently conservative Republican candidate completely shut out the unmistakably liberal Democrat in the electoral count. What is more, Nixon took a whopping 71 percent of the southern vote in 1972, while Ronald Reagan and George Bush won 63 percent and 59 percent, respectively. In 1976, Jimmy Carter won 54 percent of the southern vote, but took more than 90 percent of the electoral vote, losing only Virginia to Gerald Ford. In 1980, the situation was reversed, Reagan taking 51 percent of the popular vote and all but Georgia's twelve electoral votes. Even in 1992, when the Democrats fielded a ticket of two southerners, they won only

Figure 1.4 Percent of Southern Democrats in Congress, 1952–1992

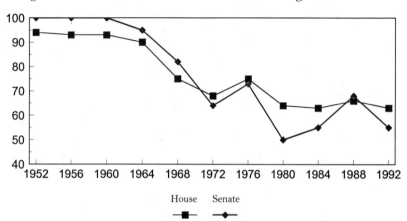

their standard-bearers' home states (Arkansas and Tennessee), Louisiana, and Georgia.

If the Republicans have been inordinately successful in winning recent presidential elections in the South, their congressional fortunes have not been nearly as good. From the 1950s, prior to the demise of Jim Crow, through 1994, Democrats held a large advantage in congressional seats (see fig. 1.4). Only with the 1994 elections did the Republicans catch up. It is striking that through the 1970s, 1980s, and early 1990s, a time Republican presidents were exceedingly popular and electorally successful in the South, southern congressional seats continued to turn over to Democrats.

Republicans did not hold any Senate seats as recently as 1960. Over the next few decades, they made some progress, and by 1980, when several conservative Republican candidates—Paula Hawkins in Florida, Jeremiah Denton in Alabama, Mack Mattingly in Georgia, and John East in North Carolina—won narrow victories, the partisan balance of southern senators was fifty-fifty. Between 1980 and 1992, however, Republicans were unable to protect their gains. In 1986, the Democrats defeated Hawkins, Denton, and Mattingly and recaptured the seat won by East, who died in the middle of his term. With these victories, the Democrats restored their two-to-one advantage in the southern Senate contingent. In 1992, Republicans won back the Georgia and North Carolina seats (and added a Texas seat), but the Democrats still held a twelve to ten advantage. Only with the loss of two Tennessee seats and the defection of Richard Shelby in 1994 have the Republicans finally captured a majority of southern Senate seats. But it was an awfully long time coming.

In the House, the trend lines are similar. Through the 1950s to 1960, Democrats held about 93 percent of the congressional seats. By the time of Reagan's victory in 1980, Democrats held 64 percent of southern congressional seats, a decline to be sure, but still a convincing majority. The Republican House contingent, however, did not continue to grow in the Reagan-Bush years. In 1980, Republicans held 36 percent of southern congressional seats; after the elections in 1992, they held 37 percent of them. Again, 1994 appears to have been a watershed year, with Republicans winning sixteen new seats and holding a small majority (51 percent) of seats in the region.[6] Again, even after the 1994 elections, the difference between Republican congressional and presidential success in the South is still marked. After all, from 1980 to 1992, Ronald Reagan and George Bush won 71 percent of southern congressional districts in their presidential contests.

It is quite noteworthy that southern Democrats weathered the Reagan-Bush years so well. Lest Democratic congressional success be interpreted as simply the result of entrenched incumbents, *open seat* elections in the South show how successful the Democrats were at the congressional level in these years.[7] From the 1980 elections to the 1992 elections, Democrats won a sizable majority (62 percent) of the 109 open seat House elections. Because Democrats had more seats to defend, they could still have been experiencing a net loss. This, however, was not the case. Democrats held a steady percentage of House seats because they were slightly more successful than Republicans at defending their own open seats. In open elections in which a Democratic incumbent retired, died, or was defeated in a primary, Democrats retained the seat 79 percent of the time. Republicans retained their seats 69 percent of the time.[8]

The weakness of congressional Republicans in this period is striking when one compares Ronald Reagan's performance in these same districts in 1984. Of seventy-nine open seat elections, only twelve were held in districts that Reagan had lost in 1984.[9] Democrats won ten of these contests. The other sixty-seven open seat elections were held in districts won by Reagan, and Democrats won thirty-eight (57 percent) of them. Where Reagan won a district by more than 60 percent, Republicans took 68 percent of the open seat contests, but this represented only twenty-eight elections.

Democratic congressional dominance is reflected further in the size and scope of these open seat victories. For one thing, when Democrats won, they won more convincing victories than Republicans. Of the sixty-eight Democratic open seat victories, 60 percent were won with at least 60 percent of the vote. Only 20 percent of the forty-one Republican open seat victories were convincing by this standard. On the other hand, 42 percent of Republican victories were narrow, with winning percentages of 52 percent or less. Only 16 percent of Democratic victories fell into this category.

The geographic scope of Democratic victories in these open seat elections is impressive as well. Democrats won at least half of the open seat elections in every state but one, the exception being Florida. The Republican party has enjoyed notable success in this state, mostly because of a burgeoning population fed by several million migrants from the North and from Latin America. Many of these northern migrants have brought their Republican identities with them. The large Cuban community in Florida also is strongly allegiant to the Republicans, the party that appeals most to their strong anti-Communist, anti-Castro sentiments. These new constituencies have helped the Republicans win twelve of Florida's twenty-two open seat elections. Although the party is doing well in this important, rapidly growing state, Florida is the least characteristically southern state in the entire region, given its diverse and rapidly changing population. Removing Florida from the picture and looking only at the other ten states of the region, one discovers that Democrats have taken 67 percent of the open seat contests. Why, in the Reagan-Bush

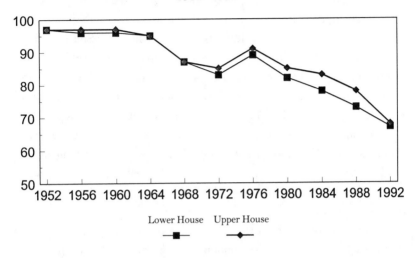

Figure 1.5 Percent of Democrats in Southern State Legislatures, 1952–1992

years, a period of popular Republican administrations, a period in which Republicans won 91 percent of southern electoral votes in four presidential elections, and a period of high Republican hopes in the South, were Republicans not very successful in winning congressional elections when their chances were best, that is, when seats opened up because of retirement or death?[10]

Republican gains have been even more limited in state legislative elections than in congressional elections (fig. 1.5).[11] As recently as 1964, Democrats held 96 percent of the seats in the lower houses of the South, a remarkable total. Through the sixties and seventies, the Democratic percentage of state house seats never dipped lower than 83 percent. In the 1980s, the Republicans did much better, and following the 1994 elections Democrats still held 63 percent of state house seats, though down from 82 percent in 1980 and 67 percent in 1992.

The story is much the same in the upper houses of the South. Democrats held almost every senate seat (95 percent of them) as late as 1964. Democratic dominance continued through the next three decades, falling to a low of 59 percent in 1994, down from 83 percent in 1984. Although the recent gains are encouraging for Republicans, the dominance of the Democrats in the state legislatures of the South is still quite impressive.

In the parlance of the literature, the realignment in the South has been slow to filter down. This review of partisanship and office holding in the region shows plainly that Republican success has not been fully achieved. The obvious question is, why not? How come so many southern whites still identify with the Democratic party? Why is it that the Republicans have so dominated at one level and that the Democrats have defended themselves so effectively at lower levels? Thirty years is a long time in political terms. Why has it taken so long for Republicans to build a party, wait out incumbents, recruit quality candidates, and see the realignment work its way down?

These questions lead to the first puzzle of this book. The region is decidedly conservative in its opinions on a great variety of issues (Nie, Verba, and Petrocik 1979; Black and Black 1987), which by all accounts should have given the Republicans a great advantage. Yet low-level Republican politicians have not fully harnessed this advantage. And if Republican presidential candidates, particularly since 1980, have provided some sort of demonstration as to how elections can be won in the region with standard conservative themes and have given lower-level Republican candidates a clear connection to conservatism, the long period of Republican mixed success is especially perplexing. Why was this connection not worth more? Even putting aside the ideological advantage, how come overwhelmingly popular figures at the top of the ticket did not do more for the rest of the party's candidates? To sum up the first puzzle, it seems the GOP should have gained more of an advantage from winning presidential elections than they did. How was this advantage spent and why did it not materialize?

The Puzzle of Race and the Realignment

If part of the Republican advantage in the South has been an ideological one, a second presumed advantage Republicans have held over Democrats is the race issue. Many have interpreted the rise of the Republican party in the region as a racial phenomenon. They link Republican growth to racial issues and to the steady flow of southern whites (both former Democrats and those new to the electorate) to a Republican party that best represents their views on race.

From this perspective, the southern realignment has been a continuation of the past. Issues of race defined and maintained the one-party system for decades in the South. By this view, the political salience of such issues did not change. They still held a powerful grip on southern whites and still influenced their political behavior. What changed was the positions the parties took on these issues and how people perceived the parties on such issues. Realignment was thus not the result of a new issue redefining the political landscape. It was the result of a new cleavage on an old issue.

As to the first element of this argument, there has been a change in the character of the race issue. Racial attitudes in the South have become markedly more progressive since the early 1960s (Schuman, Steeh, and Bobo 1985). This is not to say that racist attitudes have disappeared from the region. Only a small minority of southern whites, however, cling to segregationist views, and their numbers continue to dwindle with generational change.

What has changed since the civil rights movement is the nature of the dialogue over racial issues (as well as the issues themselves). In the face of these changes, racial attitudes have become informed by conservative ideology, not only in the South but, of course, in the country as a whole. The racial attitudes of many whites still may be characterized as conservative, reflecting resistance to government assistance to blacks as a group and applying individualistic notions and standards to the situation of blacks in this country. Some social scientists argue that much contemporary hostility to black interests stems from anti-black prejudice, which is dressed up in new ways and combined with this conservative logic (Kinder and Sears 1981; Kinder 1986). Others argue that it is simply conservative values that guide positions on racial issues (Sniderman and Hagen 1985, 110–12). Whatever one's position in this debate, it is indisputable that this racially conservative constellation of attitudes is

Table 1.1   Southern White Attitudes on Racial Questions

Generations of slavery and discrimination have created conditions that make it difficult for blacks to work their way out of the lower class.

	Southern Whites	Northern Whites
% disagreeing	43	35
% agreeing	45	53
% neither disagreeing nor agreeing	12	11
Base N	(855)	(2,316)

It's really a matter of some people not trying hard enough; if blacks would only try harder they could be just as well off as whites.

	Southern Whites	Northern Whites
% agreeing	69	56
% disagreeing	16	30
% neither agreeing nor disagreeing	16	14
Base N	(857)	(2,312)

Some people feel that the government in Washington should make every effort to improve the social and economic position of blacks. Others feel that the government should not make any special effort to help blacks because they should help themselves. Where would you place yourself [on this scale]?

	Southern Whites	Northern Whites
% saying blacks should help themselves	62	49
% saying the government should make effort	16	20
% at midpoint of scale	22	31
Base N	(819)	(2,197)

Most blacks who receive money from welfare programs could get along without it if they tried.

	Southern Whites	Northern Whites
% agreeing	76	54
% disagreeing	11	31
% neither agreeing nor disagreeing	13	15
Base N	(247)	(631)

Table 1.1 Continued

Do you think that civil rights leaders are trying to push too fast, are going too slowly, or are they moving at about the right speed?

	Southern Whites	*Northern Whites*
% too fast	40	30
% too slow	8	10
% about the right speed	52	60
Base N	(1,322)	(3,641)

Source: American National Election Studies (1980–1990 pooled).

now held by many whites who are not sympathetic to black social and economic equality or to civil rights advances.

Southern whites in particular continue to be rather hostile to black political, economic, and social progress. Using survey data from the 1980s, I show in table 1.1 that southern whites have conservative impulses on racial issues.[12] They are, in fact, much more likely to take conservative positions than white northerners, who are included in the table as a basis for comparison. A majority of southern whites, for instance, accept individualistic explanations for the black condition or at least do not ascribe present-day inequality to the legacy of slavery and discrimination. Equality is a matter of effort, and if blacks worked harder, goes this line of logic, they would achieve equal status in society. Not surprisingly, a large majority thus accept an individualistic solution to the problem. Most believe that the federal government should not work to equalize the races, socially or economically, and that blacks should not expect any preferential treatment from the government. Welfare and policies like it are viewed as such treatment and are disliked and rejected by many. Fully three-quarters of southern whites take a skeptical view of welfare and especially of black welfare recipients. Together, these related conservative beliefs and attitudes inform positions on a variety of racial issues and, most important, are socially acceptable and reinforced throughout the country, above all in the South. Even as the race issue has evolved, the South has continued to be the most racially conservative region in the country, thereby providing some continuity with the past.

The second element of the racial realignment argument is that the Democratic party has changed sides on issues of race. Since Goldwater and since the replacement of the old southern Democrats the *southern* parties have become quite differentiated on questions of government involvement in promoting racial equality and on many other questions of political significance to blacks. One way to illustrate just how differentiated the parties have become on racial issues is to look at the voting behavior of southern Republican and Democratic congressmen. The great change that has taken place in the South since the 1960s is apparent in table 1.2.[13] Southern Democrats and southern Republicans now vote very differently on civil rights issues. On two amendments to the Voting Rights Act Extension (1981), for example, southern Democrats were generally opposed to the easing of "bail out" procedures (procedures offering covered jurisdictions greater consideration in exempting themselves from the act). On one of these votes, more than three-fifths of southern Democrats voted against the amendment, and on the other, three-quarters did so. More than 80 percent of southern Republicans voted in favor of both amendments. More recently, in 1990, 86 percent of southern Democrats and but 8 percent of southern Republicans voted for a civil rights bill reversing some Supreme Court decisions that limited job discrimination lawsuits.

This pattern is also evident in votes on issues of symbolic importance to blacks. In 1986, close to three-quarters of southern Democrats voted to encourage President Reagan to urge reform on South Africa; only two of forty southern Republicans joined in. A bill in 1983 to create a federal holiday in honor of Martin Luther King's birthday garnered 85 percent of southern Democratic votes but only 37 percent of southern Republican votes. There is little doubt that on issues of race, Democrats and Republicans have been distinctively different for some time.

More important, according to those documenting a racial realignment,

Table 1.2 Congressional Votes in the 1980s

Vote Distributions on Discrimination Issues

	Southern Democrats	Southern Republicans
A 1981 Voting Rights Extension		
Vote #1	26–41	32–4
Vote #2	16–50	29–7
B 1984 Civil Rights Act	70–6	24–10
C 1990 Civil Rights Act	62–10	3–35

Vote Distributions on Symbolic Issues

	Southern Democrats	Southern Republicans
D 1981 South Africa Rugby Team	35–30	0–37
E 1983 Martin Luther King, Jr. Holiday	69–12	13–22
F 1986 Misc. South Africa Demands	52–19	2–38
G 1986 Override Reagan Veto on S. Africa Sanctions	60–4	9–30

The following descriptions come from the *Congressional Quarterly Almanac.*

A Two hostile amendments to the Voting Rights Act Extension: (1) Butler, R-Va., amendment to allow three-judge federal district courts to hear petitions by jurisdictions seeking to bail out from coverage of the Voting Rights Act. (2) Campbell, R-S.C., amendment to allow a state covered by the Voting Rights Act to bail out from coverage if two-thirds of its counties are eligible to bail out.

B Passage of the bill to make clear that the bar to discrimination in Title IX of the 1972 Education Act, Title VI of the Civil Rights Act of 1973, and the Age Discrimination Act of 1975 covers an entire institution if any program or activity within the institution receives federal assistance.

C Passage of the bill to reverse or modify six Supreme Court decisions that narrowed the reach and remedies of job discrimination laws and to authorize monetary damages under Title VII of the 1964 Civil Rights Act.

D Zablocki, D-Wis., motion that the House suspend the rules and adopt the concurrent resolution stating the sense of Congress that the Springbok National Rugby Team of South Africa, on tour in the United States, should not play rugby in the United States.

E Hall, D-Ind., motion to suspend the rules and pass the bill to designate the third Monday of every January as a federal holiday in honor of the late civil rights leader the Rev. Dr. Martin Luther King Jr.

F Wolpe, D-Mich., motion to suspend the rules and adopt the resolution to express the sense of the House that the president should urge the South African government to engage in political negotiations with that country's black majority; grant immediately unconditional freedom to Nelson Mandela and other political prisoners; and recognize the African National Congress as a legitimate representative for the black majority.

G Passage, over President Reagan's Sept. 26 veto, of the bill to impose economic sanctions against South Africa.

this partisan difference has become increasingly obvious to white southerners. Any ambiguity stemming from past party positions has now disappeared, and new party images have evolved. Survey data show that the
southern public has become quite clear about the two parties' positions
on race. For instance, as to the question of party positions on whether the
federal government "should make every effort to improve the social and
economic position of blacks and other minority groups" or "should not
make any special effort to help minorities because they should help themselves," more than 60 percent of southerners see the Democratic party as
favoring efforts to help blacks and other minorities. Fifty-seven percent
view the Republican party as opposed. Fewer than one in five southerners
views the Republicans as being on the liberal side of this issue or the
Democrats as being on the conservative side.[14]

The parties thus have become markedly different in the eyes of southern voters, and Grofman (1990), for one, argues that the Democratic
party label "[has lost] its old connotation of 'being for the little guy' and
[is] taking on a racial meaning" (9). As the term *liberal* has come to mean
"pro-black" and as the Democrats have become known as the party that
represents blacks, he writes, there has been an obvious "link between race
and 'white flight' from the Democratic party in the South" (1).[15]

The process has been self-reinforcing. As more whites have left the
Democratic party, it has become more "black." As blacks have become a
larger part of the party's constituency, they have become more involved
in party affairs, and the party has become increasingly attentive to their
concerns. Minority candidates even have emerged to represent the party.
In the eyes of the public, the Democratic party has become more closely
identified with blacks, which has led to even further white defections. As
Chandler Davidson (1990) writes about the transformation in Texas,
"The previously all-white Democratic party was now increasingly the
refuge of black and brown voters, as many whites continued to flee that
party much as they fled neighborhoods when black and brown home-
seekers moved in" (238).

What is more, the motivation of party switchers may not even have
been racial. As is well established in the political sociology literature,

when all one's friends, family, coworkers, and associates identify as Republican, the compulsion for one to do so as well is powerful (Berelson, Lazarsfeld, and McPhee 1954). In the South, so goes the racial realignment argument, people have been flocking to the white Republican party because it is the socially reinforced thing to do. "Political preferences are not constructed or sustained in a social vacuum," write Huckfeldt and Kohfeld (1989). "Prior to the events of the postwar period, it was difficult for Republican preferences to survive among white southerners. Now, in the late 1980s, it has become difficult for Democratic preferences to survive within many segments of the white electorate. In states like Mississippi, it has undoubtedly become socially unacceptable for many whites to support the Democratic party" (58). The process by which a "politically adrift white population" (40) has found its way to the Republican party thus would seem difficult to reverse.

The second puzzle I address in this study follows from these basic facts of southern politics and society and from the racial realignment scenario. For if racial attitudes continue to have vitality in southern electoral politics, if the parties have differentiated on racial issues, if southern voters recognize these differences, and if race has contributed so much to Republican strength, why did race not propel the party forward across the board? If, as Grofman (1990) writes, the effects of race are "commonsensically obvious to the informed observer" (1), how have the Democrats held on for so long? Why have many whites stayed in the Democratic fold? Are biracial coalitions really possible for the Democrats? How are they constructed and maintained? These questions are interesting because to be answered they require an examination of the assumptions that many carry as to how race and politics mix.

The two puzzles sketched out here are related, and the solutions to them are interrelated. First, conservatism and several popular Republican administrations did not give the Republicans the advantage one might expect in lower-level elections. Second, neither did race appear to be giving Republicans the lower-level advantage one would expect. Just what did the Democratic party do right in these years? Where did the Republican party go wrong? These are the questions that motivate what follows.

In this book, I offer a solution to these puzzles and some answers to these questions. My vehicle for approaching them is a study of southern congressional campaigns, for such a study affords some sense of the choices offered to southern voters and puts to the test some of the grand assumptions people carry about politics in the South.

"History is a relentless master," said John F. Kennedy,."It has no present, only the past rushing into the future." The problem I have faced in doing this work is that of describing and analyzing a moving target. Politics in the South have undergone substantial change through the 1960s, 1970s, and 1980s and continue to change in the 1990s. In fact, 1994 may be the year that demarcates a partisan system based on one set of dynamics from another. Some years must pass before this is known. Whatever happens, the tale of how Democrats held off full-scale realignment for so long a time, of decades of simultaneous Republican success in presidential elections and Democratic success in lower-level elections, of the surprisingly protracted transition from southern Democracy to southern democracy is worth telling because it adds another chapter to the fascinating political history of the region, a chapter with some important and generalizable political lessons.

What is more, the seeds of change lie within this situation. If the Republicans continue to make gains at the congressional level and at levels on down, they will likely do so because they have studied the lessons of the present and learned from them. Of course, Democratic strategy too will evolve and adjust. What follows, then, is not a prediction. Instead, it is a description and analysis of a baseline from which change can be measured and an attempt to capture a moment when the past rushes into the future.

2 The Case for Context

To understand political choices, we need to understand where the frame of reference for the actors' thinking comes from—how it is evoked. An important component of the frame of reference is the set of alternatives that are given consideration in the choice process. We need to understand not only how people reason about alternatives, but where the alternatives come from in the first place. The process whereby alternatives are generated has been somewhat ignored as an object of research. *Herbert Simon, "Human Nature in Politics"*

IN THIS BOOK, I tell a story of how Democratic and Republican candidates for Congress have campaigned for office in the South. It is a description of the strategies they have pursued, the tactics they have used, and their intentions in using them. It is, in short, an attempt to follow Herbert Simon's directive and analyze "the process whereby alternatives are generated," the Democratic and Republican alternatives posed to the southern voter. Simon's larger point, of course, is that the introduction of such political context can help resolve thorny analytical problems. By describing and analyzing elections as I do here, I aim to address the thorny puzzles of the southern realignment.

The argument I make about context is two-pronged. First, the context in which a congressional election takes place, that is, the racial balance of the district, leads candidates of the two parties to campaign in certain ways and with certain messages. The point is that much of what goes on in southern campaigns has a racial element, even if an explicit racial issue is not introduced into the contest. The racial composition of the district sets the parameters within which candidates must work and establishes the conditions for success. Their grand strategies and their specific maneuvers thus depend, to a great extent, on the size of the black and white populations in their district.

The theoretical basis of this argument is that group or racial conflict has a powerful influence on political thinking and possibly even on behavior. That is, as groups come into competition over valued resources—political power, social goods, or even symbols of group identity or pride—members of these groups are profoundly affected. Even the potential for conflict, whether real or perceived, has some bearing on intragroup attitudes and on decisions about political issues or political choices defined by race.

Substantial evidence exists that white racial-political attitudes are influenced by the racial environment or the potential for racial-political conflict in one's environment. As I show elsewhere (Glaser 1994), the more heavily black the southern county, the more racially conservative white racial-political attitudes tend to be (see also Giles 1977 and Giles and Evans 1986). This relation is strong and monotonic over a variety of racial-political measures. What is striking, though, is that negative affect toward blacks and acceptance of negative stereotypes about blacks appear to be unrelated to racial environment (Glaser 1994). This strongly suggests that it is group or racial conflict, and not just the legacy of the past, that influences attitudes that sit at the intersection of race and politics. Where blacks have more opportunity to exercise political power or to demand a larger share of societal resources, southern white attitudes reflect greater hostility to black political aspirations.

What I argue here is that the potential for group conflict shapes incentives that party politicians are very sensitive to. Of course, these incentives change as the racial balance of the district changes. Campaign behaviors, messages, and strategies—both Democratic and Republican—respond directly to the changes in these incentives.

These behaviors, messages, and strategies, in turn, shape the context of the vote choice. Herein lies the second major prong of my argument. As Simon cautions, before one attempts to analyze the individual decisions of voters, it is worth knowing something about the options they have before them. In this case, the puzzles of the southern realignment become less puzzling when the political alternatives that have been offered to southern voters are fully explored. For when analyzed in context, the political choices made by southern voters appear to make sense.

The predominant understanding of southern voting behavior starts with the observation that the Republicans have long been the more racially conservative party in the region, while Democrats are the racial liberals. As chapter 1 illustrates, this is certainly the case. But this does not take into account the Republican message that has been communicated and how it has been put out or, more important, what the Democrats have done to counter it. Voters do not behave in a vacuum. They respond *to* something: to political stimuli, to candidates, to political campaigns. Their behavior is, in part, the result of the choices that are available to them. The congressional choice posed to the southern voter at the congressional level has rarely been just "racial conservative or racial liberal" or for that matter, "conservative or liberal." It has been much more complicated than this.

Once a more useful and complete picture of the choice offered to southern voters is painted, it becomes clear that in spite of the Republicans' success in presidential elections, Democrats have had a strategic advantage over Republicans in southern congressional elections, and in fact much of that advantage has come from their handling of race. Southern Democrats have been able to keep together a tenuous black–white coalition in a variety of racial environments in the region. They have done so by blunting the edge of racial issues in these campaigns. They also have cultivated some significant offensive issues of their own with which to court white voters and to counter the conservative advantage that

Republicans have had. An analysis of Democratic campaigns shows why and how they have won southern congressional elections in thirty years of prolonged realignment and how they must operate if they are to win congressional elections in an increasingly precarious future.

The perspective that guides this study is that race has continued to influence southern politics, and in profound, if not always expected, ways. Although it is true that a New South has emerged, this characteristic of the old political system has persisted. It is not the legacy of the Old South that has led this to be the case. The region has admirably purged itself of the worst of its past. But while southern blacks have access to the ballot and to political office as never before, in fact, partly because of these developments, political incentives are such as to keep race an important electoral factor in the region.

Racial Variations and Calculations

To investigate the first prong of my argument, that the racial balance of the congressional district is a primary factor in determining the course of a southern campaign, it is worth sketching out the quantitative logic of the congressional campaign.

First, the larger the black population, the bigger the head start Democratic candidates have as they enter a contest. Democratic candidates benefit from the fact that a large majority of blacks identify with their party. But a large black population does not automatically transfer into Democratic votes, and much of the campaign revolves around the fact that blacks must be courted, their support reinforced. Table 2.1 illustrates how different assumptions about comparative turnout and black solidarity can lead to highly divergent strategic situations.

The proportion of blacks to whites in the district does not always translate into the proportion of black to white voters in an election. Much depends on the turnout rates of the two groups. A look at turnout rates that are 10 percentage points apart is illustrative. For example, in a district in which 20 percent of the population is black (about the average in the South), blacks may comprise anywhere from 16 to 25 percent of the *electorate* depending upon the turnout rate differences of the two popula-

Table 2.1   Demographic Considerations of Southern Strategists

Black Percentage of the Electorate Given Various Levels of Black Turnout
(Assumption: Turnout in Special Election is 33 percent)

	10% Black Population	*20% Black Population*	*30% Black Population*	*40% Black Population*
Black Turnout 10% < White Turnout	8%	16%	24%	33%
Black Turnout = White Turnout	10%	20%	30%	40%
Black Turnout 10% > White Turnout	13%	25%	37%	48%

Democratic Headstart Given Various Levels of Black Support
(Assumption: Black Turnout = White Turnout)

	10% Black Population	*20% Black Population*	*30% Black Population*	*40% Black Population*
80% of Black Vote to Democrat	8%	16%	24%	32%
90% of Black Vote to Democrat	9%	18%	27%	36%
95% of Black Vote to Democrat	10%	19%	29%	38%

Percentage of White Vote Needed for Democrat to Win Given Various Levels of
Turnout and Black Support
(Assumption: Turnout in Special Election is 33 percent)

	10% Black Population	*20% Black Population*	*30% Black Population*	*40% Black Population*
80% of Black Vote to Democrat / Black Turnout 10% < White Turnout	47%	44%	42%	35%
90% of Black Vote to Democrat / Black Turnout = White Turnout	46%	40%	33%	23%
95% of Black Vote to Democrat / Black Turnout 10% > White Turnout	43%	35%	24%	9%

tions. The difference is quite meaningful to both Democratic and Republican candidates.[1]

It is certainly true that most southern blacks identify with the Democratic party and vote for Democrats in elections up and down the ticket. Democratic candidates thus have to win a much smaller portion of white votes than would be the case given smaller black populations. The size of their head start does change appreciably, however, if Republicans make inroads into the black vote. In the zero-sum game of electoral politics, the difference (in a district that is 20 percent black) between strong black support for the Democratic candidate (80 percent) and almost unanimous support for the Democrat (95 percent) is a difference of three percentage points in the end result (six points when one considers that every gain is a loss for the opponent). This, of course, can be significant in a close election.

Southern campaigns are fought out on two fronts that vary in relative importance according to the racial balance of the district, turnout rates, and Republican inroads into the black vote. On one front, Republicans and Democrats battle for their share of the white vote. On the other, Democrats try to maximize the black vote as Republicans try to minimize that Democratic advantage. Democrats thus must balance their need to maximize black turnout with their quest to hold on to a significant minority of whites. They also must keep the Republican candidate from cutting into their black support. The Republican goals of maximizing their share of the white vote and depressing black turnout or cutting into the black electoral monolith are not so potentially contradictory. Nonetheless, their task is formidable.

This brief sketch of what it takes for Democratic and Republican candidates to win in the region sets the stage for what is to follow. Four main hypotheses flow from this discussion, hypotheses that both stand on their own and are interrelated.

Hypothesis 1: In majority white districts, Republican strategy should change as racial environments change. The larger the black percentage of a majority white congressional district, the greater the imperative of Republican candidates to win a larger share of the white vote and the more likely whites are to respond to an issue of race. In heavily black majority white districts, then, Republican candidates will be most likely to introduce a racial issue, an issue aimed at uniting white voters, into a political campaign and will be most likely to make it a major part of their campaign.

Hypothesis 2: For Democrats, the incentives also shift with change in the racial environment. In all majority white districts, Democrats will attempt to construct biracial coalitions. However, the larger the black percentage of a majority white district, the more likely Democrats will be to risk white votes to win black votes. At no point will they abandon one goal for the other and racial issues will always be approached in a gingerly way.

Hypothesis 3: In a majority black district, the strategic incentives should reverse. Democrats will seek to maximize the black vote, even at the cost of white votes, and racial approaches should be more likely to be embraced. This is crucial given that lower black turnout rates are more costly to Democratic candidates where blacks comprise a larger proportion of the population (see table 2.1). Republicans, on the other hand, will seek to build biracial coalitions and should handle racial issues with more moderation and more caution.

Hypothesis 4: Democrats should have more of an advantage in majority black districts than Republicans in majority white ones, mostly because the white vote is not as unified as the black vote. Given the limited Democratic goals in majority white districts, campaigns that are even modestly successful in drawing whites will win. This would be the key to Democratic success in the South and the solution to the realignment puzzles.[2]

This book represents an attempt to test these expectations, to hold them up to reality. The results of these tests reveal much about how the southern partisan system has changed and how it has remained the same. In addition, they offer more general lessons on how race and politics have mixed in the post–civil rights era.

Methodology

How politicians behave, what they say on the stump, what their campaign advertisements claim and what they charge of their opponents, whom they choose to speak to and whom they avoid, and what vehicles they use to communicate with the electorate all have some impact on voters' decisions. Yet describing and analyzing elections in this way is expensive and labor intensive. It involves going to the source and observing politics in action. It requires hustling to get people to talk with you (including conservative Republicans suspicious of a Berkeley address), dealing with unexpected circumstances (such as a hurricane threatening off the Gulf Coast), figuring out logistical nightmares (if I ride with the candidate from Alexander City to Montgomery, how will I get back to my car?), and sometimes risking personal safety (riding at seventy miles an hour on winding country roads with an unhappy, distracted campaign manager behind the wheel).[3]

From an analytical standpoint, there is another problem with participant-observer research that discourages political scientists interested in electoral behavior. It involves making generalizations based on a small number of observations and describing something not easily analyzed in a grand or more general way. As a result, many political scientists leave descriptions of elections to journalists, who generally look at each election as a separate entity. They bypass this descriptive process. They look at aggregate data or even survey data and draw conclusions based on the application of certain assumptions to their findings. Although such findings are often of great value, the assumptions are often left untouched.

The descriptions in the following chapters are all of special elections held to fill seats vacated by the death or resignation of a member of Congress. The six elections, all won by Democrats, represent more than half such elections from the 1980s and early 1990s. They took place in Mississippi's Fourth District (in the summer of 1981), in Texas's First District (in the summer of 1985), in Virginia's Fifth District (in spring 1988), in Alabama's Third District (in the spring of 1989), in Mississippi's Fifth District (in the fall of 1989), and in Mississippi's Second District (in the spring of 1993). The shaded areas of the map in figure 2.1 indicate exactly where these districts are located in their various states. Table 2.2 is a summary of the six elections, listing the candidates involved, the margins of victory, and other basic information.

Figure 2.1   Congressional Districts in the Study

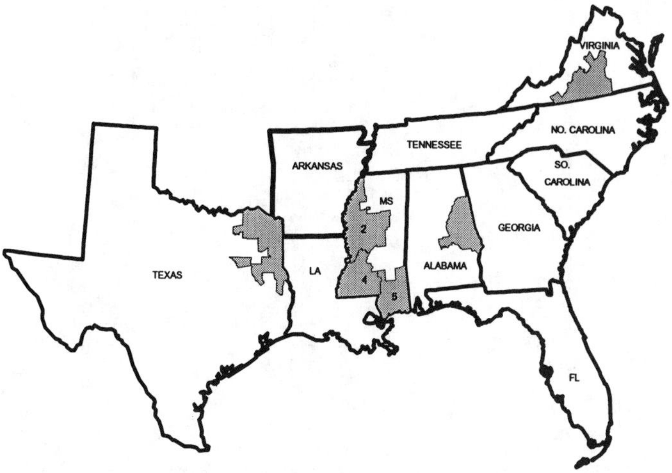

This map represents the districts as they looked through the 1980s. The 1993 congressional race in Mississippi 2 took place in a district that is marginally different from the one shown here.

I observed three of the elections at firsthand. For the elections in Alabama 3, Mississippi 5, and Mississippi 2, I traveled to the district and followed the campaigns around. I attended campaign speeches, press conferences, political rallies, church services, meetings with black ministers, commercial tapings, and candidate debates, I spoke with the candidates, and I met with numerous other actors involved in the drama. I interviewed as many people as would see me—Democrats and Republicans, journalists and candidates, campaign managers and media consultants, black ministers and white union leaders, national and state party representatives, local party hacks and campaign volunteers—thus gathering a variety of not always congruent perspectives on the same set of events. Through my interviews and observations and through local newspaper reports of the campaigns, I have pieced together fairly detailed accounts of these elections. The newspapers were especially useful in my analysis because they showed which of the candidates' messages made it to the public. Although the candidates often complained about their coverage

Table 2.2 Summary of Cases

State / District / Result	Candidates	Incumbent	Date of Election	% Black Population in District	Winner / Margin of Victory	Average Reagan / Bush % in 1980–88	Presidential Approval Rating*
Ms 4	Wayne Dowdy (D) Liles Williams (R)	Jon Hinson (R)	July 1981	42%	Dowdy 51%–49%	58%	59%
Tx 1	Jim Chapman (D) Edd Hargett (R)	Sam Hall (D)	August 1985	19%	Chapman 51%–49%	54%	63%
Va 5	L. F. Payne (D) Linda Arey (R)	Dan Daniel (D)	June 1988	25%	Payne 59%–41%	61%	51%
Al 3	Glen Browder (D) John Rice (R)	Bill Nichols (D)	April 1989	28%	Browder 65%–35%	55%	63%
Ms 5	Gene Taylor (D) Tom Anderson (R)	Larkin Smith (R)	October 1989	19%	Taylor 65%–35%	67%	70%
Ms 2	Bennie Thompson (D) Hayes Dent (R)	Mike Espy (D)	April 1993	59%	Thompson 55%–45%	48%	52%

*Percent approving the president's performance in the Gallup Survey most recently conducted prior to the election.

34

("The sorry-assed media didn't let me get my message out," said one), the part of the message that made the newspaper was of greater importance to understanding what happened than the part that was ignored.[4]

In all three cases, I spent as much as two weeks in the district during the home stretch of the campaign. This strategy had its advantages and disadvantages. The end of a campaign is a period of great activity. It is also when the media campaigns are waged. I thus had more events to observe and more commercials to view or hear by covering the final frenetic days. The downside of this decision was that the candidates and their campaign staffs were very busy and much less available at this time. Where possible, I reinterviewed people after the election when they were less hurried and more candid.

Working backward, I have reconstructed the events of the three other elections. Much of this was done by scouring local newspapers (such as the *Danville [Virginia] Bee*, the *Dallas Morning News*, and the *Jackson Clarion-Ledger*). I also interviewed candidates, campaign managers, political consultants, and reporters involved in these elections. Even with the campaign so far in the past, most of the people I talked with had clear, detailed recollections of events. In fact, these interviews often benefited from greater hindsight. The interview subjects were more candid because they were less wary of the interviewer and more emotionally divorced from the events of the campaign; and they were not talking to me in a speeding automobile heading for the next campaign event or with a lot of harried campaign workers interrupting.[5]

In conducting this research, I was confronted with some difficult choices, several of which need to be justified before I proceed. Why congressional elections rather than some other type of elections? Why special elections? Why these particular special elections when there were several others to choose from?

Why congressional elections? Most important, the first puzzle that structures this work has to do with mixed electoral results, the disparity between Republican presidential success and the party's weaker performances in congressional elections on down. In solving this puzzle, unlike Earl and Merle Black (1992), I look to the conduct of congressional

Table 2.3   Turnout in Special and Off-year Elections

	Special Election	1986 Election in Same District
Mississippi 4	32%	35%
Texas 1	27%	22%
Virginia 5	27%	23%
Alabama 3	19%	37%
Mississippi 5	37%	27%
Mississippi 2	41%	44%
Average	31%	31%

elections rather than presidential elections. This is because it is the results of these elections that have defied expectations. The more interesting question is not how Republican presidential candidates have won
votes in the South, which is not particularly surprising, but how congressional Democratic candidates have held on.

Congressional elections are preferable to state legislative elections for
very practical reasons. Congressional campaigns command far greater
public attention than elections to the state legislature. They are covered
by the newspapers. The candidates are invited to forums and debates.
Voters are more likely to have some information about these elections and
are more likely to base their decisions on information obtained in the
campaign. They are, simply put, much higher profile elections.

I look at House elections rather than Senate elections because there are
a greater number of them to choose from. Moreover, congressional elections, in most cases, involve more "local" politicians who are familiar with
the district and its inhabitants. Their campaigns are tailored to a smaller
area and are, in this sense, more diverse and more interesting. House
elections are large enough to merit public attention, but small enough to
be considered local. They best fit the requirements of this project. Moreover, Republicans have enjoyed relative success in Senate elections. House
seats are, in some sense, the line of first defense. These elections have
represented the highest level of Democratic dominance in the region.

Special elections are but a small subset of all congressional elections, and they are unique in several ways. They are held independently of other elections. They are often held in isolation, with nothing else on the ballot. They are characterized by lower turnout (Sigelman 1981).[6] Yet "specials" offer some excellent analytic opportunities, and I have tried to take advantage of them. Most important, these elections are all for open seats. In 1988, 99 percent of incumbent congressmen were reelected by an average margin of 38 percentage points.[7] The advantage of incumbency is so great that elections involving an incumbent are more predictable and less interesting. It makes most sense, from my perspective, to look at open seat elections, in which neither candidate enjoys an incumbency advantage. Almost by definition, special elections meet this criterion.

A second reason for looking at special elections is that they are, in fact, isolated from other elections. In the words of one journalist, "They're the only game in town." This is a great advantage for two reasons, one practical, the other analytical. The practical advantage is that special elections often are covered intensively by the media. Because there is usually little else of political interest going on, local and even national reporters have more time and inclination to cover these elections. They also attract journalistic attention because many political observers attach some meaning to special elections. They are "straws in the wind," precursors to upcoming elections and thus indicators of what is to come. Or they are an early electoral measure of how a president is doing. Whatever the case, there is more information available from these elections than from single contests held during the regular election cycle. This has made it possible for me to uncover information in those cases in which I did not witness the campaign. Finally, many of these special elections take place over a short period of time. The compressed nature of the election makes it easier to study, both in terms of following events in person and reconstructing events.

The analytical advantage that specials offer is that one can attribute (cautiously) the final results to the effectiveness of the campaigns, to the circumstances of the particular election. There are no coattails. If there are party levers to pull, they are less important. Most analysts of congressional elections consider local factors to be much more important than national factors in determining results. Still, congressional elections held in conjunction with national elections have another variable that must be considered in understanding the results. This research strategy thus removes a complicating factor from the analysis. Those who go to the polls in these elections are going only to cast a congressional vote and not a presidential (or gubernatorial or senatorial) vote. The campaign that more effectively gets its supporters to the polls is at an advantage, and neither side can count on voters activated by another campaign. This makes it easier to isolate the strategic factors that make the biggest difference. As this is an important objective of this project, investigating special elections makes good sense.

This is not to say that national forces are unimportant in these elections. They frequently do command national attention. Pundits interpret them as referenda on presidential performance or on some important issue facing Congress. National party leaders set them up as measures of party strength. National figures visit the districts and national money flows into the campaigns. And there is some evidence that special election voters, like midterm voters, may be evaluating the presiding administration as they cast their votes, offering support to those who interpret these elections as referenda on how the president is doing.[8] Still, even though the economy and perceptions of the president may have some bearing on voting decisions, the candidates must harness these national forces in getting their supporters to the polls. Gauging the effectiveness of the campaigns in doing this is more easily done when the congressional election is the only game in town.

The understanding of special elections as national referenda does introduce an additional methodological snare into the project. Most of the (limited) literature on the topic suggests that members of the president's party are at a fair disadvantage in midterm and special elections. Kernell (1977) argues persuasively that, in midterm elections, assessments of presidential performance affect congressional voters, particularly those disapproving of the administration. In this light, the inevitable losses to the governing party in American midterm elections and in British by-elections, an even more direct counterpart to special elections, have been understood to be the result of negative voting, of people penalizing the national government in local elections (Mughan 1986; Erikson 1988). As to special elections, Sigelman (1981) shows that three-quarters of all party turnovers in special elections from 1954 to 1978 represented losses by the president's party (there were twenty such turnovers in ninety-four special elections). Although this statistic does not properly illustrate the disadvantage that members of the president's party are at, cursory evidence suggests that special elections follow the pattern set by midterm elections and by-elections.[9]

Here the analysis runs into a potential problem. If part of the purpose of this book is to explain how the Democrats held off low-level realignment at a time the Republicans dominated presidential contests, my interpretation may be colored by the fact that I am studying special elections. Perhaps Democrats won these contests because, through the 1980s, they were the out-party and out-parties have an inherent advantage in these types of elections.

Fortuitously, the six special elections in this study enable me to address this problem—they are temporally proximate to a general election. One other finding from the literature on British by-elections is that the more time that passes after the election, the greater the likelihood the government's support will decay (Studlar and Sigelman 1987).[10] Moreover, the closer the by-election is to the *next* general election, the less likely the government's party is to be penalized by the voters (Studlar and Sigelman 1987). There is no theoretical reason to believe that American special elections are much different. To my advantage, five of the six special elections I study here were held shortly after a general election. In all but the Virginia case, the special was held three to nine months after an inauguration, not much time for hostility to the administration to build. In Virginia, the special election was held in June 1988, just five months before a presidential election.

Moreover, evidence suggests that the Republican presidents were extremely popular in these districts around the time of the elections. In four of the five districts holding elections between 1980 and 1992, Reagan and Bush won more than 60 percent of the district vote in the presidential election most proximate to the special. In the fifth, Mississippi 4, Reagan won a much smaller majority six months prior in the 1980 presidential election. That Mississippi special election, however, was held just a few months after Reagan was shot, a period during which he enjoyed enormous popularity. Indeed, the national presidential approval ratings for Reagan and Bush were very strong at the time of four of the five pre-1993 specials in this study, the exception again being Virginia (see table 2.2). The point, of course, is that a simple presidential penalty interpretation of special elections would not likely explain the Democratic congressional victories in these cases. Democrats won for reasons other than their out-party status.

The final methodological issue to be addressed here is, why these six special elections? This might be called the sampling problem, and it is a problem faced by others who do participant-observation research. As Richard Fenno (1990) writes, this is a problem with no perfectly satisfactory solution: "My answer at the beginning [of my research] was I don't know; my answer today is, I'm not sure. Nothing better characterizes the open-ended, slowly emerging, participant observation research than this admission. If I had been certain about what types of representatives and what types of districts to sample, I would already have had answers to a lot of the questions raised in [my] book" (59). Like Fenno, I found this stage of the process to be very difficult, and the defense of my choices reflects this. The research decisions involving which elections to witness were especially difficult. My original plan was not just to look at Democratic victories. Indeed, in all three of the campaigns I visited, the Republicans either were favored at the beginning or were given a good chance of winning. Limited resources made each choice difficult, and my decision to go to the Mississippi Delta, the Gulf Coast, and central Alabama instead of Houston, Miami, Ft. Worth, Dallas, or north-central Virginia had to be made without any knowledge as to how these elections would play out or who would win. The choices, in hindsight, were good ones as all three were competitive, spirited contests, if not always close in the end.[11]

Choosing the other three cases to include in this set also had to be done carefully. These choices too were made somewhat in the dark, before I knew what the final composition of my cases would be. As the project evolved, it became clear that to approach the puzzles of mixed realignment, to determine what the Democrats' congressional candidates were doing right at the same time that their presidential candidates were losing, I should study situations in which the outcome was genuinely in doubt at the beginning. Situations deemed by the press or party politicians or both to be tests of realignment were most interesting to me.[12] I also sought variation in the districts. Most important was variation in racial composition, which contributed to my ability to test a major line of my argument. Indeed, in the sample as a whole, Mississippi 2 is a majority (58 percent) black district, Mississippi 4 has a very large minority of blacks (42 percent), Alabama 3 and Virginia 5 have moderately large black populations (28 and 25 percent, respectively), and Texas 1 and Mississippi 5 have black populations slightly under 20 percent.[13]

The districts are varied in other ways, as well. There are two districts with sizable urban and suburban areas (Mississippi 4 and Mississippi 5), yet these and the rest of the districts also cover rural areas. Though Old South in character, two districts are in the outer states of the region (Texas 1 and Virginia 5); four, of course, are from the Deep South. Clearly Mississippi is overrepresented, but the districts in Mississippi that I studied are significantly different from each other and are representative of other areas in the South. In two of the elections a Republican was being replaced. The elections also were held under different electoral rules. In some, partisan primaries were held with the winners meeting in a general election; in others, nonpartisan elections were followed by an election between the top two vote-getters (if no candidate achieved a majority in the first round); in yet another (Virginia), candidates chosen in party conventions faced off in a general election. Even in the nonpartisan elections, the runoff was always between a Republican and a Democrat.

Parts of the South are not represented in this sample. There are no elections from Atlanta, New Orleans, Miami, Houston, or Dallas-Ft. Worth, or from their suburbs. These cities are so overwhelmingly Democratic, however, and their suburbs so Republican that these parts of the South have come to look like urban and suburban parts of the North, and there is not all that much to explain. The historically Republican parts of the South (eastern Tennessee and western North Carolina) are also not studied here, nor are the parts of the region most northern in character and population (northern Virginia and southern Florida). There has been no realignment in Appalachia to explain. South Florida and northern Virginia (and South and West Texas, for that matter) are interesting but rather unique parts of the region.

The six cases thus represent a large part of the Old South, that rural part of the region (though dotted with small cities) most steeped in southern values and tradition. It is now very politically competitive territory, and territory that many have been expecting the Republicans to win for years. It is the battlefield on which realignment has taken place over the past thirty years and will be taking place in the future.

3 Racial Issues in the
Congressional Campaign

RACE IS ALWAYS A FACTOR in southern congressional campaigns. As I argue throughout this book, the racial composition of a congressional district determines which strategies will be most effective, what tactics are to be used, how a candidate's time will be spent, what media are to be employed, what issues will be highlighted. Race is never far from the minds of southern campaign managers. It cannot be.

This does not mean that an explicitly racial issue arises in every southern campaign. Most campaigns, in fact, are not fought over issues that one might associate with racial politics—voting rights, affirmative action, symbolic gestures to the black community. Where such an issue does arise, though, it often becomes the focus of the campaign. The candidates keep reaching for it. The commercials and literature highlight it. The media cover it in almost every report. What follows are descriptions of two campaigns in which this happened, one in southwest Mississippi, the other in eastern Alabama. Not every southern campaign looks like these two, but they are worth studying because they illustrate dramatically how Republicans have sought white votes and Democrats have sought black votes through racial issues.

Mississippi 4—"It's scurrilous, dirty politics"

In McComb, Mississippi, a small city in the southern part of the Fourth District, the downtown is almost a ghost town. Most of the storefronts are empty and boarded up. The tenants who have stayed are suffering. No pedestrians are to be seen. Twenty-five years ago, this is where one would have found the whites-only lunch counter. No one, white or black, eats here now. About two miles toward the interstate is the mall, busy and thriving. Young couples with strollers browse the stores, and children, black and white, crowd the arcade. Inside, it looks and feels like any mall in the United States except that the fast food restaurant serves catfish and red beans with rice.

Mississippi's Fourth District is a mix of the old and the new; it is a district of contrasts. It has eleven rural counties, which are heavily black and economically depressed. It also contains Jackson, the state's largest metropolitan area, and its suburbs. Although part of the city is predominantly black and poor, the northern section of town and its suburbs are mostly white, white collar, middle class, and Republican. The district is split in a variety of ways; it is 42 percent black, 49 percent urban and suburban, and about half Republican.[1]

In this district Republicans achieved some of their first breakthroughs in Mississippi. It was here, in 1972, that Thad Cochran became one of the state's first two Republican congressmen to serve more than one term since Reconstruction (Trent Lott also was elected in 1972 in the neighboring Fifth District).[2] In 1978, Cochran became the state's first Republican senator since Reconstruction. His congressional seat was filled by another Republican, Jon Hinson, his administrative assistant in Washington.

At first, Hinson looked as if he, like Cochran, would be electorally secure and that the district would stay in Republican hands for years to come. The son of a prominent Tylertown political family, Hinson convincingly defeated John Stennis, Jr., the son and namesake of Mississippi's legendary senior senator, in 1978 and appeared to be invulnerable. Upon arriving in Washington, he was described in the *Almanac of American Politics* as likely to "vote—and to win votes—as Cochran did" (Barone, Ujifusa, and Matthews 1979, 485). In 1980, however, Hinson ran into trouble. In the course of that campaign, he was forced to acknowledge that he had been arrested for an obscene act at the U.S. Marine Corps Monument in Arlington Cemetery. He also admitted to being a survivor of a devastating fire at a gay theater in Washington. Though he denied being a homosexual, claimed to have undergone a religious experience, and offered his new wife as evidence, he clearly had a problem in the very conservative Mississippi district. Yet he was able to weather these storms. Said one supporter, "Some folks would rather have a queer conservative than a macho liberal and they may be right" (Harris 1981).

One year later, though, Hinson again found himself in difficulty after being arrested with another man for attempted sodomy in a public restroom in a congressional office building. This incident could not be ignored: Hinson's partner was black. "[That] added insult to injury here in Mississippi," said a black community leader several months after the incident. "There are still a zillion jokes about it" (Harris 1981). Under pressure from national and state Republican leaders, Hinson resigned his office, setting the stage for a special election in June 1981.

Cochran and Hinson had won the previous five elections for two major reasons. First, whites from the Jackson area had become overwhelmingly Republican. Cochran, who was from Jackson, was the first to benefit from this constituency, which has provided the base for every Republican candidacy since. Second, Cochran and Hinson were helped enormously by independent black candidates on the ballot. In 1972, Cochran won the open seat election with less than half (48 percent) the vote. His Democratic opponent fell four points short as the independent Eddie McBride siphoned off 8 percent of the vote.[3] In Hinson's first run, in 1978, a black independent took 20 percent of the vote. This actually mattered less than it had earlier because the Republican won an outright majority (53 percent) of the vote. But two years later, Hinson won reelection with just 37 percent of the vote. The black independent outpolled even the Democrat in this race, 33 to 30 percent, which was the major reason that Hinson was able to survive his first scandal. Part of Hinson's success also can be attributed to the fact that he hailed from a rural county in the southern part of the district. This helped him win enough rural white votes to add to his Republican base in Jackson.

The special election in 1981 to replace Hinson posed a problem for the Republicans. Because of the rules governing special elections, they would not be able to count on an independent black candidate in this race. The election, like many other special elections, was to be held in two stages. The first, an open, nonpartisan contest, would narrow the field to two candidates (if no one candidate won at least 50 percent of the vote). The second election would be between the top two vote-getters. Should it come to a runoff, the Democrats would not be split along racial lines.

Anticipating that several Democrats were certain to throw their hats into the ring, the Republicans calculated that their best chance for retaining the seat was in winning a majority in the first election. With this in mind, the Republicans held a caucus and settled on one candidate several months before the first election. Prior to the event, all of the major hopefuls agreed to abide by the decision of the caucus, thus allowing a Republican the opportunity to win the election while the Democrats were still divided. The caucus, after a day of intense politicking, settled on Jackson businessman Liles Williams, himself a former activist in the state Democratic party. Williams, a leader of the Religious Roundtable and a successful businessman, faced several prominent Democrats in the first round.

Republicans, in the second special election of Ronald Reagan's tenure, pumped a great deal of money and effort into the first primary. It was an especially good time to defend their seat. The primary was held just twelve weeks after Reagan was shot, and that event had built up a reservoir of support for the president. The Republicans mailed out eighty-five thousand letters under Reagan's signature to voters in the district and spent more money in that primary than in any previous congressional campaign in Mississippi history (*Jackson Clarion-Ledger* 1981). Williams did quite well, winning 45 percent of the vote in the primary, but fell short of the majority needed to avoid a runoff. Ironically, he likely was hurt by the presence on his right of two Ku Klux Klan candidates ("Vote Right, Vote White, Vote Wheems" was one electoral battle cry).[4] Even if he had won these votes, however, he would have fallen a few points short of victory.

The man Williams expected to face, if a runoff election was necessary, was Mike Singletary, who had run against Hinson in 1980. Singletary banked his campaign on making an issue of Hinson, arguing that the same "power brokers" who had backed Hinson and thus "embarrassed the district" had selected Williams (Walsh 1981). It was a message designed to appeal to conservative rural whites. Strategically, though, it was a miscalculation because another Democrat, by activating a less-competed-for black vote, made it to the runoff. That Democrat was Wayne Dowdy, the part-time mayor of McComb.

At the time of the election, legislation to extend the Voting Rights Act for five years was pending in Congress. Testimony was being heard on the legislation in Washington, and even the president was mulling over his position on the issue. Whereas Williams, Singletary, and the other candidates in the race approved of modifying the act or rejecting it altogether, Dowdy came out unambiguously in support of the extension, the only major candidate to do so (there were no black candidates in the field). Part of the reason that Dowdy's second-place finish was so surprising was that the other candidates believed that in supporting the extension Dowdy had "completely alienated his white base" (Walsh 1981).[5] Yet Dowdy pulled in enough black voters to collect 25 percent of the overall vote in the primary, considerably more than Singletary's 14 percent, third-place finish.

The extension of the Voting Rights Act also became the most important issue of the second phase of the campaign. Williams took a strong stand against extending the act in an attempt to woo white voters. His argument was basically that it was unfair that the South, which had shown so much progress in voting rights, was still being singled out. A *Jackson Daily News and Clarion-Ledger* editorial endorsing Williams summed up his position on this issue: "Progress in Mississippi must not go ignored by those who would continue to punish the South for the past and at the same time ignore that voting rights problems continue to exist in other regions of the nation" (*Jackson Daily News and Clarion-Ledger* 1981). Williams raised the issue often, and the media, both local and national, wrote about it in almost every report and editorial. It dominated coverage of his campaign.

As noted, Dowdy supported extension of the act as it was. "It was the right thing to do," he said. "I thought it had brought Mississippi far and that there were only minor hindrances associated with it, which is what I said in the campaign." While it is true that when pressed, in debates for example, Dowdy did speak of his support of the legislation, he did so in rather terse statements. His support for the legislation was not brought up in any of his campaign television commercials. And Dowdy even declined to get involved in a controversy over the order of the candidates' names on the ballot in several counties. When Republican clerks in a number of heavily black counties put Williams above Dowdy on the ballot (as opposed to listing the names alphabetically as they were elsewhere), some Democrats charged that this would confuse illiterate black voters and was thus in violation of the Voting Rights Act. The state attorney general ruled on the issue, declaring that alphabetical order had to be used. Nonetheless, Dowdy purposely chose not to pursue the matter. Although he did not dodge the issue of extension, he was not going to do anything to make it more salient than it was already. "A lawsuit would only serve to confuse the voters," he told a *New York Times* reporter (Clymer 1981a).

The message Dowdy directed toward black voters, however, was quite different. On the circuit of black churches, in front of black audiences, and on black media, Dowdy highlighted his support of the Voting Rights legislation. If his stand in public was subdued, his targeted message to blacks was loud and clear. "Martin Luther King and Medgar Evers gave their lives so you could vote," said Medgar Evers's niece in a Dowdy advertisement played on black radio stations. "Now Ronald Reagan and Liles Williams are trying to take your right to vote away. . . . Wayne Dowdy has the courage to publicly say that Wayne Dowdy would vote for the extension of the Voting Rights Act" (Treyens 1981a). The Republican state chairman, not surprisingly, was unhappy about these advertisements, calling Dowdy "one of the greatest race baiters elected to office in Mississippi in the last 20 to 30 years. It's scurrilous, dirty politics" (Treyens 1981a). But his complaints and the reporting of the radio advertisement in the Jackson newspaper had little impact on the outcome because the controversy broke after the election. The advertisement was run only on the last day or two of the campaign.

The major issue in Williams's campaign, other than the Voting Rights Act Extension, was his support of President Reagan and Reagan's support of him. Williams's polls showed the president with a 74 percent approval rating in the district (Broder 1981b), and the campaign did all it could to link their man to the president. Reagan's endorsement of Williams was included in the Republican's campaign literature and in his half-page advertisements in the *Jackson Clarion-Ledger*. As noted above, letters under Reagan's signature were sent to eighty-five thousand of the district's Republicans. At one point, the president even made a phone call to Williams that was piped over a loudspeaker to a rally. "We're waiting for you up here and need your help," declared Reagan to the candidate and his enthusiastic crowd.

Williams made support for Reagan's budget cuts a major tenet of his campaign. The dramatic cuts were being debated in Congress, and Williams sought to capitalize on the issue. He did make sure to distance himself from the cuts in Social Security proposed by the administration. Nonetheless, the *Washington Post* reported that "Williams has portrayed himself as a textbook disciple of Reaganomics preaching federal parsimony and tax cuts" (Harris 1981).

Dowdy's campaign, on the other hand, emphasized local issues, and his appeals for rural white votes had populist overtones. Dowdy railed against foreign aid. He criticized the administration's plans to send $3 billion to Pakistan, arguing that southwest Mississippi's problems should be addressed before Pakistan's. "We must balance the budget," he announced to a rally in McComb, "but while people here at home are making cuts and sacrifices, other countries are receiving our money" (Mullen 1981). On the stump, Dowdy also attacked the Federal Reserve Bank for high interest rates, Washington lobbyists, and both political parties. At one point in the campaign he even declared, "I'm running against the President of the United States, the U.S. Chamber of Commerce and every oil company in the world." (Putnam 1981a). Dowdy's style fit his populist message. He was the wealthiest candidate in the entire field of original candidates (*Jackson Daily News and Clarion-Ledger*, 1981), but his country background, his folksy manner, and his relaxed "person-to-person home-style" (see Fenno 1978) made him a good fit for the rural half of the district.

Although he took an anti-Washington, populist message to the electorate, the Democrat was cautious when talking about Ronald Reagan. Dowdy's reference to the president was that Reagan was running against him, not that he was necessarily running against Reagan. This theme was evident in Dowdy's advertisements, one of which led with, "Last year we elected a president and we have a very fine man. Our election now is for congressman and Ronald Reagan is not a candidate." Wayne Dowdy's negative message was not about the president but rather his policies and, most important, how they would affect Mississippi. Williams, so completely aligned with the president, would "rubber stamp" Reagan's program, argued the Democrat, and would not oppose cuts that would have an adverse effect on the district (Clymer 1981a).

In the end, Dowdy's strategy worked. Outspent by Williams ($372,000 to $277,000 [Ehrenhalt 1983, 843]), disadvantaged by his opponent's ties to the popular president, running in a district that had elected Republicans to Congress in the previous five elections, Dowdy won nevertheless. His margin of victory was quite small, indeed, about eleven hundred votes, leading him to joke at his victory party, "On our budget, we cannot afford a landslide" (*Washington Post* 1981a). The advertisements on black radio, the speeches in black churches, and, most important, Dowdy's message to the black community bolstered black turnout, and this, more than anything else, led to his victory.

One measure of the effectiveness of Dowdy's effort to get blacks to the polls is the increase in turnout from the first to the second election in largely black counties. As might be expected, turnout went up from the primary to the runoff in the district as a whole, a difference of three points (to 32 percent). In predominantly (75 percent) black Claiborne County, however, turnout rose nine points (to 29 percent) from the first election to the second; in 82 percent black Jefferson County, turnout rose from 25 to 35 percent. Though aggregate data make it impossible to tell for sure, the vote in these counties was almost certainly along racial lines, and Dowdy appears to have won nearly all the rural black vote. In Jefferson County, Dowdy took 77 percent of the vote and in Claiborne County, 74 percent. Dowdy overwhelmed Williams in the black neighborhoods of Jackson as well. In one Jackson precinct, for instance, Dowdy beat Williams 814 to 4. Totals from other black precincts were almost as lopsided (Treyens 1981b). In an election decided by such a narrow margin, the larger-than-expected black turnout was crucial. A black organizer who was involved in the campaign said, "I'd never seen such enthusiasm in a campaign before and haven't since. When you go after the Voting Rights Act, well, that's sacred." The state's Republican chairman also attributed Dowdy's victory to his candidate's emphasis on the Voting Rights Act, which "helped motivate the black turnout" (Clymer 1981b). Even Dowdy accepted this analysis of the election. "There are lots of folks we've [the Democrats] lost," he said pointing to the white, middle-class neighborhood outside his office window. "In an election like that one, we had to get black votes. When the Republicans went public and strong on this [the Voting Rights Act], it really energized the blacks."

Dowdy needed to do more than motivate black voters. His candidacy was premised upon an ability to win rural white votes as well. He won only 45 percent of the vote in Hinds County (Jackson), where about half the votes in the district were cast. He also lost counties holding the district's smaller cities. Williams carried Warren County (which holds

Vicksburg) with 57 percent of the vote and Lincoln County (which holds Brookhaven) with 51 percent. But Dowdy won by large margins in the rural parts of the district. In almost every county, including those he lost, Dowdy's percentage of the vote was greater than the percentage of blacks in the county. In Copiah County, a 48 percent black county, Dowdy won 61 percent of the vote. In 30 percent black Lincoln County, the Democrat took 49 percent of the vote.[6] The exceptions, interestingly, were the three most heavily black districts. Again, although aggregate data allow only a good guess as to voting patterns of particular groups, it appears that Dowdy did in fact put together an effective coalition of blacks and rural whites.

In Washington, where small pieces of electoral information become invested with great meaning, Dowdy's victory became quite significant. It was variously interpreted as a referendum on the president, a warning for conservative Democrats, and a message on the Voting Rights extension. Democrats gleefully pointed to Dowdy's victory as an illustration of public discontent with Reagan's program. "They voted their pocketbooks," said Tip O'Neill in the election's national postmortem (Clymer 1981b). Congressman Tony Coelho, chairman of the Democratic Congressional Campaign Committee, added that the victory was a repudiation of "the idea of a Solid South for Ronald Reagan" (*Washington Post* 1981a). Republicans rejected these interpretations of the election, arguing that Williams was damaged by his partisan association with Hinson. Nonetheless, the Democrats savored a moment of success after an otherwise dreary electoral season.

Insofar as Dowdy's victory was interpreted as at least a partial repudiation of Reagan in a staunchly conservative place, it became a vehicle for liberal Democrats to penalize conservatives in the party who had supported the president over the party. The chairman of the national party, Charles Manatt, and some liberals in the House used Dowdy's victory to call for the disciplining of the boll weevil Phil Gramm and others of his ilk. Manatt charged that Gramm had participated in Democratic strategy sessions on the budget and then actively worked with the administration to sabotage his own party's position (Broder 1981a). The Connecticut congressman Toby Moffett introduced a resolution to the House Demo-cratic Caucus to discipline Gramm, and though Gramm was not punished at that time, he was soon thereafter.

Finally, Dowdy's victory sent a message to Washington on the Voting Rights Act. Whereas the other two interpretations of the Democratic victory were fiercely contested, this one was not; the Voting Rights Act should be extended. As the *Washington Post* editorialized the week follow-ing the election, the "message from Mississippi" was that renewal of the act was politically acceptable and the right thing to do (*Washington Post* 1981b). Dowdy's victory was by the slightest of margins, but it carried with it symbolic value to Democrats in Washington eager to make a point.

Dowdy had a little bit of time before having to prepare for the next election cycle. He faced Williams in a rematch in 1982. The situation was even more favorable for Williams in this race because several heavily black counties were taken out of the district in an effort to create a majority black district to the north. Enjoying name recognition and run-ning as an incumbent, though, Dowdy held back Williams's challenge. He went on to win successive elections by progressively larger margins, until in 1988 he vacated his seat to run for the Senate (unsuccessfully, it turned out). He was replaced by another rural Democrat, Mike Parker. Like Dowdy, Parker faced a Jackson Republican and did not encounter an independent black candidate in the general election. Under these circum-stances, he effectively reconstructed Dowdy's winning coalition of blacks and rural voters.

Alabama 3—"It's not a race issue. It's a heritage issue"

In 1964, Barry Goldwater went "hunting where the ducks were," that is, set out to capture the South with a racially conservative message. His candidacy that year may have been a failure on a national scale, but it had an impact in the South. Goldwater won several states in the region and had some coattails, carrying seven southern Republicans to victory in the House elections of 1964. One of these seven turnovers came in Alabama's Third District (at that time the Fourth). Two years later, in elections otherwise favorable to Republicans, the Democrats won four of these seats back, including that in the Third District. As a George Wallace floor leader in the Alabama state legislature, Bill Nichols was able to defeat the Republican rather easily.

For the next twenty years, Nichols represented the district, which covers the east-central portion of Alabama. A prototypical Deep South district, it is mostly rural and has a sizable black population (28 percent). Its largest town, Anniston, has a population of just thirty thousand, but the district takes in some of the suburban areas around Birmingham, Montgomery, and Columbus, Georgia. The district's economy is based on agriculture, textiles, timber, and the military. The Anniston Army Depot, where almost all of the U.S. Army's transport vehicles and tanks are repaired, is the district's largest employer (Ehrenhalt 1987, 21). Also in the district are Auburn University, a large state university, Jacksonville State University, and Tuskegee Institute, one of the nation's first black universities, founded by Booker T. Washington more than a century ago.

Bill Nichols saw to it that the district, with its large universities and its dependence on the military, got its share of federal pork. From his senior position on the Armed Services Committee, the congressman brought millions of military dollars into the area. A solid conservative, he was renowned in the district for the service he provided and went virtually unchallenged by the Republicans throughout his tenure. When he suffered a fatal heart attack at his Capitol desk in December 1988, it set off a flurry of activity among prospective candidates, Democrats and Republicans alike. Just three hours after Nichols died, a Washington-based media consultant said that he was called by a prospective candidate. "The body wasn't even cold," he said. Such early jockeying often occurs when a seat opens up after a long congressional career.

A special election was scheduled for the following spring. Prior to the general election, each party scheduled separate primaries, which were to be held in two rounds. Unless a candidate drew more than half the votes, the top two candidates from the first primary would compete in a runoff, the winner advancing to the general election.[7] The Republican candidate was chosen in the first round. No Democrat, however, emerged from the first primary with a majority, and the top two candidates squared off.

The winner of the Republican primary was State Senator John Rice. Only months before, the thirty-seven-year-old Rice had been a Democrat but had switched parties after several battles with the Democratic leadership of the state senate. With the Republican governor, Guy Hunt, and Jack Kemp by his side, Rice publicly and proudly announced his defection. In a district in which 60 percent had voted for George Bush the previous November and 58 percent had voted for Hunt in 1986 (National Republican Congressional Committee 1988), such a move had great political possibilities. Giving some indication that Republican chances appeared to be good, party money flowed into Rice's campaign. With two weeks left before the general election, Rice had received $54,000 in cash or in-kind services from Republican congressmen and the state and national Republican parties. His Democratic opponent had only $40,000 from such party sources at that time (Smith 1989d).[8]

The two top vote-getters in the Democratic primary were the Alabama secretary of state, Glen Browder, and the black mayor of Tuskegee, Johnny Ford. The Democratic primary runoff was an interesting race, as it posed both problems and possibilities for both candidates. Ford was a strong, capable candidate, but his race (and the fact that he was married to a white woman) worked against him in this conservative district. A Browder campaign consultant, impressed with the politically savvy mayor, remarked, "If he were white, he'd be going to Congress." Several others, Democratic and Republican, echoed this sentiment. Recognizing that the black vote would not be enough to give him the Democratic nomination and that he would need white votes, Ford devised a two-pronged campaign plan. The first element of his strategy was to emphasize his conservative views and conservative background. Ford put forth conservative positions on gun control, abortion, and other social issues, positions, he contended, that were shared by the black voters of the district as well as the white. But his advocacy of such positions was aimed more at whites than blacks. Through the years, Ford had developed a reputation for being a conservative and an accommodationist. He even endorsed Richard Nixon in 1972 and George Wallace for governor in 1974 (Barone, Ujifusa, and Matthews 1979, 8). If any black candidate could make inroads into the conservative white vote in the Third District, it was Johnny Ford.

The second element of Ford's strategy was to downplay race. He avoided racial issues in the campaign and spoke often of how he thought that whites in the district could support him. This is not to say that he was blind to reality: "It would have been naive to think that it [race] wasn't in folks' minds," he said. "But you just have to smile and work on, to ignore it and move on. You have to do something constructive because white people have to be comfortable with you." This attitude permeated his campaign.

If Ford had any chance of winning, it was by energizing black voters while not stirring up resentment among white voters. In the end, these goals may not have been compatible. Bringing Jesse Jackson into the district to speak at some black rallies shortly before the Democratic runoff represented a decision by the Ford forces that turning out his black base was more important than not alienating potential white voters. Jackson drew large, enthusiastic crowds, but his visit was covered by the media and may have cost Ford some white votes, if indeed he had any to begin with.

Browder, a former professor of political science at Jacksonville State University, had specialized in the study of public opinion and voting behavior. He recognized that he too had important tactical decisions to make vis-à-vis Ford. He had to beat Ford in the runoff, but he needed Ford's help to mobilize black voters in the general election. He also had to worry about being tied too closely to Ford by the Rice campaign lest this lead to white backlash. "The one thing we worried about and were very glad and frankly surprised they [the Rice campaign] didn't do," said a Democratic media consultant, "was to run a commercial putting Browder's face next to Ford's face, trying to link the two of them together. 'Two peas in a pod' or something like that."

Given this situation, Browder completely downplayed race in his primary campaign and went to great lengths to show Ford great respect. As a front-runner, Browder had little to gain by participating in a debate that would only help to publicize his opponent. Yet he acceded to Ford's request for a televised meeting. Although confident of victory in the runoff, he treated the mayor as a serious opponent, showing Ford that he respected him as an adversary. This attitude was reflected in the debate. Browder's debate strategy, according to his campaign manager, was to draw distinctions between the two candidates while taking great pains to avoid being negative. The debate, in fact, was described as a love fest by one of the Democratic campaign consultants.

By taking Ford seriously while showing restraint in his campaign against him, Browder hoped to earn Ford's help in the general election. The strategy worked. On the night of Browder's primary victory, Ford threw his support completely behind Browder. He became a major force in turning out the black community for the Democratic nominee in the general election, campaigning quite a bit for Browder and taking him around on the black church circuit, a campaign environment, an advisor noted, that Browder was not completely comfortable in.[9] Browder's campaign manager estimated that, in the end, Ford delivered about 75 percent of his primary vote to Browder. "Johnny Ford really stepped up to the plate," the manager said appreciatively some months after the election.

Ford also had something to gain in the Democratic runoff: name recognition and public exposure in anticipation of the creation of a majority black congressional district following redistricting in 1990. Hoping that Browder's home county and the surrounding counties in the northern part of the district would be moved into another district ("Those counties don't belong in this district. They're too different from down here," he complained), Ford hoped to emerge from the election as the major black candidate of the future. Moreover, Ford saw an opportunity to cultivate important contacts through Browder. Browder received large contributions from labor (about 60 percent of his PAC contributions and one-third of his total campaign funds came from unions [Smith 1989d]), and Ford expressed interest in being introduced to some of Browder's friends in the AFL-CIO. As expected, Browder handily beat Ford, 63 percent to 37 percent, but Ford came out of the election well situated for his next campaign.[10]

From the beginning, the Browder-Rice contest attracted national interest. The election was one of two special elections taking place five months after the November presidential election. These two elections were the first tests of the partisan strength of the Bush administration. They offered some indication, at least among insiders, of how the president was doing, and in this case, how the new head of the Republican National Committee, Lee Atwater, was doing. The Alabama race became particularly important after the Democrats won a surprising and symbolically important victory in the first contest, an election to fill Vice President Dan Quayle's old congressional seat (vacated by Dan Coats, who took over Quayle's Senate term). The Republicans were quite unhappy with this development, and Atwater even expressed embarrassment over the Indiana loss (McNeil 1989). The Alabama race thus became even more important for the national Republican party.

The race quickly became acrimonious. In addition to calling Browder a "Michael Dukakis liberal" and "a national Democrat," Rice labeled him "a powderpuff" and "a wimp." At one point, a Rice press release even charged that "while our boys were dying in the rice patties (*sic*) in Viet Nam, my opponent, Professor Browder, long hair and all, was in the classroom giving lectures on the immorality of America's involvement in Viet Nam" (March 15, 1989). The charge was based on the recollection of a Rice campaign aide who happened to be one of Browder's students in the early 1970s. "He was a McGovern person," said the aide. "We discussed everything from Vietnam to welfare." Browder responded that he had held "pro-and-con discussions about Vietnam" in his classroom and that the former student had misremembered Browder's position. To support this, Browder called in another former student of his, Democratic Lieutenant Governor Jim Folsom, Jr., who recalled that his professor did not "preach against Vietnam" and that he had short hair (Burger 1989b). Browder's campaign aide later announced that Browder had absolutely supported the war at that time (Yardley 1989b).

Rice excoriated Browder further for being beholden to big labor. Given the endorsements and campaign contributions that Browder had received from various labor unions, he was an easy mark. Governor Hunt, who campaigned with Rice on several occasions, criticized Browder's labor contributions as being from "liberals . . . from Brooklyn, New York and Washington, D.C." (Yardley 1989c). Another surrogate for Rice, the vanquished Democratic primary opponent Jim Preuitt, claimed that Browder had "sold his soul to national labor unions" (Smith 1989b). Rice himself brought notice to Browder's "friends" in a debate. "There's a labor influence in this race," he said. "I believe Glen needs to answer it" (Yardley 1989d). To further highlight Browder's debt to organized labor and their own independence from "special interests," the Republicans also publicly returned almost $3,000 in contributions from "people we don't like" (Smith 1989e). Given the financial circumstances the campaign later found itself in, this was a rather bold public relations maneuver.

Browder took to the offensive as well, though it took some prodding from his campaign advisors. Browder accused Rice of holding an "off-the-wall, radical philosophy" (Burger 1989a), and he ran an extremely negative television advertisement throughout the campaign calling the Republican candidate Hand Grenade Rice, his nickname in the state legislature. Rice had a reputation in the legislature for being hotheaded and unpredictable. He even characterized himself as such. "I enjoy the lightning," said the candidate. "I like to fight. I'm not a sedentary person [or] a couch potato, and I refuse to accept defeat." But the advertisement did more than bring up his personality; it connected it to some of his more dogmatic proposals. The commercial featured a grenade ticking beneath a picture of Rice, "looking like he has a bad hangover." The grenade blows up after Rice's dangerous record and philosophy are discussed. It was a wickedly negative commercial, one that stunned the aggressive Rice. "I got my butt kicked on TV [in a commercial] that was about as low as human morals can stoop," said Rice. "It's damaged me probably for the rest of my life. It hurt my family, my mother, my business. It's sick that politics is like that." The commercial was all the more effective as Rice's campaign funds dried up in the final weeks of the campaign, making defensive or even retaliatory television advertisements impossible.

On the positive side, Browder and Rice both had well-defined strategies. Browder's campaign was devoid of controversial issues. He seemed practiced at responding to questions about issues in brief, vague remarks. On a summary of the candidates' positions given to senior citizens before a debate sponsored by the American Association of Retired Persons (AARP), Browder's answers were often just one sentence long. And his responses in the debate were not any more detailed or enlightening. In some cases, they were evasive. He supported raising the minimum wage but refused to say where it should be set, a point of contention between President Bush and Congress at that time. On his backing of Bush's "no new taxes" pledge—Browder did not sign such a pledge himself—he refused to name any specific cuts he would make to reduce the deficit. When asked about his position on abortion, Browder responded that he was personally opposed to it but that the issue was before the Supreme Court (in *Webster v Reproductive Health Services*) and that he would wait until the opinion came down (well after the election) before coming to any conclusions.

Browder's positions on controversial and ideological issues were intentionally vague because he saw little electoral advantage to be gained by taking hard-line positions. On abortion, for instance, he told a newspaper reporter, "I see no sense in me getting involved in an issue that's a highly emotional issue that might override what I consider some very substantial issues and my ability to provide my representation to this district. It is not the thing that's the most important factor or even one of the biggest factors in the issues that are important on people's lives such as defense jobs, textile jobs, senior citizens and Social Security" (Yardley 1989f). Browder's desire to avoid controversial issues annoyed some ("At least [Mr. Rice] has an answer, gives an answer," said a black minister from Anniston [Yardley 1989h]), but surprisingly neither his opponent nor the local press scored him over it.

When he did express a position, it was most often a conservative one, deflecting Rice's charge of liberalism. "We're not going to let them make this a fight about a liberal against a conservative," Browder told a *New*

York Times reporter. "I'm a moderate conservative and he's so radical that he's completely off the table" (Apple 1989). Browder's more public positions on aid to the Nicaraguan contras, taxes, and gun control indicate that the moderate conservative label was appropriate. Yet, again, his positions on many of the issues were hard to discern.

The most important element of the strategy was to stake his claim as Bill Nichols's natural successor as the district's watchdog in Washington. As illustrated in the above statement, Browder did not want his positions on issues to interfere with this impression. Nichols's reputation in the district was extraordinary. In his twenty years of service, he had brought large amounts of federal money into the district. Browder and Rice both attempted to claim his legacy, but Browder made a better case for himself. Rice held that he and Nichols had an ideological kinship, and Rice's mentor, Governor Hunt, argued that Nichols "would have felt very comfortable in the Republican Party" (Yardley 1989c). Browder's reference to the late congressman was more practical. For one thing, the Anniston newspaper reported that Howell Heflin, one of the state's two Democratic senators, and other members of the state's Democratic delegation would work to open a spot on the Armed Services Committee for Browder (Yardley 1989g). Although there is some question as to how much influence Heflin had over committee assignments in the House, Rice did not challenge the Democrats on it.[11] Heflin's declaration was important not only because it came from a popular and respected state politician, but also because this committee assignment had enabled Nichols to do so much for the district.[12]

Browder also touted his efforts to reform education in the state. In 1985, he had spearheaded legislation to institute a merit-pay program for teachers, a program supported by the Alabama Education Association (AEA), the teachers' union. The key to their support was that Paul Hubbert, executive secretary of the organization, would be able to appoint a large number of members to the board that set criteria for the evaluation of teachers. The legislation passed, though one year later, when the AEA withdrew its support of the program, it died. Nonetheless, Browder pointed to it as evidence of his practical solution for educational problems in Alabama and even used an apple on his campaign signs to make a symbolic connection with the voters.[13]

Throughout the campaign, Browder was content to let Rice talk about national issues, so long as he was able to identify himself with local issues that involved pragmatic activity and service to the district. A national Democratic campaign consultant said, "The Republicans essentially wanted to play the presidential campaign over again. Let Rice talk about national issues. We want to talk about roads and bridges and military bases." And, he could have added, education. In a nutshell, Browder's strategy was to portray himself as reasonably conservative, to talk little about divisive issues, to paint Rice as extreme and unpredictable, and to portray himself as Bill Nichols's heir apparent.

John Rice's strategy was guided by his philosophical fervor, which was both a strength and a weakness in the campaign. Rice did stake a claim to being the only "true conservative" in the race. Browder, he argued, was a genuine believer in the liberal cause. In reality, the differences between the two candidates were not all that great, as evidenced by a survey of their voting records in the House.[14] But Rice did his best to make the most of these differences and, in his rhetoric, was unquestionably the more conservative candidate.

In making this comparison, he especially criticized Browder's education bill, arguing that it showed how the Democrat was "a creature of labor interests" and tied to liberal special interests like the teachers' union. At a press conference, with a sign mocking Browder's signature apple as "Teacher's Pet Brand," Rice charged that Browder's bill had cost Alabama taxpayers $1.4 billion (Smith 1989a). It was not clear where that figure came from, and later in the campaign, he modified this estimate and charged that Browder's "liberal boondoggle" had cost taxpayers $18 million (Smith 1989b).

Not all of Rice's conservative appeal was based on building a comparison with Browder. He articulated his conservative philosophy at every campaign appearance. Zealously attacking the federal government ("In

Washington, they create chaos and call it government"), labor unions, and national Democrats, Rice spent a lot of time pledging against raising taxes and talking about reducing the size and scope of the federal government. He often highlighted his zeal for the conservative cause by taking unbudging positions on the issues. On the minimum wage, Rice was not only averse to raising it, but philosophically opposed to the very concept of a federally imposed standard. He parted company with President Bush on gun control, rejecting a ban on foreign-made, semiautomatic assault weapons (Smith 1989e). And to illustrate his opposition to taxes, he publicly signed a Taxpayer Protection Pledge sponsored by Americans for Tax Reform. When the press asked if this meant that he would not vote for a tax hike even if it was supported by President Bush or was earmarked for reducing the national deficit, Rice responded, "No, period." There was some give-and-take between the candidates on the tax issue, as Rice had voted to raise taxes while in the state legislature. The Republican argued that he had cast these votes only to keep nursing homes open (Smith 1989c), but the questions of who voted to raise state taxes, how many such votes were cast, and how much money was brought in as a result of these votes dominated much of the campaign dialogue. "Neither one of [the candidates] should be proud of their record," said the head of an independent Alabama antitax group (Smith 1989b). Rice attempted to take an uncompromising position against taxes anyway.

In his desire to express his federalist vision, Rice said early in the campaign that he would like to see the federal budget cut by 50 percent and argued that the federal government should not be funding city and county projects. In part Rice simply had a strong preference for local decision making and in part he believed that too much of the money that flows to Washington does not flow back (Smith 1989b). Rice backpeddled on some of these stands and in fact denied calling for the 50 percent cut after Browder began attacking the idea while highlighting his own pork barrel potential (and noting that for every dollar Alabama sent to Washington, $1.38 came back). Still, Rice's comment was so well publicized that Browder was able to keep Rice tied to it. "If you didn't say it then I suggest you form a posse and find [the other] John Rice out there who thinks the federal government should be cut by 50 percent," said Browder at a candidate forum.

Another part of Rice's assault on the federal government was his advocacy of local control of schools. Federal aid to education, he said on more than one occasion, came "with too many strings attached." Local governments should take on more financial responsibility, even if it means higher local taxes, because of the burdens placed on the schools by the federal government. Because he never really identified the specific burdens placed upon local school districts by the federal government, his remarks were open to interpretation. The federal government's role in the desegregation of Alabama's schools was at least intimated in these remarks. When asked to be more specific about his position on busing to achieve desegregation, the Republican told a reporter, "I just don't agree that we need to spend so much time and effort trying to reach that" (Smith 1989e).

If Rice's conservative appeals were not overtly racial in the early stages of the campaign, this changed when his campaign started losing ground in polls and in fund-raising. At this point, the candidate introduced the Confederate flag into the campaign. The issue revolved around a controversy that went back to 1985, when both Rice and Browder were in the state legislature. When some black state legislators objected to a Confederate flag being present on the House floor, Rice voted to keep the flag up and Browder did not cast a vote. Rice charged that Browder "walked out the back door and refused to vote" (Yardley 1989e). To dramatize the issue, John Rice pulled a small Confederate flag from his pocket and waved it during his final statement in a televised debate. The issue, he said, was courage, the courage to take a stand. He repeated this claim in a mass mailing, one of three to go out near the end of the campaign.[15]

When editorialists and black leaders objected to this message, Rice's campaign officials denied that the flag was a racist issue. In a most telling exchange earlier in the campaign, a Rice official said that racial issues would not be a part of the campaign. Later in the same conversation, he said that the campaign was contemplating bringing up the flag issue.

When asked if this was a racial issue, he responded, "No. It's not a race issue. It's a heritage issue. It's only a racial issue to the blacks." Despite his interpretation, the issue was laden with racial overtones and, from the perspective of many people interested in the election, was patently an attempt to stimulate white backlash.

The televised debate marked a new stage in the election. Rice's campaign manager had calculated that the Republicans would need only 15 percent of the black vote to be the majority party in the district. Near the end of the campaign, Rice, way down in the polls, running out of campaign funds, and believing that the Republican party had forsaken him, apparently abandoned even that goal in his quest for white votes. In the Anniston newspaper, a Rice official spoke of "writing off" the black vote or at least the 85 percent of the black vote that "[walked] lockstep with Joe Reed [the executive director of the Alabama Democratic Conference, the major black political organization in the state]." The reason, he said, was that "[Reed] pays them to vote" (Smith 1989g). This inflammatory statement left little doubt as to Republican intentions. Political campaigns would not write off a large bloc of votes so publicly unless there was something to be gained from it. In this case, the vote-buying charge and the flag incident were part of a desperate last-minute effort to stimulate a white backlash against Browder.

Browder's response to the Confederate flag issue and the vote-buying charges was essentially not to respond. He did not answer Rice's taunt in the debate. And he did not make any comments about it to the press. He left that to others. His campaign manager made a statement to the press that the candidate was ill the day of the vote and had an excused absence (which was, in fact, the case). In the postdebate analysis, the executive director of the Alabama Democratic Party compared Rice to the recently elected former Klansman David Duke.

Browder's public silence was purposeful. As the congressman now recalls, "I was not going to let him engage me personally [on that issue]." Nonetheless, the Confederate flag issue was highlighted in his appeals to blacks, which were made through the black churches in the district, on black radio, and in direct mail that infiltrated the black community. In one leaflet, sent out at the very end of the campaign, the Democrats used a photograph of Rice holding the Confederate flag. That piece, blasting Rice for his position, contributed to a much stronger black turnout, according to the campaign's black turnout consultant. Rice's campaign essentially handed Browder a message to take into the black community.

The week before the election, Browder met a campaign supporter who predicted his victory. "I believe the Lord is going to see you through this," said the woman. "I hope so," answered Browder, "But ya'll help the Lord out." On election day, there was concern as to how much the Lord was on Browder's side for there was a remarkable discrepancy in the weather in different parts of the district. While a series of tornadoes touched down in the northern part (Browder's home base), the southern counties (Rice's—and Ford's—turf) were in sunshine. With electric power out in some parts of Browder's home of Calhoun County, the largest county in the district, and people warned to stay indoors, the Democrats started looking into filing a lawsuit nullifying the election. It was unnecessary as Browder won and won big.

In the end, Browder took 65 percent of the vote, winning the black vote overwhelmingly and, if a pre-election poll is any indication, winning the white vote as well. In the last poll of the election, Browder had a 46 to 38 percent advantage among white voters with 16 percent undecided (Rilling 1989). Moreover, black turnout equaled white turnout in this election, according to the national party consultant. This turned a Browder victory into a "rollover." The election, which at one time appeared to be promising for the Republicans, instead was the second embarrassment for the party in a week.

Browder's victory was a model for Democratic victory in the region. Just months after George Bush's great electoral success in Alabama, Browder's strategy and, perhaps more important, his counterstrategy led him to a major victory. The result was not lost on the Democratic presidential candidate Michael Dukakis, who called Browder with his congratulations shortly after the election. Browder recalls the conversation ending with Dukakis saying, "If I had used your playbook, I'd be calling you from a different location."

Republicans and Racially Conservative Messages

At some point in all of the cases studied in this book, a racial issue arose. These two cases best illustrate the dynamics of a campaign in which a racial issue became a major issue in the campaign and serve as ideal types in this analysis. Why did Republicans in these cases bring up these issues (and it was almost always the Republican candidate who did so) and how did they generally fashion their racial message? How did Democrats respond to these issues and blunt their effectiveness?

The temptation for Republicans to raise a racial issue is always there. This is particularly true in heavily black areas, places with histories of white backlash to the civil rights movement and places where blacks now wield electoral power. Mississippi's Fourth District, 42 percent black, Alabama's Third District, 29 percent black, and Virginia's 25 percent black Fifth District, the other case in which a racial issue was prominent in the campaign, all have long histories of racial strife and racial politics. Racially conservative messages are often designed to appeal to disaffected white Democrats because Republicans and their staffs believe that there is political mileage in them. They believe that by adding white backlash votes to their loyal Republican core of voters, they can win a majority in the district.

The Republican candidates in these two cases introduced explicit racial issues into the campaigns after assessing the racial composition of the district and adding up their supporters. Liles Williams's district in Mississippi, as noted, was 42 percent black. Assuming that Dowdy would win almost all of the black vote in the runoff, and even assuming that whites would turn out in greater numbers than blacks, Williams would have to win the great preponderance (about three-quarters) of the white vote. The Voting Rights Act Extension issue had already been introduced into the campaign in the preliminary round. All the candidates except Dowdy opposed extension of the act and together polled 75 percent of the vote. Given the arithmetic of the situation, it made great sense for Williams to highlight the voting rights issue in his general election campaign.

The major play given the issue by the Jackson papers seemed to reinforce this strategy. In its editorial endorsing Williams, the Sunday edition (produced by both the morning and afternoon papers) went on at great length about the issue (*Jackson Daily News and Clarion-Ledger* 1981). In fact, more than half the editorial was devoted to an endorsement of Williams's position on the issue. Williams's campaign put out other messages, to be sure, but his opposition to the Voting Rights Act Extension was highlighted in all of his appearances and in many of his campaign advertisements. "The Voting Rights Act was the main issue of the campaign," said Wayne Dowdy. "At least, of [Williams's] campaign."

John Rice did not bring the Confederate flag issue into his campaign until the last two weeks of the campaign, though his managers were holding it in reserve in the weeks prior to the election. The issue came out near the end for several reasons. Rice's campaign started to suffer financially toward the middle of the campaign. It was unable to advertise on television during the final two weeks. With every slip in the polls, the Republican's money dried up more, and Rice lost even some national party help.[16] Rice's campaign manager had calculated that his candidate needed to win more than 65 percent of the white vote and planned his strategy accordingly. The problems faced by the campaign near the end, however, necessitated a dramatic move. The campaign needed exposure, and it was apparent that Rice's themes were not working. When the last poll of the election showed Browder to be well ahead, even among whites, Rice made some outlandish charges. He charged Browder with being a draft dodger (the Democrat was rejected by the military because of a congenital back condition) and, worse, with "teaching against the Vietnam War" in his classes. Neither charge received much attention, at least in the newspapers. At this point, Rice began waving the Confederate flag issue. Browder's campaign manager said, "He talked about it everywhere, had a very nasty piece of literature on it, just was banging away at it." The televised debate allowed him to make the point to an even larger audience. And by waiting until the closing statement, he also kept Browder from responding, should the Democrat have been so inclined. In the newspaper reports of the debate, the Rice campaign added that the Democrats were buying black votes. The racial issues injected into the campaign were more than attempts to lure white voters: they were last-ditch efforts to save the foundering campaign. The Rice campaign had planned to use these issues in the mail (which they did), but the course of the campaign required them to use it on television and in the papers.

The Republicans used racial issues because they saw them as a way of appealing to voters across ideological and party lines. When Rice's campaign manager called the flag issue a heritage issue instead of a race issue, his reasoning was that the heritage issue was one that appealed to people of many different political perspectives. Pride in the South, a sense of southernness, he claimed, were not liberal or conservative sentiments: "People are proud of the flag around here. They put 'em up in their offices. You see 'em all over the place. Even Dukakis' campaign manager had one up in his office. He's our Calhoun County director now. Man, he's constantly complaining about some of Rice's right-wing stands. But he's with us on this one." From the perspective of Rice's campaign manager, the issue had the potential to supersede other issues. Moreover, it would do so with a group of voters that both sides vie for in Deep South elections. Rural votes, in the view of many of the participants, are normally Democratic but can be lured over to the Republicans with racial issues. The Democrats agreed. "They [the Rice campaign] thought they were going to ride the [flag] issue," said a Browder campaign official. "And they could have. No doubt about it, the issue does have relevance down here, but it's mainly to the white, rural male in the district."

If Republicans have been trying to appeal to white voters like the southern Democrats of old, their message, in fact, has been quite different. How Republicans have characterized their campaign message is of great interest because it illustrates what has changed and what has stayed the same in southern politics. For the most part, southern Republicans have recognized that outright racist appeals are no longer socially acceptable. Republican campaign managers vigorously deny that they are trying to appeal to racist attitudes with their campaign tactics, and candidates take great offense when they or their tactics are labeled by others as racist. Their messages are tailored to white audiences, to be sure, but they are substantially different from the campaign messages of the old-time southern Democratic demagogues. Their message on race, they claim, is conservative, not racist.

Political observers argue that the Republican message on race is relatively new. Carmines and Stimson (1989) discuss the evolution of racial issues in the period immediately preceding the civil rights movement and the years since. Racial conservatism, they argue, is not equivalent to racism. Rather, it is "a new species, originating as a minor adaptation . . . from generalized conservatism" (190).[17] If a racist issue is one characterized by antipathy toward blacks (or black antipathy toward whites), a racially conservative issue is one based upon conservatism. A racially conservative issue may have political appeal because of widespread antipathy toward blacks, but this does not have to be the case. Whatever the intent, southern Republicans have articulated their positions on these issues in terms of individualism or distrust of the federal government or some other conservative principle.

In the elections described in this book, Republican candidates consistently raised racially conservative issues, that is, racial issues expressed in conservative terms. Most often, the Republican racial issue paralleled other campaign appeals to "get the government off our backs." In the Virginia election described below (see chapter 4), the Republican Linda Arey campaigned against a civil rights bill, calling it "an unprecedented intrusion on our private lives." Her campaign commercials highlighted her opposition to "Grove City, the *Civil Rights Restoration Act*" (emphasis added), while her opponent "favored more federal interference in our lives" (Baker 1988). Her rhetoric is interesting, first, because she used the issue to attack the federal government, a long-standing tradition in southern Virginia and one upon which many political careers have been based. Second, though she could just as easily have avoided calling the Grove City bill by its formal name, Civil Rights Restoration, she chose to use it. This allowed her to raise the racial issue in people's minds without talking about what the bill would do or how it would affect blacks and whites, indeed without even uttering the words *black* and *white*. As she shaped the issue in a thirty-second campaign spot, the choice was avoiding federal interference "in our private lives" or restoring civil rights, not much of a choice in southern Virginia.

John Rice's complaint that federal money for education came with too many strings attached also had racial connotations. Rice was playing upon sentiment against the federal government on the issue of school desegregation (and also school prayer). "We don't need the federal government telling us how to run our local affairs," said Rice at a debate. "We need to run our own affairs to support our schools financially and with our prayers." Rice's comment had two elements to it. He was attacking federal intrusion into local affairs—decisions he felt were best made at the local level. And he was making a none-too-subtle reference to one of the earliest and most volatile racial issues of the civil rights era. The issue of school desegregation is still quite touchy. In both Alabama and Mississippi, I often was told by Republican campaign workers that school integration had ruined the educational system for whites. Desegregation had brought violence, racial disharmony, and lower standards to the schools. Rice's "too many strings attached" message addressed these sentiments.

Rice also spoke of abuses in federal housing programs, another attempt to link federal government activity and race. Federal housing programs were good when they were taken advantage of "by little old ladies who kept nice gardens," said Rice at a candidate forum. They now have become "a real tragedy" and are fraught with abuses. In making these comments, the candidate was not explicitly talking about blacks and was explicitly attacking the federal government. But it was not the federal programs that were the problem, it was the people they were directed toward. In this case, such people include an inordinate number of blacks. What is different about present-day southern politics is that Rice did not say this.

In addition to these racially conservative appeals, Republicans made racial appeals in the name of fairness—fairness to whites, fairness to southerners, fairness to Republicans. Behind Rice's Confederate flag waving was the contention that whites are having to give something up to support black civil rights gains. Whether that be their heritage or the quality of their educational system, this is the sentiment that Rice attempted to tap.[18] One Rice campaign aide, a former Democratic county chairman and a college-educated mother, tried to articulate this position: "Nothing against the black folks from around here. They're a genteel people on the whole. But when you bring some folks up, when you try to equalize them, you've got to bring other folks down. And we're tired of being brought down." She was not necessarily talking about helping blacks economically, though that was part of it. Rather, she was expressing an ill-defined resentment of blacks, a belief that black economic, social, and political gains are made at the expense of whites. The Republicans believe (and may well be right) that this sentiment is widespread in the South, and they attempt to take advantage of it.

Liles Williams's opposition (and the opposition of the *Jackson Clarion-Ledger*) to extending the Voting Rights Act was framed as an issue of fairness—the fairness of singling out the South in dealing with these voting rights issues. Stating that the South had made so much progress in the area of voting rights and noting that other areas of the country also had severe problems, Williams argued that to extend the act was to *punish* the South for its past misdeeds—misdeeds that had been acknowledged and addressed. He was not arguing to take away black voting rights or to "turn back the clock," but his position was certainly unsympathetic to blacks for it called for the abolition of an important vehicle for black political progress. Although not advocating the reversal of civil rights gains for blacks, his stance was clearly an appeal to conservative whites in the district who had this in mind.

Republicans have complained about fairness in the electoral process too. Their complaints have often taken the form of charges that the Democrats are paying blacks to vote or that other illegal activities are taking place. When John Rice's campaign manager was quoted in the newspapers to the effect that the campaign was writing off the black vote because the Alabama Democratic Conference paid blacks to vote, it was part of a two-part strategy to generate a white backlash (the other part being the Confederate flag issue).

Republicans have been slowly adjusting to competitive politics in the South. Not only are they starting to field better, more qualified candidates, but they are testing various political strategies and continuing to refashion their message. Looking at the arithmetic of winning a congressional campaign in the South, Republicans have continued to rely heavily on racial issues. Not every Republican campaign is as racial as the ones described above, but some racial appeals seem to arise in nearly every election. This at least was the case in all of the elections studied here. There are problems with raising these issues, however. If they have solidified some white votes, they also have helped Democratic candidates win black votes.

How Racial Issues Help Democratic Candidates

Contrary to what one might expect, Republican candidates have often helped their Democratic opponents by raising racial issues. Democrats have been able to turn the issue to their advantage. Given how these issues play out in the campaign and given how Democrats communicate with black constituents, it is not surprising that this has been the case.

Democrats recognize how important the black vote is to their electoral prospects. But they have the difficult task as well of keeping white voters in the fold. As a result of these sometimes contradictory goals, Democrats generally do not respond with much vigor or volume to racial issues raised by their Republican opponents. They state their position, which is the racially liberal position, but they do so cautiously and softly, and they do not elaborate much. Wayne Dowdy's public response to the Voting Rights Act Extension issue, for instance, was clear but subdued. He announced his support for the measure but said little else, at least publicly or in the media. Sometimes it is not even worth it for Democrats to counter Republican charges. Glen Browder, in the Alabama race, never responded to John Rice's Confederate flag waving. "He didn't want to touch that one," said his campaign manager.

With regard to racial issues, Democratic candidates have walked a tightrope, but they seem to be good at it. If they choose to talk about racial issues in public, they do so in measured tones and in few words. They have little to gain by articulating racially liberal positions in the press or in a debate. They have much to lose. And they are willing to test white support only so far. Most Democrats figure that they benefit when the salience of a racial issue is not raised further. A restrained, brief statement of their position on the issue is all that is necessary and need not antagonize white voters sympathetic to Democrats. None of the white Democratic candidates discussed in this book would be mistaken for a champion of black issues by their public support of such issues. This is mostly because of *how* they have made their stand. Some white voters may support the Republican on the basis of the Democratic position on racial issues, but as the Democratic candidate has not vociferously and self-righteously asserted these positions, there is less of a danger that white voters will identify the Democrat as the so-called candidate of the blacks.

Emphatic public statements on racial issues are not necessary to court black votes in the South. Democrats have fared well by comparison to their Republican opponents *and* to their Democratic predecessors. At least from the perspective of the candidates, black expectations of white Democrats have not been very high and have been easily met. The Virginia Democrat L. F. Payne, for example, believed that it would take very little to generate black support in his district. Payne benefited from being compared not only to his opponent, but also to his predecessor, characterized by one Democratic activist as a "Byrd Democrat of massive resistance and a racist" (Bland 1988a). The result, according to Payne, was that blacks made no demands upon him to come out stronger on the issues raised by Linda Arey. Payne and his Democratic colleagues appeared sympathetic to blacks in sheer contrast to those who had come before and to what the alternative would be.

Black Democratic leaders appear to understand the constraints that white Democrats work under. They do not require white Democrats to take bold stands on racial issues to win their support so long as their overall record on issues of interest to minorities is good. In the context of a discussion about the Confederate flag, the field director of the Alabama Democratic Conference told me that he did not care that Browder did not respond strongly to Rice: "We would not make that issue the litmus test for our support. It's a political issue that most [white Democrats], even liberals and moderates, couldn't touch."

In spite of Democratic reluctance to champion racial issues in debates and in the press, Democrats do make strong pitches for the black vote. The Democratic position is perhaps best summed up by a black turnout specialist of the Democratic Congressional Campaign Committee, who said, "You've got to approach the black vote surgically, because the white vote in many of these places is so volatile. So you don't talk much about it [racial issues] in front of white audiences and you really drive it home in front of black audiences." Much to the advantage of Democrats, blacks can be approached "surgically." Although the South has desegregated, patterns of association there, as in the North, are still separate. Because of these patterns of association, a politician seeking to communicate with black voters can do so easily. Most important, he can reach black voters without having white voters hear his message.

The major channel to the black community has been through black opinion leaders who give the white Democrat credibility with blacks. White candidates generally have not had deep ties to the black community. The blacks they have known are those with whom they have worked in the state legislature or in party politics prior to their candidacy. These politicians provide the candidate with access to black voters. They serve as liaisons to the community and line up ministers, businessmen, shop stewards, and other black opinion leaders who, in turn, carry the Democrat's message to the black masses. Johnny Ford gave Glen Browder access to and legitimacy with black voters. A black member on the staff of the Virginia Democrat L. F. Payne escorted him to black churches and black functions. And a black state legislator from Gulfport served as a facilitator for Gene Taylor, the Democratic candidate from Mississippi's Fifth District, becoming, as another black leader put it, "Taylor's man."

With the help of these black elites, white candidates can reach black voters through a number of sources. The black pulpit has been used for several decades to reach black voters. Ministers carry great prestige in most southern black communities. When black ministers from around the district speak on a candidate's behalf, introduce him or her to their congregations, and remind their flock two days before the election to go to the polls, that candidate has a powerful advantage. When black ministers charge their parishioners, as one Jackson preacher did in 1981, with the "Christian duty" of voting for the Democratic candidate because "segregationists and racists are planning to turn back the clock" (Clymer 1981b), the message is all the more convincing. What is more, blacks who attend church are much more likely to vote than those who do not, particularly in the South. In presidential elections in the 1980s, 60 percent of southern blacks who attended church every week voted (n=97). Of those who did not attend church or who attended infrequently, only 17 percent voted (n=70).[19] Working through the black churches is all the more effective because it has allowed southern Democrats not only to reach blacks, but to reach those blacks most likely to go to the polls.

Blacks also can be reached via black media. Black newspapers offer opportunities to advertise, but an even more important channel is "narrowcasting" on black radio. Black radio is an effective medium for Democrats as it is much less expensive than television and reaches a well-defined group of people.[20] Moreover, said a Virginia media consultant, "You can hit a lot harder on radio because the other side has more difficulty keeping track of what you are saying."

Black radio was used in every one of the Democratic campaigns examined here. And, as noted above, the Republican's conservative stand on a racial issue often supplied the material used in the commercials. White Democrats were able to use the Republican's position and, in the words of a Washington political consultant, "incite people." Democratic campaign managers described their typical radio message in highly graphic terms. Said one, "[The Republican candidate] thinks niggers should be out in the field picking cotton. They don't want you to go to the polls." And another, "If you don't vote, the Republicans will think you're dumb. Don't let them take your right to vote away." These are paraphrases (by the managers themselves) of previous Democratic advertisements on black radio and illustrate how strong the message can be.

By appealing to blacks through these channels—black leaders, the black church, black media, and of course, direct mail—white Democratic candidates have appealed to blacks surgically. Whites do not attend black churches. They do not listen to or read black media. Residential segregation makes direct mail into black precincts viable. Whites simply do not hear the Democratic message directed toward blacks.

What is more, two other important sets of actors in the campaign—the media and the Republicans—do not pick up the message. The nature of campaign coverage in the general media (radio, television, and newspapers reaching a general public) has allowed Democratic candidates to run these segregated campaigns. The way congressional campaigns, even special election campaigns, are covered, the Democratic candidate has frequently been able to pursue a two-pronged strategy, one aimed toward whites (see chapter 4), the other toward blacks. First, newspapers in small cities like Greenwood and Biloxi, Mississippi, and Anniston, Alabama, generally are staffed by young, inexperienced reporters. Some are not reporters by training and are not interested in making journalism a career. Although they are intelligent and enthusiastic recent college graduates, their understanding of politics and campaigns is often limited. Few of them have much background in politics. As one reporter told me, the campaign was "a lot of fun after working on the court beat for the past year. But I don't really know very much about politics." His questions at a press conference confirmed this admission. It is difficult even for the best reporters to cover much more than the surface of any story, and those without much understanding of the topic generally do not.

Second, reporters (experienced as well as inexperienced) cover the big events of the campaign—the press conferences, the debates, the speeches, the visits by state and national dignitaries. Their coverage of candidates in the day-to-day campaign is limited. For one thing, little of the handshaking and baby kissing is newsworthy. Reporters do not have the time to cover these events, and their column inches already are filled with coverage of lively debates and press conferences. For another, even if reporters wanted to cover these types of events, they must depend upon campaign managers to tell them where the candidate will be on a certain day at a certain time. And campaign managers, even when they know where the candidate is scheduled to be (which is not always the case), do not necessarily wish for reporters to know. Thus while many important events and issue positions and controversies are recorded in local newspapers, reporters cover only a portion of the campaign.[21] Part of what does not get reported is a Democratic candidate's visit to a black church or other campaign activity in the black community.

If Democrats can count on the media not to cover their forays into the black community, they are less sure that Republicans will not catch wind of what they are saying in the black community. If Republicans do hear of Democratic charges, as in the Jackson, Mississippi, race, they respond angrily. Even in that case, however, when Williams's campaign manager accused Wayne Dowdy of being "one of the greatest race baiters elected to office in Mississippi in the last 20 or 30 years" (Treyens 1981a), it was too late. It was only after the election that Republicans became aware of inflammatory Democratic radio advertisements. As a precaution against Republican exploitation of these appeals and because limited funds almost always necessitate the saving of their media campaigns for the closing week of the campaign, Democrats (and Republicans too for that matter) save their most hard-hitting charges for the end of the campaign. Opponents thus have a limited time to respond to such advertisements, even if they do find out about them, which is not guaranteed. The last frenzied days of the campaign leave little time for monitoring radio stations in the district and coming up with a response. Keeping track of the logistics of one's own candidate is difficult enough. Keeping track of one's opponent's activities is beyond the capability of most campaign organizations. This has made Democratic tactics with regard to the black community all the more effective.[22]

In the final analysis, Republican attempts to win white votes with racial issues—a message that no doubt works with some voters—can be costly. Democrats can easily turn the issue against them in the black community, thereby bolstering black turnout. What is more, they can do so *without whites hearing their message*. "Race baiting is a classic error," said one Texas Democratic consultant. "If the Republicans can appeal to prejudice without being called a bigot, then it works. But it's so easy to create a backlash."

Republican racial issues have given Democratic candidates a platform in the black community. White Democrats do not often have much experience approaching black voters. Although they have alliances with black leaders, state legislators, and other politicians they have dealt with in their careers, white Democratic candidates and their campaign staffs often do not have informal connections to the black community. They are unlikely to have spent much time prior to the campaign in black neighborhoods, black churches, or black stores. They are not likely to socialize with blacks. On several occasions, I was told that a white candidate was not comfortable in front of all-black audiences. A racial issue introduced into the campaign gives the white Democratic candidate a reason to be in front of blacks appealing for their votes and makes the situation much more comfortable.

White Democratic candidates have needed something to generate enthusiasm among blacks. Southern blacks are neither necessarily quick to warm to white Democrats, nor do they appear to connect deeply with white candidates. Black Democratic leadership may support a white Democrat, even with good reason, but such backing does not automatically translate into an enthusiastic response from rank-and-file black voters. In the Alabama race, for instance, Glen Browder's support of black voter registration activity when he was secretary of state generated some good will among the top guard of the Alabama Democratic Conference. They wholeheartedly supported him in his congressional campaign once Johnny Ford had been eliminated. But Browder still required something to enable him to connect with the average black voter in the district. John Rice's Confederate flag gave Browder something to advertise in the black community.

It is difficult to assess exactly how many votes are won and lost through racial issues. No doubt the number varies from election to election. That all the cases here illustrate Democratic success is some indication that such issues work to the advantage of Democrats. Southern Democrats win by constructing a tricky biracial coalition, a coalition that is still possible in much of the region when they successfully finesse racial issues.

4 Courting White Voters

THE STORY UP TO THIS POINT has been about how southern Republican congressional candidates try to attract large shares of the white vote, how Democrats try to maximize the black vote, and how these two strategies are related. The margin of victory, however, comes from neither the black vote nor the white Republican vote. The difference between winning and losing turns on white votes, traditionally Democratic whites who could go either way and more often than not have gone the Republican way in presidential elections.

If Democrats are to win white votes in the South, they must do more than simply downplay their positions on racial issues. And they cannot simply hope that white Democrats will automatically vote their party label. They must give whites a reason to vote for them. Democrats do not need to win a majority of the white vote to win elections in the South (see chapter 2), but they must be able to attract a significant minority of the white vote to succeed.

The three cases to follow, one in East Texas, one in southern Virginia, and one in southern Mississippi, illustrate some prototypical southern campaigns, both Democratic and Republican. On the Republican side, the candidates have Washington connections and try to make the most of them. They put forth extremely conservative positions and charge their opponents with being liberals or with associating with liberals, which is almost as bad. On the Democratic side are three candidates who deemphasize ideology and party ties and highlight what they can do for the people of the district. The result is a campaign that pits "national Republicans" against "local Democrats." And in each case, it is the local Democrat who wins.

Texas 1—"Tora! Tora! Tora!"

In the South, a yellow dog Democrat is one who would vote for a yellow dog before voting for a Republican. That the term is used as a compliment tells much about the power of an old attachment in the face of new and powerful political forces. It is an attachment that has allowed the Democratic party to control places like East Texas since Reconstruction. From 1870 to 1985, the year of the special election studied here, Democrats represented Texas's First District.[1] From 1928 to 1985, in fact, only two congressmen served the district: the populist Wright Patman held the seat for nearly fifty years, and the conservative Sam Hall for almost ten.

But many believed that the time had come for a Republican to represent what the columnists Rowland Evans and Robert Novak (1985) called a "congenitally Democratic" district. By the mid-1980s, Republicans were winning large majorities of district votes in presidential, senatorial, and gubernatorial elections. The district went overwhelmingly for the southerner Jimmy Carter in 1976, but Ronald Reagan beat Carter by about one thousand votes in 1980 and trounced Walter Mondale in 1984. Phil Gramm dominated the district in his Senate election in 1984, and Bill Clements won there in the gubernatorial election of 1986 (calculated from Scammon and McGillivray 1986).

At the time of the election in 1985, however, Republicans had yet to win any low-level positions in the district. Democrats controlled every single courthouse in the district's twenty counties (Attlesey 1985g), and every local officeholder with a partisan identification was a Democrat (King 1985a). It is difficult to know just how large the Democratic advantage in the district actually was because the state does not register voters by party and because it is difficult to get public opinion data in an area with no major media outlets. One guess comes from a Republican pollster familiar with the area who estimated that Democrats had a ten-point advantage (Attlesey 1985d). Whatever the exact figure, self-identified Democrats outnumbered Republicans in East Texas in the mid-1980s.

Given its demographics, it is not surprising that politics in the First look so much like politics in other parts of the South. The First is actually more like neighboring Louisiana and Arkansas in character and population than it is like the rest of Texas. It is one of the poorest districts in the state and has a large population of blacks (20 percent) and few Hispanics. It has several small cities of about thirty thousand (Texarkana, Paris, and Marshall) but is mostly small town and rural. More than one-third of its voters are over the age of sixty-five (King 1985c), making it the district with the oldest population in the state.

These features have led many to identify it as a prototypical southern rural district. That and its reputation as a tenacious Democratic stronghold led confident Republicans to attempt to invest this election with a lot of meaning. Though only one seat in the House, if won it would be, they claimed, a highly symbolic bite out of the once Solid South. If this district were to fall, few others in the region could be considered safely Democratic. Yet the election meant even more. The Republicans argued that the contest would be a demonstration, that it would initiate an eastward domino effect, in which other southern districts would finally fall out of Democratic control. They, of course, were hoping that such an interpretation would bring others—voters, donors, prospective candidates—to the same conclusion, fulfilling their prophecy. "If the Republicans can win in that district," said the chairman of the state Republican party, "it is Armageddon for the Democrats in Texas" (Attlesey 1985e). National Republicans too saw this as a wonderful opportunity and put out a similar message.[2]

The opportunity was created by the Republicans in the first place. Senator Phil Gramm, himself a former Democrat, engineered the circumstances that led to the vacating of the seat when he recommended the incumbent congressman, Sam Hall, for an open federal judgeship in Texas.[3] After Hall accepted the offer, Gramm set out to recruit a Republican candidate to replace him. His first choice, Ed Howard, a popular Democratic state senator from Texarkana, could not be persuaded to switch parties and turned him down (King 1985a). Gramm then approached Edd Hargett, a rancher and a former star quarterback with Texas A&M, the Houston Oilers, and the New Orleans Saints. Hargett, having positive name recognition in the district and a ready-made network of Texas A&M alumni, was a potentially attractive candidate.[4] And though he had not held public office before, indeed because of his lack of experience he had few if any negatives going into the campaign. Hargett took up the offer.

In addition to recruiting a quality candidate, Phil Gramm encouraged other Republicans to stay out of the race. This gave Hargett a shot at winning a majority of the vote in the nonpartisan primary, thus avoiding a runoff between the top two vote-getters. In a low turnout election with a divided Democratic field, this was considered well within the realm of the possible. Gramm assured Hargett a steady supply of funding. By the time of the primary, Hargett—and Gramm—had raised almost half a million dollars (King 1985a) and spent three-quarters of a million dollars (Attlesey 1985b). By the general election, Hargett had spent one and a half million dollars (King 1985d), three times more than his opponent (Nelson 1985), and certainly more than one would expect of a first-time candidate running in a cheap media market.[5] In fact, the flow of money into Hargett's campaign compelled Democrats to charge that the Republicans were trying to buy the election. House Speaker Jim Wright decried the "outsider-funded, Madison Avenue advertising campaign" and said it was "lamentable [that Republicans] think you can buy a congressional seat just like you buy a seat on the New York Stock Exchange" (Attlesey 1985a). Finally, Gramm hired major Republican strategists—the political consultant Lee Atwater, the pollster Lance Tarrance, and the media consultant Roger Ailes—to run the campaign. In short, he was putting a fair amount of prestige and political capital at stake. A Republican victory in the First District, according to one newspaper account, "[became] a personal crusade [for Gramm], an effort to establish himself as a GOP kingmaker and unquestioned leader of the state's Republican Party" (Attlesey 1985h).

Gramm's machinations notwithstanding, Hargett did not win the majority necessary to avoid a runoff. In winning 42 percent of the vote, however, he was far ahead of his nearest competitor, the Democrat Jim Chapman, a former district attorney from one of the western counties in the district. Chapman was the only candidate from this part of the district, which likely helped him win 30 percent of the primary vote (Attlesey 1985c). A member of an old political family in the area (going back five generations), Chapman was fairly well known to East Texans. Moreover, he had used his tenure as district attorney to establish some fine conservative credentials. In that position, Chapman claimed a 99 percent conviction rate in more than two thousand felony cases (Attlesey 1985i). With characteristic Texas bravado, he boasted that he made Dallas District Attorney Henry Wade, famous for his twelve-hundred-year sentences, "look like a sissy" (Barone 1985). If Chapman had any liability going into the congressional contest, it was that he had angered some important Democrats in an unsuccessful challenge to a popular state senator, the same Ed Howard whom Phil Gramm had tried to coax into joining the race.[6] Nevertheless, Chapman appeared to be a strong candidate, at least in part of the district, going into the runoff.

Both candidates were cautious in talking about their parties. Hargett tied himself to President Reagan as much as possible, and the president made two commercials for the campaign. The candidate also brought to the district several big-name national Republicans, including Vice President Bush, Congressman Jack Kemp, and Treasury Secretary James

Baker. But Hargett's campaign literature and commercials *never* mentioned his Republican affiliation, and he rarely brought it up in campaign appearances (Attlesey 1985g). In fact, many of his campaign appearances ended in a Texas A&M "yell practice," prompting the Democratic governor, Mark White, to comment that "[Hargett is] running as an Aggie and I don't blame him. That's far more popular than being a Republican" (Hillman 1985).[7] When party label was brought up by the Republicans (in a party-sponsored commercial featuring the former Democratic congressman Kent Hance), it was to urge Democrats to "bite the bullet" and support Hargett because "the national Democratic Party is not the one we grew up with" (Attlesey 1985f). Hargett himself acknowledged that his party label was somewhat of a problem. He qualified his remarks by saying that he had encountered little hostility while out campaigning ("Except for one time when I was thrown out of a factory because I was a Republican. And that fellow may just have been mad about the economy"). Yet, as he recalled it, "There were a lot of people who were friends of mine, not bosom buddies or anything, but friends, who wouldn't vote for me because I was a Republican."

Chapman, too, was careful in talking about his Democratic affiliation. He thus took great pains to distance himself from the national party leaders. "I'm a conservative," Chapman would say. "I'm not tied to any one party" (Attlesey 1985e). In a debate with Hargett, he declined even to say how he had voted for president in 1984 (Evans and Novak 1985). Given the Democratic advantage in partisan affiliation in the district, however, Chapman was careful not to totally reject his affiliation. In striking a balance, Chapman referred to himself as a "conservative Democrat," not a "national Democrat."

Hargett's central campaign strategy was to tie Chapman to the national Democrats, to label him as a liberal, and to establish himself as the conservative standard-bearer. He first claimed that Chapman, as a Democrat, could be expected to support liberals and liberal positions on such issues as gun control and affirmative action for homosexuals. In raising the homosexual issue, Hargett was taking a page from the campaigns of several other Texas Republicans who had effectively used homosexuals as a rhetorical target.[8] In his Senate race the year before, for instance, Phil Gramm took his opponent to task for accepting a campaign donation that was collected at a gay male strip joint (Barone and Ujifusa 1987, 1133).

Chapman also was beholden to big labor and eastern bosses, argued Hargett, the hard evidence being pro-Chapman "Dear Brothers and Sisters" letters from local AFL-CIO Central Labor Councils and the United Auto Workers. When Chapman denied that he was too close to labor and claimed that he had informed the unions that he did not want their endorsements (though he had no objection to donations), Hargett attacked him again. A Roger Ailes commercial in the last week of the campaign excoriated Chapman for not acknowledging his relation to big labor (Evans and Novak 1985).[9]

Hargett worked hard to distinguish himself from Chapman, which was difficult because the Democrat was so vocally conservative. He basically attempted to paint himself as the more doctrinaire conservative and as the candidate who would not be obligated to Tip O'Neill. Such standard conservative issues as gun control and family values and standard conservative rhetoric were central to his campaign. And he aimed to damage Chapman's conservative credentials.

Indeed, Chapman's first goal was to deflect Hargett's liberal charges. He made bold declarations against gun control and abortion. He spoke in favor of a balanced budget amendment. He advocated prayer in schools. Yet Chapman was on the defensive when discussing conservative issues and sought to steer the campaign toward other issues. "We had to bash Tip. We had to come out right away on a constitutional amendment on prayer in school," said a Democratic consultant. "Then we could get on with it."

As they did. In spite of Hargett's financial advantage, the Chapman forces controlled the agenda. The Democrat's initial strategy appeared to be to capitalize upon Hargett's lack of experience. Hargett, according to a Democratic radio ad, was hand selected by Republican power brokers at "a secret meeting" and then sent to "charm school" to learn his lines: "Presto, an instant Congressman" (King 1985c). It was more than just the process that was being referred to here. The theme developed as Chapman's campaign team noticed that at Republican events, Senator Gramm would often take the microphone to answer questions directed at Hargett. In the words of Chapman, it all played into the notion that "the Republicans are trying to wow you with glitz and poor ol' Edd doesn't know what he's doing."

It was not just Hargett's inexperience that was the issue. The nature of his candidacy, argued the Democrats, compromised his independence. Anticipating this line of attack, Hargett responded to the inexperience charge by arguing that there were too many lawyers in Washington as it was. As for his independence, Hargett argued that he would not be "a rubber stamp for anyone. . . . I'll vote for President Reagan when he's right for East Texas and I'll vote against him when he is wrong for East Texas" (King 1985c).

Hargett was not as prepared to counter Chapman's two other campaign issues. The most widely discussed issues in the campaign and in press reports about the campaign were Social Security and foreign trade, both initiated by the Democrat. Given the large number of senior citizens in East Texas, Chapman, as early as the primary campaign, tried to capitalize on the Social Security issue and campaigned aggressively against a proposal to freeze Social Security cost-of-living adjustments that had passed the Republican-controlled Senate with the blessing of the Reagan administration. After the primary on June 29 and throughout the general campaign, Chapman continued arguing that the Republicans posed a threat to senior citizens, this despite the fact that the administration and Senate Republicans, under pressure from House Democrats, abandoned the freeze by mid-July, two weeks before the general election. Rep. Claude Pepper, the elderly representative wholly associated and identified with the issue, campaigned with Chapman in the district, and senior citizens were sent a letter from Pepper endorsing Chapman as the man "[who would] help us protect Social Security from the Republican onslaught" (King 1985c). A victory by Hargett would be a "terrible blow" to Social Security, warned Pepper. The message had two purposes. First, it linked

Hargett to the wrong side of the Social Security issue. Second, it linked him to the Republican party, an association that might be offensive to older Democrats.

Hargett's campaign responded to the Social Security issue in a television advertisement, a variation of an advertisement that Republicans frequently have used to defuse the issue. In this advertisement, an elderly woman shucking peas turns to the camera and chastises Chapman for trying to scare old voters with false information. "Shame on you, Jim Chapman," she scolds, all the while waving a pea pod at the camera. In another commercial, Hargett charges Chapman with distributing a campaign pamphlet on the Social Security issue that looked like an official government document. The countercharge that Chapman was not playing fair on the issue was clever, but it was a defensive response, an indication that the campaign was being waged on Chapman's turf.

The major issue in the Chapman campaign, however, was trade policy. With the oil and gas economy in shambles and a district steel plant in trouble, Chapman wanted to talk about jobs. What was most clever about his discussion was the scapegoat he found for the unemployment problem. Noting the recent layoffs at the steel plant, Chapman campaigned vigorously against the unfair trade policies of the Japanese on steel, as well as the unfair policies of other countries. "Korean steel, Canadian lumber, Argentinean dairy imports, Saudi oil and gas, Italian textiles. Right down the list, you name the industry, you name the country, we're getting our lunch eaten by subsidized foreign imports," said Chapman on the campaign trail as he called on the "greatest country in the free world" to reverse its "unilateral disarmament" on trade (Taylor 1985c). And he made the effective connection to the district. "[When American markets are] flooded with foreign goods that aren't made by Americans, it costs Americans their jobs," Chapman said, pointing out that the district's unemployment rate had increased 31 percent in the previous year (Attlesey 1985e).

This Democratic message got a big boost when a Texarkana newspaper quoted Hargett as saying, "I don't know what trade policies have to do with bringing jobs to East Texas" (King 1985c). Chapman chided

Hargett for this comment throughout the remainder of the contest and featured it in television and radio advertising that ran frequently in the closing weeks of the campaign.[10] Hargett, a self-described free trader, tried to control the damage by declaring that he knew how bad the steel plant closing was because his brothers had lost their jobs there. But again he was on the defensive. The newspapers were covering these exchanges instead of those initiated by Hargett. When Chapman gleefully pointed out that Hargett's campaign hats were made in Taiwan, the Republican's problem on the issue only got worse. There was little Hargett could do to counter this revelation. Chapman's campaign managers felt that this was the turning point of the campaign, which one called a " 'Tora! Tora! Tora!' campaign" against "Japanese imperialism."[11]

Of all the races described in this book, racial issues played the least important role in this one. Chapman's campaign aggressively pursued the black vote, bringing in numerous black campaign operatives from Austin to canvass black precincts and working the black churches. It advertised extensively on black radio stations. Chapman's advertisements attempted to portray Hargett as a stiff opponent of civil rights, but the charges had little effect because Hargett had so few racial themes in his campaign. The Hargett campaign did complain that the Democrats had a "task force of 25 hired, professional black operatives" in the district (Attlesey 1985f), a claim the Chapman campaign falsely denied. But there was little else in the Republican rhetoric on racial issues. This is, in part, because the black population in the district is not as large as it is in some of the other districts examined in these chapters. It is also likely a reflection of Edd Hargett's discomfort with these issues. Some attributed this to Hargett's football career, in which he played with and befriended many black players. Whatever the source, his reticence on racial issues surprised Democratic campaign officials, who claimed that Hargett's Republican handlers were expert in running racial campaigns.

A racial controversy did come up, however, during the campaign. The Thursday before the primary election, Assistant Attorney General for Civil Rights William Bradford Reynolds wrote to Gov. Mark White charging that the preclearance provision in the Voting Rights Act had been violated in the setting of the date for the election. Reynolds, citing the notification provision of the act (intended to keep officials from setting election dates that might discriminate against minorities), threatened White with unspecified legal action. By Monday, White had agreed to have the state formally notify the Justice Department. The primary was held as scheduled, though several media outlets reported on the confusion about the election (Taylor 1985b). In mid-July, the issue arose again, this time with the Justice Department raising the matter in federal court. A Texas election official argued that other such vacancies had been filled at least forty times since the enactment of the Voting Rights Act without the state having to preclear the date (King 1985b). Governor White, as before, argued that the demand was unreasonable, citing a 1983 federal appeals panel ruling that the setting of dates for special elections did not require preclearance. Ironically, that suit, not filed by the Justice Department, was brought in the special election of 1983 won by Phil Gramm (Sanders-Castro 1985, 7). In the Chapman/Hargett election, although the Justice Department did not allege discrimination in the setting of the date, the three-judge panel ruled against Texas, requiring the state to submit preclearance papers by August 9 (actually several days after the election) or have the election declared void.

The state ultimately did comply with the order, but Texas Democratic officials argued throughout the controversy that it was part of a Republican plan to dampen political participation. Low turnout in either the primary or the general was considered to work to Hargett's advantage, so their argument went, and Atwater was using his ties to the administration to "chill" turnout, particularly black turnout, by creating confusion about the elections. Governor White called it a politically inspired trick by the Reagan administration (King 1985b), and Rep. Don Edwards, the chair of the House Judiciary Subcommittee charged with overseeing the Civil Rights Division of the Justice Department, referred to the incident as an attempt to intimidate minority voters. "Only in the final two weeks of a hotly contested campaign, with the Republican candidate in trouble, does the Justice Department push forward to force the state to submit their plan for approval," said Edwards (Kurtz 1985). Justice Department officials responded to the charge, touting their tough enforcement of the law and denying that their decision to pursue the matter was motivated by a desire to assist the Republican candidate. "This whole matter has been worked up by career attorneys and Brad [Reynolds] just approved what they did," said a spokesman for the assistant attorney general (Kurtz 1985).[12] Looking back at it, one Democratic pollster believed the incident ended up helping Jim Chapman. He believed that the Republicans ended up raising the salience of the election for blacks with the lawsuits. If indeed this was the case, it was a tactical error.

In the end, Chapman pulled out a narrow victory, winning 51 to 49 percent by fewer than two thousand votes. National Democrats rejoiced over the victory, claiming that the Republicans had failed their own test. The notion that the South was realigning, said one campaign strategist, "was clearly not feasible," and Paul Kirk, the chairman of the Democratic National Committee, argued that "the talk about realignment is still only a Republican dream" (King 1985d). Republicans tried to paint the defeat as favorably as they could. Trying to put a positive spin on a disaster, Rep. Guy Vander Jagt, chairman of the National Republican Congressional Committee, called the loss "a smashing victory. To even be competitive in that district is indeed a historic realignment" (*New York Times* 1985). Still, it was a bitterly disappointing loss. Jim Chapman recalled meeting Lee Atwater some time after the election. "He told me that my election was the only one that ever gave him the dry heaves for three days," crowed the Democrat.

Atwater's distress was heightened because the election failed to provide his party with the demonstration they needed to initiate a broader low-level realignment in the region as a whole. He and his colleagues vowed to continue the effort. Phil Gramm, for one, issued a bold warning as the campaign drew to a close: "Win or lose this race, this is only my first involvement. We're going to keep on building the party until we're hunting Democrats with dogs" (Attlesey 1985h). His efforts continue, and several years later, this election was still on the minds of Republican strategists. "It was a phenomenal opportunity," said a Washington Republican consultant looking back "It could have been a turning point."

Virginia 5—"I'll take the district any day of the week"

Virginia is usually thought of as one of the more racially liberal states of the South. The election of a black governor there in 1989 enhanced this reputation. But parts of the state are still very conservative on racial matters. The area of the state known as Southside has been and continues to be the racially conservative bastion of the state. It was here that the most stubborn resistance to civil rights changes was met. It was here that schools closed for five years rather than desegregate. It was here, in the town of Danville, that police attacks "worse than Bull Connor's" sent almost fifty blacks to the hospital for demonstrating against downtown segregation (Branch 1988, 822). And it was here that George Wallace won 37 percent of the presidential vote in 1968,[13] one of only two Virginia districts he carried.

Most of Southside Virginia is encompassed by the Fifth District, which is heavily rural and comprises one-quarter of the territory of the state but only one-tenth of its population. Although the cities of Roanoke and Richmond sit on its border, the only sizable town in the district is Danville. Lynchburg, Jerry Falwell's hometown and what many would consider the capital of the Christian Right movement, is partially in the district. The area is mostly agricultural (the major crops raised in the area are soybeans and tobacco), but the region's soil is not overly fertile and the area is relatively poor. It has a large black population, blacks making up one-quarter of its residents. This and the other demographic characteristics of the district's population make the Fifth a district more like North Carolina than north Virginia.

The district's long-time congressman W. C. "Dan" Daniel was one of the last old-time southern Democrats. A proud boll weevil and a remnant of the Byrd machine, Daniel was one of the most conservative congressmen—Democratic or Republican—in the House of Representatives, averaging a 4 rating on the Americans for Democratic Action scale and an 87 on the American Conservative Union scale between 1980 and 1988 (Ehrenhalt 1987). According to these scales, he and Sonny Montgomery of Mississippi were the two most conservative Democrats in the House, and the old congressman was quite proud of this. Indeed, he often would boast that he voted with President Reagan more often than 77 percent of his colleagues did. Daniel was particularly conservative on racial issues, voting consistently against such measures as the extension of the Voting Rights Act, the Martin Luther King national holiday, and other issues of interest to blacks, symbolic and substantive. Nonetheless, the congressman was very partisan. He joked that he voted with Tip O'Neill only two times per session (once to vote for O'Neill as Speaker and once to close the session), but, as one Democratic official told me, he was devoted to the Democratic party and often advised the party on Democratic opportunities in the state. Despite Ronald Reagan's popularity in the district (in 1980, he won 55 percent of the vote; in 1984, 65 percent), Daniel was unchallenged throughout the Reagan years. In fact, after Daniel's death in 1988, the Republican district chairman could not recall the last candidate fielded against Daniel (Elving 1988).[14] Daniel was willing and able to hold office until his final days and died just four days after he resigned. During his final few terms, he often hinted at retirement, thereby holding off challengers, who recognized that waiting for an open seat was preferable to running against an institution.

When the open seat finally did materialize, it offered an outstanding possibility for Republicans. Political pundits saw this as a symbolic election, one in which Republicans had an excellent chance. A *Congressional Quarterly* headline declared, "G.O.P Sees New Day in Southside Virginia." They were not the only ones who saw this as a Republican opportunity. Strategic politicians did as well. Democrats were not sanguine about their prospects. Several Democratic legislators declined to join the race, and the party ended up nominating L. F. Payne at the state convention. A successful businessman from the northern part of the district, Payne had never before held public office and was a virtual unknown. The major political struggle was on the Republican side, with State Senator W. Onico Barker and Reagan White House aide Linda Arey vying for the chance to face Payne. Both candidates were attractive. Both had experience in government and a base from which to raise money. Arey had worked several jobs with the popular administration. Barker had name recognition in the district and a constituency in the city of Danville. Such quality candidates emerge when their chances are best. That a fierce nomination battle arose among Republicans is testimony to how good Republican prospects were thought to be.

The two Republicans waged a fierce battle for the nomination. Arey, who entered the race first and spent months doing the difficult "retail" work necessary to cultivate a network of delegates, had a distinct advantage over Barker, who decided to enter the race much later. Arey also had the support of the Reverend Jerry Falwell, who found her administration credentials attractive. Furthermore, Falwell was angry with Barker for having led a campaign against a tax exemption that would have benefited his church empire. Barker had some advantages, however. Most important, he had the support of Republican party officials in the district and the state who perceived that a woman might have difficulty winning a congressional race in this part of Virginia. In the end, Arey's superior organization and more ideological followers led her to victory, but it was not without cost. Barker and many of his followers left the convention bitterly disappointed.

With high expectations pinned to her, Arey's most immediate concern coming out of the convention was to attempt to bring the party together and soothe tensions with Barker. Her best efforts failed. Barker and his staff had resented Arey from the start as an outsider. The nomination battle and above all Arey's alliance with Falwell added to the ill feelings between the two camps (Elving 1988, 1009). Following the convention, several of Barker's aides came out publicly for Payne. And although Barker himself never formally endorsed Arey's opponent, he made it clear whom he was supporting. Arey described taking a seat next to Barker at a debate only to see him move to a seat next to Payne. She told of Barker snubbing a campaign rally featuring George Bush that took place one block from his house. When the Roanoke newspaper reported the state senator drinking beer from an L. F. Payne for Congress cup at the Pittsylvania County Rib Festival (Eure 1988b), the act was seen as being tantamount to an endorsement.

If the first goal of Arey's campaign was to bring the Republicans back together, the second element of her general campaign strategy was to claim the legacy of Dan Daniel. Daniel had called her "his ideological soulmate" in a Richmond paper shortly before he died, and Arey considered this to be an implicit endorsement. She talked of this endorsement often on the campaign trail and said that she would continue in his conservative tradition. Her positions on issues distinctly aligned her with "the beloved conservative congressman," and she spoke often and fondly of her personal ties to Daniel.

Along these same lines, Arey sought to strike the appropriate comparison, to characterize herself as the bona fide conservative and to tag Payne as a liberal. In her first press conference following the Republican convention, she said, "The issues will break down very clearly along liberal and conservative lines. L. F. Payne is a liberal Democrat in the Jim Wright tradition and I'm a conservative Republican in the Dan Daniel tradition" (Elving 1988).[15] If elected to Congress, Arey vowed to "fight the liberal leadership [of Congress]" (Bland 1988h). Payne, on the other hand, would have to cater to it.

Most important, Arey tried to establish the fact that she was a conservative and L. F. Payne a liberal on a highly publicized racial issue. At her first press conference, in her first response to a question as to how she and Payne differed on the issues, she brought up the Civil Rights Restoration Act. This bill, introduced in response to the Supreme Court's *Grove City* decision, required that an organization receiving federal funds in any of its parts must comply with fair hiring practices throughout the whole organization. President Reagan vetoed the bill, and Arey said that she would have voted to sustain his veto, whereas Payne would have voted to override it.[16] In a radio commercial entitled "The Clear Difference," her campaign sought to make the contrast as stark as possible. Arey's ad claimed that she "opposes Grove City, the Civil Rights Restoration Act, while he [Payne] favors more federal interference in our lives" (Baker 1988). For good measure, it added that whereas she backed George Bush in the presidential primaries in 1988, Payne "supported [either] Michael Dukakis *or Jesse Jackson*" (Baker 1988, emphasis added). The either/or construction made it a true but inflammatory statement. If Payne were to respond to the ad, he would put himself in a difficult position with either his black or his white supporters. He chose to ignore it.

Arey's attempts to establish herself as the truly conservative candidate extended to other issues as well, most notably drugs, taxes, and abortion. On drugs, Arey took a hard line, calling for the death penalty for anyone convicted twice of selling drugs to anyone under the age of nineteen (Bland 1988h). Payne's position on this was tough, though not this extreme. Arey criticized the American response to drugs coming from Central America. "In the old days before the liberals took control of the CIA and made it an impotent agency, the CIA would have taken care of Noriega," said Arey, calling for a quite aggressive approach to the problem of supply (Bland 1988h).

Trying to exploit a potential link between Payne and "tax-and-spend Democrats," Arey pounced upon Payne's refusal to sign a "No new taxes" pledge sponsored by a conservative taxpayers' organization. Payne waved the pledge off with the comment, "She's always shoving something in front of me to sign" (Baker 1988), but clearly here Arey had an edge over the Democrat in establishing herself as the real conservative.

A Roman Catholic in "the buckle of the Bible Belt," Arey took a position on the abortion issue that she believed ingratiated her with right-wing Protestants who might otherwise have been opposed to her candidacy. In one debate, in fact, she called for a "human life amendment to the Constitution" (Bland 1988d). Though it was not entirely clear what this meant, it was clear that it represented a more uncompromising position on the issue. Once again, her hard-line stance stood in contrast to Payne's position, which was that an abortion should be up to a woman, in consultation with her family and her minister.

A third major element of Arey's strategy was to take advantage of her Washington connections. Arey brought in national figures like Vice President Bush and her former boss at the Department of Transportation, Elizabeth Dole, to campaign for her. Bush, in fact, spent an entire day stumping for Arey. Each visit brought with it some front-page stories in the district's newspapers and allowed Arey to publicize her ties to the popular Reagan administration (Reagan even cut a radio commercial for her). The value of these visits for Arey was more than just being seen with political celebrities. They played into a campaign theme that the staff worked hard to develop. Part of their message, as highlighted in Elizabeth Dole's testimonial speech to a Pittsylvania County rally, was that Arey had the "intelligence, integrity, and aggressiveness" and the knowledge of Washington that would make her effective from the start. This message was inevitably reported with mention that Payne had no experience in Washington (Bland 1988i). Bringing in Bush and Dole also allowed Arey to demonstrate the clout she had with the administration and how well she could serve the district. Arey's campaign manager said, "[Bush's visit] shows what she can do for the district. Getting the vice president to the district on his 64th birthday is not exactly the easiest task" (Bland 1988k).[17]

There were nevertheless some serious problems with the conception and the implementation of Arey's campaign strategy. First, there was controversy over Dan Daniel's supposed endorsement, coming as it did from the Democratic incumbent. Arey herself told of being encouraged to run by Daniel, who, she said, wanted a conservative to take his seat. She spoke of old ties between their families (Arey's father, a country doctor, had cared for Daniel's parents in their "dotage"). She described Daniel's brother approaching her at the funeral home and reiterating the congressman's endorsement of her. She tried to muddy up the partisan difference by saying, "Labels don't matter" (Bland 1988h). One surrogate, Rep. Stan Parris, supported this by arguing that Daniel was "kind of a Republican" and noted that Daniel had told him that Arey was "a really nice lady" who was capable of replacing him (Bland 1988f). Arey's Democratic detractors, though, argued that she had filed for the Republican nomination before he had resigned and that she obviously had intended to challenge him. Daniel's son was among those who publicly objected to her attempts to claim his father's endorsement (Bland 1988g), which certainly undercut one of her strongest appeals.

Second, even though Arey was the more conservative of the two candidates, she had difficulty, as a woman candidate, in the culturally conservative district. She faced, for instance, a dilemma about whether she should use her husband's name or her maiden name. The first was the more acceptable practice in the conservative district, but her husband's name (Skladany) was foreign-sounding and ethnic (Czech), potentially problematic in the Fifth. Arey decided that her maiden name was better known in the district but felt that she was "damned either way."

The abortion issue too posed a problem for the Republican that she certainly would not have faced had she been a man. Early in the campaign, Arey was asked by a Lynchburg reporter if she had ever had an abortion. Shocked and dismayed at the question (she believed it was planted by a disgruntled Republican opponent), Arey chose not to dignify it with a response. Because she did not answer the question with an unequivocal no, however, it came up again, and her "private business" was discussed extensively in several of the district's newspapers, again undercutting an issue that should have worked to her favor.

The biggest problem Arey had as a woman candidate simply may have been that she had strong opinions and a forceful personality. These are qualities admired in political candidates, especially ideologically pure candidates, but they are not qualities appreciated in rural Virginia women.[18] The zeal with which she pursued conservative issues undoubtedly appealed to some, but her style likely worked against her in the conservative district, particularly when she was compared to L. F. Payne. One voter was quoted in the Roanoke newspaper as saying, "I think he's more a listener and she's more a talker" (Eure 1988b). To Arey's supporters, she was high energy and principled. To her detractors, she was shrill, aggressive, and hyperactive. Unfortunately for Arey, the negative impression may have won out. Said Payne in hindsight, "This was an election where issues didn't matter as much as impressions. At first Linda came across well, but I think she may have wore on people. In comparison, I came across as stable and sensible." Arey spoke along the same lines, though from a slightly different angle. She argued that her candidacy was threatening to men and women her own age and that even her best performances on the campaign trail may have contributed to this problem. "Now L.F. I like a lot," she started. "And he's a bright guy. But he's a businessman. I had just been in the public liaison office at the White

House making speeches all over. I know I did extremely well in several of the debates. Yet every time I bested my opponent, [University of Virginia political scientist] Larry Sabato would tell me that men—and women— were rushing to support L.F."[19]

Third, Arey's quest for white votes via the Grove City issue may have been undercut by another campaign appearance she made. Arey marched in the Martin Luther King Day parade in Danville, which she believed may have cost her the votes of some white Danvillians. Her appearance in the parade did not help her with blacks. Neither, as she had hoped, did her family's reputation for racial progressivism (her father crusaded to open the public library during massive resistance, her sister went to the first integrated school in the area). "I got enough black votes to fill five phone booths," said the candidate. "I can only look back and feel I was naive."

Finally, although the national visits and visits by Republican congressmen from northern Virginia were important to the campaign, they did not compensate for the lack of enthusiasm from local and state Republican elites. Arey's problems with the Virginia Republican party may have been related to her caucus victory over Onico Barker. It may have been because her return from Washington bred some resentment. Whatever the cause, Arey complained that local and state Republican officials did not help her campaign very much: "I had good support from outside the district, but no one from inside the district ever put their arm around me and said 'She's one of us.' Not one member of the Virginia state legislature from the district ever introduced me to another person. None of them ever took me up and down Main Street and introduced me to the banker, the pharmacist, or the barber." In retrospect, Arey was most disappointed by the lack of support she got from the Virginia Republican party and felt that "the hemorrhage in my own party," the lack of support from her opponent in the Republican convention and his followers, was her biggest problem in the general election.[20]

L. F. Payne was a self-made man who had developed the Wintergreen ski resort in central Virginia. Wintergreen was successful and, though a relatively new enterprise, well known in the district. Moreover the resort brought hundreds of new jobs to the area and provided Nelson County with about half of its tax base. Though Payne was a political novice, his business experience was, according to his campaign strategist, a great selling point for Virginia voters. Payne, he argued, was instantly respected in the district and had great credibility as a fiscal conservative. In fact, Virginia Democrats had had some previous success with businessman-candidates, and Payne was recruited into politics by Norman Sisisky, a Pepsi-distributor-turned-congressman from Virginia's Fourth District.

As a successful businessman, Payne had the resources to run a viable campaign. This was doubly important as he was an unknown from the sparsely populated northern part of the district. Payne loaned himself about $275,000, which gave him a fairly large financial advantage over his opponent. Arey spent $359,000 on her campaign, Payne $563,000 (*Danville Register* 1988). The large campaign chest enabled Payne to saturate the heavily populated southern tier of counties with advertising. All the television stations that serve the district are located outside of it (in Roanoke-Lynchburg, Richmond, Raleigh-Durham, and Greensboro-Winston-Salem-High Point), so that reaching district voters involves reaching many people outside the district as well. Political advertising in the Fifth is thus a fairly expensive proposition.

Of course, Payne's self-financed campaign, which was clearly an advantage, could well have turned into a liability if the Republicans had effectively put the right populist twist on it. Anticipating that the Republicans might try to use Payne's wealth against him, the Democrat's campaign consultants sought to create an image of Payne as "a regular guy." The Republicans did indeed attempt to make an issue of Payne's campaign spending. Shortly after the Democratic caucus, which was held two weeks before the Republican caucus, the state GOP chairman called Payne "a BMW liberal trying to sell himself to Chevy conservatives" (Bland 1988a). Later, a national Republican consultant charged him with being more interested in "selling five dollar hot dogs and writing checks on his mountain" than in meeting the people (Bland 1988j). The antidote to these charges was to paint a common picture of the Democrat. Payne often would talk of his humble origins, which qualified him as a self-made man as well as a regular guy. His staff, in a story in the Danville paper, portrayed him as a tobacco chewing, cowboy boot wearing, hiking and fishing enthusiast who wore jeans and open shirts and played on the Wintergreen employee basketball team (Bland 1988j). Payne's mild demeanor contributed to the image his staff was trying to cultivate. Of course, the irony of the situation was that it was personal wealth that made it possible for Payne to advertise his modest image.

Payne's campaign manager put high priority on "inoculating" the public against the inevitable charges that Payne was a liberal. Given the two-week head start granted the Democrats, they were able to refute the charge even before it was made, as it was, again and again. As with the money issue, part of the Democratic response was to highlight Payne's history, his business and engineering background, his military service, and his education at the Virginia Military Institute (VMI). "How many liberals do you know from V.M.I.?" asked his campaign manager. Campaign commercials were cut showing Payne in a hard hat at Wintergreen and emphasizing his business background. At rallies, other politicians, notably Gov. Gerald Baliles, hailed Payne's private sector success and argued that he would bring "a no-nonsense business approach to government" (Bland 1988e).

In television advertisements as well as in his appearances in the district Payne highlighted his conservative positions, especially on fiscal and military issues. He argued for the balanced budget amendment to the Constitution, adherence to the Gramm-Rudman-Hollings spending targets, and a line-item veto for the president. These positions were consistent with the conservative businessman theme his campaign was trying to develop and were highly visible in his campaign. The candidate also stressed his support for Star Wars research, aid to the Nicaraguan contras, and school prayer. He was unmistakably to the right of center on many issues of importance to Southside Virginia.

Payne, however, did not claim to be a conservative clone of Dan Daniel. His support of the Equal Rights Amendment and of choice on the abortion issue as well as his positions on a number of other issues would have been anathema to the ultraconservative Daniel. He intimated, in response to a reporter's question, that he could be expected to support the Democratic party more than Daniel had. When asked if he would vote along party lines more frequently than Daniel, he skillfully hedged the question: "I think I would vote in a manner that well represented the district, and I would vote however I felt my constituents wanted. My views and those of constituents are the same, we have the same views and values, and I could do a good job representing the district" (Bland 1988b). Nonetheless, it was quite apparent that he would offer something different from Dan Daniel.

Payne, like Arey, brought in politicians to campaign for him. But whereas Arey brought in national Republicans, Payne brought in Democrats from around the state, most notably Governor Baliles and Sen. (and former governor) Charles Robb. "With these guys and some old Byrd Democrats behind me," Payne said, "people couldn't believe that I was Teddy Kennedy." Bringing in Democrats from around the state did more than simply solidify Payne's claims to being a conservative. It helped develop a second campaign theme: Southside Virginia versus big city Washington. The Payne campaign aggressively sought to turn Arey's connections to the Reagan administration against her. The Democratic campaign claimed that Arey was "out of town and out of touch," a carpetbagger who had moved back to the district to run for Congress. They emphasized an insider-outsider theme at every campaign stop. As Baliles said to a local crowd, "We can choose to send Virginia values to Washington or we can choose to bring Washington values to Virginia." He left little doubt as to which was the preferable option. The Democrats predicted even that Arey would put her house up for sale the day after she lost the race (and so she did).[21] They tried to make her Washington resume a "negative," and in this way, said Payne's campaign manager, "The more Washington showed up, the more it played into our hands."

The Payne forces likewise highlighted district issues in their campaign, emphasizing jobs and fair trade practices instead of ideology and the president. The seven hundred jobs that Payne had created in the district complemented the theme of "jobs . . . being stolen from Virginia by unfair foreign trade." In touting his support for a trade bill that had recently passed in Congress, Payne claimed that he would "be a watchdog over unfair foreign practices involving district products" (*Danville [Virginia] Bee* 1988). Arey, on the other hand, opposed the trade bill because of a provision requiring businesses to notify workers of a plant closing at least sixty days prior to the closing. Though she said that the rest of the bill was acceptable, she reiterated her opposition to trade quotas of all kinds. The answer, she asserted, was for "the President [to] work diligently to find timely and effective remedies to correct the problem [of unfair trading practices]" (*Danville Bee* 1988). These responses illustrate Payne's more activist approach to the problem. Payne's campaign manager, who also advised the Texas race described above, claimed to be the first to use the unfair trade message effectively and repeated it in many of the southern campaigns he advised. He especially emphasized how the issue tied into the local theme the campaign tried to develop. "She emphasized Washington and we emphasized the district," he said. "I'll take the district any day of the week."

As to Arey's position on the Grove City legislation, Payne's response was subdued. He stated his support for the legislation but did not make it a centerpiece of his campaign. He did, however, use Arey's position and the *Richmond Times Dispatch* editorial excoriating Payne for his stand on the issue in appealing for black votes. A black turnout expert from the Democratic Congressional Campaign Committee (who also worked the Alabama and Mississippi 5 races) noted that Arey's stand on the issue "was played to the hilt" in every piece of Democratic literature sent to the black community.

Payne himself felt that black support would be easy to court, not only because he compared favorably with Arey on this issue, but because he compared favorably with Dan Daniel. Payne said, "[Daniel] was so conservative, I was a breath of fresh air [for blacks]." For these reasons, Payne did not feel that blacks "made unrealistic demands on me." He did not have to appear as a champion of black issues to win their support. But he did do those things necessary to win black votes. He advertised on black radio. He lined up black opinion leaders. And, accompanied by a black assistant campaign manager, he visited dozens of black churches in the district.[22] His attempt to reach out to the black community and his moderate positions generated a lot of support, said a black community organizer: "He was a refreshing change. He came in to listen and didn't make promises we all knew he couldn't keep. We said to him, listen, we know you can't change the world, but at least you know we're here."

In the end, Payne defeated Arey rather convincingly, 59 percent to 41 percent. He ran against another conservative Republican six months later in a closer race. His opponent in that contest was a state senator who had not introduced a bill in his entire eight-year tenure ("Lots of people around here kind of liked that," said Payne), but the Democrat turned back this challenge. In 1990, the Republicans did not even field a candidate against him. Being assigned to the Public Works and Transportation Committee and the Veterans' Affairs Committee, Payne was well positioned to deliver on the local promises he had made in his first campaign and to do what was necessary to defend his seat over time.

Mississippi 5—"Gene Taylor and Friends Welcome George Bush"

On weekends, the beautiful white sand beaches of southern Mississippi are filled with sun worshipers and volleyball nets. The focal point of the coast is the town of Biloxi. Biloxi ends at the beach in seafood shacks, a boardwalk, and gift shops advertising souvenirs from hurricane Camille, which devastated the region in 1969. This town caters to tourists. Indeed, the Gulf Coast is known as the Redneck Riviera, and the area makes the Fifth District unlike any other in the state.

The Fifth is different from the rest of Mississippi in other ways as well. Demographically, it is quite distinctive. The three counties on the coast, which contain the cities of Biloxi and Gulfport and more than half the district's population, are urbanized and, compared to the rest of Mississippi, fairly white collar and affluent. Even Hattiesburg, the only city in the eight and one-half inland counties of the district, has a large white-collar population, as it is home to a large state university. The rural area in the district is unlike the rest of the state. Its land is not as rich as the land along the Mississippi River, and the economy is based more on timber than agriculture. The coastal area is distinctive in that it is home to many Roman Catholics, many of them migrants from the New Orleans area, and has a smaller black population than the rest of the state. Blacks comprise only 19 percent of the district while Mississippi as a whole is 31 percent black.

Economically, the district is also rather unique. In addition to the tourism and timber industries, the seafood industry is important to the coast. Although it is not unusual for a southern economy to be dependent upon the military, this district is especially so. It is home to numerous military bases, the Stennis NASA Center, a major shipbuilding industry, other industry dependent on military contracts, and two Veterans Administration hospitals. Up and down the coast these military installations provide jobs and feed service industries, which are especially important when the tourist season ends. As one local put it, "We'd starve to death without military money around here."

The demographics and economics of the district have made it hospitable to Republicans for a number of years. This dominance has been overwhelming in presidential elections since the early 1970s. Indeed, in 1972, this was the most Republican district in the country in a most Republican year; Nixon won 87 percent of the vote in the Fifth. At the congressional level, the district also has been very supportive of the GOP. The district was represented for sixteen years by former House Minority Whip Trent Lott. Lott, an aide to the longtime boll weevil congressman William Colmer, changed parties for the 1972 election and was the first Republican to represent the district since Reconstruction. He enjoyed huge support throughout his tenure, and when he decided to leave the House in 1988 for a run at the Senate seat being vacated by John Stennis—a position he won—the Republicans kept the district in the fold.

Larkin Smith, formerly the Republican sheriff of Harrison County (which includes Gulfport and Biloxi), succeeded Lott by defeating a popular Democratic state senator from the coast, Gene Taylor. Smith designed his campaign's theme around his resume. His experience as sheriff and his role in bringing a federally funded drug-interdiction organization to Gulfport gave a certain credibility to his law-and-order and antidrug message and made him a heavily favored candidate in the conservative district. He also held a great advantage over Taylor in funding (he outspent

Taylor by more than three to one), and, more important, he had a huge advantage at the top of the ticket. Indeed, in 1988, George Bush's 69 percent in the district was bettered in only a dozen districts in the entire country. Although Smith's ten-point margin of victory was somewhat smaller than many in the media and in politics expected, it was assumed that he would hold the seat for many years.

Larkin Smith did not have much time to make his mark on Washington. He had been in office only six months when he was killed in a plane crash near Hattiesburg. His death set into motion special election procedures. Because Mississippi law dictates that the seat be filled within one hundred days of the vacancy in a nonpartisan election, the campaign was to be short and frenetic. This was especially the case because the runoff was scheduled by the governor to follow only two weeks after the primary (if no candidate won a majority in the primary). Three candidates—one Republican and two Democrats—emerged in the weeks following Smith's death to make the race.

The Republican in the contest was Tom Anderson, Trent Lott's administrative assistant in Washington. Anderson had served Lott for sixteen of the prior eighteen years, taking two years off to serve as the Reagan administration's ambassador to six island nations in the Eastern Caribbean. Republican leaders approached the election with confidence. One national Republican consultant told me as he headed down to Mississippi to advise the campaign that a runoff would be unnecessary. This, after all, was a district very partial to Republicans. Even though Anderson was relatively unknown and even though party labels would not appear on the ballot, he was sure to have the resources to saturate the district with his name and to fully advertise his GOP connection.

Anderson also had a major advantage in that he was the only Republican in the race. To maximize his chances, other Republican candidates were forced out of the race even before it started. Because there was only one Republican in the race, it was hoped a runoff could be avoided. At the very least, Anderson was absolutely certain to make the runoff. With this in mind, his boss Trent Lott engineered the best of circumstances for his employee.

Lott's task was tricky. The plane crash had essentially martyred Larkin Smith. Following his death, many Republicans had urged his widow, Sheila Smith, to run for the seat, and she did unofficially declare that she would announce her candidacy with the support of Republican dignitaries, including Senator Lott. Although Lott, Anderson, and Smith all denied it, it was widely believed and was reported in the local press that Lott forced Mrs. Smith out of the race before she officially got in. Other declared Republican candidates bowed out of the race as well, the papers reporting that the senator watched from the doorway as two Republican state legislators announced their change in plans at a news conference (Cassreino 1989).

The Democratic candidate whom the Republicans were most concerned about was Mike Moore, Mississippi's attorney general. The young, aggressive Democrat had taken fully 87 percent of the vote on the Gulf Coast in his campaign for attorney general in January 1988. He had the backing of several prominent national Democrats and was the leading Democrat and "the man to watch" according to Democratic insiders. Enjoying strong support from blacks and labor and a promising reputation among national Democrats, Moore looked like a formidable opponent. Also in the race was Gene Taylor, the young state senator from the coast who had won 45 percent of the vote against Larkin Smith in 1988. The low-key Taylor had name recognition and the basis for a campaign organization already in place. Nonetheless he was considered the lesser of the two Democrats and was underestimated by both of his opponents.

The three candidates were close on most major issues. All three were antiabortion, tough on drugs, budget-balancing, pro–school prayer, anti–gun control conservatives. The major issues in this part of the campaign thus became the candidates themselves. The two favorites, in particular, had some immediate problems to face.

Ironically, the effort to create favorable circumstances for Anderson (and the public knowledge of this effort) created unanticipated problems for the candidate. Despite the fact that Lott was enormously popular in the district ("You've got God and Trent on a popularity index and I'm not sure who comes first," said one Democratic campaign official), his role in the campaign became an issue. Foremost, Lott's involvement created an image problem for Anderson, who, previously unknown in the district, now had to make the case that "he was his own man." The press started to pick up on this, asking Anderson in debates whether he was an independent thinker. And, of course, the two Democrats also worked on this theme. Moore said, "I'm really incensed about one of our leaders picking someone out for everybody else to vote for. If Trent wants to run for Congress, he ought to" (*Gulfport Sun-Herald* 1989a). Taylor said, "The people of South Mississippi, not Washington, should pick the next congressman" (Cassreino 1989). Interestingly, it was Lott, not Anderson, who responded to the charges in the newspaper. To Moore, he said, "I tell you what he'd better do: Instead of talking about me, he needs to be looking after his own knitting. The fellow asked to be attorney general. I say, 'let's let him be attorney general'" (*Sun-Herald* 1989b). To Taylor, Lott responded, "Gene Taylor better tend to his own knitting. He's got to deal with Mike Moore" (Cassreino 1989). These responses, of course, made it appear that Lott was looking after Anderson's knitting.

As the campaign progressed, the problem refused to go away. Democratic and Republican elites continued to speculate whether Sheila Smith had been blackmailed or enticed out of the race by Lott. There was discussion about whether or not Mrs. Smith would have been a strong candidate, a sympathetic favorite who might have scared the strong Democrats out of the race. Mike Moore's campaign manager, in fact, said that his candidate probably would not have run had Mrs. Smith stayed in. The press ran several stories containing denials from the parties involved. And there was some concern that Mrs. Smith would not fully back the Republican ticket. Even after she cut a television commercial for Anderson (dressed in black in a poorly lit funeral home setting), some local Republican party leaders fretted that her endorsement appeared half-hearted.

Anderson also had to deal with Democratic charges of impropriety. Following a Jackson newspaper report that Anderson had received free air travel but had not reported the gift on financial disclosure forms, the Democratic Congressional Campaign Committee called him a "walking scandal." The committee even added to the charge, claiming that he was reimbursed for automobile travel on the same day he received free air travel (Peterson 1989b).[23] Anderson first responded that he had reported the air travel. When the newspaper obtained the reports that showed he had not, Anderson's press secretary claimed it was simply an oversight, that the candidate did not have his own records available, and that the reports would be corrected (*Sun-Herald* 1989b; Peterson 1989b).[24] On top of this, Anderson had to contend with reports that he had improperly impeded a federal investigation of a Louisiana toxic waste firm (Peterson 1989b). The firm, which was fined $6 million for pollution violations, had enlisted the assistance of Lott and Anderson and also had contributed to Lott's Senate campaign and Anderson's congressional campaign. Anderson responded in a debate that he had called the Justice Department simply to get status reports on the case and that he wanted to be sure that the company got a fair hearing. As might be expected, he excoriated the Democrats for their desperate "smear tactics" (Peterson 1989b).

On the positive side, Anderson had a large campaign fund to address these problems and to counter the negative publicity. He attempted to close the name recognition gap with massive direct mailings, one from President Bush, and a television advertising blitz. Whether it was because he was unable to shake his own negatives or because he failed to build up enough name recognition or both, Anderson did not win the first-round majority that the Republicans had hoped for. In fact, he did not win a plurality. Anderson aggressively pursued the Republican northern area of the district in this first campaign and won all of the northern counties, but came in second overall (with 37 percent of the vote) because he did not fare very well on the more populous coast.

Mike Moore followed standard southern Democratic strategy in the campaign, defining himself as a conservative while pursuing some important constituencies, specifically blacks and labor. He actively pursued the black vote, hiring the same Congressional Campaign Committee get-out-the-vote expert who had worked in the Alabama and Virginia races described above. Based on his statewide run for office, he and his staff felt that they had a clear idea of how to pursue the black vote while at the same time retaining white voters. Though he was not considered "a champion of black issues," said one black leader, "he was a friend of ours," and black opinion leaders generally lined up behind him. Moore also had the backing of the labor unions in the district. Though the area is notoriously hostile to unions, an AFL-CIO endorsement enabled him to generate some money with which to run a credible campaign.

Moore originally used that money to advertise his record as attorney general. In his quest for white votes, however, Moore, like Anderson, had an unexpected strategic problem: public opinion polls showed his positive was also a negative. These polls showed that people objected to his running for another office so soon after becoming attorney general. Being perceived as tenacious and aggressive had served him well in his campaigns for district attorney and attorney general. But "aggressive" translated into "overly ambitious" in this contest, and Moore's handlers had difficulty addressing this public perception. "In playing up Moore's record as attorney general, we were playing right into our negative," said his media consultant. "Frankly we tried a lot of things to deal with this problem and none of them worked." Moore ended up coming in third, winning but 21 percent of the vote, a great deal of it from the black community.

Unlike Anderson and Moore, Gene Taylor did not have an albatross around his neck as he entered the first campaign. He had, in fact, some underrated strengths. Although he had lost to Larkin Smith just six months before, he had done better than expected. That race and his tenure as a state legislator gave him an organizational base and some name recognition in the district. As the most underrated candidate, he was spared the attacks of the other two candidates, who built each other's negatives up further. At the same time, Taylor, mostly staying out of the fray, was able to enhance his well-crafted image as Clean Gene. He called even for the state party to remove its commercial attacking Anderson for the airplane and toxic waste matters, self-righteously insisting that he did not want to be associated with negative advertising. When a popular radio disc jockey took to calling him Opie Taylor, after the young do-gooder on the old Andy Griffith show, and his opponents Trent Anderson and Geraldo Moore, it was illustrative of the public images the three candidates had created for themselves.

Conceding the black vote to Moore and the hard-core Republican vote to Anderson, Taylor tried to stake out the middle (a decidedly right-wing middle), calling himself the "bipartisan conservative candidate." It was an appeal that worked well. In spite of the fact that Taylor's opponents were much better financed (Taylor spent only $34,000, while Moore spent $83,000 and Anderson $220,000—Souther 1989b), Taylor actually beat them both with 42 percent of the vote. His moralistic, middle-ground strategy worked so well in the primary that he continued talking about the same things in the runoff. The question was whether this appeal would work with only two candidates in the field rather than three.

The runoff thus featured a race between a very conservative Gene Taylor and an ultraconservative Tom Anderson. The contest was interesting because there was so little philosophical difference between the two candidates. Yet both candidates tried to highlight the differences that did exist, at least as they saw them.

Anderson's grand campaign strategy for the runoff had three major components. First, he attempted to get across the fact that he was the *more* conservative candidate. Because Taylor made a convincing case that he was truly conservative, Anderson did this by taking memorably extreme positions on various issues. The drug issue was one that Anderson emphasized, particularly given Larkin Smith's success with it in 1988 and given the candidate's record in the Caribbean. During one debate, Anderson appeared to advocate assassinating the Panamanian dictator Manuel Noriega (Souther 1989c). In the same discussion, he called for the dispatch of U.S. troops anywhere in the world to fight drugs at their source, and he urged that convicted "drug lords" be subject to the death penalty. His extreme positions were not confined to the drug issue. Anderson said in one debate, "I want to see that we restore prayer in school, not just in classrooms but at football games and sporting events. That's something we need to work very hard at" (Souther 1989d). On taxes, he signed an ironclad pledge to refuse to raise taxes, hoping to force Taylor into an uncomfortable spot. As Anderson happily anticipated, Taylor refused to sign the pledge. The Democrat's reasoning was clever though. He certainly was opposed to raising taxes but would vote to do so if it meant saving an industry or a military base in the district.

Anderson tried to distinguish himself from Taylor in other ways. He called Taylor a "backbencher," made a commercial that questioned Taylor's effectiveness by showing the number of his bills passed in the Mississippi Senate, tried to tie Taylor to "big labor" and "eastern bosses," and argued that Taylor would not be able to get things done in the liberal Democratic party. Republican campaign literature highlighted Taylor's passage rate, his support of a gasoline tax increase, and, rather deceivingly, his "liberal" stands on issues. Taylor pretty effectively responded to these charges. In a story written by a reporter who was to become Taylor's press secretary in Washington, it was noted that Taylor's passage rate was higher than Trent Lott's most recent eight years. It was also reported that the gasoline tax proposal was introduced by a Republican and approved unanimously by the state senate (Souther 1989f). As to a campaign flyer that quoted Taylor as saying, "I think it's crazy that we continue to spend money in law enforcement," the Gulfport newspaper reported that the statement was taken out of context. In making the statement, Taylor, in fact, was calling for more prisons and tougher sentencing: "I think it's crazy that we continue to spend money in law enforcement, and those in law enforcement catch the same people" (Peterson 1989a).

The second part of Anderson's strategy was to activate all those people who had made the Fifth District the Republican stronghold of Mississippi. Part of this attempt can be seen in the allocation of Anderson's time, above all in the primary. He campaigned a lot in the heavily Republican, heavily black northern part of the district in the primary and considered this to be his base even though he came from the coast. But it was obvious from the primary results that the less populated northern counties could not provide him with enough of the vote and that for the runoff, something else was needed. Those voters, Democratic and Republican, who had supported the Republican ticket in the past had to make the connection between Reagan and Bush and Tom Anderson. The answer was to bring in the president himself.

His influence in the district put to the test, particularly after Anderson's disappointing second-place finish in the primary, Senator Lott arranged a one-hour presidential visit to Gulfport. Bush's speech, attended by thousands, televised live, and covered extensively by the newspapers, included an announcement that the president would be attending a drug summit in South America (which fit well into one of Anderson's campaign themes). The president also gave a warm and personal endorsement of Tom Anderson. It was the type of event and media coverage that most candidates can only dream of. Anderson hoped the wonderful publicity would bring wayward Republicans back to his side.

The third prong of Anderson's strategy involved the black vote. Anderson's strategy vis-à-vis blacks was to encourage them to "sleep in," to stay at home on election day. There was little hope that he would win much of the black vote, especially as Mike Moore, who had the preponderance of this support in the primary, had endorsed Taylor in the runoff. But because the black leadership in the district was lukewarm toward Taylor, Anderson's strategy was to attack Taylor in the black community. While in the state legislature, Taylor had voted to close a hospital that served a black community elsewhere in the state. He also voted with the governor to close two historically black colleges, Mississippi Valley State University and Alcorn State University.[25] Many blacks were unhappy about losing schools and hospitals that had served the black community for so long and that were a source of jobs, and Anderson hoped to capitalize on this discontent in his negative campaign.

The point man for this campaign was C. F. Appleberry, a black minister from Meridian, a town outside the district. Under his name, a crude, xeroxed handbill was distributed throughout black neighborhoods in Gulfport and Ocean Springs. Denouncing Taylor for voting to close the colleges and the hospitals, as well as for a vote against allowing "small businesses and minority owned firms to have a guaranteed portion of all State Contracts (*sic*)," the handbill announced, "It is time for us to

WAKE-UP!" and "Mr. Taylor IS NOT OUR FRIEND." There were also several references to black votes being taken for granted by Democratic politicians:

> Join me the Reverend C. F. Appleberry in sending Mr. Taylor a message. No longer will we be fooled by electing somebody that says one thing, while he is running for the job, but forgets us after he has been elected!
>
> SEND A MESSAGE—No longer can our votes be taken for granted, just because a candidate has the Democratic Mark beside his name.
>
> SEND A MESSAGE—This Tuesday, October 17, 1989 let Mr. Gene Taylor and other democrates (*sic*) know there are other chices (*sic*) for our votes.

The tag line "VOTE FOR TOM ANDERSON FOR CONGRESS. HE HAS YET TO VOTE AGAINST US" hardly inspired confidence that Anderson would serve blacks effectively, but it was the best reason Anderson's campaign could come up with for staying home.[26] A slightly less inflammatory commercial on black radio stations also featured the Reverend Mr. Appleberry. While gospel singers sang "Amen" in the background, Appleberry declared that "Taylor is not a friend to minorities, to poor people, or to small businesses" and "What is going to happen to your Social Security, Medicare, and Medicaid if Taylor is elected?" The radio ad repeated the flyer's closing line.

Black leaders in the district heaped scorn on Appleberry, one Taylor supporter calling him "a prostitute." Another black leader, not a strong supporter of Taylor, discounted the effectiveness of the Appleberry campaign: "He's from out of town. No one around here knows him and no one's going to listen to him." Nonetheless, the Democrats did not take any chances and responded immediately. They got an injunction against further distribution of the flyer for not being properly attributed to the Anderson campaign. The Democrats were able to move quickly, a state party official said, "because we were expecting something like this," and that may have diminished the effectiveness of the attack flyer.[27] However effective the attack was, it was more an attempt to depress black turnout than to generate support for Anderson.

Anderson's runoff strategy of outflanking the conservative Taylor, reaching out to perennial Republicans, and depressing the black vote had the potential to succeed. Yet, there were several problems—some old, some new—in the execution of the strategy. What was supposed to be the pinnacle of the campaign, Bush's appearance in Gulfport, may actually have worked against Anderson. Once again, there was much speculation that Lott's involvement in the race may have backfired, in part because of the media's reaction. The fact that Bush and Lott were so prominent in his campaign raised anew questions as to what Tom Anderson could do on his own. Editorial cartoonists began to lampoon him as a "lap dog" and as a talking doll whose string was pulled by Trent Lott. Debate moderators continued to ask him how he differed from Lott and Bush and what he had accomplished independently. From the perspective of many different people—journalists, Republicans, and Democrats—Anderson never really came up with a satisfactory answer.

Other difficulties plagued the Republican campaign. It is not clear how much Anderson's problems with his travel reporting or his involvement with the Louisiana toxic waste company hurt him in the end. Taylor refrained from bringing up these issues, confident that the media would publicize them (as they did). But Taylor did bring up Anderson's military record. Like Dan Quayle, Anderson was a National Guardsman during the Vietnam War. In a debate in which the candidates were allowed to quiz each other, Taylor questioned how Anderson could advocate sending American troops abroad to fight drugs: "Do you value those people's lives less than your own? Are you willing to make a commitment with them that you would not make on your own?" Anderson, like Quayle, argued that he was proud of his stint in the National Guard ("right here in Mississippi"), that he could have been called "anytime, anywhere," and that "it would be a delight to serve my country and do anything necessary to protect the freedoms of this country" (Souther 1989c).

Though this was a politically sensible response, it did reveal another of

Anderson's weaknesses. It was one thing to say "I served my country and I'm proud of it"; it was quite another to say that it would be a "delight" to do so. It is perhaps unfair to evaluate one word spoken in the heat of a debate, without a script, but Anderson's choice of words is illustrative of a larger problem. He came across as effete and "arrogant" (Barone and Ujifusa 1990, 696) and "above people," particularly in comparison with the "down-home" Taylor (Barone and Ujifusa 1989, 696). Other factors played into this perception as well. Next to the handsome Taylor, Anderson, wearing thick, horn-rimmed glasses, looked bookish.[28] As one Democrat asked me, "Who's gonna vote for some guy with pink glasses?" His $2 million net worth also made the newspapers. Both Anderson and Taylor refused to publicly release their income tax returns, but Taylor was able to cloak himself in the image of the humble, corrugated box salesman. Anderson was unable to portray himself as a man of the people.

Gene Taylor's campaign was either very well designed or very lucky or both. His campaign themes played into Anderson's weaknesses (and Moore's, for that matter), and he did not have to face the major problems that Anderson did. He had some name recognition in the district, he had an easily resurrected campaign infrastructure (though he was still in debt from his previous run for Congress), and, as one advisor said, "He had the stamina to shake five hundred to two thousand hands a day. Add to that all the hands he shook last time and you've got quite a base to start with."

As noted, Taylor's main campaign theme was that he was the "bipartisan conservative candidate for Congress." This involved distancing himself from liberals (like Ted Kennedy) and identifying himself with conservatives, even Republican conservatives. When President Bush came to Gulfport, signs along the highway read, "Gene Taylor and Friends Welcome George Bush." In a televised debate shortly thereafter, he said that he was "closer to George Bush than people realize. I like him. . . . I'm glad he was here" (Souther 1989e). Of course, Taylor did not attend the rally. When asked by a television reporter why he had missed it, Taylor gave the ironic response, "I'm not a party crasher. If I'd been invited, I'd have been there." Though Taylor adroitly handled questions like these, projecting the right public relation to Bush was complicated and posed the campaign some challenges. At a press conference at a military facility, for example, Taylor found a photograph of the commander-in-chief hanging behind him. Before the television camera went on, and after some discussion about what to do, the picture was taken down.

In addition to the attempts to blur party lines, Taylor staked out very conservative issue positions. He "respected all life, including that of the unborn," advocated family values, and favored school prayer. He touted his authorship of one of the country's toughest drug laws (giving mandatory lifetime sentences to anyone convicted of selling more than ten pounds of marijuana or two ounces of cocaine). He promoted himself as a friend of the taxpayer and abhorred wasteful spending. He desired "a nation not afraid to say 'In God we Trust.'" He was, in short, boldly conservative on the campaign trail. In a humorous moment at a Taylor press conference with the conservative Mississippi Democratic congressman G. V. "Sonny" Montgomery, a journalist noted that Taylor was sitting to Montgomery's right. "That's where I'm going to keep him," quipped Montgomery. Taylor laughed and nodded his head in agreement.

One problem with Taylor's attempt to position himself so far to the right was that Anderson, members of the media, and even some callers to a television phone-in show asked how he would get along with his party's leadership.[29] Taylor's response was that there were plenty of conservative southern Democrats in Congress, for example, fellow Mississippians Sonny Montgomery and Jamie Whitten, who were effective and powerful. He claimed that with the help of the Democratic Mississippi delegation, he would have immediate influence. To bring home the point, he spent a day touring military installations and campaigning with Montgomery, a powerful member of the Armed Services Committee and chairman of the Veterans' Affairs Committee. At some press conferences, Montgomery announced that he had secured a spot on Armed Services for Taylor.[30] Having additional letters from House Speaker Tom Foley and the chair of the Armed Services Committee to pass on to the press, Taylor was assured a spot on the committee. In a district where the military is so important to the economy, this was a real boon to his campaign. And Taylor had a specific battle to join. His first priority once in Washington was to keep the Mississippi Army Ammunition Plant open and operating.[31] Taylor also was appointed to the Merchant Marine and Fisheries Committee, another committee overseeing business important to the coastal district.

Besides promising to work for a continued military presence in the district, Taylor spoke of local issues to a much greater extent than Anderson did. He talked incessantly about dredging the Gulfport port channel so that larger commercial ships could pass through. In an area where the seafood industry is important, Taylor talked tough on Turtle Excluder Devices (TEDs). Shrimpers are required by federal law to use these devices to avoid catching the endangered Kemp's Ridley turtle. Taylor was the only candidate to promise legislation to make the TED voluntary (Souther 1989a). As one shrimper was quoted in the newspaper, in support of Gene Taylor, "This is the only country in the world where it's legal to kill a baby, but it's illegal to kill a turtle" (Dockins and Peterson 1989).

Taylor's emphasis on local concerns fit well into his campaign rhetoric, which had a decidedly local flavor. As "South Mississippi's Choice," Taylor made much of the fact that he was from the area. Although Anderson was born and raised on the coast, he had lived in Washington for the past eighteen years, and Taylor labeled him an outsider.[32] Taylor spoke of how his campaign contributions came from local people. Whereas Anderson received a great deal of money from the national party, Taylor in the preliminary election did not receive any, in part because there was more than one Democrat in the field. Taylor claimed that 97 percent of his campaign funds came from local people, a figure from the primary that went down considerably as he received money from Washington during the two-week runoff campaign. He argued, as he had in his campaign against Larkin Smith in 1988, that the lack of support from Washington was evidence that he had not passed a liberal litmus test. National Democrats simply were not much invested in him, argued Taylor, because he was too conservative. With this rhetoric, Taylor catered to the idea expressed by a Hattiesburg television journalist that "Mississippi is an island." Anderson did not.

Taylor emphasized that he was an "average joe," a corrugated box salesman, a middle-class family man with the same problems and aspirations as his constituents. His campaign, he assured people, was run on a shoestring, and his staff did everything possible to make this point. His campaign signs, which were everywhere, were corrugated cardboard with "Gene Taylor for Congress" spray-painted across a crude stencil. His opponents' signs were slick and professional. The Democrat's television advertising also had less elaborate production values, though, interestingly, he had the resources to buy expensive commercial time during the World Series. When the Gulfport newspaper ran a front-page story featuring photographs of a goat wearing a Gene Taylor for Congress sandwich board and a rural tin-roof headquarters advertising new and used tires and Gene Taylor, Taylor's staff rejoiced. The accompanying story reported that because they were "short of funds for voter research, Taylor supporters are calling everyone in the phone book—inviting them to come by the headquarters for a cup of coffee and reminding them that Taylor will be speaking at the George County Fair on Friday" (Peterson 1989c), and it too was well received. This was just the homely image they were projecting. Noting that the pictures and story ran the same day as President Bush's visit, Taylor said some time after the election, "I'm convinced that goat got me more votes than Bush's visit. I heard it so often in the coffeeshops that it had to be true."

Perhaps the most interesting thing about Taylor's attempts to portray himself as humble and his campaign as low-budget was the Republican response to it. Taylor's claims of poverty were met with great derision by Republican officials, who knew better. At Anderson headquarters, visitors were handed editorial columns not about Taylor's wrongheaded positions or his terrible record, but rather a column from the Jackson paper headlined, "Some people tired of Taylor getting fat on 'humble pie.'" The columnist wrote, "But Lord, his beholdin'-to-nobody (*sic*) bit is beginning to wear every bit as thin as the sack-cloth he would have us believe his suits are made of" (McKenzie 1989).

Taylor's campaign was somewhat different from some of the other Democratic campaigns described here in that Taylor did not aggressively pursue the black vote. Perhaps because the payoff is smaller in this 19 percent black district, perhaps because he did not want to change his strategy from the primary (when Moore pulled in most of the black vote) to the runoff, Taylor did not court blacks very actively. One local black leader said, "I'm going to vote for him but that's about it. He didn't reach out enough so I'm not going to try to reach back." As noted, some of Taylor's Senate votes were quite unpopular in the black community, and he did little to indicate that he would be much interested in black issues in Congress.

Taylor's campaign did advertise extensively on black radio, a common practice in southern Democratic campaigns, but did not target the audience. The advertisements were the same as those played on country-western, Top 40, and evangelical Christian stations. These advertisements dealt with jobs, drugs, and the death penalty and did not discuss Anderson's positions on racial issues. As for the black church circuit, Taylor did meet with black ministers the weekend before the election, but he did not appear at the one black church on his Sunday schedule. And the pastor at that church did little more than remind his congregation to vote. Though he mentioned Gene Taylor, it was not a bold endorsement. It was apparent that neither the black community nor Taylor had all that much enthusiasm for the relation.

Though Taylor did not energetically appeal to blacks, his campaign did work hard to turn out blacks on election day. Mike Moore's black turnout expert came over to the Taylor campaign and attempted to establish a network in the black community. Taylor posters went up in barber shops and diners in black neighborhoods, and teams of blacks were recruited to work for Taylor. Taylor's basic strategy vis-à-vis blacks was to line up a few black leaders who had networks in the community and could deliver a bloc of votes. For this to work, he did not need to make a connection with black voters so much as with black leaders. "I have found that in the black community they truly have opinion leaders," said Taylor. "There was a time when it was more prevalent in the white community too. But that's not the case anymore and it sure makes a difference in how you reach for black votes."

In the end, Gene Taylor scored a 65 percent to 35 percent victory. Not his association with Trent Lott, not even a visit from President Bush kept Tom Anderson from losing by an embarrassing margin. In fact, Anderson's percentage of the vote actually went down from the first election, when he won 37 percent of the vote. Taylor's effective campaign strategy and his mastery of what Richard Fenno would call a "person-to-person homestyle" (Fenno 1978) led not only to a victory but to a rout for the Democrats. One year later, in the 1990 election, Taylor solidified his position in the district: Sheila Smith finally got her opportunity to run and was trounced as Gene Taylor took 81 percent of the vote.

Resentment Issues

Democratic candidates must do more to win in the South than just appeal to black voters. They must appeal to whites, and, given the dearth of southern white liberals in the electorate, they must find some issues that endear them to moderate and even conservative whites. I argue that southern Democrats have adapted well to this new environment, to a situation in which they have had to put together a coalition of blacks and whites.

One set of issues that southern Democrats (and to a lesser extent, Republicans) have used to appeal to whites are what I call resentment issues. Resentment issues define an in-group and an out-group. They allow a politician to assess blame and responsibility for the problems of the in-group on an out-group. And they introduce situations that are interpreted as being threatening to the interests of the in-group. That is, they bring group conflict into focus.

Racial issues are resentment issues, but they are a subset of all such issues. Southern politicians, particularly southern Democrats, have latched on to another subset of these issues. Like racial issues, they involve an easily distinguishable out-group. Like racial issues, they feed upon the natural inclinations people have to view the world from an "us against them" perspective. I contend that these issues have been used much like racial issues in political campaigns and have been an important part of continued Democratic success after the Voting Rights Act.

The foreign trade issue, so much a part of Jim Chapman's campaign and also prominent in the campaigns of the Democrats Taylor in Mississippi, Browder in Alabama, and Payne in Virginia, is an excellent example of such an issue. Foreign trade was raised in these campaigns not so much because these politicians expected people to understand the intricacies of tariff policy or international economics. Rather, it spoke to the concerns people had about the suffering U.S. economy and provided an easily accessible answer to the problem. The Japanese were not responsible for the oil bust that devastated East Texas, but when a steel plant closed down in the district, Chapman blamed unfair foreign competition, and the Japanese were an easily identifiable villain that he could point to. When his Republican opponent said that he did not know what trade policies had to do with bringing jobs to East Texas, Chapman's campaign gained further momentum. Hargett spent the rest of the campaign on the defensive, trying to explain his statement. The issue played further to Chapman's advantage when Hargett's campaign hats were found to have been made in Taiwan. The Democrat gleefully pulled the hat out of his pocket during the only televised debate of the campaign in what he described as "the defining moment of the campaign." In the end, it was widely believed that Jim Chapman rode the issue to Congress. The issue was effective, said a Democratic analyst, because "it [seemed] to cut with everyone—farmers, workers, seniors, small businessmen" (Taylor 1985c).

Although Chapman won by a small margin, the Texas election served as a demonstration to other southern politicians, and not the demonstration that the Republicans had hoped for. The power of the issue was apparent to Democratic officials even before the election was over. "The good news out of the Texas race, win, draw, or lose, is that we have an issue we know we can use next year," said the executive director of the Democratic Congressional Campaign Committee (Taylor 1985c). Indeed, a Democratic campaign consultant argued that because of the Chapman campaign, the trade issue had become a standard piece of the southern Democratic repertoire.

The way these Democrats and Republicans talked about drugs also illustrates how an issue can be shaped to generate resentment. Many of the arguments sounded here against drugs were supply-side arguments. It is not surprising that in these campaigns there were many Republican and Democratic calls for the death penalty for drug kingpins (with expansive definitions of the term). Neither is it surprising that little was said about drug treatment centers or education programs, which, of course, are more liberal approaches to the problem. What is surprising is how much of the drug dialogue centered on assassinating the Panamanian leader Manuel Noriega and the effective interdiction of foreign drug runners. Tom Anderson even called for military action against drug cartels in Central America. Voiced in a part of the country where the drug problem is comparatively less severe, these seemed to be rather dramatic proposals.

The foreign aid issue that came up in the Dowdy campaign is a third issue that fits into the resentment category. In highlighting this issue, Dowdy was not only blaming "our problems" on "them," he was making the case that what was rightfully ours was going to them. When he attacked President Reagan's $3-billion package of foreign aid to Pakistan, he argued that while Americans—and Mississippians—were sacrificing under Reagan's plan, "other countries [were] receiving our money." Reagan's budget cuts did not spare Amtrak, farm programs, and veterans' programs, he argued, why should they spare foreign aid? Dowdy's campaign strategy with regard to this issue was masterful. His message had two strands, two elements of a zero-sum game. He talked about who was losing and who was sacrificing as a result of Republican budget cuts and who was benefiting from Republican policies. Taking advantage of his position in the out-party, Dowdy found a comparative advantage where Williams was vulnerable, where the Republican's hands were tied by his public endorsement of the administration.

What do these three issues have in common? For one thing, in each case people of a different race or nationality or both are benefiting at the expense of Americans. These issues are not explicitly racial in content. They nonetheless derive some of their political appeal from the fact that the target of political rhetoric is some racial or foreign out-group, at least in the minds of political strategists seeking any advantage they can.[33] They are often issues with a racial twist, a twist that broadens their appeal. And it is not just that the Japanese, the Latin Americans, and the Pakistanis are easy targets because they are not white. The advantage of resentment issues is that there are so few representatives of these out-groups in the district that the strategy has little electoral cost. There is no one to challenge the legitimacy of these issues, to cry "foul," and politicians are unfettered and unchallenged in making their inflammatory remarks.

The references by campaign managers to Tora! Tora! Tora! and "Japanese bashing" also indicate that it is the adversarial aspect of these issues that they feel is most important. A Democratic campaign consultant said that it was not necessarily the trade issue, per se, that was important to the campaign, but "how it played into the big patriotism thing." In his mind, such rhetoric worked and was employed in his election because it not only highlighted a problem, it created an adversary. And Chapman himself believed that it was not that people understood the issue, but they "sensed it. They had this nagging fear that foreigners were buying up our industry, that no VCRs were being made in America." The dual goal of these resentment messages is thus to create a threat and, in the words of a Democratic consultant, "[to] get at some of those pro-American chords that Reagan sounds so well" (Taylor 1985c). In other words, these issues allow Democrats to redefine "us" as well as to blame "them."

Both Republicans and Democrats have used resentment issues in their campaigns on occasion, but Democrats have used them with greater frequency and with more effect than Republicans. The Republicans already have racial issues in their arsenals and, as will be discussed, other campaign themes to play. Democrats have had to do something specifically to "keep whites home," as one Democratic politician put it. Racial issues have not been available to them for obvious reasons. Out of sheer necessity, other ways to appeal to whites have had to be devised.

The trade issue has been especially good for Democrats as Republican efforts to portray themselves as pure conservatives (and even their conservative convictions) have gotten in the way of taking a protectionist stand. For instance, the Virginia Republican Linda Arey, extraordinarily consistent in the application of her ideological principles, took a strong free trade position in her campaign against L. F. Payne. In this, Arey was not much different from other southern Republicans. For example, in the House, southern Republicans almost unanimously opposed the protectionist Gephardt Amendment to a 1987 Omnibus Trade Bill (only one of thirty-nine congressmen voted for it), while over three-quarters of southern Democrats (sixty of seventy-seven) accepted the amendment.[34] Other votes on trade issues generated similar results. The point, of course, is that Democrats had come upon an issue that distinguished them from Republicans, one that they perceived to be electorally profitable. Said a pollster from the Chapman campaign, "I think the Democrats can win in the South if they take these symbolic tools away from Charlie Black [a national Republican advisor], if they capture the symbols of the campaign from the beginning." Trade has been one such symbol for the Democrats. Resentment issues offer others as well.

A second element of the Democratic resentment strategy to keep white voters in the fold has been to pepper their campaigns with populist appeals in the best of the southern tradition. In these cases, Democrats made class-based appeals of us versus them and attacked large banks, corporations, insurance companies, and other large institutions in their rhetoric. As conservative as the southern electorate is, these southern Democrats believed such appeals to be effective and relied on them to activate and capture the rural white vote and the working-class white vote. As Jim Chapman put it, "People in my district are suspicious of anything big and institutionalized. You can even be a progressive Democrat in my conservative district if you understand this."

These efforts involved more than just selecting the right enemy. They involved capturing an image, forging a connection with the common man. The Democrats spoke at length of their humble roots and the difficult times in their lives and linked their own stories to the issues they were highlighting in their campaigns. Glen Browder's mother, widowed at twenty years of age with three children, was testimony to the need for Social Security. Mississippi Democrat Gene Taylor's advertisements told of how he and his siblings had to move from southern Mississippi to find jobs. Even Virginia's L. F. Payne, a millionaire developer, had modest beginnings and often talked of his father, a retired state trooper, and his mother, a teacher, and their service to the state.

While identifying themselves as common men, these southern Democrats labeled their opponents pawns of the rich and powerful. "Edd Hargett," declared a Jim Chapman radio commercial, "is a *Republican* backed by the *rich*" (Attlesey 1985b), not a popular combination in East Texas. On a television call-in show, Gene Taylor spoke of his supporters as "humble folks" who sent in five-dollar donations to the campaign while Anderson's supporters were rich "fat cats" from far away. Wayne Dowdy borrowed a page from Huey Long, who once observed that corporations (particularly oil companies) "are the finest political enemies in the world" (Williams 1969, 416). Dowdy's television advertisements portrayed his opponent as a stooge of the oil industry (Clymer 1981a), and he declared at campaign rallies, "I'm running against the President of the United States, the U.S. Chamber of Commerce, and every oil company in the world" (Putnam 1981a). When an airplane towing a Williams streamer flew over one rally, Dowdy added that his opponent had "the backing of the big oil companies and now has a hot air balloon and an airplane as well" (Mullen 1981). As this illustrates, populist issues and themes afforded another vehicle by which southern Democrats could appeal to white voters, above all, rural white voters.

The Republicans in these races also had populist chords to ring. Their attacks on big institutions were directed at "big labor," "big eastern labor unions," "big eastern labor bosses," or some other such bugbear. These charges usually came about when Democrats had taken money from labor, sometimes a considerable percentage of their overall campaign fund. It was more difficult to link them to the big forces of eastern liberalism, though, as these were not usually credible charges. Nonetheless, the AFL-CIO and the National Education Association made excellent rhetorical enemies, and the Democrats were guilty by association.

If there has been a problem with an antiunion populist attack, however, it is that some members of labor unions may be offended by the rhetoric.

Republicans have tried, as John Rice tried in Alabama, to create a fine distinction when they make the case that "organized labor and the working man are two different things." Newspaper stories about Rice's old union pals feeling betrayed, though, may have undermined his point (Smith 1989f) and cost him as much support as he gained.[35] Linda Arey also experienced difficulties in wooing labor votes with statements (in front of a labor audience) that she did not trust "big labor bosses in Washington" and that some union members might resent their dues going to support presidential candidates they did not prefer. Both statements were loudly jeered (Bland 1988c).[36] These incidents illustrate how the target that best fits the rest of the Republicans' campaign message—big labor—has been problematic, particularly as many white swing votes in the district are union members. They also show that while Republicans sometimes do attack large institutions in the populist tradition, their natural targets are fewer. One lovely enemy for Republicans, of course, is big government, and inasmuch as they can harness this populist theme, they will be very effective.

That Democratic campaign managers keep returning to populist messages and other resentment issues and winning elections with them is some indication that they have resonance among white (and black) southern voters. But this evidence is only suggestive. Survey research is needed to investigate further the relation between attitudes on racial issues and attitudes on resentment issues as well as the relation between attitudes on resentment issues and the vote. Nonetheless, as these cases show, the choices offered to southern voters are shaped very much by the belief among campaign officials that these types of issues work.

Conservatism and Parochialism in Southern Elections

"Conservatism," write Earl and Merle Black (1987), "occupies an exalted ideological position in the South" (213). This, of course, gives the more conservative Republicans a decided advantage. Black and Black predict the continued growth of the Republican party given the force of conservative politics in the South: "In most southern states, . . . campaigning as a Republican is a diminishing liability, for the GOP is rapidly growing and has excellent future prospects. Our analysis has shown key sectors of the southern electorate—whites, in general, but especially the conservatives, the college-educated, and the youngest generation—either realigning in favor of the Republicans or strongly moving in that direction" (255–56). The conservative advantage in white public opinion, as Black and Black label one of their chapters, favors the Republicans more than ever, and it is little wonder that analysts of southern politics have pointed to this as an indicator of a bright Republican future.

Republican congressional candidates recognize the strategic advantage that conservatism gives them, and they borrow extensively from the presidential campaigns. They run as staunch conservatives, highlighting the issues and messages that Reagan and Bush used so effectively in the South. There is a big difference between these campaigns and the presidential campaign, however. Republican congressional candidates do not face northern liberals. Their Democratic opponents are often highly conservative, and they must approach the southern electorate somewhat differently.

First, a number of issues have offered some possibilities for Republicans to distinguish themselves from Democrats. To start, they have tried to exploit "no new taxes" pledges, as Bush and Reagan did so effectively in their presidential campaigns. In these cases, the Democrats consistently refused to sign a strict pledge put out by a conservative national taxpayers organization. The Republicans signed it with great ceremony. Still, it was hard to paint their Democratic opponents as wild-eyed liberals, even on this issue. Although Democrats did not sign the pledge, they did affirm their commitment to fighting tax increases. Sometimes, they even tried to turn their refusal to sign the pledge into something positive. Gene Taylor, for example, refused to sign the pledge because it prevented him from voting to raise taxes if a military base or an industry in the district was in great trouble.

On other issues, southern Republicans have tried to "out-conservative" their conservative opponents. Linda Arey's proposal to post the Ten Commandments in every schoolroom and Tom Anderson's declarations on school prayer, for instance, illustrate candidates trying to differentiate themselves on a specific issue. But how much room was there for Arey, Anderson, and their colleagues to the right of their Democratic opponents? Did Anderson's declaration make him the purer conservative? Did this difference matter to Mississippi voters?

Emphasizing their superior conservatism does not appear to have been enough for Republicans to win over the numbers of white southerners that are required to overcome the Democratic advantage among blacks. Mostly this has been because southern Democrats have been conservative enough, particularly on social issues like abortion, gun control, and school prayer but even on some economic issues, like lowering the capital gains tax. Moreover, southern Democrats have been greatly concerned that people will judge them by their association with the national Democratic party and thus have taken great pains to separate themselves from the national party, its more recognizable celebrities, and its leadership. "I wouldn't know Ed Kennedy if he stepped on my foot," said Gene Taylor. Whether intentional or not, his reference to Kennedy as Ed proved his point. A *New York Times* reporter wrote about the Texas Democrat Jim Chapman, "[He] has so often called himself a 'conservative Democrat' as opposed to a 'national Democrat,' that some people here say they are beginning to think he is a member of some new party" (King 1985c). L. F. Payne, Wayne Dowdy, and Glen Browder also carefully dodged association with such nationally known Democratic figures as Walter Mondale, Michael Dukakis, Edward Kennedy, Jesse Jackson, Barney Frank, and the entire national party apparatus.

The Democrats' conservative positions on the issues, their alienation from the national party, and their connections with state and local conservative Democrats are the ways they have attempted to deflect the inevitable charges of liberalism. Scattered evidence suggests that they have been successful and that southern voters do not perceive them to be liberal. An *Anniston Star* poll, for example, showed that only 19 percent of registered voters ($n=606$) thought of Glen Browder as a liberal despite his being barraged with this charge by the Republican candidate (Rilling 1989). A large number (34 percent) could not place Browder on an ideological spectrum (not an easy task given Browder's skilled evasiveness).

Nonetheless, among registered voters Browder clearly was not thought of as a liberal. This conclusion is in line with other evidence on southern perceptions of southern Democrats. Only 34 percent of southerners place the Democratic candidate for Congress in their district on the liberal side of a seven-point liberal-conservative attribution scale, and well over half these people (20 percent of all southern respondents) see the candidate as only moderately liberal. Of course, many respondents are unable to place themselves or the candidates on this scale, but of those who do, a large majority do not consider them liberal. This is not the case for Democratic presidential candidates. Michael Dukakis, for instance, was perceived by 54 percent of southerners as liberal, and most (38 percent of all southern respondents) did not perceive him as moderately liberal.[37]

The point is that southern Democrats have strategically and success-fully placed themselves on the right, but to the left of Republicans, to capture the votes of white moderates and liberals (few as they may be) and to compete with Republicans for the conservative white vote. In Downs-ian terms, southern Democrats have situated themselves near the center of the distribution of political opinion, a decidedly conservative location. Republicans work hard to establish themselves as the bona fide conserva-tives and to many white southerners, this matters. But local Democrats have been conservative too, and conservative enough to blunt the effect of Republican charges of being "too liberal." In the Virginia case, for exam-ple, L. F. Payne's campaign manager argued that Linda Arey thought the district was more conservative than it actually was: "Partially, this was because of Dan Daniel. She also had to run to the far right to get the nomination. Once we inoculated L.F. as a conservative, though, we were okay."

A second Republican strategy in the congressional elections of the 1980s and early 1990s was to highlight the candidates' connections with popular Republican administrations. All the Republicans in this small sample but one (Hayes Dent, who ran in 1993) ran radio and television commercials featuring Presidents Bush and Reagan. They sent out letters under the president's signature. When possible, they brought the presi-dent or high-ranking administration officials into the district. Vice president and presidential candidate Bush campaigned for a day with Linda Arey in Virginia and made a presidential appearance in the Gulfport election. These events were always good for a front-page story or two.

In addition, the Republicans adopted themes from the presidential campaigns and from the president's agenda. Liles Williams talked about Ronald Reagan's budget cuts throughout his campaign. Tom Anderson obtained and was photographed with a satchel of cocaine shortly after George Bush held up a package of drugs in a nationally televised speech. Linda Arey, dubbed by *Congressional Quarterly* "an overnight symbol of the South's Reagan-era Republicanism" (Elving 1988, 1008), supported the president's veto on the civil rights bill, even when many southern Republican congressmen were not prepared to do so. The Republicans in this sample unabashedly tied themselves to both administrations.[38] Given the overwhelming victories of the Republican presidential candidates in these districts, such a strategy seemed sensible. But the major shortcoming of this strategy is that it made the Republicans vulnerable to an effective Democratic counterstrategy.

In the Reagan-Bush years, Democrats obviously did not play up their ties to Republican administrations. They attempted to find other issues to differentiate themselves from Republicans and tended to use local issues to fill this role. Republicans have often been so enamored of conservative issues that they have failed to diversify their campaigns. Southern Democrats have, and they believe that the local angle has been an important contributor to their success in the past thirty years. Whereas Republicans have emphasized their superior conservatism and their connections with the president, Democrats have highlighted issues of service to the district and discussed opportunities to deliver federal money and federal projects to the highly dependent area. In Alabama, the Democratic consultant said, "The Republicans essentially wanted to play the presidential campaign over again. Let Rice talk about national issues, we want to talk about roads and bridges and military bases." In Virginia, the sentiment was similar. "She [Arey] emphasized Washington and we emphasized the district," said a consultant to the Payne campaign. "I'll take the district any day of the week."

This difference between Democratic and Republican campaign themes was highly evident in all of the elections observed here. While Tom Anderson talked about his relation with the president, Gene Taylor talked about his relation with the area's shrimpers. Linda Arey, though possibly less accepted in the staunchly conservative district, spoke of hard-line conservative principles like "local control" and "private enterprise." L. F. Payne spoke of the local jobs he personally brought into Nelson County with his business enterprise. John Rice made cutting taxes and federal spending the centerpiece of his campaign. So did Glen Browder, but he talked about protecting the district from cuts in the federal budget (the Dick Armey bill to close down obsolete military bases was in the news at the time of the campaign). Campaign mottos captured the local image these Democrats were trying to create: Gene Taylor was "South Mississippi's Choice," L. F. Payne's motto was "Virginia Values, Virginia Leadership," and Glen Browder's was "Alabama Thinking, Alabama Values." Compare these to their Republican opponents' taglines: "Leadership, not Politics," "A Congressman We Won't Have to Train," and "Experience Where it Counts!" The key for Democrats, insisted one media consultant, has been to "parochialize the race," to make a local connection with every issue.

Toward this end, Democratic political promises have been more locally oriented. Military installations are important to the prosperity of many southern districts. Establishing one's dedication to taking care of the district on military issues has been crucial to Democratic candidates. The best way to do this is to have a position on the Armed Services Committee, from which a congressman can bring defense pork home to the district, pork that will supply jobs and support service industries in the area surrounding a military base or a veterans' hospital. It is no accident that fifteen of the thirty-one Democrats on the House Armed Services Committee after the elections of 1988 were southerners. Running for office the first time, Democrats can promise only to ask for a seat on the committee. Democrats in the Alabama and Mississippi 5 races went somewhat further: they solicited the assistance of powerful Democrats from the state delegation, Sen. Howell Heflin from Alabama and Congressman Sonny Montgomery from Mississippi. In the days immediately preceding the election, Heflin and Montgomery announced that they would attempt to assert their institutional influence to open a spot on Armed Services for their new colleague. Montgomery even spent a day campaigning with Gene Taylor, visiting military installations and veterans' hospitals and providing Taylor with an important headline. Gene Taylor did receive an Armed Services assignment upon coming to the House. Browder did not, though he got on the committee shortly thereafter. What were the hopes and promises of the Republican candidates opposing Taylor and Browder? Anderson aimed for the Energy and Commerce Committee or the Small Business Committee, picking up on some of his experience in Washington. John Rice, whose personality and ideological fervor guided him throughout his campaign, wanted to get on the Interior Committee. "I firmly believe those are going to be the hot issues," he said, "and I want to be where the heat is" (Smith 1989e).

The Republicans have recognized the strategic advantage this local angle gives Democrats. One Republican leader attributed the narrow loss in Mississippi's Fourth District to Liles Williams's "[failure] to develop any local issues" (Broder 1981b). Yet none of the other Republicans in this small sample appeared to have learned from Williams's mistake. Part of the reason is that Republicans, as mostly rational actors, have subscribed to the idea that "Nothing succeeds like success." As sensible politicians, they have done what works. But they have looked to the wrong example, the presidential election, rather than adopting the successful strategy of local Democrats. Republicans, experiencing so little success at the local level, have fixated on Washington politics, which has inhibited the development of local campaign themes. Although Republican candidates have recognized that they must make a local connection on the stump, they also have tried to capitalize on the party's national success, to use the conservative formula that won the South for Reagan and Bush. These two goals may not be complementary. Superior Republican conservatism actually may have hindered them from taking the local angle and from identifying themselves as the district's guardian in Washington.[39] Strong (1971) argued in the early 1970s that "[Republicans] take their ideology seriously. This seriousness prevents them from being flexible enough to broaden their bases of support" (254). Things did not change much in this regard in the following two decades.

A newspaper debate between L. F. Payne and Linda Arey over transportation issues illustrates the point. In the debate, Arey said that America's interstate highway system was starting to show its age and that federal money should go toward repair and renovation. At the same time, she lambasted a spendthrift Congress and "those most special of political pork barrel plums—unnecessary construction contracts." Payne, on the other hand, talked about the plum he would like to deliver to the district, the "construction of a Danville bypass for U.S. Routes 58 and 29" (*Danville Bee* 1988). On foreign trade issues, a similar contrast emerged. Arey, supporting the free trade principles that had been championed by Ronald Reagan, came out strongly opposed to trade restrictions. Payne, on the other hand, used the issue to characterize himself as the district's guardian. He talked about "inequities against American jobs in the present world trade situation" and "[working] on behalf of our district with the U.S. trade representative to increase exports of our district's products and to be a watchdog over unfair foreign practices involving district products" (*Danville Bee* 1988). The two candidates used the newspaper forum to stress different things, Arey her support of the conservative principles of President Reagan, Payne his dedication to protecting the district.

The Alabama case is another, vivid example of a Democrat neutralizing and even capitalizing on his opponent's conservative message. John Rice declared that federal money for schools came with "too many strings attached." The message was intended to strike a conservative chord, but it left Rice vulnerable to Glen Browder's message of district advocacy. For every dollar in taxes that left Alabama, argued Browder, $1.38 was spent in the district. "I like the balance of trade we have with the federal government," said the Democrat. At another point, he said, "John Rice's philosophy would devastate this district. . . . I believe that Bill Nichols worked hard to bring federal money to the district and we ought to keep it" (Yardley 1989a). Browder also argued that Rice's proposal to cut federal spending by 50 percent would threaten $85 million in benefits for district veterans as well as other valuable programs. Rice's conservative plans—Browder labeled them Ricenomics—were irresponsible and would cost people in the district (Burger 1989a).

At another point in the race, as discussed in chapter 3, Rice's campaign manager was quoted as saying that the campaign had returned $3,000 in donations from "people we don't like" (Smith 1989b). Again, Rice's intent was to win conservative votes (particularly given that his campaign was financially strapped). But again, the comment played into Browder's campaign strategy. In the words of the Democrat's media advisor, "That business came off sounding like 'I don't want to represent everybody in the district.' It was hyperideological. Glen said he would serve all the people of the district and it made him seem more constituency oriented, which is just what we were aiming for." Browder and Rice alike attempted to tie themselves closely to the late Bill Nichols, both taking notice of Nichols's extraordinary service to the district. Nichols delivered and so long as he did, Republicans were loathe to challenge him. When the opportunity arose to replace him, Rice tried to connect himself ideologically to the conservative Nichols, which was sensible given that he had a strong case for this. Browder, however, appears to have been more effective at positioning himself as Nichols's natural successor, as the individual best able to carry on his work.

These Democrats also tried to turn the Republican candidates' connections to the president into an advantage, or at least into less of a disadvantage, again by characterizing the contest as one of home versus Washington. As noted above, their opponents tied themselves to the popular Reagan and Bush administrations as much as possible, and Presidents Reagan and Bush, intent on party building to a degree that their predecessors were not, were cooperative. In fact, Reagan, Bush, and other prominent Republicans played important roles in all of these Republican campaigns. The connection to the Republican administration, notably in places where Reagan and Bush had won by overwhelming margins, was a source of great pride for the Republican candidates. But in an observation that directly addresses one of the puzzles of the southern realignment, the Democrats often salvaged some advantage from their precarious situation, and that advantage stemmed from their outsider status.

As is good campaign practice, southern Democrats blamed Washington insiders for all of the country's problems. In the 1980s and early 1990s, the Democrats had a broad target in a federal government headed by Republicans, and these conservative southern Democrats took aim at it. In one of the more clever and far-reaching claims of the campaigns observed here, Gene Taylor took credit for balancing his budget for the previous six years, while charging that Tom Anderson had not balanced his budget in the whole time he had been in Washington. A campaign aide admitted that Taylor's budget was in fact the Mississippi state budget (Mississippi has a balanced budget amendment in its constitution) and Anderson's budget was the federal budget. Anderson tried to link himself to the administration, to characterize himself as an insider. This allowed Taylor, the outsider, to lay the problems faced by the federal government at Anderson's door. His charge was outrageous, to be sure, but it went unchallenged.

The Democrats here depicted presidential efforts on behalf of Republican candidates as outside interference. They tried to turn these visits to their favor, and the general sentiment of both Democratic and Republican officials was that it worked. "The more Washington showed up, the more it played into our hands," said the Virginia Democrat L. F. Payne. In the Mississippi 5 race, claims of outside interference were a major part of Taylor's campaign, and campaign insiders on both sides felt that Anderson was seriously damaged by them. The Republican was plagued with the problem of being perceived as a pawn of Trent Lott and George Bush. Unflattering editorial cartoons and biting disc jockey comments about what was supposed to be the most important event in his campaign, Bush's appearance in the district, only reinforced that image.

The outsider image that southern Democrats had was doubly effective as they disassociated themselves from *both* national parties. They played an us versus them game and "them" included both the Republicans and the national Democrats. Political necessity thus led to an effective campaign tactic. "I will only listen to the people of the district," said Wayne

Dowdy at a McComb rally, "not the lobbyists in Washington or either political party" (Mullen 1981). Gene Taylor's argument that his campaign was poor because he failed to meet the liberal litmus tests of national Democratic donors also illustrates the point. Anti-Washington, anti-Congress campaign rhetoric is effective in most places and is a common tactic in congressional campaigns (Fenno 1978, 163–69). It was doubly effective through the 1980s and early 1990s for southern Democrats, who took advantage of their position in the party out of office and of their minority position within the Democratic party. They were outsiders in Washington, so they claimed, which gave them currency with their future constituents.

Finally, Democrats have been able to keep a local edge in that their candidates are more likely to have risen through local and state political institutions than Republicans. That is, Democrats have been more likely to come into the race having held local office or with political experience at the state level. Republicans have been more likely to come to the race with considerably less experience. In part this is a national phenomenon. As Alan Ehrenhalt (1991) argues, the Democrats, as the party of government, are better situated to recruit able candidates for low-level offices:

> Consider two bright, glib, personable twenty-five-year-olds with a natural talent for salesmanship. One is a liberal Democrat who sees government as a benevolent instrument of social policy. The other is a conservative Republican who agrees with the national GOP leadership that government itself is a large part of the problem. Which one is more likely to put his talents to work selling himself to the voters as a candidate for public office? Which one is apt to decide that it is more respectable (as well as more lucrative) to sell insurance or real estate or computers? (224–25)

Ehrenhalt's argument is that while it is not so difficult to find high-quality candidates for high-profile positions, the Republicans have been less successful, and understandably so, at recruiting superior candidates for state legislative or city council positions. Ehrenhalt's argument is even more powerful when applied to the South, where decades upon decades of Democratic dominance have made it difficult for Republicans to recruit candidates for low office. This advantage is certainly reflected in my sample; five of the six Democratic candidates were state senators or city councilors or district attorneys. They had been elected before, if not in the entire district, then in a significant portion of it. L. F. Payne was the only Democrat who came to the race with little or no political experience.

Only one of the six Republicans in these cases came into the race with previous electoral experience. Tom Anderson and Hayes Dent (see chapter 5) were aides to Republican politicians. Linda Arey held an appointive position in the Reagan administration. Liles Williams was a former Democratic party leader, and Edd Hargett had no previous political experience. John Rice was a state senator who represented a significant part of the southern half of the Third District of Alabama. Of course, Rice had been elected as a Democrat and had switched to the Republican side shortly before the election, an event that many southern Republicans see as the most important way to build the party. The point is not that these were unattractive candidates. Well funded and with political resumes that had some appeal in these districts, they had good chances to win these elections. They were not as attractive as their Democratic opponents, however. They had not won elections in the district before and, in a couple of cases, they had built their careers elsewhere, notably in Washington. In an interesting twist, when their old Republican bosses came to town to vouch for them, their Democratic opponents all further played the populist independence theme. They asserted that the Republicans were handpicked (the nature of the special election primaries had something to do with this) and argued that "powerful folks in Washington" were interfering in the local political process. It was a minor theme in the Democratic message, but it was consistent with many of the other points they were trying to make.

The local strategy Democrats pursued in these cases is likely to be most effective when the candidates are able to disassociate themselves from the national Democratic party and national Democratic figures. In this sense, the Democratic quest for white votes becomes more difficult when a Democrat is in the White House. During the Reagan-Bush years, congressional leaders or controversial Democratic figures like Barney Frank, Jesse Jackson, and Jim Wright made inviting targets for Republican candidates. Democrats, however, easily deflected the charge that they had some tie to these people. With a Democratic president in office, southern Democratic candidates have had a new problem. The president is so much more visible to the public, and the connection between a president and members of his congressional party is so much easier to make that their ability to run independently of the national party has been diminished.

Take, for instance, a special election held in Kentucky's Second District in May 1994 after the death of the venerable Democratic congressman of forty years, William Natcher. Though Kentucky is a small reach out of the South (as most scholars define it), this district, in the rural, west-central part of the state, has a southern character. Containing a very small population of blacks (5 percent of the district), the character of the district nevertheless was such that appeals to white voters were of utmost importance to gaining victory.

Not surprisingly the winning Republican candidate, a Christian bookstore owner named Ron Lewis, emphasized his outsider status. President Clinton was weakest at the time of the election, his disapproval ratings bettering his approval ratings for only the second time in his term. As a result, Lewis's out-party campaign was certainly different from the Democratic outsider campaigns detailed here. Whereas a Democrat like Gene Taylor did not portray himself as being opposed to the Republican administration and its policies (which were popular in his district), Lewis ran against the president and his policies at every opportunity, and his campaign rhetoric tied his opponent, the state legislator Joe Prather, to the president. A television commercial showing an image of Prather slowly "morphing" into an image of Bill Clinton was widely shown. Noting that the president's legislation was winning by small, even one-vote margins, Lewis would tell crowds, "A vote for me . . . will be a vote against Bill Clinton" (Kocher 1994b). In some regards, Lewis's message was not much different from the other Republican messages I describe in these cases. His attempt to nationalize the campaign, however, carried more pungency because a Democrat was in the White House.

Joe Prather's campaign message also did not differ much from the Democratic messages discussed in this book. Prather's main appeal was local in character. He associated himself with state, not national, Democratic leaders. He painted himself as the defender of tobacco interests in the district, which were vulnerable given antismoking developments. Patterning himself after Natcher, Prather refused to take money from so-called special interests (defined as money from out of state).[40] Said the candidate, "[Natcher used to say], 'if you take their money, the minute you go there to serve they have their hands all over you.' I'm here to tell you that the hands I want on me are the hands of the people of the 2nd District" (Kocher 1994a). Prather attacked Lewis for taking money from the national Republican party and accepting help from national Republican politicians. He tried to tie the two points together after Minority Leader Bob Dole visited the district on Lewis's behalf. Dole was not interested in the people of the Second District, ranted Prather: "You know I'm not going to Congress and tell Sen. Dole that I'm going to be for taxing Kansas wheat. And I darn sure don't want him in here telling us that he's going to tax that cash crop that is the economic foundation [of the Second District]" (Kocher 1994a).

Statements like this reinforced the widely held belief that Prather was a poor candidate, which certainly contributed to his loss. Nonetheless, if his campaign illustrates anything, perhaps it is that being in the out-party is not so much an advantage for Democrats in the years of Republican presidents as being associated with the party in power is a disadvantage in Democratic years. As part of the purpose of this chapter is to explain how Democrats survived a lengthy period of popular Republican presidents, I focus here on the small things Democrats did to take advantage of their out-party status or at least to neutralize the disadvantage of not being linked to Bush or Reagan. What is striking is that whether the White House was occupied by a Republican or a Democrat, Democratic congressional candidates knew their advantage lay in running local campaigns, while their Republican opponents honed in on their national advantage. In the Texas, Virginia, and Mississippi contests, the local campaigns were quite effective. In the Kentucky case, with an unpopular Democrat as president, the Republican's national theme paid off. That the largest Republican gains in Congress in the past thirty years have occurred in the midterms of Democratic administrations is some indication that the nationalizing of the congressional election is possible if the circumstances are right.

The cases in this book illustrate that Democratic candidates have adapted to and even flourished in a hostile political environment. As the Kentucky election shows, they must be prepared to adjust to continuous changes in that environment. Nonetheless, what they have accomplished to this point, and how they have accomplished it, is impressive.

The mathematics of these elections require that Democrats win only a minority of white votes in their districts, and sometimes only a modest minority of that vote. Increasingly, southern whites, even a majority of southern whites, are supporting congressional Republicans, for racial reasons or for conservative reasons or both. By cultivating new issues and refining some old ones many Democrats have been able to attract white votes and court enough of them to keep the Republicans from taking over southern delegation after southern delegation.

5 The Majority Black District

ONE RECENT CONSEQUENCE of the Voting Rights Act of 1964 has been that southern states have created new majority black congressional and state legislative districts. The number of majority black districts in the South has gone from zero in 1970 to sixteen following the 1990 redistricting. The number of black members of the House of Representatives from the South has risen accordingly from two (first elected from 45–50 percent black urban districts in 1973 [*Congressional Quarterly* 1982]) to seventeen over this period. As of the 1990 Census, blacks comprise 19 percent of the population of the South, and, as of 1992, black representatives represent almost 14 percent of southern congressional districts.[1]

The large and growing number of these districts is only one reason I include a majority black case here. The districts are located in many of the places where race has most pervaded politics in the past. And these are the places where race is still a big and very obvious issue. Moreover, including an election from a majority black district in this book offers an opportunity to test one of the major hypotheses from chapter 2. What happens when the racial balance tips the other way? Do contests in majority black districts mirror those in majority white districts? How does partisan strategy differ in these districts, and in what ways is it the same? The election described here, pitting a black Democrat against a white Republican, allows one to broach these questions. The primary election, in which five black Democratic candidates, two white Democratic candidates, and one white Republican candidate vied to get into the runoff, also provides insight into the formation of racial-political strategy.

Mississippi 2

The election that took place in Mississippi's Second District in the spring of 1993 brings this study full circle. Like the election in Mississippi 4 discussed above, this was one of the first special elections of a new administration.[2] The districts, in fact, are adjacent, even sharing some of the same territory. Claiborne and Jefferson Counties, in the Fourth in 1980, were moved to the Second when a majority black Second District was created.

The district comprises the heavily black parts of the Jackson metropolitan area, the city of Vicksburg, the overwhelmingly black Claiborne and Jefferson Counties, and the entirety of an area of the state misnamed the Delta. The area is not a triangular piece of land at the mouth of a river, the usual definition of the term, but a flat floodplain of the Mississippi in the west-central part of the state. The river's work has defined the area geographically. Rolling hills border the region to the east and the north, and the Yazoo River defines its southern border. As the Mississippi River has flooded and receded over the centuries, the soil is rich in organic material and very fertile. As one local put it, "Spit and plant a seed and it'll grow."

The seed, of course, has long been cotton. It is said that cotton was king in the Old South and no more so than in this area. Large plantations and large-scale cotton gins dot the region, and much of the Delta's other business is dependent on a healthy farm economy.[3]

The other major "crop" of importance to the area is catfish. Although catfish have long been part of the southern diet, the large-scale farming of catfish is a rather new phenomenon. In 1970, close to six million pounds of catfish were shipped in the United States. By 1989, three hundred million pounds were shipped, 87 percent from Mississippi ponds, and Delta ponds at that (Forman 1989). The big difference between catfish and cotton is that the catfish industry is providing jobs. Technology has made unskilled labor much less necessary in the cultivation of cotton, and the farms are no longer a major source of employment. The catfish processing industry, however, is located in the Delta, and this has created manufacturing as well as agricultural jobs.

Most of these jobs have gone to poor blacks, who greatly outnumber whites in the region. Indeed, the legacy of the cotton industry is the large black population. The cotton plantations of the Deep South initially operated with large numbers of slaves and were the slowest to adopt more modern agricultural techniques that made slavery much less profitable. The region even served as a market for excess slaves from the developing Upper South (Genovese 1967, 90, 247). To this day, the Delta is the most heavily black area of the country's most heavily black state in spite of the huge migration of Delta blacks northward. Many people have returned to the Delta to retire, yet the out-migration of young blacks continues to this day and is of concern to many.[4]

Not only is the district heavily black but it is extremely poor, by some measures the second poorest congressional district in the nation. At the time of the 1990 Census, 44 percent of people in the district lived below 125 percent of the poverty line, and 61 percent lived below 200 percent of that mark. More than 20 percent of the district's residents received public assistance. More than 22 percent of people over age twenty-five had less than a ninth-grade education (U.S. Bureau of the Census 1992).[5] And, as elsewhere, it is blacks who suffer disproportionately, creating a huge racial gap that shows no indication of closing. As of 1990, the unemployment rate for district whites was 4 percent; for blacks it was 18 percent.

The mean income for whites was $33,581; for blacks, it was $15,385. Whereas 71 percent of the district's whites had graduated from high school, only 43 percent of blacks had reached that milestone. Still, the statistics do not prepare the visitor for the sheer depth of the poverty that pervades the black communities in the area.

The poor, heavily black Delta experienced some turmoil during the civil rights movement. Greenwood, Ruleville, Drew, and other towns in the area had their share of confrontation and violence in the early 1960s. The major chapter that the Delta adds to the story of black political progress, however, comes later. With the passage of the Voting Rights Act and the widespread registration of blacks, black political power in the Delta (and elsewhere in the South) should have grown. But, of course, it did not. One way the white political establishment was able to dampen the effect of new black voters, particularly in heavily black places like western Mississippi, was to redefine political boundaries. In 1960, the Second Congressional District fully embraced the Delta (as it had for the prior eighty years). A redistricting in 1966 (following the Supreme Court's one-person, one-vote decisions) carved the Delta into three separate districts by running boundaries east-west across the state. The practical effect and the all-but-expressed purpose of dividing up (or "cracking") the Delta was to dilute the political strength of blacks, to keep any one district from being majority black. This districting plan remained in effect until 1982, when the Delta was glued back together (and added to) by a federal court relying upon a new judicial interpretation of the Voting Rights Act.[6] Following this redistricting, the Delta, now part of an almost-majority black district (over 48 percent), played host to the first congressional election in the rural South in which a black candidate had a fair chance of winning. Those chances improved further when the white Democratic incumbent, weighing his chances in the new district, chose to retire.

The election of 1982 pitted a black Democratic state senator, Robert Clark, against a white Democrat-turned-Republican, Webb Franklin. Clark's victory in the Democratic primary over two better-known white candidates (one the son of a segregationist governor, the other the cousin of the powerful senator James Eastland) was a major victory in and of itself. Clark, however, was politically unsophisticated and disorganized. Though he generated an enormous amount of enthusiasm among Delta blacks, whites turned out in even greater numbers, and Clark lost a very close election marked by almost complete racial-line voting. In 1984, after the district was redrawn once again to incorporate even more black population (almost 53 percent of the district), Clark once again took on Franklin. Once again he lost, this time by a little more than three thousand votes.

In 1986, Democrats fielded a different black candidate, a younger, more sophisticated state official, Mike Espy, to run against Franklin. Espy, a superior candidate to Clark, defeated Franklin, though narrowly (52 percent to 48 percent). Although Franklin attributes his loss to Espy and not to the redistricting (Fava 1993), this contest too was marked by racial-line voting. Espy won almost all of the black vote; Franklin took 88 percent of the white vote. The key to Espy's victory appears to be a dropoff in white turnout, which went from 63 percent in 1984 to 51 percent in 1986 (Lightman 1987).

Though he started at a great disadvantage, Espy built on that narrow victory to establish himself as an invulnerable incumbent. By 1990, running against an erratic black Republican, Espy won 84 percent of the vote and, of course, much of the increase in support came from white voters. That he did not emerge from the civil rights movement and that he came from a prominent family in the region (his family owned and operated funeral homes in the Delta) made him less threatening to whites and made this increase in support possible. As a local attorney put it, "All the things were there to make him perfectly acceptable to a Greenville Kiwanis Club" (Hall 1986). But it was Espy's active courtship of whites and a conciliatory message on race that generated so much goodwill. His activities in Washington—championing the catfish industry from his position on the House Agriculture Committee and taking comparatively conservative issue positions—further cemented his standing with Delta whites.[7] At the same time, many blacks remained enthusiastic about him. One black activist, who found Espy too moderate, nonetheless greatly admired him and fully supported him: "He [Espy] broke barriers. That was a great accomplishment. He was an advocate for our feelings. He was somebody we could touch. Talk to. He called us back. We haven't had anyone else in this district or even this state in over a hundred years." Forging this black-white coalition in the Delta was a most impressive accomplishment and destined Espy for even greater things.

Mississippi 2 Primary—"They're both playin' to a racist theme"

By late December 1992, President-elect Bill Clinton had made most of his decisions on cabinet appointments, but he had yet to fill the position at the Department of Agriculture. For weeks, Mike Espy's name had been mentioned as the leading candidate for the job. Only with the last set of appointments, though, did Espy win the job he quite aggressively sought. In fact, it was reported in the *Washington Post* that he pushed too much for the position and that this almost cost him the appointment (Balz and Marcus 1992).

Espy resigned his congressional position following his confirmation in late January, thereby setting into motion special election procedures in Mississippi. Like the other two Mississippi elections described above, this was a nonpartisan election to be held in two rounds if, as is likely in these situations, no one candidate received a majority of the vote in the first round at the end of March. Should the second election be necessary, it would be held two weeks later. As in the cases above, the absence of an incumbent and the opportunity for low-level officeholders to run without having to abandon their present position made for a large and talented field of candidates.

The low-salience special election also provided Republicans with a real opportunity to win a seat that would otherwise be considered beyond their reach. "We've been on the bottom so long, you know," said a finely dressed woman at a midafternoon rally for the Republican candidate. "We really are hopeful about this one." State party officials were optimistic as well but recognized that some things could be engineered to further heighten the possibility of capturing the seat. Foremost among these was to organize a caucus well before the primary election to settle on one

Republican candidate (as they had done in the Mississippi 4 special election described above). Premised on the likelihood that the Democrats would not be able to follow suit, Republican state party officials believed that a candidate chosen by caucus would assure that a Republican made the runoff. A single Republican candidate in a large field posited even the possibility of a first-round victory. Indeed, the publisher of the largest black-owned newspaper in the district unhappily predicted this to me some weeks before the first election. Republican strategists were not that optimistic, but they felt that a bitter contest between Democratic candidates in the first round could well dampen support for the Democrat who emerged from the first election. Making this pitch, state party officials were able to get all the potential Republican candidates to participate and bound them to the decision of the caucus. The party's political director described the process: "It was open and fair. We treated everybody equally. All the candidates filed with us and we gave them the names and phone numbers of every delegate. Secret ballots, of course. It worked real well. As a party official, I felt good about it."

The Republican caucus did work well, as all six Republicans participated. The clear favorite going into the caucus was Hayes Dent, a thirty-one-year-old aide to Republican Gov. Kirk Fordyce. The other major candidate was Bill Jordan, a black attorney from Jackson. Jordan, however, was clearly at a disadvantage with the caucus delegates. According to one observer of the Republican scene, "He would have been an ideal candidate for that district, but those people [the delegates] just weren't ready for it." Yet race was not the only determining factor. Jordan lived outside of the district, albeit only a couple of blocks from the district line, and this may have hurt him. And Dent had been courting important Delta Republicans for a number of years.[8] The support of the governor, the first Republican governor of Mississippi since Reconstruction, also strengthened Dent's position with the delegates. He won the caucus with ease, and, in the next two days, all the other Republican candidates dropped out, Jordan included, and publicly endorsed him. With the Republican field cleared, Dent was able to turn to his primary goal, as a Dent aide put it, "turning out our core constituency . . . can we say that?"

As anticipated by the Republicans, the Democrats were unable to settle on one candidate. A caucus similar to the Republican one was planned, but the incentives for candidates to join the process were much weaker. Although several Democratic candidates announced their early intention to participate, some of them boycotted it from the beginning and others dropped out when it appeared that one candidate, Hinds County Supervisor Bennie Thompson, was at a great advantage. In the end, only Thompson and some minor candidates agreed to be bound by the results of the caucus. The Democrats who did not participate complained that they were unable to get lists of the delegates, that Thompson and state party chair Ed Cole were co-workers, that white Democratic leaders were not invited, and that the Jackson power brokers "conceived a black political caucus in Jackson for a Jacksonian, playing us Delta folks for dummies." Upon his inevitable victory, Thompson unapologetically touted himself as the Real Democrat and the Unity Democrat and did so at every campaign appearance and in every piece of literature. His claim to such status was disputed throughout the primary campaign, but the course of events certainly worked to Bennie Thompson's advantage. All of the other candidates complained about the process and were quite defensive about their decision to pull out of the caucus. The matter came up at many of their appearances and dominated much of the media's coverage of the election, crowding out other issues that possibly could have worked to the advantage of someone other than Thompson.

While one would not describe Bennie Thompson's career as meteoric, he had advanced steadily through several elected positions. As the first black alderman and black mayor of Bolton, a town of about eight hundred people just west of Jackson, and as one of the first two black supervisors in Hinds County (following the conversion from at-large elections to district elections), Thompson had been a "trailblazer," as his campaign literature described him. It was more than just his electoral victories that made this description accurate. Thompson had been a plaintiff and an expert witness in lawsuits aimed at opening up electoral possibilities for blacks in Mississippi, possibilities that he himself had taken advantage of. As an elected official and a director on the Hinds County Human

Resources Board, Thompson had been a strong advocate for blacks, seeking better services for the black community, a share of county contracts for minority businesses, equal funding for historically black universities, and better housing, transportation, and education for his black constituents. What is more, in his career as a black advocate, Thompson developed a more confrontational approach to whites, one that he defended as effective: "The bottom line is results. If you can get results with consensus building, fine. If you get results with confrontation, fine. But for black people in Mississippi, confrontation has been one of the main means of survival" (Applebome 1993).

Six other Democrats joined Thompson and Dent in the open primary. The most prominent of them was Henry Espy, the mayor of the town of Clarksdale and elder brother of the new secretary of agriculture. Espy entered the race as a major candidate with huge name recognition (at least surname recognition) and a considerable campaign war chest. As of the week before the election, Espy had raised $168,000, compared to $152,000 for Dent and $84,000 for Thompson. Whereas no other candidate in the race had raised more than $8,500 from political action committees, Espy had $30,000 in such donations, most of it from agricultural PACS that had contributed to his brother's campaigns (Curran 1993). Espy began the race as the frontrunner, but never entered the caucus process. Without his participation, the caucus would not have served its purpose anyway, and that may have been the reason it unraveled so quickly.

The other candidates were an interesting assortment of unknown and well-known long shots, including two icons of the civil rights movement. One was Unita Blackwell, one of the founding members of the Mississippi Freedom Democratic Party and a protégée of its leader, Fannie Lou Hamer. Blackwell, the daughter of sharecroppers, founded a model Head Start program and a low-income home ownership program. In 1976, she incorporated the town of Mayersville and became its first mayor. She later became the president of the National Conference of Black Mayors. She was a frequent advisor to Jimmy Carter and was well connected to Bill and Hillary Clinton (one of her campaign brochures showed her whispering into Bill Clinton's ear). Most recently, she had received a generous MacArthur Foundation award for "creativity in public affairs."

The second icon in this race was James Meredith, the man who thirty years earlier had integrated the University of Mississippi in one of the most dramatic events of the civil rights struggle. Meredith's civil rights experience was highlighted in his campaign. His campaign literature featured a picture of him lying wounded from a gunshot wound, and his main campaign event was a two-week "march" through the district. Meredith's peculiar past, though, was a political liability as well as a strength. He had worked for Jesse Helms in Washington ("Yes, I sure did. Since I went to OLE MISS, the only man to give me a job was him") and had endorsed David Duke in his Louisiana gubernatorial race ("I did that because twelve years ago, he called me and told that because of a speech I made at a college in Louisiana, he had decided to QUIT the KLAN because he now believes that what he had been saying and doing was wrong. Ten years later, his record was clean").[9] The centerpiece of Meredith's campaign was a call for "40 acres and a mule" for all black Americans. The reference, of course, was to an unfulfilled promise from emancipation. Though he later said that this was a symbolic statement and that what he really advocated was giving $40,000 to all black Americans, many people in the district were befuddled. As one Henry Espy supporter said to me, "Now what the heck am I gonna do with a mule?"

Three other Democratic candidates rounded out the field. Brian Neely, a young black attorney and former Marine, languished in obscurity. David Holbrook, a white Democratic state representative who had obtained biracial support in his previous campaigns, was unable to generate much enthusiasm outside his home base. Steve Richardson, a dentist who campaigned under the slogan, "I want to be your cotton pickin' congressman" and made health care his signature theme (and campaigned in a white smock to illustrate the point), was not to be taken very seriously.

Henry Espy started with a formidable lead. An internal Democratic party poll in February showed him well ahead of any of his competitors. Espy had the support of 40 percent of those with an early preference; none of the other candidates was named by more than 14 percent of the respondents. Espy led among both blacks and whites and even ran on a par with Hayes Dent among Republicans. Much of this lead had to do with the popularity of his brother. Espy did what he could to build on this, claiming his brother's strong support and arguing that he could do the most for the district with his family (and thus his administration) connections. "The commitment continues" was the tagline on his literature, and wherever possible Espy's brother, grandfather, and family were highlighted ("When Mike comes home, is he going to be sitting at the dinner table with any other candidates?" asked Espy's campaign spokeswoman of a reporter [Walton 1993]).

The themes that had worked so well in his brother's four campaigns also found their way into Espy's campaign. Targeting the same voters—moderate blacks, liberal and moderate whites, and strong Christians—Espy preached a message of racial harmony and racial healing. According to his staff and the media in the Delta, he was the only major candidate occupying this electoral space, Thompson being hostile to whites, Dent to blacks. "They're both playing to a racist theme," argued an Espy campaign advisor. "It doesn't matter if you paint it white or black." Espy's major black competitor received most of his attention on this count: "If Bennie Thompson captures enough of the black vote, he can become a black congressman. Then we [the district] will get zilch." Given the campaign's promise of using excellent connections to deliver progress to the district, this was a major point of comparison.

Espy encountered some problems with his electoral strategy, however, that cost him dearly. For one thing, his brother did not endorse his candidacy. Although Henry Espy had said, "Mike is in this campaign just as deep as you can put your hand in a cookie jar," Mike Espy denied that he was involved in the campaign the week before the election. "I've got my hands full running the ag department and I am not involved in anyone's campaign," he said in a statement released to the press, "I wish my brother well. There are many qualified candidates in the race. He is certainly one of them. The 2nd District's voters will choose the best candidate" (Walton 1993). Whatever his reasons, Mike's lack of support hurt his brother because the issue consistently came up in debates and interviews. By linking himself to his brother, Henry Espy also invited comparisons that may not have worked to his benefit, and he spent some time talking defensively about coattails. "I'm Mike's older brother," he said at a candidate forum. "I'm the first Afro-American in the Clarksdale City Council and the first Afro-American mayor of Clarksdale. It kind of looks like Mike came up on my back."

Another problem Espy faced was that he actually shared the ideological middle with Unita Blackwell. And Blackwell, unlike the other minor candidates, was well funded. She was willing to spend part of her Mac-Arthur grant on the campaign, and, having connections to Hollywood and to women's groups (including the political action committee Emily's List),[10] she raised a sizable amount of national money in the weeks preceding the primary. With this money, she was able to buy thirty-two huge billboards across the region and lots of air time for radio and television commercials featuring the sonorous voice of her friend the actor James Earl Jones. Blackwell also had a biracial campaign team, including several people who would have worked for Espy had Blackwell not run. Making statements like "Freedom is freedom and it has no color" and "I'm not tryin' to isolate black folks, white folks, green folks, or polka dot folks. Who's serving the Second District needs to serve the people who need it most," she portrayed herself as conciliatory on racial issues. Blackwell certainly had some electoral liabilities. She was not a particularly good public speaker. A laudatory *Los Angeles Times* article described her as "speaking in the rhythms of the Delta" (Mills 1992), which probably hurt her with white voters. And although she ran on her ability to get things done ("I've done somethin' with nothin' and in the Second District, we have nothin'. We have to find creative ways of doin' somethin'"), and on how she planned to do practical things in the future ("I'm thinkin' about the House Appropriations Committee, which is a very important situation that we need to do somethin' about"),[11] she was somewhat of a philosopher, which likely made her less accessible to voters. Whether or not she had a chance to win a spot in the runoff, Unita Blackwell clearly shared philosophical and electoral space with Henry Espy and posed a problem for him.

Espy's biggest problem nevertheless was self-inflicted. In response to a badgering questioner at a white taxpayers' forum, Espy said that he would consider repealing Section 5, the preclearance provision of the Voting Rights Act. Worse yet, a tape of the forum came to the attention of Bennie Thompson, who used it to fullest effect. Although Espy denied making the statement and charged that the tape had been doctored, Thompson brought it up at campaign appearances because, as his campaign manager said, the Voting Rights Act was the vehicle for black political progress: "With statements like that you bring black people out of the woodwork. Black politicians are saying, 'That's how I got elected and this man wants to repeal it?'" The black press, unabashedly allied with Thompson, excoriated Espy with even more flourish. Charles Tisdale, publisher of the *Jackson Advocate*, editorialized,

> Henry Espy is immersed in a dumb, bitter and unnecessary confrontation with voters and the media over whether or not he told a white Greenwood voter that he would oppose the Voting Rights Act. He denies that he did. Having seen the tape of Espy's conversation with that Greenwood voter, however, there is no doubt in my mind that Espy agreed to—in his words—"fight" the Voting Rights Act, thus dumping on the dreams, hopes, and aspirations of generations of African Americans long dead and as yet unborn; the dreams of Medgar Evers, Martin Luther King, and hundreds of unknown martyrs who fought for the right to vote in this state when hope unborn had died. (Tisdale 1993)

The issue received a large amount of local press coverage, in part because Thompson supporters called a series of press conferences through the district to publicize and criticize the gaffe, in part because the candidates sparred over the issue at a debate televised throughout the district. With Thompson supporters calling him "a nappy-headed white man" in the newspapers (Stewart 1993b), Espy was again on the defensive.

The effort to discredit Espy worked. As the campaign manager for Hayes Dent put it, "He dropped like lead." And Espy could not afford a drop in support because his following was less devoted in the first place.

A Republican poll taken just before the primary showed that Espy's voters were much less likely to turn out. Among the 40 percent of voters who knew the date of the election, Espy fell back to third place.

The main beneficiary of Espy's unraveling was Bennie Thompson. Thompson, who had name recognition in the heavily black Jackson area (which had been added to the district in the Voting Rights refinements of the 1980s and 1990s) and financial support from organized labor, started with a solid base. Although he did not have the backing of the religious leadership in the district, which was predominantly in Espy's camp, he had cultivated the support of other black leaders over the years. As noted above, Thompson was closely tied to the most important black newspaper in the district, a weekly based in Jackson—the publisher described Thompson's campaign manager as being "like a brother to me". He had developed relations with other black officeholders throughout the region and indeed the state. He was a founding member and past president of the Mississippi Association of Black Mayors and the Mississippi Association of Black Supervisors and the founding chairman of the Mississippi Institute for Small Towns. He was part of the active civil rights community, as a plaintiff in voting rights litigation and in the *Ayers* case.[12] In short, Bennie Thompson had developed a strong network of supporters who were opinion leaders in their various communities, and they turned out his vote.[13]

Henry Espy was not the only candidate who had to deal with damage control in the closing days of the primary campaigns. Unfortunate stories also came out about the Republican Dent, though as the only Republican in the race, he appears to have had fairly stable support. The Jackson newspaper reported in a front-page story the Friday before the election that Dent had a drunk driving conviction and had been arrested for driving with a suspended license after that conviction. Dent also had been arrested at a Jackson nightclub for belligerent behavior. Obviously intoxicated, he had thrown a bottle at an off-duty police officer. Dent's lengthy college record was also mentioned in the story (it took Dent ten years to earn his degree). His staff fumed that the story came out so late in the contest and that Dent's responses were only to be found on page 9 of the newspaper.[14] Expressing regret over the incidents, Dent said he had "sowed some wild oats" during college but argued that he had since "stepped into manhood" in the Gulf War (Mitchell 1993a). The only candidate who used this material against Dent at this stage was David Holbrook, the white state representative, who attempted to drain off the Republican's white vote. Operating under old rules that held the Republican label to be a liability, he also brought up Dent's party label. Of course, he did not take much out of Dent's vote totals.

Dent won a spot in the runoff, leading the field with 34 percent of the vote. Bennie Thompson, with strong support in Jackson, won the other spot with 28 percent of the vote. Espy took only 20 percent and even with Unita Blackwell's 7 percent would not have made the runoff. The other candidates split the remaining 10 percent of the vote, with James Meredith coming in last, receiving but 360 votes of the 101,000 cast.

Mississippi 2 Runoff—
"It's like the chicken voting for Colonel Sanders"

There was only a two-week break between the primary and the general election, so the winners had no time to celebrate their victories. Dent and Thompson had to escalate their campaigns and redirect their sights in a very short period of time. Both were up to the task. Throughout the primary, Dent's staff had predicted a race against Thompson, and Dent, possibly in an attempt to activate whites in the primary, had publicly predicted that Bennie Thompson would be his opponent (Stewart and Fava 1993). Indeed, this was wishful thinking. When it became clear that Dent was not going to win the first round outright, his staff formulated a two-campaign strategy that was premised upon his facing Bennie Thompson instead of Henry Espy. Upon hearing the final preelection poll results showing that Espy's lead had dissipated, Dent's staff celebrated. One of Dent's campaign directors instructed an underling to call the media: "Issue a statement saying, 'The king is dead. Long live the king.'"

Inasmuch as they could influence the result, Dent's prediction was quite possibly a self-fulfilling prophecy. There is evidence that the Republicans did what they could to ensure a race against the more extreme black candidate. For one thing, reporters were investigating whether Republican money was being directed toward the Thompson campaign for the first election. Thompson denied it, but there is some indication that this was in fact the case. Although there is no way to determine motivations, a review of Federal Election Commission Reports from the Thompson campaign and the most recent Mississippi senatorial elections shows that a fair number of people who gave money to Trent Lott and Thad Cochran in their previous campaigns also gave money to Bennie Thompson. More important, it was the Republicans who originally had the videotape of Henry Espy's voting rights gaffe. They managed to get the tape to Bennie Thompson, who predictably used it very effectively. An advisor to the Republican campaign, savoring the final preprimary polls and taking the luxury of looking beyond the first election, said, "I never thought we'd get rid of Henry Espy. But, damn it, we have."

The Republicans celebrated Bennie Thompson's victory because they perceived him to be threatening to whites. A Chicago-based Republican advisor compared Thompson to Rep. Gus Savage of Illinois but made a distinction: "Both have strong racial components to their campaigns. The difference is that Savage was stupid and Bennie is a smart man. It's gonna be a serious two weeks." An important Delta Republican leader also made the point that Thompson would be unpalatable to whites: "If white people know how bad Bennie Thompson is, they'll go out and vote for Hayes Dent. Bennie Thompson is not what we need in the Mississippi Delta."

The Republican project for the second phase of the election was thus to get this message out to whites. Several hours before Sen. Robert Dole was to appear at a rally in the district, the finance director of the Dent campaign was spotted at lunch at the next table. When asked if Dole's visit would make a difference, he mumbled, "Well okay, sure it'll help, but we want to make Bennie the issue. We hope that will happen and it will." How to do this effectively was tricky. Dent attempted first to portray Thompson as threatening and hostile to whites. At a "debate" in Greenwood the week before the election,[15] Dent amplified purported statements by Thompson to the effect that he did not need white farmer support (Thompson denied making the comment) and argued that Thompson was aiming to racially polarize the electorate. Copies of the column in which Thompson's comments were first reported were widely circulated among white voters (Walton and Howard 1993), and editorials throughout the Delta harshly criticized Thompson and his campaign. The managing editor of the *Clarksdale Press Register* wrote in a column that became a piece of Dent literature, "Which identifier might Bennie Thompson least care for—the 'white' or the 'farmer'? . . . It is quite possible that Bennie Thompson's idea of agriculture could well be limited to the raising of hell. . . . [He] has no interest in farmers, doesn't care much for white folks and doesn't care much for anybody else who might. Holding one's nose to vote—even for a Republican—is superior, I would suggest, to drowning within the race-baiting and divisiveness of the alternative (Mosby 1993a). "The Choice is Yours," said another piece of Dent literature, which placed an underexposed photograph of the light-skinned Thompson next to a photograph of Hayes Dent.[16] It went on to compare the two candidates. Under Thompson's scowling picture were captions such as "Bennie Thompson tied up the courts in an effort to dodge the draft," which compared nicely to "Hayes Dent is a war hero." Dent's tough stand on crime was compared to Thompson "lobb[ying] to reverse the death sentence for a savage killer."

If these types of messages were intended to bring whites to the polls, the Republicans believed as well that they could claim the mantle from Mike and Henry Espy and portray their campaign as the racially moderate one. If they were successful in doing so, perhaps they could win moderate whites and even some blacks who had supported Espy, Blackwell, and Holbrook in the first round. "Our issue," rambled a Republican strategist, "is that Bennie is no Espy. Bennie is somewhat threatening. If I were a black person, I'd think he wouldn't provide the good relations we need. We'll make race the issue in this campaign. Who is the moderate on the race issue—Hayes or Bennie?"

In fact, Henry Espy appeared to tacitly support them. He refused to publicly support Thompson and, according to Republican officials, was doing what he could to support Dent. It is not clear if this is because he was angry with Thompson over the voting rights tape or because he believed that his future political interests lay in a Dent victory (Dent likely being more vulnerable in a 1994 general election than Thompson in a 1994 primary). The Republicans also hoped that Mike Espy's support of Bennie Thompson would be lukewarm and checked to see if he had filed for an absentee ballot prior to the general. Dent, for his part, paid homage to Mike and Henry Espy at every campaign stop, lauding them for their efforts to heal racial wounds and for their nonconfrontational style. He claimed to be the racially moderate candidate battling against the extremist.

The Republican campaign argued further that Thompson was a corrupt politician, a charge that may have been more potent given that the corruption trial of a high-profile black official, Congressman Harold Ford, was taking place in nearby Memphis and receiving much attention in the media. Though Ford was acquitted a few days before the election, the corrupt black politician theme clearly was being played. "We've known about Bennie Thompson for a long time," said Dent at the Greenwood event. "He's got serious problems and they all revolve around his professional life." Dent's television and radio ads were especially hard hitting. With a newspaper masthead and damaging headline in the background and the words "indictment," "kickbacks," and "corrupt" flashing red across the screen, a deep-voiced narrator recounts some charges against Thompson and intones, "Bennie. Bennie Thompson. What makes you think at a time when people are voting corrupt politicians out of Congress [a jail door is heard to slam], they'll vote you in?"

The Republican strategy here was clever. According to one reporter, the Republicans peddled the stories around. Although this reporter's newspaper did not pick them up, two Delta papers (owned by the same person) did. One of the problems the Republicans had here was that charges were never filed against Thompson. The essence of the most damaging story was that authorities *considered* a criminal investigation into Thompson's dealings with a private gravel company, but that the Democratic state auditor (later governor) Ray Mabus failed to pursue it. The *Clarksdale Press Register*, in an article titled "Friends in high places saved Thompson," quotes Pete Johnson, Mabus's Republican successor as state auditor, as saying that "there is no question that Bennie Thompson would have been indicted (given the evidence)." The article also reported that Mabus was supporting Thompson in the election and that Mabus's former chief of staff was Thompson's assistant campaign treasurer (Mosby 1993b). Since the campaign could not attack Bennie Thompson for indictments that never happened, the two damning front-page articles suggesting that Democratic officials "fixed" Thompson's situation became the source and the backdrop for the television advertisements (the audio also played on radio).[17] The newspaper reports gave some legitimacy to the advertisement, which with the sound muted made Thompson into a convicted felon.

If the first major element of the Dent campaign was to emphasize the race issue, the second was to reframe the election as a struggle between city and country, between Jackson and the Delta. The Republicans argued that Thompson was urban and unconcerned with the problems of the rural areas that comprised most of the district. They highlighted Dent's experience in agriculture, and Dent indeed appeared to have picked up some valuable agricultural expertise in working for Governor Fordyce. He spoke impressively about agricultural problems and solutions. The campaign even compared the politicians brought in to campaign for the candidates. Minority Leader Robert Dole and Mississippi's Thad Cochran, both on the Senate Agriculture, Nutrition, and Forestry Committee, stumped for Dent. Thompson, noted Dent, hosted "those noted agricultural experts" Tipper Gore and Rep. John Conyers of Detroit. Dole and Cochran made appearances in the district, one of them at the Stoneville Agricultural Research Center. Tipper Gore (and Democratic party Chair David Wilhelm) came to a fundraiser in Jackson, but "they never stepped foot in the district."

The third major element of the Republican strategy was to establish and publicize Dent's conservative credentials. Bringing Robert Dole into the campaign was part of this effort. Dole, who was involved in a filibuster of President Clinton's economic stimulus bill at the time, flew in with Thad Cochran for a few hours to campaign with Dent. Dole clearly did not know Dent very well (in an interview with a local print reporter, he strongly urged people to vote for Dent Hayes), but, being experienced at this type of campaigning, he learned a lot about him in the car going from the first event to the second. At the second event, he saluted Dent's military service in the Gulf War and his Bronze Star and talked about him more specifically. With Dole and Cochran vouching for him, Dent gained some credibility with white conservative elites.[18] Not surprisingly, the visit got a lot of press coverage throughout the district.

Dole's visit also played into the Republicans' attempt to link their campaign to the national political scene. Dole (and Dent in almost every appearance thereafter) railed against various aspects of Clinton's initial program. Clinton's BTU tax (Dole called it the big-time unemployment tax), an economic stimulus bill filled with pork ("a live hog wouldn't stand a chance in the U.S. Senate"), and Labor Secretary Robert Reich ("He's an aggressive fellow and very close to the President . . . and Mrs. Clinton") all were targets of Dole's sharp wit. "Don't give Teddy Kennedy any more help up there," Dole urged a well-heeled Republican crowd at the Greenville airport. "As you can see from this filibuster effort, every single vote counts. It could mean the difference between higher and lower taxes or bigger and lesser government." Had Dent run against Henry Espy, President Clinton would have been an even larger target for the Republicans as the race issue would have been diluted. Dent still spent a great deal of time and energy attacking a Democratic president who was not popular among whites in the district. Clinton's poor performance in the district was brought up by almost every Republican I talked with.

Other conservative issues were prominent in the Dent campaign as well. Abortion was brought up to win conservative and Christian fundamentalist votes, although Dent was not a hardliner on the issue. Commercials highlighting Thompson's support for abortion on demand and "the radical Freedom of Choice Act" were narrowcast on Christian radio. The advertisement bluntly offered its instructions: "It's your civic obligation and Christian duty to vote on Tuesday for Hayes Dent. . . . Vote as if millions of babies' lives are at stake. They are." Raising abortion served not only to activate white votes but to raise volunteers, according to a Washington-based Republican consultant. In his general experience, right-to-life activists were excellent campaign workers and in this case, much better than "the old southern ladies who are more concerned with making their gumbo than with stuffing envelopes." Dent also berated the spendthrift Congress, the bloated budget deficit, environmental over-regulation, and big government in general. His proposal on the budget deficit, to cut congressional salaries by 10 percent every year until the budget is balanced, was obviously unrealistic but combined several of these conservative signature issues.

Whereas Hayes Dent tried to win moderate black votes, votes that had previously gone to Espy, Bennie Thompson made little effort to reach out to white voters. In part, he believed that such an effort was fruitless. Asked at a Lexington meeting with about thirty core supporters if he expected to get any white vote, Thompson responded, "I expect to get about as much as Mike Espy got the first time and you know that's not that much. Let's face it, black elected officials are a rarity, and whites aren't used to dealing with us. We're like blue jeans. When you first put them on, they're a little difficult to get used to. But then you get comfort-able in them." Thompson's intuition was that Mike Espy's coalition of blacks and whites was not possible for him. His reluctance to pursue white votes was more than just a calculation that he would not win white votes, however. It stemmed from a belief that the interests of most blacks in the district were not congruent with those of most whites. Recogniz-ing that there is great poverty among Delta blacks, that agriculture is no longer supplying many jobs, and that a fair proportion of blacks in the district have come to live in urban areas, Thompson promised to confront the various problems that the average black person in the district faced. "There are a lot more voters out there than just farmers. We've gotta focus on others than the farmers," he said at the Lexington meeting, a comment that probably was similar to the "white farmer" remark that the Dent campaign was feeding on.

The issues Bennie Thompson talked about on the campaign trail and those that were highlighted in his literature had to do with improving housing, water and sewage systems, rural transportation, veterans' hospitals, programs for the elderly, day care, educational opportunities, and other social programs for minorities and the poor. These were things he had done for Bolton and for Hinds County and that he would seek for the district as a whole.[19] He talked a little about improving the economy in the district and, noting that all the cotton in the district was sent to textile mills in North Carolina, advocated bringing processing industries into the district. Mostly, though, he promised to "work with elected officials to solve problems, to deal with nuts and bolts problems that people in this district have."

Thompson argued that the Republicans were hostile to blacks and would be unable to handle these problems. In a line that got such a good response he repeated it throughout the campaign, he told voters, "If you vote for my opponent, it's like the chicken voting for Colonel Sanders." He also argued that he was far more qualified to deal with these problems than Dent not just because he was black and Dent was white but because he was experienced and Dent was not: "Hayes Dent has no track record. He hasn't done anything for anybody. You know how they say an empty wagon makes a lot of noise? Well, he's makin' a lot of noise." He would be even more effective because "a Democrat can do a heck of a lot more than a Republican, especially during a Democratic administration," and he would be able to "sit down with Clinton and make some sense." Mike Espy's presence in the administration was brought up, and, much to the chagrin of the Republicans, a commercial featuring Espy's endorsement was played repeatedly over the last few days of the campaign.

Issue positions, however, were not really central to the Thompson campaign strategy. The key to the campaign was getting black voters to the polls, and it was not Thompson's stands on issues that were of crucial importance here. In this context, Bennie Thompson's stated reason for skipping the televised debate in Greenwood is interesting. When asked by the former candidate Robert Clark at the Lexington meeting to explain his rationale, Thompson responded, "There just aren't any issues left to debate. Besides, this election is based on who gets their folks out. We hope to get ten thousand votes in Jackson. I had two hundred volunteers there and they were more important." Yet his deeper reason for avoiding the forum was that he did not perceive it to be politically profit-able enough to warrant meeting Dent in what he perceived to be a hostile setting. "If you look at the *Greenwood Commonwealth* and Channel 6 [the sponsors of the debate], there's always somethin' negative about some-body black and we deserve better. If you're invited to the lion's den and if you go and get eaten alive, it's your fault."

What sort of message, then, did Thompson use to get his supporters to the polls? The main way to activate voters was to emphasize race and the racial history of the area. The guiding principle of the campaign could be found on a poster pinned to the cork walls of campaign headquarters: "It's a power thing. Vote April 13." Campaign flyers (provided by the NAACP national headquarters) had pictures of small black children and messages like "Three good reasons why you should vote April 13" and "I Can't Vote April 13 . . . You Can." Thompson also spoke frequently of his involvement in lawsuits to open the political process up to blacks in the wake of the Voting Rights Act, of his effort to increase minority set-asides in Hinds County, of his involvement in the *Ayers* case, and of the right of blacks to represent the Second District. That there were no black congressmen from Mississippi, a state with a 36 percent black population, was "an indictment of our state" and necessitated that the Second be represented by a black congressman.

Sounding this message and many variations on the same theme, Thompson conducted an aggressive campaign. The only matter that put him on the defensive involved Henry Espy. The campaign was concerned that, as Espy had not endorsed Thompson, Espy's followers might stay home on election day. When Mike Espy agreed to endorse Thompson in a television commercial, however, that concern appeared to ease. In the scheme of things, Mike Espy's endorsement was much more important than his brother's.

However important Mike Espy's endorsement, Thompson's solid or-ganization of black opinion leaders, a network that had been cultivated over a decade and a half, was his most important source of strength. This network carried Thompson to his primary success, and much of the two-week stretch run to the general election was spent reinforcing his ties to those who would represent him in a major grass-roots campaign to turn out black voters. His schedule on the Saturday before the election illustrates this well. It started with a prayer breakfast meeting with housing officials and community leaders in Tutwiler at 7:00 A.M. The leader of the meeting urged the group to get through the morning's business quickly because they had much campaign work to do. Thompson then went to Greenwood to meet with a dozen ministers, again over a meal.[20] Most of the group, including the organizer of the meeting, had supported Henry Espy in the primary, and it was important to reestablish a positive tie to Thompson. (Fortunately for Thompson, the following day was Easter Sunday, the best-attended church day of the entire year.) Traveling at ninety miles an hour, Thompson reached Grenada two hours later for a barbecue in his honor in the town square. He was quite late. A fair number of people had gathered to listen to a band playing blues and gospel favorites. An old woman introduced Thompson by singing, "Gimme that ole time religion" ("because it's good for electin' Democrats"), and the candidate gave a vigorous get-out-the-vote speech to the crowd as a small parade of police cars circled the square with sirens wailing in a salute to Thompson. After another hour's drive, the candidate held a lengthy meeting with Holmes County volunteers in which he answered questions and calculated how many votes were expected from the county. His pep talk was basic G.O.T.V.: "We got the votes if they come to the polls. At some point, we need to know who hasn't shown up. Whether they're fishin' or takin' a nap, we gotta go get'm." By six in the evening, he was in Canton, seat of Madison County. Giving a speech to party faithful, he again talked about turnout and made a public wager with the county chair. If the county produced four thousand votes, one expense-paid charter would be provided to take county volunteers to his inauguration. If the county failed to meet this goal, the county party would have to pay some other group's expenses to Washington.[21]

The final two days were devoted to maximizing black vote as well. On Easter Sunday, Thompson visited the largest church in the Jackson area, not only because of its size but because the service was broadcast over the radio throughout the district. The congregation of about three thousand listened as the Democrat gave a very humble two-minute speech, after which he was blessed by the bishop (the blessing included an admonishment, "We're prayin' for you on Tuesday. Amen. You know we'd pray for you more if you came to church more often. Amen"). On Monday Thompson toured the district with Jesse Jackson.

As election day neared, there was a marked preoccupation with ballot security, ballot integrity, voter intimidation, and the buying of votes—by both whites and blacks, Republicans and Democrats. Stories of election fraud and intimidation beyond the usual demonization of one's opponent were told by people in and around both campaigns. Republicans, party activists, and members of the rank and file were particularly worried about irregularities in the black precincts and related many stories about them. A New Jersey transplant at a Republican rally was amazed at the way elections were run in the area. "I've never seen anything like it," he said indignantly. "Here, they'll take people into the voting booth and actually vote for them." A white woman who lived in a heavily black town told of an election official watching her vote in a curtainless polling booth. After she marked the ballot for an unopposed candidate, the friendly official informed her that she did not have to vote for unopposed candidates. A Republican official recounted several instances of laxity on the part of election officials—leaving the polls open while going out to lunch, transposing vote totals, counting two boxes at the same time in the same room (leading to some double counting). He was even more concerned with ballot security. Noting that "sometimes elections are won around here after the polls close," he told of boxes disappearing, ballots being run through scantrons multiple times, and interns who were assigned to "babysit" boxes from the closing of the polls to the reporting of results.[22]

On the other side, black political operatives mostly worried about the intimidation of black voters, which, they claimed, happened when Republicans pursued ballot security measures. Democrats argued that these measures, taken almost wholly in minority precincts, are thinly veiled attempts to keep blacks from the polls. They noted that in the Robert Clark campaign, signs were posted around polling places in black neighborhoods with the warning, "Anyone posing as an illiterate and asking for help will be FINED and JAILED" (Neilson 1989, 187). In other recent southern elections, black precincts had been saturated with postcards to this effect.[23] Republican poll watchers (in suits and sunglasses) were placed in front of black precincts, a maneuver, it was believed, that was intended to scare away some black voters. In a place with a history like the Delta, such concerns were not outlandish.

Many Democrats in the Delta also were anxious about the possibility of last-minute vote buying by the Republicans. Such fraud appeared to be enough a part of politics as usual (among Democrats and Republicans alike) that even rank-and-file blacks expected it. In a most amusing illustration, the blues band at a Thompson rally sang several songs dealing with these themes. One number, "Gonna Make up Your Mind and Let Bennie Be the Man" instructed voters who were confused at the polls to get some help ("but make sure it's the right person"). In another song, voters were told, "If they put a little honey in your hand, tell'm to take their business to someone else."

If the Republicans did try to buy some votes—and I know of no evidence that they did—it did not help them much. Blacks stayed almost entirely in the Democratic camp. Whites were overwhelmingly Republican in their preferences. According to a Republican consultant, polls showed that only 1 percent of people voted for the candidate of the other race. Under these circumstances, Thompson was able to activate enough black voters to overcome a racial differential in turnout. Whites clearly were motivated to vote against Bennie Thompson. But blacks also turned out in substantial numbers, and Thompson ended up winning the election with a rather comfortable 55 percent of the vote.

Racial Politics in a Majority Black District

Race continues to dominate people's political thinking in the Delta, "the most southern place on Earth," according to a local politician. Outsiders are struck by it immediately. "Race here is like sex at a horny prep school. You can't have a conversation without discussing it," said a Washington political consultant working in the district. Those who live in the area, and especially those involved in Delta politics, are also well aware of it. It is, as various locals put it, an "obsession," a "preoccupation," an "albatross hanging around all our necks."

That race dominates politics in this territory is not terribly surprising.[24] One would most expect racial conflict to define political conflict in areas where blacks pose a numerical threat to the political dominance of whites (Huckfeldt and Kohfeld 1989). In fact, numerous studies provide evidence that racial conflict shapes whites' attitudes toward politics, above all in places where the black population is large and concentrated enough to ensure that blacks will be courted by politicians as an important constituency (Giles 1977; Giles and Evans 1986; Fossett and Kiecult 1989; Glaser 1994). The tradition of racial-line voting in this district, a tradition upheld in this election, further supports this theory and supports it with evidence of black political behavior as well as white. Precinct returns from the general election give some indication of how divided the electorate actually was. Thompson won overwhelmingly black precincts by overwhelming margins (374–4, 355–12, 516–6, 233–2); Dent won the largest white precinct 2484–87.

Assessing how group conflict shapes politics, however, involves more than simply looking at what people think or how votes fall. The virtue of this review of events in the Second District is that it illustrates the extent to which race pervades political strategy in places like the Delta. This is not to say that every election here is fought over racial issues, but rather that politicians continually seek to address concerns about group position and group power. Bennie Thompson's campaign was premised upon the right of blacks to be represented by a black. As the poster in his office declared, this election was "a power thing." Thompson also pointed to what he had done for his black constituents in the past and talked about what he would do for black people as their congressman. His oft-repeated line comparing the Republican to Colonel Sanders was only partly in jest. Dent, he argued, would not look out for their interests and indeed was hostile to them.

Much of Hayes Dent's campaign message was based upon the threat that Thompson posed to whites. The key to the campaign was not to build up Dent's positives, his connections to Fordyce, Cochran, and Dole, or his work in the Mississippi Department of Agriculture. Neither was his staff notably concerned about his negatives, his brushes with the law, or his inexperience. This campaign was about making sure whites understood what the election of Bennie Thompson meant to them. In the words of a Republican advisor, their goal was "to make Bennie the issue." They understood very well that cultivating the impression that Thompson was antiwhite would activate large numbers of white voters throughout the district.[25]

Democrats and Republicans Change Places

A recounting of events in this election gives some sense of what group conflict between blacks and whites looks like in the political arena. It breathes some life into the equations and the numbers that support this argument. But the importance of this chapter is not just to illustrate how racial conflict shapes politics in places like the Delta. From an analytical point of view, the value of this case history is also that it offers an excellent opportunity to test a central idea of this piece. As discussed in chapter 2, part of the point of this exercise is to show how political strategy is linked to the ratio of blacks to whites in a district. This case allows the most direct test of the proposition that racial balance is a determining factor in Democratic and Republican strategy. If the racial balance in a district tips the other way, with blacks representing a larger proportion of the electorate than whites, do the incentives for candidates to behave in certain ways reverse as well? Do candidates then approach the electorate differently?

The evidence from this election suggests that they do. These candidates did reverse roles in terms of their basic plans and their approaches to the black and white electorates. Bennie Thompson's campaign looks much like the Republican campaigns described above in its strategic plan. Just as Republicans in these other races made few overtures to the minority black population and ran racially based campaigns oriented toward a white audience, Bennie Thompson ran an unapologetic racial campaign oriented toward blacks and virtually ignored the white minority. This certainly is not the only way for a black Democrat to win in this district:

Mike Espy projects another model. Nonetheless, one of two mutually exclusive choices must be made. Black Democrats must either maximize the black vote and ignore the white vote or take a racially moderate approach and hope to put a coalition of blacks and whites together, as Mike Espy did. Thompson looked at the absence of white support for Espy in his first election and noted that the district had become more heavily black since the 1990 redistricting and chose the former, probably safer, course. It was a strategy to which he was better suited in any case.

Hayes Dent's campaign approached the election more like the Democratic campaigns than the Republican campaigns described in this book. Whereas Republicans in most of the above elections made little effort to court blacks, the Dent campaign did what it could, particularly given how little credibility it had in the black community. For one thing, Dent hired a black press secretary and gave him an enormous role in the campaign. The job was twofold. First, he became the other "front-man" for the campaign, appearing on the evening news if Dent did not, interacting with local print reporters, and visibly organizing Dent's appearances. Although he was the only black on the team, he represented the campaign's visible goal of biracial progress and harmony. College educated and refined, he was well received by whites, at least from the perspective of the campaign. Second, the press secretary served as the campaign's liaison to the black community. He was the one sent to meet with black groups, often by himself, to make the case for Hayes Dent. He had held a similar position in the successful Senate campaign of the Republican Paul Coverdell in Georgia in 1992 and, according to his boss, a Washington political consultant, had managed to help dampen the black vote, if not activate it behind the Republican. One difference between that race and this one, however, was that Coverdell ran against Wyche Fowler, a white Democratic incumbent who had less appeal to blacks than Bennie Thompson.

Dent too made a public effort to reach black voters, at least in his words. His attempts to claim the legacy of Mike Espy, his praise of Espy's approach to race relations and racial progress, his support of Mississippi Valley State in the controversy over the *Ayers* case, and his attempts to portray himself as a racial moderate were all part of a strategy to win the small proportion of middle-class black vote or devout Christian black vote that would provide him with a majority. Though Dent did little actual campaigning in the black community, his public message was conciliatory on the race issue.

Still, his campaign sought to activate whites by painting Bennie Thompson as a racial threat and certainly savored the prospect of running against him as opposed to Henry Espy for that very reason. "If we go against Bennie Thompson, we'll use scare tactics. Bennie Thompson won't get any of the white vote," said one of Dent's aides before the primary. This was, of course, the strategy they adopted. For all Dent's public statements of racial moderation, the Republicans did run a racial campaign. Like the Democratic campaigns described above, they had two messages: publicly claiming racial moderation while charging the opponent with extremism when they could.

The most important difference between Dent's strategy and that of the Democratic campaigns described above is that the Democrats were able to appeal more effectively to blacks and whites through separate channels. In the runoff, the Republicans attempted to establish relations with some important black leaders, notably Henry Espy and some of those who supported him. Their avenues to the black community, though, were too few and ineffective and their Bennie Thompson scare tactics too public. Lacking the ability to communicate separately, they were unlikely to cut into the majority black vote as the Democrats have been able to cut deeply into the white vote in majority white districts.

Like the Democratic races described above, the Republican campaign attempted to redefine the election on more favorable terms in its effort to win black votes. At an obvious disadvantage in a black-white election, they tried to reinterpret the race as a Delta versus Jackson election. Indeed, the other great advantage of running against Bennie Thompson instead of Henry Espy was that he was from the Jackson area. "This campaign is no longer about white and black or Democrat and Republican, it's about downtown Jackson and the Delta. That's who he wants to represent," Dent said at an airport rally. At every campaign stop, it was the Delta against the city, the problems of agriculture versus the problems of the cities, one of us or one of them. It was the tint given to every issue and event in the campaign. Dent's strategists even pointed out (time and again) that national Democratic figures visiting the Thompson campaign never even set foot in the district. And Robert Dole's visit to Greenville was planned with this in mind. Dole himself apologized for being an outsider but added that at least he had enough respect for the people of the Second to come into the district itself.

The irony of this Republican strategy is that the Delta had been split up in the 1970 redistricting so as to preserve white representation in all of Mississippi's five districts. It was put back together to create a majority black district in the 1980s, which makes Dent's redefinition of "us" and "them" so interesting. But the tactic held some possibility because the Delta is such a self-conscious and well-defined place, the type of place where outsiders could be resented.[26] This redefinition of the electorate was also without much risk because Jackson was Thompson's power base and because the area carved out of Jackson and added to the Second was almost entirely black. Dent had little to lose in attempting to attract some black votes from the Delta by painting the choice as city versus country and by tapping into resentment among blacks who supported other candidates in the first round. The hope was that these Delta voters, excluded by "the Jackson power brokers" in the caucus process or simply resenting Thompson's victory over their candidate, would support their cause.

Finally, like the Democrats described above, Dent tried to characterize himself as the local candidate, Bennie Thompson as the national candidate. He did his best to tie Thompson to President Clinton, who did not do well among Mississippi or Delta whites in the presidential election of 1992.[27] Campaigning with Robert Dole at the peak of a Republican filibuster of Clinton's economic stimulus plan, the less experienced candidate picked up some pointers on how to attack the administration as well as some good jokes.[28] Following Dole's lead, he attacked the plan as wasteful (all the more wasteful as it did nothing for the Delta) and full of pork. The president, his wife, and his economic stimulus plan became Dent's favorite targets for the remainder of the campaign. Had Dent run against Henry Espy, this would have been an even more important part of the Republican strategy because Espy did not pose as much of a racial threat as Thompson and because Espy's brother was in the administration.

Dent claimed to be not just an outsider to Washington, but an insider in the district, one who understood the local problems of the Delta far better than his opponent. He spoke of his unrelenting opposition to raising taxes and singled out an increased barge tax as an excellent example of how Clinton's tax proposals would hurt the area. Most important, he juxtaposed his agricultural experience with Thompson's. "My opponent just this week has discovered the meaning of the word *agriculture* and only at the urging of the National Democratic Party," he announced at a rally at the Stoneville Agricultural Research Center. He, on the other hand, had been intimately involved in shaping agricultural policy in the Fordyce administration.

In that Bennie Thompson highlighted his Democratic affiliation and his ability to "sit down with Clinton and make some sense," the patterns of the majority white districts appear to be reversed here as well. Bennie Thompson, like the Republicans described above, linked himself to the national party.[29] Thompson kept a local angle to his campaign, however, in making this national link. He spoke of how he intended to use his connections to "bring home the bacon," a rally cry not at the disposal of Republicans decrying the proliferation of pork. Thompson pulled his national message and his local message together as the Republicans described in the other cases were not able to do.

Moreover, Dent's attempt to raise local issues did not really put him in a position to woo the sizable number of black voters required to put him over the top. Although agriculture is a large part of the Delta's economy and identity, only 8 percent of the district's population work in "Agriculture, forestry, fisheries, and mining" (U.S. Bureau of the Census 1992), and that includes both blacks and whites. This is rather small compared to the percentage of people in the district who are on public assistance (20 percent) or who work in public sector jobs (22 percent), both heavily black local constituencies that Bennie Thompson courted. Dent's plan to make the local connection as forcefully as he could was smart but misguided because it was directed, for the most part, toward local whites and not local blacks.

The strategic considerations posed by the racial balance of the district and the particular circumstances under which the election was held were well understood by both campaigns. As a result, I would argue, this election followed the pattern described in the two previous chapters, but with a twist. The twist, of course, is that this election is a mirror image of the other elections. From a strategic perspective, Bennie Thompson pursued a southern Republican strategy. This is not to say that he articulated more racially conservative positions. Rather, he pursued a strategy that required maximizing the turnout of the majority race without attempting to build a racial bridge across the electorate. At the same time, it was the Republican who attempted to maximize his white base with racial rhetoric while reaching into the majority black vote with racially moderate appeals and a redefinition of the electorate. The difference, for Hayes Dent, was that he was not well positioned to do either of these things. And blacks were not very receptive to his message, which is generally a problem for southern Republicans.

6 Resolving the Puzzles

TO REPEAT THE WORDS OF V. O. Key with which I began this book, "In its grand outlines, the politics of the South revolves around the position of the Negro" (5). Perhaps the most intriguing element of this argument was that racial context profoundly influenced the course of southern politics. It was the concentration of blacks in a particular area that shaped white racial attitudes, political incentives to suppress black aspirations, and political dialogue in that area.

The South has undergone dramatic changes since Key analyzed the southern polity in 1949. But while the specifics are different, his argument is still compelling. Racial context continues to be a crucial variable in understanding southern politics, at least at the congressional level. In this book, I look at the relation of racial context to political strategy and

find that it remains quite strong. Both Democratic and Republican political strategy are sensitive to racial context, and to a marked degree. The
result is that the interplay of political campaigns in heavily black areas of
the South is still predictably different from what it is in areas of smaller
black concentrations.

I hypothesize in chapter 2, for instance, that Republicans, as members
of the racially conservative party dependent on white votes, are more
likely to introduce racial issues into a campaign in which blacks are more
numerous in a district. These are the places where the political attitudes
related to racial conflict are most likely to be evoked. The political rationale is that racial issues, particularly those that evoke group or racial
conflict, are most likely to rally whites and to maximize the Republican
share of the white vote. Democrats also should adjust their strategy to
the racial balance in the district. Where blacks comprise a larger share of
the population and make a potentially large contribution to victory, Democrats will focus on boosting black turnout levels, even to the point of
risking some white votes. Where blacks are less numerous, the major
focus should turn to taking a larger share of the white vote.

Although the small number of cases in this study compel one to draw
cautious conclusions, clearly these expectations have been met. In Mississippi 4, Alabama 3, and Virginia 5, those majority-white districts where
blacks made up a large proportion of the population, racial issues became
central to the Republican campaign. In an effort to unify white voters, Republican campaigns introduced racial issues into the political exchange.
By talking about the extension of the Voting Rights Act, *Grove City*, the
Confederate flag, and vote buying in the black community, they made
direct and none-too-subtle appeals to white voters. In Mississippi 5 and
Texas 1, where blacks represented only about one in five people, racial
issues were not used to win white votes, and other conservative themes
were tapped instead.

Republicans did have a strategy vis-à-vis blacks in these two congressional districts, however, and racial issues were part of it. While
neither Tom Anderson nor Edd Hargett made an effort to court blacks,
both had a message directed at black voters that their colleagues in the

heavily black districts did not. The message was designed to encourage blacks to "sleep in" by making their Democratic opponent look bad or by confusing the election. The major racial issues in these Republican campaigns, Reverend Appleberry's charge that Gene Taylor was unsympathetic to blacks in Mississippi 5 and the Voting Rights controversy in Texas 1, were employed not to sell the Republican to whites but to weaken the Democrat in the eyes of the black community. Trying to make the Democrat unappealing with racial issues was not a feasible strategy in the more heavily black districts, where Republican racial conservatism designed to win white votes also activated blacks for the Democrat. Skirmishing over the black vote in less black districts was thus very different than in heavily black districts.

Democratic campaign strategy varied with changes in racial balance as well. Wayne Dowdy, in heavily black Mississippi 4, strategically courted black votes and spent inordinate resources to reach and activate them. Gene Taylor, in a neighboring Mississippi district with far fewer blacks, made only modest efforts to attract black voters, devoting scarce resources, time, and energy to winning a larger share of the white vote. The other campaigns in the majority white districts fell between these two, though none of these Democrats appealed to black votes so publicly as to jeopardize their chance to win white votes. And it was not just the relative attention Democrats paid to blacks as opposed to whites that varied in these districts, but also the tenor of their campaigns, the risks they were willing to take, and the severity of their message. Wayne Dowdy highlighted the threat to the Voting Rights Act in his campaign in order to outrage and inflame black voters and to maximize black turnout (though he still did it through separate channels to black voters). Gene Taylor's message to blacks was not much different from his message to whites. These differences, of course, were partly a function of the ammunition provided to them by their opponents' campaigns. Nonetheless, it is again clear that the dynamic of the campaign in black communities varied with change in the racial context of the election.

The election in the majority black district also fits well into this scheme. As I hypothesized, the Democratic and Republican campaigns reversed strategic places in Mississippi 2. The Democratic campaign, in this 58 percent black district, spurned coalitional politics to generate excitement among blacks, to maximize the black vote and their portion of it. The white Republican attempted to forge a racial coalition, however fruitless the task appears to have been in retrospect. Looked at together, these special elections do reveal a pattern that illustrates how racial context determines the course of southern elections. The dynamic of the campaign, premised both on the original strategies of the two camps and the responses to these strategies by their opponents, was closely tied to racial balance in the district.

Demonstrating this, however, is only one purpose of this book. The philosophy guiding this research strategy is that understanding the political strategies of candidates, that is, understanding the context of the vote choice, gives insight into the results of elections. This is not an ironclad explanation for why Democrats have been congressionally successful. There are other important explanations to consider (see below). Still, I argue here that given the strategies pursued by congressional Democrats and Republicans, Democrats have had an advantage in a great many southern districts. It is this argument that guides my contribution to the resolution of the southern realignment puzzles.

Understanding Mixed Republican Success

The evidence that more and more southerners are calling themselves Republican is irrefutable. Yet this phenomenon has been very slow to translate into electoral success below the presidential level. Why have Republican presidential candidates so dominated, while prior to 1994 Republican congressional candidates have had only limited success? Why have Republican presidential candidates been able to take advantage of a strong conservative bent in southern public opinion while southern congressional Republicans have not? Why has a partisan connection to popular presidents not been worth more? Finally, if race is so potent a force in the South, why has the "filtering down" realignment process been so slow? By all accounts, it should have occurred as Republicans up and down the ticket benefited from being associated with the racially conservative party.

The reasons for mixed Republican success are complex and multifaceted, and it is worth reviewing them first before proceeding to my explanation. One aspect of the GOP problem is perfectly evident. Simply put, it takes time to build a party. The Republican party in the South started from nothing in the early 1960s, and many compelling explanations for the lack of Republican local and congressional success start with the very problems of building a party upon the foundation of presidential victories. "Ever try to build a pyramid from the top down?" asked one Republican campaign manager in explaining his party's fortunes in the region. The problems that vex Republican party leaders have been problems of doing just that.

For one thing, the choices that the Republicans have been able to offer southern voters simply have not been as good as those offered the Democrats. It takes more than having the right message. The right messenger must deliver it. As a general proposition, Democratic candidates have been stronger than Republican candidates. In some measure the Republicans have had a recruiting problem that Democrats did not. And the problem is self-perpetuating, for without Republicans at the lowest local and county offices, there has been no political—or electoral—training ground. In the cases studied here, the Democrats recruited stronger politicians with low-level "seasoning," candidates who had more experience at the local and state level, who had run for office before and had a sense of what it took to succeed, and who enjoyed name recognition within at least some portion of the congressional district. The Republican candidates, though able to raise money and campaign effectively, generally had shorter political resumes and less electoral experience.

A rather ironic aspect of this problem is that in the absence of some evidence of Republican success, capable conservative candidates have stayed Democratic in low-level elections. Republican party officials claim to have difficulty convincing even ideologically appropriate people to run under their banner for low-level offices. A Republican party official in

Mississippi told of bumping into a woman he had convinced to run for a local office in one Delta county. When she told him she had won, he was delighted. His pleasure was short-lived though because she had run as a Democrat. "Otherwise I wouldn't have had a chance to win," she explained. Perhaps, as Alan Ehrenhalt argues, it has been more difficult all over the United States for Republicans to recruit viable candidates for low-level offices, but it has been particularly a problem in the South. Yet there are indications of change. As recently as the early 1970s, said an official of the South Carolina Republican party, "we really had to scrape the bottom of the, um, to look everywhere to find candidates. Now we're holding competitive primaries. It's a real sign that we're healthy." Still, he and Republican party officials carry an underdog mentality when talking about recruitment.

This comment raises another recruitment problem that Republican party builders have faced. Over the time Republicans have been winning presidential contests in the South, they still have been much less likely to hold competitive low-level primaries than Democrats (Thielemann 1992, 129). Some analysts argue that intraparty competition is important to a party's health. Competition leads voters to gain an early awareness of candidates and issues and leads candidates to cultivate relations with groups of voters (Sorauf 1984). In evolutionary terms, it also may be argued that competitive situations lead to the success of candidates who develop more "adaptive" messages and characteristics. That is, running in a primary may help successful candidates to identify what works best in the district. Most important to the puzzle at hand, competitive primaries may give southerners a reason to abandon a Democratic affiliation reinforced in Democratic party primaries, which are much more likely to be competitive and thus meaningful. "The lack of primary competition means that southern voters instinctively think of themselves as Democrats below the presidential level and the GOP gives them little reason to change their minds," writes Gregory Thielemann on the Republican "stall" in Congress (1992, 127; see also Jewell and Olson 1988). In this argument, Republican party competition thus would break the last tenuous connections to the Democratic party and presumably allow many to overcome a last psychological hurdle to voting Republican in congressional and local elections. Although Thielemann's empirical demonstration of this point is unconvincing, Republicans certainly will benefit at every electoral level when they fully break the impression that the only meaningful participation in party affairs is within the Democratic party.

Yet intraparty competition has its disadvantages. Candidates must devote resources to winning primaries, resources that can be used to win general campaigns. Primary battles also bring out negative material that can be used by a general election opponent. And they may lead to bitterness between candidates that is difficult to repair and may cause problems for the victor. Glen Browder, for one, argued that his hard-fought first primary victory over a well-financed competitor with a sizable following made the ensuing campaigns quite challenging: "The question was, could I rebuild a base that had fragmented?" Mending relations with the losers became an important priority for the Alabama Democrat. Intraparty competition is thus a mixed blessing. What Republican party competition really reveals is that strategic politicians are increasingly recognizing that the Republican label is no longer the liability that it once was. From this perspective, what primary competition exists in the South is more a by-product of Republican growth than a cause of it, and situations like that in South Carolina indicate that the Republican recruitment problem is easing.

Harold Stanley (1992) points out a related Republican recruitment problem, one that has the added virtue of helping to explain the mixed-results phenomenon in the South. Having lots of opportunity for upward mobility and with fewer entrenched Republican incumbents, notes Stanley, the most successful Republican representatives have been more likely to leave the House and run for higher office than Democratic representatives. A count of retirements from the House between 1968 and 1992 shows this to be the case. Three-quarters (76 percent) of Republican retirees, but only one-quarter (26 percent) of Democrats, left the House to pursue another political opportunity (usually a Senate seat or a governorship). Congressional representatives are often the best candidates the Republicans have to offer in statewide races, and they frequently win. But this poses a problem at lower levels as Republicans have had to constantly replenish the lower ranks, which brings one back to the problems the party has had in recruiting high-quality candidates. This argument gives some insight into why the realignment has worked its way from high- to low-level offices. It does not, however, explain why this process has been so slow and difficult for the Republican party. For if it had been disadvantageous to run as a Democrat over this time, politicians would have flocked to the Republican party. The question remains, why have Democrats been perceived to be at such an advantage?

It is not just recruitment problems that Republicans suffer from. There are other problems with trying to build the pyramid from the top. Democrats have long controlled a large majority of county courthouses throughout the South, and this has given them another great advantage. The large number of Democratic mayors and sheriffs and judges affords Democratic candidates a strong, ready-made network of opinion leaders and important local officials. These networks, built on loyalty and patronage as well as a common affiliation, provide the basis for a campaign organization. Indeed the organizations of several of these Democrats were stocked with people, officials and citizens, who had some direct interest in a Democratic victory. The white organizer of a Bennie Thompson rally in the Mississippi Delta explained, "We just try to keep everything Democratic around here." He added, smiling, "We're in the construction business. That speaks for itself." The strength of the Democratic networks was noteworthy next to the weaker Republican networks, which had much less to bind them together. Linda Arey and John Rice, in particular, complained vociferously about the lack of support they received from local Republicans.

Democrats have in addition controlled electoral machinery throughout the region, which can be a great resource for keeping power, as has been demonstrated repeatedly throughout southern history. Although there is some check on election officials in the Voting Rights Act, they still make many decisions of importance. Consider the decisions of the election officials in the three Republican-controlled counties in Mississippi's Fourth District. These officials changed the order of the candidates' names on the ballot with the almost certain intent of confusing illiterate and uneducated (and most likely black Democratic) voters. It is no coincidence that these were the only counties that did not use alphabetical order on the ballot: all the other counties in the district were run by Democrats. The incident illustrates only one possibility offered by Republican control of electoral machinery, and a small one at that. But in a place where there is great concern about poll operations, ballot security, and vote counting, Democratic control of the county courthouses has made a big difference.

Given their reduced presence in the state legislatures, the Republicans also have not had much say in the drawing of district lines. Although Republicans have controlled statehouses in several southern states, in the early 1990s, while redistricting was going on, they held only four of them. This, of course, compounded the Republicans' difficulty in contributing to the line-drawing process. Redistricting can offer a growing minority party the opportunity to grow further, but unless a critical mass of state legislators is achieved, the process simply perpetuates partisan imbalance. Holding only a bit over one-quarter of all southern state legislative seats in 1990, Republicans were unable to realize that critical mass. As Republicans continue to make gains in state legislatures, this should change.

Even in 1990, though, there was a vehicle for Republican advantage in redistricting—ironically, the Voting Rights Act. Finding themselves allied with black Democrats, Republicans were greatly advantaged by the creation of additional majority black districts in several states. When heavily black areas were cut from several districts, many white Democrats lost their strategic advantage. It is not surprising that in 1992, black Democrats and white Republicans won contiguous districts in Alabama, Georgia, and South Carolina while white Democrats lost those seats. In 1994, several other Republicans claimed seats in the more heavily white districts created with majority black districts after 1990. The new districts explain part of the reason for recent Republican breakthroughs in the South. Republican presidential candidates were winning big in the old districts, however. District lines are thus not the only explanation for the lack of Republican progress in the Reagan-Bush years.

Of course, there may in fact be a relation between Republican success at the presidential level and Democratic success at the congressional level. Republicans have made their largest gains since 1964 in midterms during Democratic administrations. In 1966, 1978, and 1994, years in which southern Democrats were least able to "denationalize" their local elections, Republicans reached new plateaus of success. Where southern Democrats can run on their own game plan, proven through time to be effective, they have an advantage. I have attempted here to illustrate this advantage. With a Democrat in the White House, they lose this control. The slow filtering down of the realignment ironically may be a function of Republicans' doing so well in the presidential elections. It is nonetheless worth understanding how Democrats have prolonged their local advantage for so long.

Finally, in the days of total Democratic dominance, the Republican party was a totally impotent force in the South. Key (1946) describes Republican party leaders as politically naive and ineffective. They were interested in doling out a little patronage from the national party or in interacting with national politicians but had "only the foggiest notion where the Republican voters in the state live[d]" and "[were] overwhelmed by the futility of it all" (293). Their legacy has been devastating. Given that the party was so immature at the beginning and has worked under such a disadvantage to the Democrats, many argue that it is little wonder that a full realignment has yet to take place. Simply put, there is a strong line of argument that given the huge obstacles, all described here, it just has taken time for change to occur.

Still, the first major Republican gains occurred several decades ago, and since that time the party has almost completely dominated in presidential contests in the South and has won a share of Senate and gubernatorial contests. Add to this the advantage that race has given the GOP, and it is astounding that the forces of the past continue to make themselves felt. Other realignments have filtered down in much less time than this. Large numbers of Republican candidates in the 1850s and Democratic candidates in the 1930s, to take the two best examples of previous large-scale realignments, were elected within a few years of the large shifts in mass partisanship (Sundquist 1983, 92–98, 214). As an explanation of the southern Republican condition, the argument that it just takes time for a party to mature begs the question, why so long?

Understanding the presidential-congressional dichotomy requires analysis of the dynamics of both presidential elections and other elections. The nature of the choice is so different in these two sets of elections that it is not surprising there has been dramatic variation in Republican success. Republican presidential candidates have been able to stake a claim to the right half of the political spectrum without being crowded by their Democratic counterparts. Democratic nominees, emerging from a series of primaries and caucuses increasingly dominated by issue activists, have had to pass the liberal litmus tests of many of the Democrats' constituent groups. Although these candidates (with the exception of Carter and Clinton, northern liberals) have attempted to moderate their views during the general election, they have had few conservative credentials. Attempts to present themselves as moderate or to downplay ideological differences (such as Michael Dukakis's claim, "This is an election over competence, not ideology") were hard to accept and often futile. The choice at the presidential level has been clear-cut: A conservative faces a liberal. In the South, this is little choice.

This is not to say that race has had nothing to do with Republican success at the presidential level. Some contend that Republican tactics in recent campaigns were designed to tug at racist or racially conservative attitudes. The Republican Willie Horton television commercial in the presidential race of 1988 is a case in point. Many Democrats attacked this advertisement as a thinly disguised racial appeal. "If you were going to run a campaign of fear and smear and appeal to racial hatred you could not have picked a better case to use than this one," said Dukakis's campaign manager, Susan Estrich (Jamieson 1992, 474). In the postmortem of the election, some academic consensus has formed around the conclusion that "the Bush campaign trafficked in racially loaded stereotypes" in its use of the furlough issue (Kinder et al. 1989, 14; see also Woodward 1988; Pomper 1989; Black and Black 1992). More broadly, the Republican law and order message and Republican complaints about welfare abuse and wasteful social programs are seen through this prism (Sears and McConahey 1973; Kinder et al. 1989; Gilens 1990; Edsall and Edsall 1991). This is not to say that Democrats have not employed some of the same themes in their campaigns. But generally they have been in greater evidence in Republican presidential campaigns and party platforms.

Whether or not these appeals are racial in intention or in effect or both, I argue that the choices in recent presidential elections, in those elections since Barry Goldwater broke through in the Solid South, have been ideologically stark enough that race simply has not mattered much. There in fact may be some racial appeal to conservatism (that is the basis of another book), but when faced with a conservative and a liberal, white southerners have taken the conservative, the Republican, time after time.[1]

Southern congressional elections, however, have been different. The ideological choices offered there have not been as stark. For the most part, Democratic candidates have not paid homage to liberal constituencies. They have usually been more liberal than their Republican opponents, but not markedly so and not dangerously so. Southern Democrats have often been indistinguishable from southern Republicans on social issues like abortion and capital punishment, on defense issues, and on patriotism issues. They have presented themselves as probusiness, anti-tax fiscal conservatives. They have differed from their Republican opponents, to be sure, but the differences have been a matter of degree, not of kind. In southern congressional elections, Democrats have generally been moderate-to-conservative, which likely has blunted the effectiveness of the inevitable Republican charge that Democrats are too liberal.

There are several reasons to believe that Democratic congressional candidates have even been at an advantage in these elections. Ironically, Republican congressional candidates in the South, like some Republicans throughout the country, occasionally have been hampered by ideology (Barnes 1988). Democrats are philosophically consistent when they portray themselves as better able to serve the district. On the other hand, the doctrinaire conservative policy stands of Republican congressional candidates, the same ones that have served Republican presidential candidates so well, often have conflicted with the need to promise local benefits or to fight for protected markets, to name the most important examples. Such conflicts certainly make a difference in congressional elections. Indeed, Gary Jacobson (1990) attributes mixed national electoral results to differences in what voters find attractive in presidential and congressional candidates. He offers evidence that presidential candidates are evaluated according to their views on national policy while congressional candidates are evaluated on their ability to defend their district from the repercussions of that national policy. Although this is not just a regional phenomenon, the South, with its strong support of both Republican presidents and Democratic congressional candidates, has been contributing more than its share to what Jacobson seeks to explain.

In addition to their heavy use of local issues, southern Democrats have relied on an important feature of their districts to win elections. Many congressional districts in the South have large black populations. Blacks comprise 17 percent of the South's population, and, in the Deep South above all, there are large enough concentrations of blacks in most districts to give the Democrats a decided advantage. It is an advantage that Democrats must use carefully, and here is where racial issues have carried importance.

In a great many elections in the South, racial issues are raised. Racial issues do not automatically win elections for Republicans, however. In fact, oftentimes they damage Republican chances. The key to understanding this paradox lies in how the issue gets played out in the campaign. While Republicans raise the issue, Democrats often do not respond in public. If they do respond, it is in moderate tones, perhaps expressing their support for the racially liberal position but not vocally and not to the extreme. In the black communities, however, these issues play well. Democrats use the issue handed to them by their opponent in front of black audiences, in commercials on black media, and in direct mail to black neighborhoods. It is the segregated nature of many aspects of southern life that has allowed this strategy to work. Democrats can make strong appeals to blacks without losing the moderate or even the conservative white support they initially have because whites, for the most part, do not hear these appeals. So long as the Democratic candidate does not appear to spearhead black causes, he or she does not put significant white support at risk.

Democrats have been advantaged further in implementing this process because black political leaders do not expect white Democrats to be vocal advocates of black political interests. Black leaders give white Democrats considerable leeway in negotiating their tricky course. As an important official in the Alabama Democratic Conference put it, white candidates were not held to a litmus test on black issues. His organization understood the constraints that white Democrats operated under and took a pragmatic view of their campaign behavior. A black leader from Virginia also voiced this opinion, "[L. F. Payne] didn't have to come across as some big liberal on our issues [to get our support]. We knew he had to walk a tightrope. We knew that he had to maintain a core constituency." This freedom to deal with the sensitive issues of race quietly has enabled white Democrats to combine enough of the white vote with a heavy and monolithic black vote.

Democrats have won congressional elections because they take advantage of heavy support from blacks without risking a large proportion of their white support. Republicans have won congressional elections in the region, but many of their victories in the 1970s, 1980s, and early 1990s were in the traditionally Republican hill country of Tennessee, Arkansas, and North Carolina, the growing areas of Florida, and the affluent suburbs of the larger cities, places with fewer blacks than those required to make a biracial coalition viable. Throughout the rest of the region, local Democrats continued to win open seat competitive elections in the Reagan-Bush years. The racial composition of their districts and the strategies by which they pursue two separate communities have made this possible. If they are to continue to win in a very uncertain future, they must continue to to forge a racial coalition.

The Republican Future

This book is really devoted to what Democrats have done right in the South in the post–civil rights era. Analysts have been predicting for decades that the Democrats would fall, that ultimately the Republicans would break through and win at lower political levels as they have at the presidential level (Sundquist 1983; Stanley 1987; Bullock 1988b), yet Democrats have survived long odds. What of the future? How much longer can the Democrats hold out? Their dominance in the South has faded. With the 1994 elections, Democrats lost significant ground. Although they still dominate state legislatures, even this advantage has been eroding. The Republican future is bright, yet one cannot count southern Democrats out yet. Their remarkable success over the past thirty years, their winning formulas, show how adaptable they are to new circumstances. That in the 1994 House elections, 89 percent of southern Democratic incumbents retained their seats while only 83 percent of non-southern Democratic incumbents did so is some indication of their ability to weather a storm that raged against Democrats across the country.

The question thus becomes, what must Republicans do to achieve full-scale realignment. What are they doing right? What must they continue to do? What strategies hold the greatest potential for electoral payoff? This analysis offers some clues.

One possibility for further Republican growth involves Democratic politicians switching sides either in a slow trickle or en masse. The task of Republican party leaders is to make conversion attractive and to court young, conservative Democrats. Every so often the Republicans score a big coup when a congressional incumbent like Phil Gramm or Andy Ireland of Florida switches parties and is reelected as a Republican. This, however, has been a relatively rare event, and the contention here is that Republicans should be directing their attention to low-level officials, those holding the types of offices that have eluded the party. The key is to identify young, upwardly mobile politicians whose paths are blocked by senior Democrats and whose prospects improve in less crowded and less competitive Republican primaries. What the Republicans have to offer is a less cluttered career ladder. For someone willing to take the risk, there is more opportunity to achieve quickly in the Republican party in the South. Although not likely to carry large numbers of followers with them, these young politicians will improve the Republican pool of candidates, which will in turn improve the party's fortunes in the long run.

The other great advantage of converting Democratic elites is that with every conversion, the stigma carried by a Republican affiliation is broken down further. Conversion generates legitimacy for the party. When a high-profile individual makes the change, it helps dispel the idea that Republicans cannot win. That idea has been a very damaging one over the decades, and each switch makes it more likely that others will reassess the electoral consequences of doing the same.[2] Indeed, with a high-profile convert like Richard Shelby and a large number of new southern Republicans in the House and Senate in 1994, the perception may now be that the Republican label is advantageous, and this probably will lead other Democratic elites to follow suit. With each defection, with each loss of a seat, the remaining conservative Democrats also lose some cover, some comfort in their numbers, some sense of being a meaningful minority in the national party. This could inspire further defections.

Republicans have been able to convert some Democratic officeholders and other potential Democratic candidates.[3] This obviously has contributed to the growth of the party. But Republican candidates, whether they started out as Democrats or not, need to have winning campaign strategies. John Rice's campaign in Alabama (see chapter 3), shows that Democrats-turned-Republican have not necessarily been ready to run winning campaigns.

If there is a key to southern Republicans reaching dominance in upcoming years, it may be in directing their attention to the black vote in one of two ways. First, Republicans would benefit from breaking the Democratic lock on the black vote. A second possibility may be to "deracialize" their campaigns. On the first point, as is apparent from some of the cases discussed above, southern Republican strategists, even in areas where blacks do not comprise a majority, are beginning to recognize that some black votes may help Republicans win close contests. Even 20 percent of the black vote can make the difference between victory and defeat (see table 2.2).

It has taken a change in Republican leadership for this idea to be considered in party strategy. The first post–civil rights generation of leadership had no desire to direct appeals toward blacks. Nor did they think it was necessary. Their party was building, after all, on the defections of racially motivated southern whites. After nearly thirty years of stunted Republican growth at low levels, a new generation of pragmatists has begun to rethink party strategy. An Alabama campaign manager put it bluntly: "The old breed said, 'Fuck 'em. Don't pander to 'em.' We can't afford to take that attitude anymore. We want to win elections, and the reality of the situation is that we've got to win over black independents." Others, notably the late national Republican party chairman Lee Atwater, have spoken publicly about the importance of cutting into the overwhelming Democratic advantage among blacks.

If some Republican strategists now believe that the party must, in the words of a Mississippi party official, "be evangelical to blacks," they are not fully certain about how this is to be done. A Washington-based Republican consultant discussed the problem faced by the southern wing of the party: "Southern Republicans genuinely want racial harmony. And they want to do something for blacks. But they don't really know what to do." The stated desire "to do something for blacks," of course, has a certain paternalistic ring to it, but it illustrates his point well.

Part of the problem may be that many southern Republicans believe that they have a legitimate claim to at least some of the black vote, a claim that blacks do not appear to recognize. They argue that their party has been more supportive of civil rights and black progress than is commonly believed and that the Republican party was instrumental in the passage of civil rights legislation. "We cast the tough votes," said Linda Arey, arguing that historically the Republicans were the racially liberal party. Moreover, this argument goes, the Democrats, the party of segregationists, have "gotten a free ride." Complained a longtime Republican leader in Mississippi, "We had a window of opportunity in '69–'70 when blacks were grateful. I assumed they were very grateful, but they weren't grateful enough for all that we had done." He went on, "Since then, we've taken a bum rap. Sure race has been a factor in our growth but not how the liberals portray it. By the time we got on the scene, the battle was over. The Citizens' Councils, almost to a man, their leadership was Democratic. By the time we came on the scene, no one would believe you if you said, 'We gonna save you from desegregation.'" It was not that he is wrong here, but through the past two decades southern Republicans have been unable to balance this message with their appeals to whites, a finesse that requires more than just an appeal to the past.

How might southern Republicans appeal to blacks? Recruitment of black candidates is one way to break the notion that there is no room for blacks in the party. Several Republican officials talked about this as a development and noted that a few candidates were being groomed. Indeed, in Oklahoma, considered by some as having a southern political culture, a black Republican, J. C. Watts, was elected in 1994. In more heavily black places, though, such candidates invariably will be characterized as Uncle Toms, alienating rank-and-file blacks instead of attracting them to the Republican camp. Bennie Thompson's effective campaign against Henry Espy in the Mississippi 2 primary suggests that this is always a possibility.

In addition, Republicans have sought to appeal to the sentiment, either already held or easily evoked, that blacks as a group would benefit by having their votes competed for. "It would be good for blacks, the country, and the Republicans if blacks became competitive," said a resentful Republican political consultant. "The Democrats could nominate David Duke and get all the black vote." The strategy now appears to be to approach black opinion leaders who hold this sentiment and have them carry the message into the black communities. In the Mississippi Gulf Coast election, for example, the Republican campaign located a black minister from a neighboring congressional district who was unhappy with the Democratic candidate's votes in the state legislature and wished to call him to task. While this minister claimed to be a Democrat, he felt that the Democrats needed to be more accountable to the black community. "The only time they come to us is when they're running for office. We wanted to let Gene Taylor know that there's a segment out there not to forget. That's the reason we threw a little potshot at him," said the minister. He added, "Those people [the Democrats] are just usin' us to perfection."

Some Republicans assert that a number of their standard nonracial themes that work well among whites could be directed effectively toward black independents and middle-class black voters. Believing that some blacks would be receptive to "the gospel of individual initiative" and to free enterprise, antiregulation, antigovernment rhetoric, Republicans have attempted to carry this message to black audiences. Hayes Dent argued at several points throughout his campaign that the black middle class had made more progress in the 1980s than any other group in American society. "That doesn't totally absolve Ronald Reagan and George Bush," he backtracked, "but they did provide opportunity to blacks." He believed, even in retrospect, that 15 to 20 percent of the black vote could be won with the "uncomfortable" message, "You shouldn't rely on the government." Specific issues like opposing a rise in the minimum wage and welfare reform were taken to audiences of black businesspeople in Alabama and Mississippi in hope of cutting into solid Democratic support. This is possible. Both of Mississippi's senators, Thad Cochran and Trent Lott, have won portions of the black vote in their Senate races by tenaciously building a small network of black supporters. Their success in building that network has come over time, though, and southern Republicans running for Congress, at least those in this sample, have not successfully courted blacks with their conservative message.

Finally, there is some evidence that Republicans have tried to buy the support of black ministers and other black leaders in attempts to divide the black vote or at least to discourage the idea (among blacks) that their leadership is so unanimously behind the Democrats. Either by contributions to black churches or by making direct payments to individuals, the Republicans have made efforts to reach black leaders with money. One Republican campaign manager told of several instances in which Republicans had solicited black ministers in their campaigns. His most vivid example of vote buying involved a campaign official who, not trusting his new allies to deliver their congregations, gave them only half the promised money up front: "It was literally half the money 'cause he took a paper cutter out and sliced all those bills in half. Man, their eyes were about poppin' out of their head."

A second grand Republican strategy vis-à-vis blacks would direct itself not to attracting blacks to the party, but to demobilizing them. As things stand, Republicans recognize that, Lott and Cochran notwithstanding, they have little to no support from the black community. Even campaigning in the black community appears to be fruitless to Republican candidates, which is a source of great frustration. Linda Arey's comment that, even after marching in a Martin Luther King Day parade, she had only enough black votes "to fill five phone booths" illustrates this point. She believed that her public support of the parade, moreover, was part of the reason she lost so much of the white vote in Danville. John Rice argued that it did not really matter what he did, there was no way he could win any black votes: "It all came down to, 'Are you willing to lay money on the table?' . . . We went into Hobson City, a 100 percent black town, and had a blast. Played basketball. Had a parade in the downtown. A barbecue. I got no votes out of that town. My philosophy and my voting record were out the window. Meant nothing." The public opinion polls and electoral statistics show that Rice was right. He did not get any support from blacks in his election, and he was probably correct in his belief that such support was not possible. Many southern Republicans have been unable to win black votes within the confines of their present electoral strategy. Their message to whites has been incompatible with a message that would be appealing to blacks.[4] Moreover, in reaching whites, they are heard by blacks.

Perhaps because of this reality or because of the Republican perception of this reality, previous efforts to demobilize blacks have had a "low road" quality to them. Twenty-five years after the civil rights movement, there are still accusations that Republicans attempt to discourage black voters by intimidation and deceit. Most commonly, it is charged that the Republicans place people or threatening signs (offering rewards for those documenting voter fraud) outside black precincts to scare off prospective voters. Black leaders have become increasingly vigilant and active in responding to these tactics, a Texas state legislator threatening even to send out "big, black and burly" ex-convicts to watch Republican poll watchers being sent to minority precincts in a coordinated campaign (Davidson 1990, 236). Still, it is clear that these programs help keep the black vote down and that some Republicans continue to engage in them.

This is not to say that Republicans are the only ones responsible for fraud and intimidation. They, in fact, respond that the Democrats violate election rules so frequently that it has become necessary to station observers at the polls, particularly in black precincts. Their list of such violations is long and varied, and many southern Republicans vehemently defend their right to try to keep fraud in check, notably in those areas where they expect to do worst. Perhaps most important here is that the accusations from both sides relate to how the parties treat the black vote. This, of course, says much about how southern politics has changed as well as how it has stayed the same.

Although intimidation may in fact work, it is problematic in many ways. And it is surely not a tactic upon which to build a party. A more attractive route for dealing with the black electorate may be to deracialize the Republican campaign. If the campaigns described in this book are any indication, introducing race into the campaign introduces a problem. It mobilizes the opponent's base. It also relieves a white opponent of having to make an affirmative case for himself or herself before the black electorate. As I have noted, the racial issue offers the Democrat a vehicle through which to approach black voters.

Racial conflict has without doubt brought many southern white voters into the Republican party. Race issues have taken the party from nothing to something (and something substantial). Republican candidates have continued to rely on them. I argue that at this point, perhaps racial appeals are counterproductive, especially in places with large black populations. The racial balance in many districts in the South has led Republicans to believe that generating group conflict is to their benefit, and herein lies part of the pattern of campaign behavior illustrated in this book. The ability of Democrats to turn these racial appeals around in the black community and to overcome them with a large enough minority of white voters to win indicates that Republicans may benefit when they adjust their perceptions of the costs and benefits of racial issues. Having other conservative populist themes in their quiver, Republicans, I argue, could abandon racial issues with little cost.

It is certainly not time to read the Democratic party its last rites in the South. The Solid South has given way to a decidedly two-party system. The Republican party has been invigorated. Yet even as a majority of whites have turned Republican, southern Democrats have continued to win much more than their share of congressional elections by sticking to a formula that has kept them on top in recent decades.

What is ultimately remarkable is that the Democrats in the South have a long history of survival and dominance. At the turn of the century, Democrats were challenged by a surging populist party and were able to beat back that challenge with Jim Crow laws and virulent racial rhetoric. What is more, they established a system of politics that they completely dominated for almost six decades.

In the past several decades, Democrats have again survived a challenge to their superiority. This time, they did not have much in their favor except perhaps a little momentum from the past. With the Republicans holding the race card that Democrats had played successfully throughout the previous regime and holding a conservative advantage in public opinion, Democrats have had to manage to survive in a hostile new political world. Through tough times, their dominoes remained standing.

In hindsight, 1994 may be viewed as marking a transition to a new era in southern politics. If this is the case, the thirty years following the Voting Rights Act constitute a period in southern political history marked by a surprisingly resistant and resilient Democratic party, a period in which race continued to matter in southern politics and matter a lot, but not in the way most expected it to. The lessons here are thus analytical as well as political. Race, racial issues, racial conflict may affect political thought and behavior in some predictable ways, yet not yield predictable electoral results. It is by looking at political campaigns, at the context within which political choices are made, that such choices make more sense.

Notes

Chapter 1 The Puzzles of the Southern Realignment

1 The South is defined by Key and many other analysts of southern politics as the eleven states of the former Confederacy: Alabama, Arkansas, Florida, Georgia, Louisiana, Mississippi, North Carolina, South Carolina, Tennessee, Texas, and Virginia. This is how I define the region as well. The South covers a large area, one that is geographically, demographically, and politically diverse. Much of what is to follow is an analysis of "the politics of the South." As such, it highlights what is common to the various parts of the region and downplays some intraregional differences. This is not to say that such differences do not exist, only that they do not fall within the scope of this research.

2 The black belt is a wide strip of rich land that runs across the Deep South. It is the part of the South where plantation agriculture was most practiced and slaves were most relied upon. It is, to this day, the area with the heaviest nonurban concentration of blacks in the South.

3 Like Democratic dominance in the region, Republican success in hill country also

goes back to events of the Civil War. These areas were not suited to plantation agriculture, and the poor white farmers who lived there generally did not own slaves and were unwilling to join the Confederacy in the Civil War. This area comprises eastern Tennessee and western North Carolina and Virginia.

4 Neither of them was that much of an exception when it came to the use of race in their campaigns. Long, writes his biographer, "more frequently than has been supposed, [did] indulge in race baiting. He never did it very well, however, and obviously did not enjoy doing it when he felt . . . that he had to" (Williams 1969, 327–28; see also Brinkley 1982; Hair 1991). Watson abandoned his populist goal of a black-white coalition and supported the disenfranchisement of blacks when it became apparent that this was politically necessary (Woodward 1938, 370–72).

5 The data for this exercise come from the American National Election Studies and were made available by the Inter-University Consortium of Political and Social Research through the archive at U.C. DATA of the University of California, Berkeley, and through Computer Services at Tufts University. The data were originally collected by the Center for Political Studies of the Institute for Social Research, the University of Michigan, under a grant from the National Science Foundation. Neither the original collectors of the data nor the Consortium bears any responsibility for the analysis or interpretations presented here.

6 Although 1994 was certainly a bad year for Democrats in the South, it was no better for Democrats outside the South. Almost 13 percent of all southern seats went from Democratic to Republican hands; 12 percent of nonsouthern seats were taken from the Democrats.

7 This open seat analysis is based upon data extracted from the biennial *Almanac of American Politics.*

8 Elections from the 1992 cycle are not included in these percentages because major redistricting often made it difficult or impossible to designate an incumbent. Seats created after the 1980 redistricting are not included here either.

9 These figures also do not include the 1992 elections because of major changes in district boundaries.

10 Republicans have picked up some ground by defeating incumbents. Nineteen Republican challengers defeated Democratic incumbents between 1980 and 1992, while only thirteen Democratic challengers unseated Republican congressmen.

11 The data upon which this discussion are based come from various editions of the *Statistical Abstract of the United States.* The data for 1994 were supplied by the National Conference of State Legislatures.

12 All these data are from American National Election Studies surveys conducted in the 1980s. These surveys have been pooled to maximize the number of cases.

13 It is instructive to look at congressional votes because even though they may not perfectly reflect a representative's personal sentiments, they do represent his political stands. A member of Congress may not be called upon by his next electoral opponent to defend his vote, but he must always be prepared for this eventuality. Roll call votes

are thus useful quantitative data on the public positions of members of Congress. Of course, there are ways for them to hide their actual positions by voting one way on procedural questions and another on the substantive issue. I have chosen to look at the more substantive votes, as I am most interested in the positions a congressman might have to defend in public.

14 Again, these data come from the American National Election Studies (1980–90 pooled).

15 Empirical tests of this idea have not all been confirming. Petrocik (1981), for example, argues that white backlash may have led to changes in the southern party system but has not sustained them. See also, Stanley (1987).

Chapter 2 The Case for Context

1 Turnout in these special elections varied but was usually rather low. In the elections studied here, turnout averaged 31 percent of the voting age population. For ease of presentation, the calculations in this table are based on the assumption that a normal turnout in special elections is 33 percent, though this is simply a convenient base. The general principles being discussed here are applicable whether normal turnout is 20 percent or 50 percent.

2 Many of the observations I make about the effectiveness of various strategies and tactics require inferences based on fragmentary evidence. Such is the nature of this type of research. Some of my conclusions are based on what people have told me in the course of interviews, how they have viewed the effectiveness of various issues. At several points in this book, I am able to test propositions with survey data. For the most part, however, where such data existed, they were almost impossible to obtain. Where they were obtained, they rarely offered the relevant variables to test my hypotheses. Aggregate data from these elections also offered limited ability to test hypotheses. I have resorted to using these data in places, if only to get a partial confirmation of my expectations.

3 This man drove his car off a bridge on election night. His injuries were minor.

4 In spite of the fact that candidates are inevitably dissatisfied with their coverage, not one of the candidates discussed here was ignored by the media. Indeed, what is striking was how much of their message got into the newspapers as intended and even unfiltered. Many of the press reports and television stories as well were very uncritical pieces on the candidates. Others came right from press releases.

5 In the pages to follow, numerous people are quoted. Most of these quotes come from personal interviews with participants in the campaign. As the names of these people are of no import to the story being told here, I have identified most speakers by their role in the campaign, for example, "Democratic media consultant" and "Republican campaign manager." Where names have been used, the person involved is one of the candidates or the quote came attributed from a newspaper or both. Quotes not followed by a newspaper citation come from personal interviews.

6 The six cases studied here do not conform to Sigelman's findings. In these special elections, turnout averaged 31 percent of the voting age population. This is certainly much lower than turnout in presidential elections, and the average turnout for the 1988 presidential election in these six districts was 52 percent. But turnout in the 1986 elections, a better comparison because it was an off-year, also averaged 31 percent in these districts (see table 2.3). Indeed the average turnout in all southern congressional districts in 1986 (not including uncontested Louisiana elections) was only 34 percent. Clearly these special elections were not unique on this count. They generated as much turnout as elections held on the regular cycle.

7 This is the average margin of victory for victorious incumbent congressmen who faced major party opposition. Those who did not face major party opposition are excluded here (seventy-two congressmen—17 percent of all congressmen—fell into this category). These numbers were calculated from data provided in Duncan (1989).

8 Jacobson and Kernell's (1983) important "strategic politicians theory" is yet another way to conceive of how national forces impinge on congressional elections. They argue that national conditions many months prior to the election influence the decisions of politicians to run for office and lead party elites and supporters to donate money to or withhold it from campaigns. These decisions determine the relative strength of Democratic and Republican candidates running for Congress and the "local choices" offered to voters in various districts.

9 The finding that fifteen of twenty turnovers went against the president is of somewhat limited value because Sigelman does not give information on how many seats the president's party and the opposition party defended in this time (he gives only the total number of contests in which there was no change in party control). The more relevant statistic would be the percentage of seats successfully defended by the president's party and by the opposition party. Although presenting the findings this way would likely show that the president's party has been somewhat less successful at defending its seats than the opposition party, it would still be quite evident that both defend their seats much more frequently than they lose them.

10 Studlar and Sigelman actually look at both British by-elections and American special elections in their research note. They are unable to test their time-passage hypothesis for special elections, however, given the poor quality of some of the American election data.

11 As Mark Westlye (1991) argues, margin of victory is not a particularly good measure of campaign intensity, and indeed, "the two concepts are theoretically distinct" (18). By his criteria—quantity of news coverage, paid advertising, campaign expenditures—these cases could all have been expected to be, and in fact were, "hard fought campaigns."

12 There were five other special elections won by Democrats in the South in the period from Ronald Reagan's first victory in 1980 to the early months of the Clinton administration. They were held in northwestern Georgia (Georgia 7; 1983), central Louisiana (Louisiana 8; 1985), Nashville (Tennessee 5; 1988), Houston (Texas 18; 1989), and Fort Worth (Texas 12; 1989).

Seven special elections were won by Republicans over this period—in the corridor between Dallas and Houston (Texas 6; 1982), western North Carolina (North Carolina 10; 1986), northwestern Louisiana (Louisiana 4; 1988), Knoxville (Tennessee 2: 1988), Miami (Florida 18; 1989), Dallas (Texas 3; 1991), and north-central Virginia (Virginia 7; 1991).

13 These percentages apply to the district at the time of the election. The 1990 redistricting changed some of the districts in marginal ways. Mississippi 4 even has gone through two changes. Nonetheless, the districts remain recognizable in the 1990s.

Chapter 3   Racial Issues in the Congressional Campaign

1 The district's boundaries changed shortly after the 1981 election looked at here. In an effort to create a majority black district in the Mississippi Delta, several predominantly black counties on the Mississippi River were taken out of the Fourth. Following the redistricting, the district became 37 percent black. Nonetheless, this description remains pretty accurate, even following the 1990 redistricting.

2 In 1964, the Third District elected a Republican congressman who was unable to defend his seat in 1966.

3 Cochran also benefited from an independent black candidacy in his first run for the Senate. Cochran beat his Democratic opponent 45 to 32 percent, while Charles Evers, the brother of the slain civil rights leader Medgar Evers, won 23 percent of the vote.

4 Robert Wheems, the former grand chaplain of the Klan, attacked the Democrat Wayne Dowdy as "a scalawag who wilfully aid[s] and abet[s] the Black Power Movement," and Liles Williams as a member of the "sinister Common Cause." "Can we afford less moral courage in 1981 than in 1964?" he asks in a *Jackson Clarion-Ledger* advertisement. In a crowded field, Wheems received less than 1 percent of the vote. "I was hoping the race would come down to me and a Negro," he explained to the *Clarion-Ledger* (1981a). In fact, Wheems miscalculated. No blacks were in the field.

5 Dowdy had a different concern vis-à-vis whites. He avoided bringing up the homosexual scandal because Hinson also was from the southern part of the district, and he feared offending any rural whites who might have connections to the political Hinson family.

6 These data were compiled from Putnam 1981b.

7 Such an arrangement, Parker (1990) notes, makes it extraordinarily difficult for minorities to win nominations (74).

8 This difference is actually a bit understated because Browder ran in two primaries and Rice ran in one. Under campaign finance laws, this allowed Browder to accept larger donations from the national party. Browder's connections to labor allowed him to raise more money overall. In their final Federal Election Commission reports, Browder reported spending $679,000 to just $443,000 for Rice (Barone and Ujifusa 1989, 15).

9   Browder himself agreed that he was not comfortable campaigning in churches, but that went for all churches, black and white.

10 Unfortunately for Ford, this opportunity did not arise. Although a majority black district was carved out of the black belt running across the central part of the state in the 1990 redistricting, it was in the western part of the belt. In 1992, the Third District remained roughly intact, and two white Democrats lost their seats to black Democrat Earl Hilliard and white Republican Spencer Bachus.

11 Browder did not receive an appointment to the Armed Services Committee upon his arrival in Congress; he was assigned to the Public Works and Transportation Committee, another fine place for congressmen interested in bringing home federal money for their districts. Later in 1989, however, Browder switched to the Armed Services Committee, where a seat became available when the Arkansas congressman Tommy Robinson defected to the Republican party.

12 Heflin was not the only statewide Democratic figure brought into the district. Browder tried to build on the district's traditional Democratic ties with highly publicized endorsements from Jim Folsom, Jr., and George Wallace, Jr., the sons of two major Alabama political figures. Even George Wallace, Sr., despite being ill, appeared in a Browder radio ad.

13 Browder's campaign manager became a little concerned when a scare over a pesticide used on apples (alar) became newsworthy during the campaign.

14 The two candidates, who both came to the Alabama House of Representatives in 1982, voted together twelve of twenty times on key votes between 1982 and 1986. They took the same side on issues like gambling, abortion, and tort reform, but diverged on taxes (allowing the public to vote in referendums for various tax increases) and education reform. On Browder's legislation to create a merit pay system for teachers, Rice had been a major and vocal opponent. He had argued that the AEA would control the teacher evaluations and that teachers' raises would cost the state millions of dollars (White 1989).

15 What was most interesting about this particular mailing is that it, unlike the other two, was not sponsored by the Republican National Campaign Committee. Their decision was likely informed by David Duke's election to the state legislature in Louisiana, which was considered an embarrassment to the national party.

16 Elite political behavior is almost as effective as a public opinion survey in assessing the direction of a campaign. In this case, the national committee's representative to the Rice campaign spent the closing weeks of the election working in Florida (Yardley 1989d).

17 The authors acknowledge that racial conservatism may simply be "racism dressed up, made respectable" (191), but they refrain from tackling the question of whether or not this is the case.

18 Rice, as noted, also called his support of the Confederate flag an act of courage, an indication that he acted on what he believed was right. The courage headline on his campaign literature again illustrates how these appeals are made less directly than in

years past. It also indicates that candidates often require a justification for taking such a stand. Rice's campaign manager said, "The issue is courage. John Rice had the courage to stand up and be counted. Everybody knows John Rice isn't a racist" (Yardley 1989d).

19 Both figures are from the American National Election Studies and represent validated vote.

20 Other radio stations often are used to reach specific groups with well-honed messages. Evangelical Christian and Spanish-language radio stations, for example, also offer excellent opportunities to narrowcast.

21 The political scientist and former congressional candidate Sandy Maisel (1986) reports that he and many other congressional candidates found the coverage of their campaigns to be unsophisticated and skewed toward bigger, local events (119).

22 Occasionally, a Republican campaign will be able to make Democratic radio advertisements a campaign issue. In the North Carolina Senate race in 1990, for example, the Republican candidate, Jesse Helms, attacked his Democratic opponent, Harvey Gantt, for using "racial ads" on black radio. His commercial accuses Gantt of running a "secret campaign": "Why doesn't Harvey Gantt run his ad on all radio stations, so everyone can hear it instead of just on black stations? Doesn't Harvey Gantt want everyone to vote?" (Toner 1990). This race was unusual, however. Gantt, running against a nemesis of liberals, had a large campaign fund and was able to advertise widely before the election, thus giving Helms the opportunity to attack him. Moreover, Helms, who was waging a racially charged campaign of his own, knew what was coming and had a ready response. In most elections, Republicans are not able to respond to the black campaign ads because they come so late in the campaign.

Chapter 4 Courting White Voters

1 Even the Republican who held the seat in 1870 did so for less than one term (King 1985a).

2 Because Republicans called great attention to the election and because little else was going on, the election attracted a lot of national attention. Even the national press paid a great deal of attention to developments in East Texas. And because the Republicans defined the situation so clearly, the election did become an important test of southern realignment in numerous reports in the *New York Times* and the *Washington Post* and in columns by various political analysts such as Mark Shields (1985), Jack Germond and Jules Witcover (1985), Michael Barone (1985), and Rowland Evans and Robert Novak (1985).

3 Gramm, after a highly publicized fight with the Democratic leadership in the House, renounced his Democratic affiliation, resigned his office, and won a 1983 special election for his congressional seat as a Republican. His bold move and the publicity surrounding it positioned him to run for and win in 1986 the Texas Senate seat vacated by the retiring Republican John Tower.

4 In 1968, as Edd Hargett was leading Texas A&M to its first Cotton Bowl victory in twenty-seven years (and first appearance in twenty-six years), Phil Gramm was teaching in the Economics Department at the university. In 1985, Texas A&M had not yet returned to the Cotton Bowl. Needless to say, Hargett's stature among alumni was great.

5 To give some perspective, in 1986, the average major party campaign raised close to $180,000 for both primary and general election activity (Stanley and Niemi 1988, 94).

6 Howard refused to endorse Chapman after the primary.

7 Hargett made his Aggie connection a major part of his campaign. His campaign speeches were peppered with Aggie jokes and his yard signs and bumper stickers were maroon and white, the school's colors. Most important, the Texas A&M alumni network proved to be a major source of his campaign funds (Watson 1985).

8 Indeed, the state Republican party officially defined homosexuality as "an abomination before God" and "indicative of a society's moral decadence" (Shields 1985).

9 Big labor was a particular bogeyman in this election. Responding to charges that he was beholden to "East Coast labor bosses," Chapman pointed to a one-thousand-dollar donation to Hargett from the Teamsters and argued at a debate that "Hargett's support is coming from some of the most crooked unions in the country" (Germond and Witcover 1985).

10 "Frequently" is perhaps not strong enough. Chapman's pollster contended that they used the trade advertisements on radio almost constantly with "700 grps [gross rating points] a week." Seven hundred gross rating points translates into almost 100 percent of the listening audience. This amount of advertising, according to a radio station account executive, is astounding for a political campaign.

11 County-level electoral results give some indication that Chapman's trade appeals were effective. The Democrat won 59 percent of the vote in Morris County, home of the steel plant and struggling under a 33 percent unemployment rate. The neighboring counties also had high unemployment rates and, with the exception of Hargett's home county and Bowie County (Texarkana), went into the Chapman column. Turnout in these counties was three points higher than in the rest of the district. Except for one county that is 36 percent black, blacks comprise about one-fifth of the population of these counties. It is thus fair to conclude that rural whites in this depressed area (near Hargett's hometown) were voting for Chapman. Their reasons for doing so cannot be determined with these data (public opinion data would be much more effective in assessing the impact and import of the issue), but these findings suggest that the "Japan bashing" may have had some effect. All these data were compiled from results reported in the *Dallas Morning News* on August 4, 1985.

12 The Justice Department, later in 1985, sought to codify the requirement to preclear special elections in some revisions of procedures for the administration of Section 5 of the Voting Rights Act. In oversight hearings before the Subcommittee on Civil and Constitutional Rights, a staff attorney for the Mexican American Legal Defense and Educational Fund , based in Texas, supported the provision with reference to the elec-

tion in the First District. Noting the Gramm election in 1983 and arguing that the Department of Justice had filed suit here because the Democrat was likely to win, she concluded that the lesson was that enforcement of Section 5 was arbitrary and selective. "I think what it clearly demonstrates is if you give the Department of Justice room to move, room to make selective decisions, they will make selective decisions on such enforcement. And we can't afford ambiguity in these regulations" (U.S. Congress 1985, 127).

13 This figure was calculated for the counties and cities comprising the Fifth District of the 1980s, which has slightly different boundaries from the district of the 1960s. These data were compiled from Scammon (1970).

14 His last contested election, in fact, was in 1970.

15 Jim Wright served as an all-purpose villain for Arey throughout the campaign. At one point, she told a reporter, "My mother always said that there's a little good in everybody; I just haven't been able to find it in Jim Wright. I think he's an archliberal, interested in power, not the people, and that is reflected in his leadership" (Bland 1988d). In reality, Jim Wright was not particularly liberal. His ADA scores were always quite moderate (between 40 and 50), which is what one might expect from a Texas Democrat. It is unlikely that the voters of the Fifth would have known this, however, and Wright was a high profile target because he was getting particularly bad press at the time of the campaign. Just under way was a probe of his financial dealings, which ultimately led to his resignation.

16 Arey's position on this issue was not even in the mainstream of the Republican party. House Republicans originally voted 124 to 29 on the issue, with less than half of the southern Republicans voting against it (see table 1–1).

17 Arey's manager said that Arey herself had called Bush to request his assistance, but it was also reported in the Danville paper that Virginia congressmen and the Reverend Jerry Falwell had appealed to Bush to visit the district.

18 Arey told of a letter received after the campaign relaying a barbershop conversation about her candidacy. When asked what he thought of Arey, one man responded, "Is she the widdah? No. What business does she have then running for the seat then?"

19 Public speaking was not Payne's strong suit. One reporter described him as being "shy" and "uncomfortable" giving a speech and noted that "he put some people to sleep" (Bland 1988a).

20 Another problem her campaign faced was hemorrhaging within her own campaign. Arey had four campaign managers and had difficulties with all four of them. She also fired a campaign consultant and a press aide (Eure 1988a).

21 Arey's deep disappointment at losing, particularly in her hometown and own neighborhood, led her to burn her political bridges. At her election night party, Arey blamed her Republican rival, Onico Barker, for her defeat, saying that he should have endorsed her (Stanbury 1988). She also resigned the Republican nomination for the congressional election to take place the following November. The next morning, she moved back to Washington, where her husband was a corporate lobbyist.

22 Arey also tried to reach black voters through the churches. It was an effort black leaders appreciated, though her position on *Grove City*, according to one prominent black leader, "raised a red flag" and made it difficult for blacks to support her.

23 The national Democratic party kept both stories alive by filing multiple complaints with the House Ethics Committee at different times. As anticipated, a high-profile story in the Gulfport newspaper followed.

24 In 1988, the Jackson paper published a story on the businessman who had provided Anderson and others with the free travel. In an investigative piece, the story raised questions about some low-interest Farmers Home Administration loans he had received, implying some sort of deal. The businessman lost a libel suit against the paper, and the records used as evidence in the suit detailed Anderson's free rides.

25 Taylor never explained his position on the first vote. His rationale for the second vote was that black-only schools were no longer needed because blacks could attend any state college. Why not consolidate the resources?

26 Reverend Appleberry became involved in the Anderson campaign because of the hospital and school issues. His organization produced more than a hundred thousand petitions from all over the state prior to Gov. Ray Mabus's veto of a bill to help the Charity Hospitals. Although one of the three Charity Hospitals in the state is in Meridian, none are located on the Gulf Coast. Appleberry's organization vowed to remember the governor and his legislative allies at the next election. Said Appleberry, "There's got to be a reckonin' day. We've got petitions from every county and we're gonna let them know there's a segment out there not to forget." Appleberry's support of the Republican was clearly motivated by his dislike of Taylor, not by any particular attachment to Anderson.

27 The events surrounding the injunction are not exactly clear. Reverend Appleberry claimed that, in fact, no injunction had been issued and that the whole thing was a Democratic ploy.

28 He not only looked bookish, he was bookish. Upon graduating from college, Anderson did graduate work in English (Brownson 1982).

29 The television and radio phone-in show have become an important part of southern campaigns. This is not only because they offer free media time (and lots of it), but because they are situations that can be controlled by the campaign. Friends and supporters are encouraged to phone in and even members of the campaign staff will call with questions that the candidate wants or needs to answer.

30 This press conference at a veterans' hospital illustrated who the most important player was. The television cameraman was about one half-hour late, leaving a half-dozen print journalists waiting patiently. Taylor and Montgomery took a second tour of the facility rather than start without him.

31 Taylor was successful in keeping the plant in the House budget, but the appropriation was stricken in the Senate.

32 Taylor's preoccupation with his local roots angered some of Anderson's supporters, who also were fixated on who was and was not local. As I watched the taping of a de-

bate with some Anderson supporters, several of them complained to me that Taylor went to high school and college in New Orleans. "And his company [the company he worked for] is based there too. Can you imagine?" exclaimed one woman.

33 Many southern politicians rail against nonracial out-groups as well. Homosexuals are a particularly vulnerable target. Although they are not a visible group in these districts, the stereotype politicians can call upon in their campaigns is accessible to most people. Both Democrats and Republicans try to link their opponents to gays and declare themselves against such things as affirmative action for gays, as Edd Hargett did in Texas and Gene Taylor in Mississippi 5. Their hostility to gays is astounding given the invisibility of the group in these areas. But again, they make an excellent target.

34 The vote was taken on April 29, 1987, and reported in *Congressional Quarterly Almanac.*

35 Rice had been a dues-paying member of the United Rubber Workers of America, an AFL-CIO union, for several years in the early 1970s.

36 Arey's positions on labor issues generated some hostility. The Virginia Republican opposed some legislation pending in Congress requiring a sixty-day notification to workers before a plant could be closed down. She believed in retrospect that her position on the issue made her appear more antagonistic to labor than she actually was and required "two-step reasoning" to generate support from the public. That is, its virtue was not apparent on its face and needed too much of an explanation to be effective. It was her biggest regret in looking back on the campaign.

37 These percentages come from the American National Election Studies. The House figures come from the 1986 survey (n=338). The Dukakis figures come from the 1988 survey (n=441).

38 Southern Republican congressional candidates sometimes find themselves pursuing a peculiar strategy with regard to their national party. In some places, like southern Mississippi, the resentment against Republicans has worn away. In other places, as in East Texas, it is still a liability to run as a Republican, and the party's candidates do not try to evoke party ties. Yet, these Republican congressional candidates do all they can to link themselves to national Republican figures if not to the Republican label. The great irony of the Texas case is that Republicans before the election and Democrats after the election claimed it was a test of southern realignment, yet neither candidate fully embraced his affiliation in the campaign.

39 This has been a problem for many doctrinaire conservative Republicans, southern and nonsouthern. The Indiana congressman John Hiler, who beat minority whip John Brademus on Reagan's coattails in 1980, is one example. Upon reaching Congress, Hiler did nothing to bring pork to the district, rebuffed the mayor of South Bend, who was seeking a federal loan guarantee, and stood by while South Bend's largest employer left for the Sunbelt ("Capital should be allowed to move freely," he explained). After some very close elections, Hiler swallowed his conservative principles and became a much stronger advocate for his district (Barnes 1988).

40 Natcher refused campaign contributions from any source (Barone and Ujifusa 1991). Prather was not quite so principled, accepting contributions from Kentucky interests.

Chapter 5   The Majority Black District

1   While the Supreme Court's ruling in *Shaw v. Reno* may put some of these districts in jeopardy,—at this writing it is not clear how this decision will play out—some if not all of these majority black districts will survive.

2   There were several other special elections pending at the time of the election, though all were scheduled for the following months.

3   When one crop feeds so much money into an area's economy, it is little surprise that it becomes important to the identity of the area. In an incident that illustrates the Delta's attachment to cotton, when the Greenville newspaper reported that Sen. Trent Lott's wife modeled polyester for a congressional wives' charity fashion show, it caused a furor. "All hell broke loose," said the reporter who wrote the piece. "That story brought in more letters to the editor than any other issue this year."

4   A striking number of middle-class blacks are returning to the area to retire, citing the difficulty of urban life up North and the lower cost of living in the region. These people have had a profound effect on the politics of the area because they have the skills and the time to volunteer in campaigns as well as some previous experience in politics.

5   As a point of comparison, in Mississippi as a whole, 32 percent of residents lived below 125 percent of the poverty line and 50 percent below 200 percent of the poverty line. Almost 13 percent of households were on public assistance. Sixteen percent of adults had less than a ninth-grade education.

6   *Jordan v. Winter*, 541 F. Supp 1135 (N.D. Miss. 1982) *vac'd and remanded sub nom. Brooks v. Winter*, 461 U.S. 921 (1983), 604 F. Supp. 807 (N.D. Miss. 1984), *aff'd sub nom. Mississippi Republican Executive Committee v. Brooks*, 469 U.S. 1002 (1984).

7   Espy is conservative compared to other black members of the House. Before the election of the Republican Gary Franks in Connecticut in 1990, he was consistently the most conservative member of the black delegation. Americans for Democratic Action gave him a rating of 67 in 1990. The average score for black members of the House that year was 91.

8   Dent told me, for instance, that while serving in the Persian Gulf during the Gulf War he made sure to write letters to Republican activists back home in order to "stay in the loop." He also had worked on numerous Republican campaigns, which he cited as the reason it took him so long (ten years) to get his college degree.

9   Both quotations are from the prepared text of a speech Meredith gave at the Democratic caucus.

10   Emily's List, in addition to the endorsement, sent a freelance campaign consultant to assist the campaign. Though she was able to raise money through women's groups, Blackwell perceived her sex to be a liability in the election: "Sometimes I think we got a menfolk-womenfolk problem more than a black-white problem in this state of Mississippi," she said in a televised debate.

11   These quotes come from a personal interview and from comments made at a candidate forum.

12 The *Ayers* case involved the unfair distribution of resources between "white" and pre-
    dominantly black educational institutions. The victory of civil rights forces in the case
    may have been a Pyrrhic one as the state of Mississippi responded by proposing to
    close some historically black institutions (including the Delta's Mississippi Valley
    State University) to resolve the issue. Thompson's involvement in the case tied him
    closely to those defending the school from closure as well as the administration and
    faculty of the school. Indeed, a few days before the primary election, a peculiar rally on
    Thompson's behalf was held during a huge sociology class at Mississippi Valley State.
    The speaker, who had argued the *Ayers* case before the Supreme Court, gave an alarm-
    ist speech in which he endorsed his friend Bennie Thompson as students took notes.
    Thompson won 49 percent and Espy won 37 percent of the vote at the Mississippi
    Valley State precinct; he won 16 percent of Leflore County (home to Valley State)
    while Espy took twice that countywide.

13 The Republicans underestimated how connected Thompson was with the black lead-
    ership in the district. One official expressed surprise that the moderate black political
    leadership in the district had lined up almost completely behind Thompson in the first
    campaign.

14 A *Jackson Clarion-Ledger* reporter defended the timing of the story by noting that it
    took a long time to locate the policeman involved in the incident.

15 Bennie Thompson refused to debate Dent, and the televised forum thus occurred with
    Dent facing a panel of three reporters while sitting next to a conspicuously empty
    chair.

16 "The Choice is Yours" literature came from previous congressional elections in the
    Second District. In both of the Robert Clark–Webb Franklin elections, Republicans
    produced literature that used the same format and the same heading, though the origi-
    nal Franklin material also had a not-so-subtle tagline, "He's one of us" (Neilson 1989,
    95).

17 The front-page treatment of these allegations makes it quite apparent that coverage of
    the election by the media in the Delta was extraordinarily tilted. That Hayes Dent's
    brushes with the law merited only brief mention (mostly on the editorial page) further
    illustrates the biased reporting of the Clarksdale and Greenwood papers. The Jackson
    paper appeared to tilt the other way, though. It did not run any news stories on
    Thompson's legal problems but did highlight Hayes Dent's problems on the front page.

18 Dole was actually the second choice of the campaign. Jack Kemp, however, had turned
    down an invitation, saying he was philosophically opposed to a white person repre-
    senting a majority black district. Dent's top campaign staff were bitter and Dent in-
    troduced Dole with "Ladies and gentlemen, I bring you the man who's probably going
    to be the next President of the United States." It was supposed to be a dig at the ab-
    sent Jack Kemp.

19 The Republicans excoriated Thompson for his tenure in Bolton, where, they claimed,
    the number of city employees went from fewer than ten to more than seventy during
    his tenure. The town has about eight hundred residents.

20 It helped that the good-sized Thompson had a good-sized appetite. Thompson stood in front of the brunch buffet at the ministers' meeting and told me that in the past two days he had eaten six catfish meals.

21 Madison County gave forty-five hundred votes to Thompson on election day.

22 Republicans also tell of poll watchers being intimidated by precinct officials. In an extreme example, one Republican official described being locked in a closet for several hours in a black precinct in Tennessee.

23 In the North Carolina senate race in 1990 between Jesse Helms and Harvey Gantt, postcards informing voters that "it is a federal crime, punishable by up to five years in jail, to knowingly give false information about your name, residence or period of residence to an election official" were sent out to voters in heavily black areas. Though the state Republican party promised not to use residence information obtained from returned mail, they argued that the postcards were legitimate. While the Republican National Committee had pledged by consent agreement in federal court in the early 1980s to "refrain from undertaking any ballot security activities in polling places or election districts where the racial or ethnic composition of such districts is a factor," it was argued (and accepted in federal court) that this was solely a state party effort (Edsall 1990; Ayres 1990).

24 Some argue that this is not the case. "I hope you haven't come in here with any racial predispositions. That business is over and done with here," said one Republican official to me before talking about political strategy in almost exclusively racial terms. Others pointed to Mike Espy, who courted and won over many whites during his moderate tenure as the Delta's congressman and, by this argument, "deracialized" politics. But they overlooked the fact that his first victory came without white support and also that the Republicans did not seriously challenge him after that.

25 The idea that Bennie Thompson was hostile to whites was pervasive among Delta whites, even among some of his white friends. A white Democratic activist who was deeply involved in the Blackwell campaign said, "Bennie is less antiwhite than people think he is." Though it was part of her rationale for working in the general election for the Thompson campaign, her phrasing illustrates that she clearly believed there was something to this characterization.

26 At least this was the belief of the Republican campaign. "Yankees" from the Republican National Committee staff were not allowed to answer the campaign telephone.

27 Clinton did not do particularly well with southern whites in general. In a *New York Times*/CBS News exit poll, 34 percent of southern whites reported voting for Clinton, while 49 percent reported voting for Bush and 18 percent for Perot. Mississippi whites and especially Delta whites were hostile to the Democratic nominee.

28 Although Dent was quite polished, especially given that he had never run for office before, his lack of experience was most apparent when he tried to tell a joke. Whereas Dole could tell the same joke to great effect at two consecutive functions, Dent had trouble remembering his good punch lines.

29 This, of course, is not so much a function of racial balance as of timing. All the Demo-

crats in the other cases described here were able to run against Washington during the Reagan and Bush years.

Chapter 6 Resolving the Puzzles

1 White southerners have voted for the Republican candidate over the Democratic candidate in every presidential election since 1964. From 1952 to 1964, the white vote was split about evenly.

2 Not every high-profile conversion of a southern Democrat has provided the desired demonstration. For every Andy Ireland, there has been a Bill Grant, another Florida congressman who switched parties in the middle of his term. Though Grant ran unopposed as a Democrat in 1986 and 1988, he announced his conversion in 1989 and was defeated resoundingly in the 1990 election by an opponent who made the switch a major issue of the campaign. For every Phil Gramm who left the Democratic party after feuding with Democratic leaders, there has been a Tommy Robinson, who also switched parties after many conflict-ridden years in the Democratic party. Robinson, like Gramm, tried to parlay the publicity into a run for higher office (the Arkansas governorship). Not only did he fail to win his party's nomination for governor, but the Democrats recaptured his congressional seat.

3 A survey of partisan switching among officials in 1993 reveals some variation state to state. In Arkansas, Florida, Georgia, Louisiana, and South Carolina, for instance, two or three elected officials changed parties in this calendar year. In Mississippi, twelve Democratic officials (state legislators, county supervisors, municipal aldermen, and a mayor) changed their affiliation. The state party of Tennessee reported no switches in 1993. Several state parties did not gather such information. Data were compiled by the state Republican parties of all these states.

4 This is not just because of racial issues in the campaigns. Tying themselves so closely to Reagan and Bush does not appear to be a fruitful way to appeal to blacks. As Katherine Tate persuasively shows, attitudes toward Ronald Reagan further bolstered Democratic attachments among blacks (1993, 65–70).

References

Apple, Jr., R. W. 1989. "House Race in Alabama Takes on a Biting Tone," *New York Times*, March 31.

Applebome, Peter. 1993. "Racial Lines Seen as Crucial in Mississippi Runoff," *New York Times*, April 12.

Attlesey, Sam. 1985a. "Wright criticizes GOP campaign," *Dallas Morning News*, June 4.

———. 1985b. "Candidates in 1rst District race make their last-ditch maneuvers," *Dallas Morning News*, June 27.

———. 1985c. "Hargett, Chapman in Runoff," *Dallas Morning News*, June 30.

———. 1985d. "Hargett, Chapman camps plot runoff tactics," *Dallas Morning News*, July 1.

———. 1985e. "1rst District runoff race focussing on jobs, trade," *Dallas Morning News*, July 28.

———. 1985f. "1rst District candidates target key groups in campaign," *Dallas Morning News*, June 29.

———. 1985g. "Democrat Chapman edges Hargett in runoff," *Dallas Morning News*, August 4.

——. 1985h. "Volunteers credited for Chapman win," *Dallas Morning News*, August 5.

——. 1985i. "Chapman says he's ready to go to work," *Dallas Morning News*, August 5.

Ayres Jr., B. Drummond. 1990. "Judge Assails G.O.P Mailing in Carolina," *New York Times*, November 5.

Baker, Donald P. 1988. "Two vie for conservative title, house seat in Virginia's 5th," *Washington Post*, June 9.

Balz, Dan, and Ruth Marcus. 1992. "Clinton Said to Fill Last Four Cabinet Jobs," *Washington Post*, December 24.

Barnes, Fred. 1988. "The Unbearable Lightness of Being a Congressman," *New Republic*, February 15, pp. 18–22.

Barone, Michael, Grant Ujifusa, and Douglas Matthews. 1979. *The Almanac of American Politics, 1980*. New York: E. P. Dutton.

Barone, Michael, and Grant Ujifusa. 1985. *The Almanac of American Politics 1986*. Washington, D.C.: National Journal.

Barone, Michael. 1985. "Running in the 'East Texas Tradition,'" *Washington Post*, June 25.

——. 1987. *The Almanac of American Politics 1988*. Washington, D.C.: National Journal.

——. 1989. *The Almanac of American Politics 1990*. Washington, D.C.: National Journal.

——. 1991. *The Almanac of American Politics 1992*. Washington, D.C.: National Journal.

Bartley, Numan V., and Hugh D. Graham. 1975. *Southern Politics and the Second Reconstruction*. Baltimore: Johns Hopkins University Press.

Beck, Paul Allen. 1977. "Partisan Dealignment in the Postwar South," *American Political Science Review* 71:477-96.

Berelson, Bernard R., Paul F. Lazarsfeld, and William N. McPhee. 1954. *Voting: A Study of Opinion Formation in a Presidential Campaign*. Chicago: University of Chicago Press.

Black, Earl, and Merle Black. 1987. *Politics and Society in the South*. Cambridge: Harvard University Press.

——. 1992. *The Vital South: How Presidents are Elected*. Cambridge: Harvard University Press.

Bland, Laura E. 1988a. "Payne nomination: How did he do it?" *Danville (Virginia) Bee*, March 28.

——. 1988b. "Democratic candidate stresses views of defense, education," *Danville (Virginia) Bee*, April 21.

——. 1988c. "Union members jeer Arey, but may not support Payne either," *Danville (Virginia) Bee*, May 27.

——. 1988d. "Payne takes pro-choice stand; Arey stresses anti-abortion position," *Danville (Virginia) Bee*, June 1.

——. 1988e. "Democrats tout virtues of being in majority party," *Danville (Virginia) Bee*, June 7.

——. 1988f. "Trible says a vote for Arey important to Virginia," *Danville (Virginia) Bee*, June 7.

———. 1988g. "Daniel's son counter claims in 5th," *Danville (Virginia) Bee*, June 8.

———. 1988h. "Arey draws on D.C. experience," *Danville (Virginia) Bee*, June 8.

———. 1988i. "Dole says Arey understands how Washington works," *Danville (Virginia) Bee*, June 8.

———. 1988j. "Democrat Payne 'regular guy,'" *Danville (Virginia) Bee*, June 8.

———. 1988k. "Bush urges vote for Arey, criticizes Wright inquiry," *Danville (Virginia) Bee*, June 13.

Branch, Taylor. 1988. *Parting the Waters: America in the King Years, 1954–1963*. New York: Simon and Schuster.

Brinkley, Alan. 1982. *Huey Long, Father Coughlin and the Great Depression*. New York: Vintage Books.

Broder, David S. 1981a. "Democrats, Cheered by a Victory, Leery of Disciplining Renegade," *Washington Post*, July 9.

———. 1981b. "Party chiefs launch post-mortems of Miss. election upset," *Washington Post*, July 10.

Brownson, Charles B. 1982. *1982 Congressional Staff Directory*. Mt. Vernon, Virginia: Congressional Staff Directory.

Bullock, III, Charles S. 1988a. "Regional Realignment from an Officeholding Perspective," *Journal of Politics* 50:553-74.

———. 1988b. "Creeping Realignment in the South," in Robert H. Swansbrough and David M. Brodsky, eds., *The South's New Politics: Realignment and Dealignment*. Columbia: University of South Carolina Press.

Burger, Frederick. 1989a. "Browder, Rice off to a spirited start," *Anniston (Alabama) Star*, March 9.

———. 1989b. "2 more rally for Browder," *Anniston (Alabama) Star*, March 22.

Carmines, Edward G., and James A. Stimson. 1989. *Issue Evolution*. Princeton: Princeton University Press.

Cassreino, Terry R. 1989. "Republicans clear the way for Anderson," *Gulfport (Mississippi) Sun Herald*, September 3.

Clymer, Adam. 1981a. "Mississippi to choose successor to Hinson today," *New York Times*, July 7.

———. 1981b. "Mississippi loss: 2 warnings for GOP," *New York Times*, July 9.

Congressional Quarterly. 1988. "Review of Congressional Election Winners," November 12.

Congressional Quarterly Almanac. 1981. "House Passes Bill to Extend Voting Rights Act," 415–18.

Congressional Quarterly's Guide to Congress. 3d ed. 1982. Washington, D.C., Congressional Quarterly.

Converse, Philip E. 1966. "On the Possibility of Major Political Realignment in the South," in Angus Campbell, Philip E. Converse, Warren E. Miller, and Donald E. Stokes, eds., *Elections and the Political Order*. New York: John Wiley and Sons.

Curran, Tim. 1993. "Henry Espy Tops Field in Race for Brother's Seat Tuesday, But Delta Contest Now Tight," *Roll Call*, March 25.

Danville (Virginia) Bee. 1988. "Issues and Answers: 5th District '88," June 1.

Danville (Virginia) Register. 1988. "Payne fund lead helped with 5th win," July 22.

Davidson, Chandler. 1990. *Race and Class in Texas Politics*. Princeton: Princeton University Press.

Dockins, Metric, and Patrick Peterson. 1989. "Diverse crowd shows democracy in action," *Gulfport (Mississippi) Sun Herald*, October 13.

Duncan, Phil, ed. 1989. *Politics in America: Members of Congress in Washington and at Home*. Washington, D.C.: Congressional Quarterly.

Edsall, Thomas B. 1990. "Helms Makes Race an Issue," *Washington Post*, October 31.

Edsall, Thomas Byrne, and Mary D. Edsall. 1991. *Chain Reaction: The Impact of Race, Rights, and Taxes on American Politics*. New York: W. W. Norton.

Ehrenhalt, Alan, ed. 1983. *Politics in America: Members of Congress in Washington and at Home*. Washington, D.C.: Congressional Quarterly.

——, ed. 1987. *Politics in America: Members of Congress in Washington and at Home*. Washington, D.C.: Congressional Quarterly.

——. 1991. *The United States of Ambition*. New York: Times Books.

Elving, Ronald D. 1988. "GOP Sees New Day in Southside Virginia," *Congressional Quarterly*, April 16, pp. 1008–09.

Erikson, Robert S. 1988. "The Puzzle of Midterm Loss," *Journal of Politics* 50:1011–29.

Eure, Rob. 1988a. " 'High energy' helps GOP candidate," *Roanoke Times and World News*, May 29.

——. 1988b. "Fifth District's Campaign Subtlety Faces Media Age," *Roanoke Times and World News*, June 1.

Evans, Rowland, and Robert Novak. 1985. "Realignment at the Cuthand Fish Fry," *Washington Post*, August 2.

Fava, Al. 1993. "Franklin sees race with inside point of view," *Greenwood (Mississippi) Commonwealth Delta Advertiser*, March 24.

Fenno, Jr., Richard F. 1978. *Homestyle: House Members in Their Districts*. Boston: Little, Brown.

——. 1990. *Watching Politicians: Essays on Participant Observation*. Berkeley: IGS Press.

Forman, Gail. 1989. "Catfish Achieve Upward Mobility," *New York Times*, February 1.

Fossett, Mark A., and Jill K. Kiecult. 1989. "The Relative Size of Minority Populations and White Racial Attitudes," *Social Science Quarterly* 58:412–17.

Genovese, Eugene D. 1967. *The Political Economy of Slavery*. New York: Vintage Books.

Germond, Jack W., and Jules Witcover. 1985. "1rst District campaign as test of Dixie realignment a phony," *Dallas Morning News*, July 27.

Gilens, Martin. 1990. "Racial Attitudes and Opposition to the American Welfare State." Unpublished paper, Department of Sociology, University of California, Berkeley.

Giles, Michael W. 1977. "Percent Black and Racial Hostility: An Old Assumption Revisited," *Social Science Quarterly* 30:469–85.

Giles, Michael W., and Arthur Evans. 1986. "The Power Approach to Intergroup Hostility," *Journal of Conflict Resolution* 30:469–85.

Glaser, James M. 1994. "Back to the Black Belt: Racial Environment and White Racial Attitudes in the South," *Journal of Politics* 56:21–41.

Glazer, Amihai. 1990. "A Formal Model of Group-Oriented Voting." Paper presented at the conference, "Modeling the Links between Race and U.S. Electoral Politics," University of California, Irvine, May 19.

Grofman, Bernard. 1990. "One Dozen Easy Ways to go Wrong in Modeling Race and Politics." Paper presented at the conference, "Modeling the Links between Race and U.S. Electoral Politics," University of California, Irvine, May 19.

Gulfport (Mississippi) Sun-Herald. 1989a. "Candidates work Lucedale crowd," September 10.

———. 1989b. "Anderson: Free rides overlooked," September 24.

Hair, William Ivy. 1991. *The Kingfish and His Realm: The Life and Times of Huey P. Long.* Baton Rouge: Louisiana State University.

Hall, Carla. 1986. "Espy's Mississippi Milestone," *Washington Post*, December 19.

Harris, Art. 1981. "Hinson's memory haunts his Mississippi district," *Washington Post*, June 17.

Hillman, G. Robert. 1985. "White assails suit in First District race," *Dallas Morning News*, July 25.

Huckfeldt, Robert, and Carol Weitzel Kohfeld. 1989. *Race and the Decline of Class in American Politics.* Urbana: University of Illinois Press.

Jacobson, Gary C. 1990. *The Electoral Origins of Divided Government.* Boulder: Westview Press.

Jacobson, Gary C., and Samuel Kernell. 1983. *Strategy and Choice in Congressional Elections.* 2d ed. New Haven: Yale University Press.

Jackson Clarion-Ledger. 1981. "Williams, Dowdy to meet in runoff," June 24.

Jackson Daily News and Clarion-Ledger. 1981. "We back Williams," July 5.

Jamieson, Kathleen Hall. 1992. *Packaging the Presidency.* 2d ed. New York: Oxford University Press.

Jaynes, Gerald David, and Robin M. Williams, Jr., eds. 1989. *A Common Destiny: Blacks and American Society.* Washington, D.C.: National Academy Press.

Jewell, Malcolm, and David Olson. 1988. *Political Parties and Elections in American States.* Chicago: Dorsey.

Judis, John B. 1988. "Black Donkey, White Elephant," *New Republic*, April 18, pp. 25–28.

Kernell, Samuel. 1977. "Presidential Popularity and Negative Voting: An Alternative Explanation of the Midterm Congressional Decline of the President's Party," *American Political Science Review* 71:44–66.

Key, Jr., V. O. 1949. *Southern Politics in State and Nation*. Knoxville : University of Tennessee Press.

Kinder, Donald R. 1986. "The Continuing American Dilemma: White Resistance to Racial Change 40 Years after Myrdal," *Journal of Social Issues* 42:151–72.

Kinder, Donald R., and David O. Sears. 1981. "Prejudice and Politics: Symbolic Racism versus Racial Threats to the Good Life," *Journal of Personality and Social Psychology* 40:414–31.

Kinder, Donald R., Tali Mendelberg, Michael C. Dawson, Lynn M. Sanders, Steven J. Rosenstone, Jocelyn Sargent, and Cathy Cohen. 1989. "Race and the 1988 American Presidential Election." Paper delivered at the annual meeting of the American Political Science Association, Atlanta, Georgia, September 2.

King, Wayne. 1985a. "Texas G.O.P. Seeks to Win U.S. House Seat Today," *New York Times*, June 29.

———. 1985b. "U.S. Court Says Texas Erred But Doesn't Delay Election," *New York Times*, August 2.

———. 1985c. "Texans Pick a Congressman Today," *New York Times*, August 3.

———. 1985d. "Democrats Cheer Results in Texas," *New York Times*, August 5.

Kocher, Greg. 1994a. "2nd District race takes off," *Owensboro (Kentucky) Messenger-Inquirer*, May 21.

———. 1994b. "Lewis makes a final sweep of 2nd District," *Owensboro (Kentucky) Messenger-Inquirer*, May 24.

Kurtz, Howard. 1985. "Texas to Obey Election Edict," *Washington Post*, August 2.

Lightman, Allan J. 1987. "Racial Bloc Voting in Mississippi Elections: Methodology and Results." Trial exhibit presented in *Martin v. Allain*, 658 F. Supp. 1183 (S.D. Miss. 1987).

Lubell, Samuel. 1966. *White and Black: Test of a Nation*. Revised edition. New York: Harper Colophon Books.

Matthews, Donald R., and James W. Prothro. 1966. *Negroes and the New Southern Politics*. New York: Harcourt, Brace and World.

Maisel, Louis Sandy. 1986. *From Obscurity to Oblivion: Running in the Congressional Primary*. Revised edition. Knoxville: University of Tennessee Press.

McKenzie, Danny. 1989. "Some people tired of Taylor getting fat on 'humble pie,' " *Jackson Clarion-Ledger*, October 2.

McNeil, Robert B. 1989. "Atwater pats Rice on back, but won't predict victory," *Anniston (Alabama) Star*, March 30.

Mills, Kay. 1992. "Unita Blackwell: MacArthur Genius Award Caps a Creative Political Life," *Los Angeles Times*, August 2.

Mitchell, Jerry. 1993a. "Assault 'mistake,' Dent says," *Jackson Clarion-Ledger*, March 26.

Mosby, Ray. 1993a. "Dent seen as preferable to Thompson," *Clarksdale (Mississippi) Press Register*, March 3.

———. 1993b. "Friends in high places saved Thompson," *Clarksdale (Mississippi) Press Register*, March 8.

Mughan, Anthony. 1986. "Toward a Political Explanation of Government Vote Losses in Midterm By-Elections," *American Political Science Review* 80:761–75.

Mullen, Bill. 1981. "Candidates Williams, Dowdy share platform in McComb," *Jackson Clarion-Ledger*, July 4.

National Republican Congressional Committee. 1988. Report in *The Presidential Hotline*, December 14.

Nelson, Mark. 1985. "Candidates rely on congressmen," *Dallas Morning News*, July 25.

Neilson, Melany. 1989. *Even Mississippi*. Tuscaloosa: University of Alabama Press.

New York Times. 1985. "Democrat Wins Congressional Race in Texas," August 4.

Nie, Norman H., Sidney Verba, and John R. Petrocik. 1979. *The Changing American Voter*. Cambridge: Harvard University Press.

Parker, Frank R. 1990. *Black Votes Count: Political Empowerment in Mississippi after 1965*. Chapel Hill: University of North Carolina Press.

Peterson, Patrick. 1989a. "Liberal language flies in 5th District," *Gulfport (Mississippi) Sun Herald*. September 21.

———. 1989b. "Environmentalists, Bush jump in fray in 5th District," *Gulf Coast (Mississippi) Sun Herald*, September 30.

———. 1989c. "Taylor HQ takes town by the horns," *Gulfport (Mississippi) Sun Herald*, October 12, 1989.

Petrocik, John R. 1981. *Party Coalitions: Realignments and the Decline of the New Deal Party System*. Chicago: University of Chicago Press.

Phillips, Kevin P. 1969. *The Emerging Republican Majority*. New Rochelle, N.Y.: Arlington House.

Pomper, Gerald M. 1989. "The Presidential Election," in Gerald M. Pomper, ed., *The Election of 1988: Reports and Interpretations*. Chatham, N.J.: Chatham House.

Putnam, Judy. 1981a. "Dowdy beats Williams by paper thin margin," *Jackson Clarion-Ledger*, July 8.

———. 1981b. "Dowdy sworn in; Final tally shows 912-vote margin," *Jackson Clarion-Ledger*, July 10.

Rilling, Paul. 1989. "Poll shows hefty lead for Browder," *Anniston (Alabama) Star*, March 28.

Sanders-Castro, Judith A. 1985. Prepared testimony before the Subcommittee on Civil and Constitutional Rights of the Committee on the Judiciary, House of Representatives

(99th Congress, 2nd Session). *Proposed Revisions of Procedures for Administration of Section 5 of the Voting Rights Act of 1965.* November 13.

Scammon, Richard M., ed. 1970. *America Votes 8.* Washington, D.C.: Congressional Quarterly.

Scammon, Richard M., and Alice V. McGillivray, eds. 1986. *America Votes 16.* Washington, D.C.: Congressional Quarterly.

Schuman, Howard, Charlotte Steeh, and Lawrence Bobo. 1985. *Racial Attitudes in America: Trends and Interpretations.* Cambridge: Harvard University Press.

Sears, David O., and J. B. McConahey. 1973. *The Politics of Violence: The New Urban Blacks and the Watts Riot.* Boston: Houghton Mifflin.

Shields, Mark. 1985. "East Texas Wind," *Washington Post,* August 2, p. A17.

Sigelman, Lee. 1981. "Special Elections to the U.S. House: Some Descriptive Generalizations," *Legislative Studies Quarterly* 6:577–88.

Simon, Herbert A. 1985. "Human Nature in Politics: The Dialogue of Psychology with Political Science," *American Political Science Review* 79:293–304.

Smith, Christopher. 1989a. "Rice hits Browder on home turf," *Anniston (Alabama) Star,* March 10.

———. 1989b. "Rice: A far journey to Congress," *Anniston (Alabama) Star,* March 15.

———. 1989c. "Rice on taxes: 'Never,'" *Anniston (Alabama) Star,* March 19.

———. 1989d. "Browder's war chest is fattest," *Anniston (Alabama) Star,* March 24.

———. 1989e. "Rice dedicated to conservatism," *Anniston (Alabama) Star,* March 26.

———. 1989f. "Work ethic strong in Rice background," *Anniston (Alabama) Star,* March 29.

———. 1989g. "Rice workers all but write off black vote," *Anniston (Alabama) Star,* April 1.

Sniderman, Paul M., and Michael Gray Hagen. 1985. *Race and Inequality: A Study in American Values.* Chatham, N.J.: Chatham House.

Sorauf, Frank. 1984. *Party Politics in America.* Boston: Little, Brown.

Souther, Sharon. 1989a. "Goal is balancing nature, economy," *Gulf Coast (Mississippi) Sun Herald,* September 28.

———. 1989b. "Taylor, Anderson make run-off," *Gulf Coast (Mississippi) Sun Herald,* October 4.

———. 1989c. "Anderson: U.S. must 'get rid of Noriega,'" *Gulfport (Mississippi) Sun Herald,* October 11.

———. 1989d. "Anderson, Taylor air their differences," *Gulf Coast (Mississippi) Sun Herald,* October 12.

———. 1989e. "5th District candidates work to keep from being stereotyped," *Gulf Coast (Mississippi) Sun Herald,* October 14.

———. 1989f. "Democrats attack ads by Anderson," *Gulfport (Mississippi) Sun Herald,* October 15.

Stanbury, Beth. 1988. "Barker will not run for 5th, calls Arey's charges 'absurd,'" *Danville (Virginia) Bee,* June 16.

Stanley, Harold W. 1987. *Voter Mobilization and the Politics of Race.* New York: Praeger.

——. 1992. "Southern Republicans in Congress: Fallen and Can't Get Up?" *Social Science Quarterly* 73:136–43.

Stanley, Harold W., and Richard Niemi. 1988. *Vital Statistics on American Politics.* Washington, D.C.: Congressional Quarterly Press.

Stewart, Steve. 1993b. "Loss may not be end for Espy," *Greenwood (Mississippi) Commonwealth,* March 31.

Stewart, Steve, and Al Fava. 1993. "Dent, Thompson prevail in primary," *Greenwood (Mississippi) Commonwealth,* March 31.

Strong, Donald. 1971. "Further Reflections on Southern Politics," *Journal of Politics* 33:239–56.

Studlar, Donley T., and Lee Sigelman. 1987. "Special Elections: A Comparative Perspective," *British Journal of Political Science* 17:247–56.

Sundquist, James L. 1983. *Dynamics of the Party System.* Revised edition. Washington, D.C.: Brookings Institution.

Tate, Katherine. 1993. *From Protest to Politics: The New Black Voters in American Elections.* Cambridge: Harvard University Press and the Russell Sage Foundation.

Taylor, Paul. 1985a. "GOP Hopes to Undo East Texas Tradition," *Washington Post,* June 26.

——. 1985b. "Dispute Settled, Texas House Race To Be Held Today," *Washington Post,* June 29.

——. 1985c. "Anger over Imports Fuels Texas Campaign," *Washington Post,* August 1.

Thielemann, Gregory S. 1992. "The Rise and Stall of Southern Republicans in Congress," *Social Science Quarterly* 73:123–35.

Tisdale, Charles. 1993. "Tisdale's Topics: Elect Bennie G. Thompson," *Jackson Advocate,* March 25–31.

Toner, Robin. 1990. "North Carolina Senate Contest Down to Wire," *New York Times,* October 31.

Treyens, Cliff. 1981a. "Dowdy takes seat in capitol today," *Jackson Clarion-Ledger,* July 8.

——. 1981b. "Surge in black, rural turnout put Dowdy over top," *Jackson Clarion-Ledger,* July 8.

U.S. Bureau of the Census. 1967. *County and City Data Book 1967.* Washington, D.C.: U.S. Government Printing Office.

——. 1983. *Congressional District Profiles, 98th Congress* (Supplementary Report PC80-S1-11).

——. 1986. *Statistical Abstract of the United States 1987.* 107th ed.. Washington, D.C.

——. 1992. *Population and Housing Characteristics for Congressional Districts of the 103rd Congress (Mississippi).*

U.S. Congress. 1985. Oversight Hearings before the Subcommittee on Civil and Constitutional Rights of the Committee on the Judiciary, House of Representatives (99th Congress, 2nd Session). *Proposed Changes to Regulations Governing Section 5 of the Voting Rights Act*, November 13 and 20.

Walsh, Edward. 1981. "Reagan Assists GOP Candidate for Hinson's Seat," *Washington Post*, June 23.

Walton, Steve. 1993. "Will Espys build empire on politics?" *Jackson Clarion-Ledger*, March 21.

Walton, Steve, and J. Lee Howard. 1993. "Feathers flying, 2nd District fight enters final round," *Jackson Clarion-Ledger*, April 11.

Washington Post. 1981a. "Democrat Wins Race for House in Mississippi," July 8.

———. 1981b. "The Message from Mississippi," July 18.

Watson, Tom. 1985. "Hargett Faces Chapman in Texas 1rst Runoff," *Congressional Quarterly*, July 6, p. 1336.

Weiss, Nancy J. 1983. *Farewell to the Party of Lincoln*. Princeton: Princeton University Press.

Westlye, Mark C. 1991. *Senate Elections and Campaign Intensity*. Baltimore: Johns Hopkins University Press.

White, David. 1989. "Some issues find Browder, Rice on the same side," *Birmingham News*, March 19.

Williams, T. Harry. 1969. *Huey Long*. New York: Vintage Books.

Woodward, Comer Vann. 1988. "Referendum on Reagan," *New York Times Review of Books*, December 22.

Wright, Gavin. 1986. *Old South, New South: Revolutions in the Southern Economy since the Civil War*. New York: Basic Books.

Yardley, Jim. 1989a. "It's Browder against Rice," *Anniston (Alabama) Star*, March 8.

———. 1989b. "Campaign charges escalate," *Anniston (Alabama) Star*, March 16.

———. 1989c. "Campaign is 'sleazy,' 'sickening,'" *Anniston (Alabama) Star*, March 17.

———. 1989d. "Browder, Rice clash on funding," *Anniston (Alabama) Star*, March 21.

———. 1989e. "Candidates charge each ducked votes," *Anniston (Alabama) Star*, March 24.

———. 1989f. "Browder targets the middle class," *Anniston (Alabama) Star*, March 26.

———. 1989g. "Heflin wants military committee for Browder," *Anniston (Alabama) Star*, March 29.

———. 1989h. "House race foes visit opponent's home field," *Anniston (Alabama) Star*, April 2.

Index

Abortion, 55, 60, 86, 96, 98, 107, 117–18, 129, 160–61

AFL-CIO, 57, 86, 110, 126, 207*n*35

Agriculture Committee (House), 146

Agriculture, Nutrition, and Forestry Committee (Senate), 160

Ailes, Roger, 84, 86

Alabama 3 district, 32–33, 41, 53–54; primary election in, 55–58, 181; congressional election in, 58–66, 68–69, 71–75, 79, 125, 129–30, 132–35, 182, 190, 194, 201*n*8, 202*nn*9, 12–13, 15, 16, 18

Alabama Democratic Conference, 18, 65, 72, 74, 79

Alabama Education Association (AEA), 61, 202*n*14

Alcorn State University, 113

American Association of Retired Persons (AARP), 60

American Conservative Union, 92

Americans for Tax Reform, 63

Americans for Democratic Action, 92, 205*n*15, 208*n*7

Anderson, Tom, 34, 106, 110, 119, 121, 126, 138, 206*nn*24, 28, 32; problems with campaign, 107–09, 115–16; campaign strategy, 111–15, 123, 128–29, 131–33, 136; and black vote, 113–15, 176–77, 206*n*26

Anniston Star, 129

Appleberry, C. F., 113–14, 177, 206*nn*26–27

Appropriations Committee (House), 153

Arey, Linda, 34, 100, 102, 104, 138, 182, 191, 194, 205*nn*15, 17–18, 20–21, 207*n*36; use of racial issues, 70, 74, 95, 103, 131, 205*n*16, 206*n*22; in party convention, 93–94; conservatism of, 94–96, 128–30, 132, 134; problems with campaign, 97–99; and trade policy, 125, 127

Armed Services Committee (House), 54, 61, 117, 132–33, 202*n*11

Armey, Richard, 132

Atwater, Lee, 58, 84, 90–91, 191

Ayers case, 155, 164, 170, 209*n*12

Bachus, Spencer, 202*n*10

Baker, James, 85

Baliles, Gerald, 101–02

Barker, W. Onico, 93–94, 99, 205*n*21

Barone, Michael, 203*n*1

Black Belt of South, 2–4, 197*n*2

Black, Charlie, 125

Black church, 75–76, 79, 120

Black, Earl, 10, 35, 127

Black, Merle, 10, 35, 127

Black opinion leadership, 74–76, 79, 103, 110, 113, 114, 120, 154, 164, 188

Black radio, 48–49, 76, 120, 203*n*22

Black voters: appeals to, 48–49, 50–51, 103, 120, 174–77; mobilization of, 56, 163–66; charges of vote buying, 65, 167, 193–94; demobilization of, 90–91, 113–15, 176–77, 194, 206*n*26; intimidation of, 166–67, 194–95 (*see also* Electoral fraud and ballot security); Republican appeals to, 170–71, 190–94, 206*n*22

Blackwell, Unita, 150, 153, 156, 158, 210*n*25

Brademus, John, 207*n*39

British by-elections, 39, 200*n*10

Browder, Glen, 34, 68–69, 129–30, 133, 181, 201*n*8, 202*nn*9, 11, 13–14; in Democratic runoff, 55–58; pursuit of black votes, 57, 75, 79; general election strategy, 59–63, 122, 125, 132, 134–35, 202*n*10; response to racial issues, 64–66, 73–74

Bush, George, 13, 117, 133, 139–40, 184, 188, 193, 210*n*29, 211*n*4; in 1988 and 1992 presidential elections, 10–11, 40, 55, 66, 95, 106, 210*n*27; political positions of, 60, 63, 128; involvement in congressional campaigns, 84, 94, 96–97, 109, 113, 115–16, 119, 121, 130–31, 135–36, 205*n*17

Capital gains tax. *See* Tax policy

Carmines, Edward G., 70

Carter, Jimmy, 9, 11, 81, 150, 185

Catfish, farming of, 144, 146

Chapman, Jim, 34, 84, 90–91, 204*n*6; and foreign trade issue, 88–89, 122, 124–25, 204*nn*10–11; campaign strategy, 85–88, 126, 129, 204*n*9

CIA, 96

Civil rights movement, 9

Civil Rights Act of 1964, 5

Civil Rights Restoration Act (*Grove City* Act), 70, 95, 103, 176, 206*n*22

Clark, Robert, 145, 163, 166, 209*n*16

Clarksdale Press Register, 158–59

Class-based politics, 3–4, 125

Clements, Bill, 81

Clinton, Bill, 139–41, 150–51, 161, 172–73, 185, 210*n*27

Clinton, Hillary, 150, 161, 172

Coats, Dan, 58

Cochran, Thad, 44–45, 157, 161, 168, 193–94, 201*n*3

Cole, Ed, 149

Colmer, William, 105

Confederate flag, 64–66, 68–69, 71–73, 79, 176, 202*n*18

Congressional voting, 20–21

Congressional Quarterly, 93, 131

Congressional elections, 35–36; Democratic advantage in, 12–15, 27–28; influence of racial balance, 28–31, 169–74, 175–78; media coverage of, 33, 35, 77–78, 203*n*21, 209*n*17; national vs. local forces, 38–40, 200*n*8

Connor, Bull, 92

Converse, Philip, 5

Conyers, John, 160
Cotton, cultivation of, 143, 208*n*3
Coverdell, Paul, 170

Dallas Morning News, 35
Daniel, Dan, 92–93, 95, 97, 101–03, 130
Danville (Virginia) Bee, 35
Davidson, Chandler, 22
Death penalty, 120, 123
Democratic Congressional Campaign Committee (DCCC), 75, 103, 108–09, 122
Democratic National Committee, 91
Democratic party: in Old South, 2–5; "white flight" from, 23, 199*n*15; candidate distance from, 85, 102, 116, 118, 129, 136–41, 173, 184; control of county courthouses by, 182; electoral advantages of, 186–87; weakening of, *see* Partisanship, trends in South
Dent, Hayes, 34, 130, 138, 148, 150, 152, 154, 163–64, 168, 209*n*18; problems in campaign, 155–56, 208*n*8, 209*n*17, 210*n*28; use of race issue, 157–60, 171; political strategy, 160–62, 170–74, 209*n*15
Denton, Jeremiah, 12
Dixiecrats, 4, 5
Dole, Elizabeth, 96–97
Dole, Robert, 140, 157, 160–61, 168, 209*n*18, 210*n*28
Dowdy, Wayne, 34, 123, 129, 201*nn*4–5; use of Voting Rights Act, 47–49, 51–53, 67–68, 73, 78, 177; populist appeals of, 49–50, 126, 136–37
Drug policy, 96, 107, 111, 117, 120, 122–23
Dukakis, Michael, 58, 66, 69, 95, 129–30, 185, 207*n*37
Duke, David, 65, 151, 192, 202*n*15

East, John, 12
Eastland, James, 146
Education policy, 61–62, 64, 71, 134, 202*n*14
Edwards, Don, 90
Ehrenhalt, Alan, 137–38, 180
Eisenhower, Dwight, 5, 10

Elections of 1994, xii, 15, 24, 189, 196, 198*n*6
Elections of 1958, 5
Electoral vote, in South, 9–12
Electoral fraud and ballot security, 166, 194–95, 210*nn*22, 23. *See also* Black voters, intimidation of
Emily's List, 153, 208*n*10
Energy and Commerce Committee (House), 133
Environmental policy, 162
Equal Rights Amendment, 101
Espy, Henry, 150–51, 156, 161, 164–65; as racial moderate, 152–53, 158–59, 162, 171, 173; and Voting Rights controversy, 154–55, 157, 192
Espy, Mike, 34, 146–47, 152–53, 158–59, 162–64, 170, 173, 209*n*12, 210*n*24
Estrich, Susan, 185
Ethics Committee (House), 205*n*23
Evans, Rowland, 81, 203*n*1
Evers, Charles, 201*n*3
Evers, Medgar, 48, 154, 201*n*3

Falwell, Jerry, 92, 94, 205*n*17
Fenno, Jr., Richard F., 40, 121
Florida, 14
Foley, Tom, 117
Folsom, Jr., Jim, 58, 202*n*12
Ford, Gerald, 11
Ford, Harold, 159
Ford, Johnny, 55–58, 66, 75, 79, 202*n*10
Fordyce, Kirk, 148, 160, 168, 173
Foreign aid, 49–50, 123
Foreign trade, 87–89, 102–03, 122, 124–25, 134, 204*n*11
Fowler, Wyche, 170
Frank, Barney, 129, 139
Franklin, Webb, 145–46, 209*n*16
Franks, Gary, 208*n*7

Gantt, Harvey, 203*n*22, 210*n*23
Gephardt Amendment (1987 Omnibus Trade Bill), 125
Germond, Jack, 203*n*1

Goldwater, Barry, 5, 9, 11, 20, 53, 186
Gore, Tipper, 160
Gramm, Phil, 52–53, 81, 83–84, 86, 90–91, 189, 203n2, 204n4, 205n12, 211n2
Gramm-Rudman-Hollings measure, 101
Grant, Bill, 211n2
Greenwood Commonwealth, 164
Grofman, Bernie, 22–23
Group conflict theory, 26–27, 168–69, 176
Gulf War, 156, 161, 208n8
Gun control, 55, 61, 63, 85–86, 129

Hall, Sam, 34, 81, 83
Hamer, Fannie Lou, 150
Hance, Kent, 85
Hargett, Edd, 34, 83, 126, 138, 204n4; campaign strategy of, 84–88, 204nn7, 9, 207n33; and trade issue, 88–89, 122; and Voting Rights controversy, 89–90, 176–77
Hawkins, Paula, 12
Heflin, Howell, 61, 132–33, 202n12
Helms, Jesse, 151, 203n22, 210n23
Hiler, John, 207n39
Hilliard, Earl, 202n10
Hinson, Jon, 34, 44–47, 52, 201n5
Holbrook, David, 151, 156, 158
Homestyle, 50, 121
Homosexuality, 44–45, 85–86, 204n7, 207n33
Horton, Willie, 185
Howard, Ed, 83–84, 204n6
Hubbert, Paul, 61
Huckfeldt, Robert, 23
Humphrey, Hubert, 11
Hunt, Guy, 55, 59, 61

Ideology, 60–63, 86, 95–96, 101, 111, 127–31, 133–35, 160–62, 185–86, 205n15
Interior Committee (House), 133
Ireland, Andy, 189, 211n2

Jackson Advocate, 154
Jackson Clarion-Ledger, 35, 48, 49, 68, 72, 201n4, 209n14

Jackson Daily News and Clarion-Ledger. See *Jackson Clarion-Ledger*
Jackson, Jesse, 56, 95, 129, 139, 166
Jacobson, Gary, 187, 200n8
Johnson, Pete, 159
Johnson, Lyndon B., 5, 10
Jones, James Earl, 153
Jordan, Bill, 148

Kemp, Jack, 55, 84, 209n18
Kennedy, Edward, 102, 116, 129, 161
Kennedy, John F., 5, 24
Kentucky 2 district, 139; congressional election in, 139–41, 207n40
Kernell, Samuel, 38, 200n8
Key, V. O., 2–4, 7, 175, 184, 197n1
King, Jr., Martin Luther, 48
King national holiday, 20–21, 93, 99
Kirk, Paul, 91
Kohfeld, Carol Weitzel, 23
Ku Klux Klan, 47, 151

Labor unions, candidate ties to, 57–59, 86, 110, 112, 126–27, 204n9, 207n36
Lewis, Ron, 139–40
Lincoln, Abraham, 9
Line-item veto, 101
Long, Huey, 4, 126, 198n4
Los Angeles Times, 153
Lott, Trent, 44, 105–09, 112–13, 115, 136, 157, 193–94
Lott, Tricia, 208n3
Lubell, Samuel, 6

Mabus, Ray, 159–60, 206n26
Maisel, Sandy, 203n21
Majority black districts, 31, 142–43, 169, 172, 183–84, 201n1, 208n1, 209n18
Manatt, Charles, 52
Matthews, Donald R., 6
Mattingly, Mack, 12
McBride, Eddie, 45
McComb, Mississippi, 44
McGovern, George, 58

Media coverage of elections. *See* Congressional elections, media coverage of

Media strategies, 78, 206*n*29; use of narrowcasting, 48–49, 76, 161, 203*n*20

Medicaid, 114

Medicare, 114

Merchant Marine and Fisheries Committee (House), 118

Meredith, James, 151, 156, 208*n*9

Methodology of study, 31–35; choice of House elections, 35–36; choice of special elections, 37–40; choice of cases, 40–42

Mexican American Legal Defense and Educational Fund (MALDEF), 204*n*12

Military presence in South, 54, 61–62, 105; Democratic protection of, 54, 117–18, 131–33, 202*n*11, 206*n*31

Minimum wage, 63

Mississippi 2 district, 32–33, 41, 143–44, 168, 173; previous congressional elections, 145–47; primary election in, 147–56, 192; congressional election in, 156–69, 170–74, 182, 193, 208*nn*9–11, 209*nn*12–18, 210*nn*20, 21, 24–26, 28

Mississippi 4 district, 32–33, 41; congressional election in, 40, 44, 47–53, 67–68, 72, 75, 78, 123, 126, 129, 133, 136–37, 177, 201*nn*5, 6; primary election in, 46–47, 201*nn*4, 5; electoral results, 51–52

Mississippi 5 district, 32–33, 41, 104–05; primary election in, 107–11; congressional election in, 111–21, 123, 125–26, 128–29, 131–33, 136–37, 177, 192–93, 206*nn*26–28, 30, 32, 207*n*33

Mississippi Association of Black Mayors, 155

Mississippi Association of Black Supervisors, 155

Mississippi Delta, 143–45, 149, 153, 157, 160, 167–69, 171–72, 201*n*1

Mississippi Freedom Democratic Party, 150

Mississippi Institute for Small Towns, 155

Mississippi Valley State University, 113, 170, 209*n*12

Moffett, Toby, 53

Mondale, Walter, 81, 129

Montgomery, Sonny, 92, 117, 132, 206*n*30

Moore, Mike, 107–11, 113, 116, 120

NAACP, 164

Natcher, William, 139–40, 207*n*40

National Conference of Black Mayors, 150

National Education Association, 126

National Republican Congressional Committee, 91

Neely, Brian, 151

New York Times, 129, 203*n*1

Nicaraguan contras, 61, 101

Nichols, Bill, 34, 54, 61–62, 134–35

Nixon, Richard, 10–11, 56, 105

Noriega, Manuel, 96, 111, 123

Novak, Robert, 81, 203*n*1

O'Neill, Tip, 52, 86, 93

Parker, Mike, 53

Parochialism, 62–64, 118, 131–41, 172–74

Parris, Stan, 97

Participant-observer research, 32

Partisanship, conversions to Republican party, 1–2, 22–23, 55, 189–90, 203*n*3, 211*nn*2, 3; trends in South, 7–9; of southern blacks, 8–9

Party switching. *See* Partisanship, conversions to Republican party

Patman, Wright, 81

Payne, L. F., 34, 93–99, 125, 138, 205*n*19; relationship to black voters, 74–75, 103, 188; political strategy of, 100–02, 122, 126, 129–32, 134, 136

Pepper, Claude, 87

Perot, Ross, 210*n*27

Petrocik, John R., 199*n*15

Phillips, Kevin, 6

Populism, 3–4, 49–50, 100–01, 125–27

Prather, Joe, 139–40, 207*n*40

Preuitt, Jim, 59

Prothro, James W., 6

Public Works and Transportation Committee (House), 104, 202*n*11

Quayle, Dan, 58, 115

Racial attitudes, in South, 17–20, 26
Racial issues, 43–44, 154; in Old South, 2–3; Republican use of, 67–73, 95–96, 124, 157–58, 176; Democratic response to, 73–79, 103, 187–88
Reagan, Ronald, 13, 20, 46, 50, 52, 87, 113, 123–24, 128, 131, 133–34, 139–40, 184, 188, 193, 200*n*12, 210*n*29, 211*n*4; in 1984 and 1988 presidential elections, 11, 40, 81, 93, 96; involvement in congressional campaigns, 49, 130, 135
Reagan administration, 90, 102, 106, 138
Realignment, predictions of, 5–6; mixed nature of, 7–16, 184–85; as a racial phenomenon, 16–23; Republican hopes of precipitating, 82–83, 91
Reed, Joe, 65
Reich, Robert, 161
Republican National Campaign Committee, 202*n*15
Republican National Committee, 210*nn*23, 26
Republican party, 202*n*15; in Old South, 3, 184; and racial appeal in South, 5–7; growth in South, 7–16, 128; problems with label, 84–85, 190, 207*n*38; intraparty competition in, 99, 180–81, 205*n*21; conservative advantage of, 127–29; candidate connection to, 130–31, 133, 135–37; recruitment problems, 179–82
Resentment issues, 121–27, 171–72
Reynolds, William Bradford, 89–91
Rice, John, 1, 34, 55, 131, 138, 182, 190, 194, 201*n*8, 202*nn*14, 16; political strategy, 58–63, 127, 132, 134–35; use of racial issues, 64–66, 68–69, 71–74, 79, 202–23*n*18
Richardson, Steve, 151
Richmond Times Dispatch, 103
Robb, Charles, 102
Robinson, Tommy, 202*n*11, 211*n*2

Sabato, Larry, 99
Savage, Gus, 157
School prayer, 71, 101, 107, 111, 117, 128–29
Shaw v. Reno, 208*n*1
Shelby, Richard, 13, 190
Shields, Mark, 203*n*1
Sigelman, Lee, 39, 200*nn*6, 9, 10
Simon, Herbert, 25
Singletary, Mike, 47
Sisisky, Norman, 100
Small Business Committee (House), 133
Smith, Larkin, 34, 105–07, 110–11, 118
Smith, Sheila, 107–08, 121
Social Security, 60, 87–88, 114, 125
Special elections. *See* Methodology of study, choice of special elections
Stanley, Harold, 181
Star Wars research, 101
State legislative elections, 15–16, 36
Stennis, Jr., John, 45
Stimson, James A., 70
Stoneville Agricultural Research Center, 160, 173
Strategic politicians theory, 200*n*8
Strong, Donald, 133
Studlar, Donley, 200*n*10
Sundquist, James L., 5
Symbolic racism, 17

Tarrance, Lance, 84
Tate, Katherine, 211*n*4
Tax policy, 60, 61, 63, 96, 111–12, 128–29
Taylor, Gene, 34, 105, 112, 121, 206*nn*30–32; relationship to black voters, 75, 113–14, 120, 177, 193, 206*nn*25–26; in primary election, 107–08, 110–11; campaign strategy in general election, 115–19, 125–26, 128–29, 132–33, 136–37, 139, 207*n*33
Teamsters, 204*n*9
Texas 1 district, 32–33, 41, 81–83; primary election in, 83–84; congressional election in, 84–91, 122, 124, 126, 129, 177, 203*n*2, 204*nn*6, 7, 9–11, 207*n*33; electoral results in various counties, 204*n*11

Texas A&M, 83, 85, 204n4

Thielemann, Gregory, 180

Thompson, Bennie, 34, 156, 161, 167, 168–72, 182, 209nn12, 17, 19, 210nn20, 21; primary campaign strategy, 149–50, 152, 154–55, 192, 209n13; and relationship to whites, 157–60, 169, 171, 173, 210n25; runoff campaign strategy, 162–66, 170, 174, 209n15

Tora! Tora! Tora!, 81, 89, 124

Tower, John, 203n2

Truman, Harry, 4

Turnout, special elections, 36–37, 199n1, 200n6

United Auto Workers, 86

United Rubber Workers of America, 207n35

University of Mississippi, 151

Vander Jagt, Guy, 91

Veterans' Affairs Committee (House), 104, 117

Vietnam War, 58, 68, 115–16

Virginia 5 district, 32–33, 41, 92, 205n13; congressional election in, 39, 70–71, 74–75, 94–104, 125–32, 134, 136, 182, 188, 194, 205nn15–21, 206n22, 207n36; nominating conventions in, 93–94

Virginia Military Institute (VMI), 101

Virginia, Southside, 92

Voting Rights Act, xii–xiii, 121, 142, 145, 155, 164, 182–83, 196; extension of, 20–21, 52–53, 93; as campaign issue, 47–49, 51, 67–68, 72–73, 154, 176–77; Texas preclearance controversy, 89–91, 177, 204n12

Wade, Henry, 84

Wallace, Sr., George, 9, 11, 54, 56, 92, 202n12

Wallace, Jr., George, 202n12

Warren, Earl, 5

Washington Post, 49, 53, 147, 203n1

Washington, Booker T., 54

Watson, Tom, 4, 198n4

Watts, J. C., 192

Webster v Reproductive Health Services, 60

Welfare, 186

Westlye, Mark, 200n11

Wheems, Robert, 47, 201n4

White, Mark, 85, 89–90

Whitten, Jamie, 117

Wilhelm, David, 160

Williams, Liles, 34, 46, 50, 52–53, 123, 138, 201n4; and Voting Rights controversy, 47–49, 51, 67–68, 72; relationship to Reagan administration, 49, 131, 133

Witcover, Jules, 203n1

Women candidates, problems of, 97–99, 205n18, 208n10

Wright, Jim, 83, 95, 139, 205n15